MW01535387

In the Garden of Aeden

M. Pilotte

Published by Wexford Falls Independent Press, 2018.

IN THE GARDEN OF AEDEN

First edition. September 28, 2018.

Copyright © 2018 M. Pilotte.

ISBN: 978-1393159223

Written by M. Pilotte.

Table of Contents

Chapter ONE | (Spring 2015 - Litchfield County, Connecticut)..1

Chapter TWO | (December, the previous year)....................... 11

Chapter THREE.. 23

Chapter FOUR.. 31

Chapter FIVE.. 41

Chapter SIX 61

Chapter SEVEN 77

Chapter EIGHT.. 95

Chapter NINE...105

Chapter TEN 111

Chapter ELEVEN 121

Chapter TWELVE...131

Chapter THIRTEEN | (Christmas Eve) 153

Chapter FOURTEEN 161

Chapter FIFTEEN | (December 2014, Christmas afternoon)..167

Chapter SIXTEEN...173

Chapter SEVENTEEN 187

Chapter EIGHTEEN | (The following morning)................207

Chapter NINETEEN 221

Chapter TWENTY...235

Chapter TWENTY-ONE...241

Chapter TWENTY-TWO...253

Chapter TWENTY-THREE..265

Chapter TWENTY-FOUR 277

Chapter TWENTY-FIVE 281

Chapter TWENTY-SIX..293

Chapter TWENTY-SEVEN..301

Chapter TWENTY-EIGHT 313

Chapter TWENTY-NINE...321

Chapter THIRTY 331
Chapter THIRTY-ONE 345
Chapter THIRTY-TWO 363
Chapter THIRTY-THREE 377
Chapter THIRTY-FOUR 391
Chapter THIRTY-FIVE 397
Chapter THIRTY-SIX 413
Chapter THIRTY-SEVEN 419
Chapter THIRTY-EIGHT 431
Chapter THIRTY-NINE 441
Chapter FORTY 447
Chapter FORTY-ONE | (Weeks later) 453
Chapter FORTY-TWO 457
Chapter FORTY-THREE | (Later that winter) 463
Chapter FORTY-FOUR | (Spring—weeks later) 475
Chapter FORTY-FIVE 479
Author's Note 495

This book is dedicated to my husband and family.

Chapter ONE

(Spring 2015 - Litchfield County, Connecticut)

———— ✿ ————

THE YOUNG MAN NEVER expected their friendship to wear as thin as an old rag, certainly not since that bond had been so solid. Then all hell broke loose. And now as he forged on to his destination, his mind was cluttered with jarring thoughts of the past few months—potentially life changing events. In his frame of mind, he failed to appreciate the sights of Litchfield County that lure hoards of tourists each year: colonial townships, their public gardens sprouting the first blooms of spring, and vistas with hints of mist drifting downward like so many stray angels on a mission.

Driving along in the hills, in moments of clarity, he was reminded of childhood trips he'd taken to auction barns where his parents discovered crafted furniture dating from the eighteenth century. Once in a while when the price was right they would make a purchase, sometimes two or more. Like so many other bargain hunters, they had hoped to hit the jackpot: come upon a rare painting ensconced in a dusty old frame. But no such luck.

His mother once took him and his sister to the *Regina Laudis* Abbey in nearby Bethlehem for a wedge of Mother Noella's divine

1

cheese. He relished the taste of it and, after all these years, the very recollection of it cleared his head of his cares, but only temporarily, and took him to a brighter place in his mind. He wondered if that qualified as a Proustian moment. He couldn't quite get everything straight. His mind was so troubled.

But other than locals or tourists, family and friends come to this place in northwestern Connecticut, Hillside Manor, white, de rigueur, and Jeffersonian in style, with an imposing entry and art-filled corridors leading to smartly appointed rooms and suites. The mansion sits regally on acres of rolling hills dotted with English gardens and koi ponds where delicate mists descend, rendering it a delectable tableau. Local artists have captured it in various media; however, its charm is often overlooked by those souls who are confined there for rehabilitation. It could be a perfect Bed and Breakfast getaway in another life at another time. But sadly, for some, it's their last stop.

The young man, more likely a GQ cover model heading to a photo shoot than a casual visitor, parked his dusty vehicle in the last available spot, defying the sign that read 'Personnel Only.' His sun kissed face and dark wavy hair bore lighter streaks from a Caribbean cruise he'd taken weeks ago. But he was back now, and it was imperative that he make this visit.

The old man in Suite 115, the most luxurious with views in two directions, didn't seem to care much about his surroundings, interior or exterior. At times, he could figure out where he was and even why he was here, so it was thought. Since his arrival at the Manor, he would count the days in sunsets and sunrises. Evenings he would watch the shrinking sphere through the bay window as it slipped out of sight beneath the hills. The other window provided southern exposure to welcome the same sphere in luminous pastels as it repeated its daily voyage.

But when it rained, that threw off the count. Didn't matter. He was just there. That was indisputable. That late day sun, like him, the older man, gradually lost its colors, and faded into oblivion, a void of blackness until, presto! His room was flooded with harsh, artificial light, like his life there at the Manor, artificial, not the way it was, or should be. Same thing, day after day, night after night. He showed no interest in what the flat screen TV on a corner wall could offer. He didn't need to be reminded of how others lived, whether fact or fantasy. He was trapped in a world of bright hopes and gray despair, a confusion of time and space.

They would say he had failed to thrive, like the flower arrangements in his bedside vase. The older man insisted they remain there even as they crumbled and flaked onto the nightstand. For some reason or another, he couldn't tell you, he wanted them there, until of course new ones arrived, and they always did. It was something else he could count on.

At the arrival of the young man, the older man showed a modicum of relief from his humdrum existence. A brightening of his rheumy blue eyes, a little more focus. He cocked his head toward his visitor. The older man couldn't tell you how often this visitor came. Was it every other day, once a week? His thoughts wouldn't let him go there. For that matter, it could have been the first visit. His mind played such tricks.

And so he tried to fashion a smile, at least he thought he did, and with his good hand accepted the out-stretched hand from his visitor. The young man rubbed the older man's good hand and proffered fresh flowers to replace the skeletal remains. A thought ran through the older man's head that maybe this young man had brought him flowers before. Then the thought vanished as quickly as it had invaded his conscious mind. He wasn't sure. It seemed to him he was never sure about much of anything. What was dream, what was reality. Thoughts swam in at random and ran amok like little fishes in an aquarium. But he did feel a sense of gladness that the young man was here, but only for a moment.

The young man was much younger, by a good 30 or so years. He addressed his elder by name. Yes, it felt comfortable to the older man to hear his name, his proper name. It felt familiar, right, good.

"Well, how are you today? In good spirits, I hope?" The young man knew better. Hoping for a verbal response was probably useless, but the older man did pause to let it sink in just the same. The young man noticed that. He wished he could read his thoughts, but feared what the older man still might be thinking. "Look," he said, smiling. You could see where the young man's laugh lines were pale in contrast to his tanned, finely chiseled face. "I've brought you some of my first blooms of the season, white lilacs. Remember you were almost excited as I when those harbingers of spring first appeared in the garden. You quoted from Whitman, 'When lilacs last in the dooryard bloom'd.' You told me that white lilacs are symbolic of the holiness of life. You know, I never knew that. "

He waited again for some recognition, some sign, but the older man only grunted a guttural sound, seemingly an attempt at intelligible speech, and then he gestured with his good arm, motioning for him to exchange the old flowers for the new.

"The garden's looking especially nice this spring," the young man said as though nothing out of the ordinary had happened. He addressed the older man in a normal tone of voice. There was no need to be condescending. After all, the older man was still his superior. "I wish you could smell the lilacs, don't you? Or maybe you can. Here." He moved the lilacs toward the older man's face, but was rebuffed. In response, the older man motioned again toward the vase. Then he nodded, almost imperceptibly, uttered the same sound, and rested his chin onto his chest. The young man noticed the lightweight robe was in need of a good pressing. The older man in his right mind would have frowned upon wearing a wrinkled garment, especially in the presence of others. He was a proper man of habit, liked things just so. Back then, that was.

The young man began to speak a little louder. He couldn't be sure how much the older man's hearing was impaired, or if at all. It was hard to read him. He turned abruptly as an aide knocked first and then strode in to tend to the flowers. The young man wondered who had summoned her. She must have seen him enter with the bouquet. He hadn't signed in. The woman at the main desk had merely waved him through. They hadn't spoken. And he hadn't even taken in the surroundings. He was intent only on seeing the older man, searching his face, checking for signs of progress, and hoping, hoping for a return to normalcy and healing, not just for the older man, but for himself and the others.

His last visit, an austere, starched looking woman, the head nurse, had informed him that she thought the older man might be depressed and that could be hindering his progress. Her lips were pursed even as she formed her words. Strange, he thought. She was not very agreeable looking. She stated that the older man needed to work harder at getting back to his former self, and he was not a very willing resident, even recalcitrant. Not patient, but *resident*, she'd called him, connoting the idea of permanence to the young man. It saddened him to hear her harsh words.

But did he believe them? He tried not to hold much credence in any prognosis. He knew the older man too well as being a man of conviction. He'd improve if he willed himself to, if he believed there was a need for him to do so. But what was really going on that mind of his? The young man feared the worst. The older man seemed lost in his own world. He had to will himself back. Fight to return to his former self and continue where he had left off, to resume their friendship, if it was ever possible. Some things could be fixed. Others...he let go of that thought.

"Where are your beads?" The young man broke the silence. The older man reacted to the increase in volume. He seemed to register the weight of the question as he lifted his head and moved his lips to speak but only managed something like 'eer'. He sagged. Then he moved his good hand down into a pocket and with gnarled fingers fished them out. He brought the crucifix to his face, searching for his lips. He missed the target and kissed the air instead. Then he dropped the beads. They landed in his lap and slid down the trouser leg of his baggy pajamas.

The young man retrieved them, smiling weakly. Then he turned to reposition the fresh flowers. The aide had disposed of the dead ones, refilled the water and plopped the new flowers in the vase where they rested as they may, lacking any sense of creative arrangement, all within in a matter of seconds, then she disappeared without a word like a ghost.

It was late afternoon and nearing the older man's supper hour. Except for the sun's position, it could have been any time of the day. The young man was about to take leave when he heard a knock at the door. Too late for a doctor's call, and the older man's sister or nephew would know not to come at this hour. This time no one entered. The knock came again, gentle but a little more persistent. The older man turned his head, but wasn't about to respond so the young man rose to answer the door.

In sailed a teen-aged girl, tallish, elegant but casual in appearance. The young man's eyes opened wide as did his mouth. What could she be doing here? And with flowers, too? What is wrong with her? Has she no sense of propriety? The flowers, he noted, were the same as those from his garden. He knew the variety well. He had cultivated them and designed every inch of his garden after studying book after book on the subject. It was an interest that came along at an opportune time in his life and served to meet a need. It soon became a passion.

Well, the young man said to himself, that girl was capable of just about anything. There were no rules in her book. Rather, she created her own to suit her needs and whims.

She beamed when she saw the young man who returned to his seat, a floral overstuffed chair. He, in turn, recoiled as she approached him. "Oh, I get it." She smiled shamelessly at the two men. The older man grew agitated, distressed. He looked down at his hands.

She addressed the young man first. "The lilacs. I see you beat me to it. I, uh, borrowed a few but I thought you wouldn't mind so much since I didn't take all of them. There's a lot left, even though they're mostly still buds." She paused a moment, hoping he would look at her. She softened her voice. "I didn't know you'd be here."

"No, I'm sure you didn't." The young man tried to neutralize the hostility in his voice, to conceal what he felt. There was a sensation of pulling at the back of his throat. He gulped involuntarily. He couldn't help it. Her presence always unnerved him. He wished it wouldn't show but it did, and she knew it, but she thought it meant something else. Still he couldn't look her straight in the eye and so he looked down, averting those sensational hazel eyes, then over at the older man. He had to do something.

"Can I squeeze my flowers into the same vase as yours?" Her tone was sensual. She always managed to sound that way to him no matter the circumstances. He wondered what made her that way.

"Why not?" The young man answered glibly, still avoiding eye contact. "You'll do what you want." He wished he hadn't said that.

"Well, they'll match." She ignored the gravitas of his remark. "And why have another vase on that little stand? It'd be too crowded or maybe he'd knock it over." She looked over at the older man. She had tempered her sensuality with a dose of sweetness.

Without invitation, she hopped onto the older man's bed, pausing to straighten the spread, then asked directly and very slowly, "How are you doing today?" She made a point to use his proper title, which she'd always forgotten or chosen to ignore. She reached out to touch his hand, the lame one. The good one was now in the pocket with his beads. He felt nothing. The young man thought he detected a frown on the older man's face. With him in that condition, it was hard to tell. "I come again to ask your forgiveness," she said to him, hoping he could hear her. "I'm truly sorry. I am. I didn't realize..." Her tone was anything but sensual as she tried to unlock the older man's fixed countenance. She actually looked contrite or else she had put on her face of remorse as she could, as she had too often.

"I don't know if he heard me." She addressed her comment to the young man who was self- absorbed. He appeared to be studying the blank TV in the corner. "Maybe he's deaf too. Do you think he can hear what I said? "

"I think he does hear you." The young man sounded absentminded. "Yeah, he does."

"Well, he's not saying anything," she insisted, fiddling with a garish maroon claw of a fingernail – the same color as her hair. "I can ask him again. I want him to know how sorry I am. Really." Tears welled in her eyes. The young man tried to avoid them. There was too much in those eyes.

The young man fidgeted with his shirt collar. He glanced at his watch, then turned to address the older man. "You know, I'm heading out now. I'll be back to keep you up to snuff with all the news. Everyone's been asking when you'll be back. We miss you. I miss you."

To her, he said, "You'd best be leaving too. You don't want to tire him out. His supper will be wheeled in a few minutes." His dismissive tone had little effect.

"I just got here. I can't tell if he's heard me say that I'm sorry." Now she was whining. That little girl voice. Her petulance bothered him.

After a moment. Now the young man knew it—that she'd been there before. She should leave things alone. Let it be. The more you scrape at it, the deeper the wound. And some things never heal; they leave the scar for you to contemplate forever, a searing reminder. And who would know it better than he? He screwed up his courage to speak again to her, still not facing her. "You can't take all the blame. Sometimes things just happen." He spoke this to the picture window, out to the hills beyond, and to the vista that the older man saw day after day. And for her.

He hoped the older man had some peace amidst his jumbled thoughts—unlike his own and the girl's. He heard her leave, waited a few minutes, then gently touched the older man's shoulder and closed the door behind him.

Chapter TWO
(December, the previous year)

CONSIDER THE FAIRY circles in the sands of the Namib Desert on the southern coast of Africa. The mysterious origins of their perfectly round shape, devoid of vegetation, has intrigued experts in many fields, generating explanations from countless theorists, ranging from ecologists to computer scientists. These circles of sand over time morph from a pure sand surface to one of complete vegetation, and then revert to the sand circles, from order to chaos and then the reverse, ad infinitum. Does not that phenomenon bear resemblance to the vicissitudes of human existence, the peaceful times yielding to chaotic upsets, and then back again—just about anywhere in this world?

FATHER CHRISTOPHER Tosi passed through the small town of Birch Valley, Connecticut, near enough to his parents' home, a roomy Dutch cape, circa 1970. It was the only real home he'd remembered since moving into St. Aeden's rectory and sharing the quarters and parish duties with his pastor and mentor, Father Bernard Monahan, so he decided to pay his mother a visit. But it had to be brief. She, of course, was delighted to see her son whenever he had a few minutes to spare. Since the opportunity presented itself, she offered to send him back with Christmas presents, for him and for Father Bernie, as he was known to most, but Chris declined, saying he'd see her later on Christmas day, and that Father Bernie, still a kid at heart, would be tempted to open his gift, then rewrap it, hoping no one would discover this furtive act that he'd perfected in his childhood along with his brothers and sister.

She wanted her son to stay for lunch—always the doting mother—food plus gentle reminders equals love—the all too familiar equation. But he was far too busy to take that much of a break. He was way behind in his schedule of duties. And to add insult to injury, he had consented to be interviewed by the local newspaper reporter for the last of her seasonal articles on his prayer garden. Another hitch in his already overloaded schedule.

He was pleased he'd caught his mother at home. He feared she might be out doing last minute shopping. It would take her days to prepare for Christmas dinner, and each year it was different. One year she might invite old friends or relatives he'd hardly remembered. Other times someone who had no place to go would show up at the table for the holiday dinner. He never knew whom to expect. It gradually became the one holiday that his mother put her heart into. She would pass over the other holidays, a practice that stemmed back from the tragedy that altered the course of all their lives, the one that extinguished so much of the holiday spirit in her. But for Christmas, Marie Angela Tosi made the effort to supercharge it, even if for only a day, and then it left her entirely, making her feel selfish that she was able to enjoy herself.

"Christopher," Marie said joyfully. She always called him by his given name, and she always tried to be upbeat in his presence. She thought it would do both of them good, and it did. But Chris couldn't help notice how his mother had changed over the past ten years. Her dark eyes dulled. Some days, they seemed to hold so much pain, and her hair was almost completely gray, unstylish. She wore it shorter now, and would nervously pluck at an errant curl, evidence that her thoughts were elsewhere other than in her kitchen. And she didn't seem as tall either or else she didn't stand up to her full height almost as though she made the effort to crawl inside herself. As for her husband Fred, Chris's father, he looked about the same, but kept his emotions guarded as if expressing them might effeminate him. Marie's strained, unnatural cheerfulness only annoyed him, got him drinking too much when she got into those moods, those moods to try to show people she was fine, just fine. She wasn't. It was hard to fathom and so she tried to stay even-keeled whether she felt it or not. But seeing her son, the priest, always put her in a better frame of mind. She thrived on his visits.

She broke a moment of silence between them. "I do hope Father Bernie will be able to make it to dinner his year. I'll be making his favorite roast with all the trimmings. Please ask him if you haven't already. But I'll bet you probably did. I like to think of him as part of our family."

"You might say that he is. I will remind him, Mom," Chris responded. "He should come if he doesn't go to his sister Molly's. You know he goes there for other holidays mostly. But I'm not sure if she's up to cooking for the holiday this year. She hasn't been in great shape lately, according to what Bernie tells me. Not that her lazy son would consider getting help for her or taking her out to a restaurant dinner."

"I won't hear of that," she retorted. "Out to dinner, imagine that, on Christmas day. Then that would mean Father Bernie too." She tsk-tsked audibly. Then she brightened. "I've got it. When you invite Bernie, why don't you ask him to bring his sister along? We'd be happy to have her."

"That's extra work for you, Mom. What does that bring your number up to now?" he asked. Frown lines appeared on his forehead. He didn't want his mother to feel overly stressed. His mother was strong but he knew she'd get little help from his father.

"Now don't you worry about that, Christopher," she reassured him. "It'll be very pleasant having them with us. Please tell them so. And I, uh, I hope you don't mind, but I have asked Jack and Ada Powers to join us for dinner this year, and they have accepted." She stopped to gauge his reaction. It wasn't slow coming. She took a deep breath and continued, "Face it, Christopher, it's about time. We, uh, I have to move on. All of us do. It's been, what is it now, ten years, hasn't it?" She stopped to contemplate. "Now let's see how many we've got."

Chris's reaction caused her to stammer. She took a moment to regroup then forced a smile, taut, uncomfortable. Unnatural. Chris knew better. He didn't know how it would feel with the Powers couple there, not that he had anything personally against them. There was no reason to. But have they forgotten, have they been able to move on as though nothing had happened to fracture the two families? Could they pretend that everything's just fine now? Not very likely, he decided.

Marie recomposed herself. She had a knack, a habit she'd acquired for self-preservation, of segueing from an uncomfortable topic to an entirely different one in a split second. And the timing was perfect in this case. "By the way, Christopher, how is that beautiful garden of yours these days?"

Chris broke into a grin at his mother's skill. But then a not so subtle glance at his watch prompted a quick sobering. "Oh Mom, it's winter. My garden's dormant now, well, mostly. Nothing much is happening there. Nothing is supposed to. It's fine. Everything needs rest now and then, even my flowers and shrubs," he answered. "They're, uh, hibernating." He shifted his weight from one leg to the other, then added, "Except for maybe one or two plants."

"Well, I don't think Beryl Baines would decide to write about nothing at all," she said resolutely. The local reporter had already extolled the magnificence of his garden in the three previous seasons. Winter was next, as Chris well knew. It would complete the series. Baines had received highly positive response to her previous articles, and almost over night Chris had become a minor local celebrity, which he could have done without. He wished that she could conduct the interview on another day. Today was too full.

"She will have to be very creative to find anything much to say in her winter article. I guess we'll have to see," he remarked impatiently. "That would be a challenge—really not much at all to write about." He turned towards the front door, zipping his jacket. Marie arranged his scarf as only a mother could or would do.

"You know, Mom, I really have to get going. I only stopped by to say 'hi'. Tell Dad the same too. Hope he's OK." Marie shrugged which could have meant anything or nothing. Chris hugged and kissed his mother. Then they both did their private little wave, something Marie initiated when Chris and his twin sister Beth went off to kindergarten. These days it made both of them feel good. Then the practice ended abruptly at that traumatic time in their lives. She was happy to see it reinstituted quite by chance after Chris received Holy Orders, one of the most joyous moments in their lives. She had tried to erase the memory of spring semester of his high school days and the three years he'd been to college when much of his communication was monosyllabic, when he was shrouded in a state of perpetual gloom. Once it lifted, it drifted and morphed. At times it threated to envelop him, but he was better able to slough it off when he became a seminarian. Father Bernie was probably the best person for him to be around in times when the gloom reemerged. It was to Marie's benefit that she knew very little of what was still troubling her son.

Chris had adjusted fairly quickly and well to Wexford Falls and to St. Aeden Church and community. He would always refer to his habitat as the little big town, reminiscent of the famous country group by the same name, not that he was a big fan of their music but it was how he characterized his new location. He thrived there until inevitably the anniversary of the Christmas week tragedy came around, dredging up feelings of resentment and discomfort leading to depression.

Wealthy homes, veritable chateaux sprang up in the outskirts of Wexford Falls over the past decade. Manufacturing companies, small businesses and franchises employed many of the town's inhabitants, some of whom pride themselves in tracing their heritage back to the founding fathers of the county. In the center of town, Main Street and its immediate environs was an ongoing project, undergoing renovation and restructuring, to include some welcome gentrification, all of which was sorely needed as time had whittled away the newness and threatened the soundness of so many older structures.

But this was not so for Chris's beloved St. Aeden Church, which dates back well over a century. Built from field stones and mortar and the sweat and toil and calloused hands of master masons, it was solid, elegant in its Romanesque simplicity. All things considered, it was a perfect fit, newly ordained Father Christopher Tosi and St. Aeden's with his own outdoor design, the meditation garden, clearly an integral part of it.

MARIE TOSI WAS THRILLED that her son the priest was assigned to a parish only twenty-five minutes away, that being only if her husband was driving. She, on the other hand, preferred the back roads, which undoubtedly added time to her trip. She was also thankful that Chris had made the choice to live at home with his parents and commute to State University, having relinquished his basketball scholarship to Providence College. Among the many life changes was his major, which may have led to a shift in his career path. But he was needed there at home at that time and not hours and miles away, and he surely needed his parents. The three clung tenaciously to each other as if to life rafts in a turbulent sea until the day he made a surprise announcement.

Chris wanted to join the priesthood. And yes, he was certain of his choice. There was no doubt in his mind. A period of discernment in Italy after graduation set him straight. He would enter the seminary to prepare for his life as a priest. He felt now as though his life had a keen sense of direction, a purpose. Marie though had mixed emotions. Now for sure, she would never have grandchildren like the Mullins family whose rafters echoed with the squeals of delight as their brood descended upon them Christmas Eve. From that awful day on, their good neighbors invited Chris and his parents to join them on Christmas Eve. And they would go, laden with food and gifts, and in the midst of their company they would enjoy the festivities, or at least go through the motions; then the gloom would gradually descend upon them once they were back home. The bright spot was when Marie decided a few years ago to celebrate anew Christmas dinner in all its glory.

What it took was Marie Tosi's having a long talk with herself. She told herself to break loose and make a big deal of Christmas day, to start with one special day—to make it joyful for others, hoping it would spread to her, that it would bathe her in the joy of the Christ child's birth. She then began coming to St. Aeden Church to attend mass celebrated by her son. Dinner therefore had to be later in the day as Chris's mass was usually the last one and she needed sufficient time to put the finishing touches on the dinner. Father Bernie nabbed the earlier mass, as he always rose with the proverbial chickens. Plus he could pull rank, being the elder.

For his first Christmas at St. Aeden's, Marie gifted her son with books and manuals on gardening. She had read somewhere that gardening was salubrious, even therapeutic, or maybe it was her psychologist who had suggested that she herself take it up. Instead she passed it on to Chris. And so he credited his mother with getting him into the pursuit of gardening. She thought it would be beneficial for her son, working out of doors, beautifying grounds for a prayerful purpose, not realizing that he'd have little time to cultivate anything other than his spirit. Father Bernie agreed wholeheartedly with Marie that Chris could do something that he himself had only dreamed of. Of course, Chris knew next to nothing about gardening. The only experience he'd had with anything growing outside was mowing the grass when his father was too busy. If it was green, Chris would cut it down per his father's instructions. Plus he remembered it being fun zooming around on the riding mower. It was the part of yard work he liked best especially before he was old enough to get a driver's license.

Father Bernie had a plan. He laid it out to his young curate emphatically: there's an empty lot adjacent to the church grounds that was bequeathed to St. Aeden's some years ago, and it had served no purpose at all. It had remained just a weed infested vacant lot that had to be mowed flat so as not to look ugly. They already had adequate parking on the premises so why not make a garden there? Not a vegetable garden; there were farmers markets galore, but a flower garden with anything in the world he wanted to plant as long as it was beautiful and inviting. Bernie could not tolerate the proliferation of weeds; he felt it was an open invitation to invite pests and other undesirable invaders so close to the church. Chris didn't want to start out on the wrong foot with his pastor, so he said he'd give it a try.

A few years later it was the talk of Wexford Falls. Chris was interviewed for a regional publication which featured several flattering shots of the garden and a few interesting facts about the young priest who had designed and maintained it. The reporter called it quite 'fetching', a strange descriptor for a prayer garden, Chris thought. But the garden became his refuge and his pride and joy. When things ate at him, he would go out there and watch the birds and the butterflies flitting about his flowering shrubs. That many of his plantings had religious or symbolic meaning only added to the charm of his garden. It set him at ease praying in the midst of such natural beauty.

Fortunately there was very little to maintaining the garden in the winter so his efforts could be channeled to the Christmas duties and activities of which there were more than he and Father Bernie alone could manage. If it weren't for the generosity of the parishioners they could hardly handle all the extras. There was the outdoor pageant and the special music program. Once everything came together, it would be spellbinding. It was just days away, and so much more to set in place.

FATHER CHRIS TOSI EASED his dusty blue Ford 150 pickup into the long gravel driveway of St. Aeden's behind the charming old Victorian style rectory, cream colored with dark brown and green trim everywhere trim could possibly be. He preferred leaving the vehicle outside whereas Father Bernie parked his shiny black Chrysler in the far left of the three bay garage, always the far one. It was habit, as the other two bays were rarely occupied. The garages were repainted to match the rectory, although much of the trim was cream as well. Since it was way in back no one made any move to repaint it.

Chris couldn't help but notice a stack of old lumber of motley sizes and shapes heaped haphazardly in front of the right bay of the garage. He shook his head in disbelief. Could those boards ever be fashioned into a respectable looking manger? The sorry sight served as a sobering reminder that they had to get a move on to get it done before the annual Christmas pageant just days away.

Chris yanked the emergency brake and the pickup obeyed with a grinding squeak. He had parked it dangerously close to that woodpile of dubious value. Chris got out and checked some of the planks, shaking his head in disbelief. Next year they'd probably need to replace the lumber, although the manger needn't look brand new either. Somehow they would get it to work.

Chris spotted Mrs. Hopkins, the housekeeper, getting into her Toyota. He gave her an energetic wave. She had stayed on later than usual. Chris wondered why. He supposed that everyone was working overtime or on all eight cylinders because of the demands of the holiday season. And Mrs. Hopkins was no exception.

The one he did not expect to see was Beryl Baines from The Hillside Journal. She had pulled into the driveway just as Chris was heading toward the back door. Then it hit him. He had forgotten their appointment for the interview, but she obviously hadn't, and she was persistent, a requisite quality reporters tend to possess to get the job done.

"Hey there, Father Chris," she yelled running after him, panting and huffing, her ample bosom heaving under a voluminous silk scarf. Wispy yellow bangs peeked out of her beret. Once she caught her breath she said, "Remember, Father, we had a three o'clock today?" He knew he hadn't.

"So then, how about now?" she asked almost frantically, wiping her forehead with the back of her hand. "I have a deadline."

He wanted to say, so do I, but he did not wish to appear rude. She had done much for St. Aeden's and for him as well through her folksy articles centering on his prayer garden. Membership in their parish had increased since the articles were published. Father Bernie commended Chris for that, and the bishop, in turn, commended Father Bernie for such growth and what it translated to for the diocese.

"OK for here and now, Mrs. Baines?" he asked hopefully. Maybe like this, on the fly, she could get her information faster. Father Bernie would wonder what was keeping him. He certainly would have heard the pickup make its presence known.

"Oh, OK, Father Chris," she relented. She dreaded the flight of stairs that awaited her. "Sure, why not? Come sit in my car, please. If that's not all right, I suppose I could come upstairs. And, by the way, Father, remember it's Beryl. Skip the formality, please."

Chris anticipated Bernie's reaction at this hour and said, "Sure, Beryl it is. No, that's fine with me if it works for you here, but I've only got a few minutes. Really." She nodded. What else could she do?

"Ah, yes, winter, a good time to get the story done before the snows cover it all up. We're lucky or you would say blessed that they're a trifle late coming this year—much to our benefit, " she began. She couldn't help notice his end of the day weariness, regretting that she was taxing him so. Dutifully, she whipped out her note pad and pencil from her worn canvas tote bag and surveyed her list of questions, wondering how she was going to make this do in just minutes, and by the light of her flashlight.

Chapter THREE

WITHOUT FURTHER ADO, Beryl Baines edged herself onto the driver's side of her compact sedan, adjusting her bulky car coat for comfort sake. She patted the passenger seat, inviting Chris to be seated, and he accepted. He fiddled around with the seat levers to make room for his long legs. Beryl's were a good foot or so shorter than his, he estimated.

Not wasting any time as she'd promised, she began. "Oh, by the way, Father Chris, Emil, you know my son Emil, I guess everybody does, well he came along with me, uh, earlier, at the time we had set for our, uh, appointment. And, uh, as long as we, he and I, were here, he, uh, was the one who took the pictures, not I. I hope you don't mind, but Emil likes to come along and help, and he really does a fine job, so people say. He did do some of the pictures for two of the seasons' articles. Remember he was at a special camp for, you know, the challenged, at the time of the summer article. So I did the pictures myself for that one."

Chris noticed that she had her camera handy to refer to the photos, as needed. This is going take forever, he feared. He was already feeling cramped. The seat didn't go back as far as he'd have liked. He replied, "No, of course, why should I mind? The articles have been great, exceptional I should say, the photos too, both Emil's and yours."

Beryl smiled broadly, revealing a row of recently crowned teeth, licked the tip of her pencil and got right into it, gazing at him intently. She asked him how he felt about the faded remains of his garden in the bleakness of winter. She knew he'd kept as much of the color alive, covering various plantings until the first habitual frost robbed them of their vitality.

A slow to form smile told her as much as words could. Faded remains? Look what actually did remain. Is different less than vibrant where the plantings are concerned? He'd let her carry the ball.

"I was amazed at what we noticed this afternoon out there in the garden," she gushed. Beryl was an astute reporter as well as part time editor who knew exactly how to capture her interviewee's attention. But still the doting mother that she was, she credited her special needs son for noticing, or she said as much. "Emil spotted it, the star, the star that is. You have a star configuration, in your walks, those paths, five rays emanating from a center, I mean. I didn't see that when I covered your garden for the paper the past seasons. The floral presence seemed to overtake the design of the paths. So I never noticed. The eye was drawn to the color, the variety and arrangement of your plantings—to the sheer beauty, the totality of it. But now with the plants all in hibernation," she paused to chuckle, "the star design predominates. What a clever idea, Father."

Chris by nature was modest, unassuming. "That was quite by chance, I assure you. For me, each path led to a different destination—a statue, a birdbath, a bench, for example. That there turned out to be five rays radiating from a center was, I should imagine, a divine working. I can't really take credit for it, no, not at all."

"Oh, but you can, Father Chris, and why not?" she said, scrawling furiously on her little pad, flipping pages at an alarming rate, nodding, getting it all down verbatim, Chris figured. She paused a second to anchor her flashlight more securely on the dashboard." Then she added, "The star, ah yes, so appropriate to the season, to Christmas tide, the star of Bethlehem, wouldn't you say?"

Chris seemed to be weighing her words. He nodded, pleased with the direction her article would take. He was amazed that this chatty, motherly matron was so observant and perceptive in taking in what she saw and heard, giving it a particular slant.

"I'm sure our readers can't wait to see this last of the seasons articles. And I promise—I'll see it gets out right away, in time for Christmas. Now, where was I? Oh yes. Father, I assume you have planted mostly perennials, am I right?" she looked directly at him. She thought she knew flowers pretty well, having written so many articles about the Wexford Falls Garden Club. Millicent Tewksbury, the long time president and master gardener, had instructed her well, always volunteering much more information than requested.

He nodded, hoping to avoid discussing what was and what wasn't a perennial. It was winter. It didn't matter. She got the hint and moved on.

"I suppose you miss those charming little hummingbirds, don't you Father?" she asked. "I assume you know what they represent."

Oh, she was leading him. Yes, he knew full well what they stood for. He looked forward to their arrival each year, to their fragile daintiness, their delicate grace, to their celebration of life as only they can express themselves. Spring was always a relief to him, the rebirth of nature in all its splendor and glory.

"Yes, by all means. I make sure that I provide for them. To see them floating above my flowers is a very peaceful feeling, such natural beauty and elegance, but I thought we were focusing on my winter garden," he added with a sense of urgency. " I imagine you noticed the suet packs and sunflower seeds that I leave for the winter visitors."

"Ah, yes. And I'll bet you just go right across the street to the Swenson's Hardware for your seeds, don't you?" she asked with a sweet smile. "You can find just about anything in that place. And Eva Swenson is such a darling lady. Everybody loves her so."

Well, of course, he'd go locally, to Swenson's. He was surprised she'd even ask, but he figured reporters do ask all kinds of questions since an unanticipated one may lead to something of interest.

"Father, let's focus a minute on your holly bushes, so many of them. I've only given them lip service, if you will, in the other articles. There was so much to concentrate on when the garden was in bloom, but holly is a Christmas plant and this is where we are, right now, just days away." She directed Chris who feared a lengthy explanation would be in order, but, oh, why not?

He sneaked a quick peek at his watch before answering. Bernie would be wondering what was going on. "The hollies, yes. If you recall, I chose hollies as a border on the two sides facing the street for a hedge to keep onlookers from gazing into the garden. My aim was to give it a secluded sense of peace, considering how this garden is planted on a corner lot."

Beryl flexed the fingers of her right hand and nodded. She noticed that Chris appeared to be having an 'aha' moment. She always hoped for those moments to occur when interviewing since one idea often led quite unexpectedly to another, and provided richness to an article.

"Now, Beryl, this may be of interest to readers. So, you know the leaves of the hollies are prickly; well, it has been said that they represent the crown of thorns that Jesus wore on Good Friday, and the red berries on the female bushes symbolize the drops of blood shed at the Crucifixion. But you can't have these female bushes without the presence of the male bushes...no fruit without pollination, that is. We can thank the bees for that. Those red berries appear once a year in the fall. But you may have mentioned that in the autumn article. I can't remember." Chris just realized that he'd gone from the sacred to the profane in his explanation, but he'd leave it up to Beryl as to what she chose to include in her article.

Beryl continued to scribble as she nodded for him to go on. Her head seemed to him to be in perpetual motion. He smiled and resumed. "I'm probably going off track, but I thought you might want to consider this. Are you familiar with the Christmas song, 'The Holly and the Ivy'?"

He observed her nodding, now more emphatically, affirmatively. Yes, she knew the song. She'd heard it each year at Christmas time. It was definitely not one of her favorites though, couldn't hold a candle to "O Holy Night".

"Now, I'm sure you noticed ivy climbing on the larger rocks. We hauled them here and put them where they'd look best. Actually we weren't sure where that was. You can see them a lot better now that the flowers are dormant. Did you know that ivy is actually an evergreen? Love the name evergreen. Explains it nicely. OK now, for support, ivy must cling onto something to survive in the way that we cling to Christ in our lives, and note how the ivy also becomes entwined into the hollies," he said, pausing for a reaction. He handed her camera to her so she could check for a photo of the ivies, which she did. Again, her familiar nod.

"Oh, I almost forgot," she said twinkling with renewed energy. Another idea just struck her. "All right, we have talked about flowers that bloomed and died prior to winter, but what about those new blooms I'm seeing near your Mary shrine?" She located the photo on the camera. Chris beamed.

"Now that is a story," he said. "You may need to sharpen your pencil." The heck with time. He needed to tell her what would give her article something special, something many people might not know.

"No problem, Father," she said. "I've got several sharpened ones. I'm ready. Go on." She opened her case and showed him pencils of various lengths ready for action.

"What you see blooming on either side of my shrine to Mary is the Glastonbury rose, which is not really a rose at all, but it does have thorns and leaves and looks somewhat like a rose, a wild rose, one might say. It is considered an evergreen. There again. We are so blessed. I am so blessed. It grows and blooms all winter, fortunately in this zone, in frozen ground. You can see for yourself.

"Mrs. Tewksbury deserves the credit for these plants. A few years ago when I undertook this project, my garden, she came to me and asked if I wanted any guidance—that's what she called it—not help but guidance. I thought having the gardening manuals would be enough, but, no, she had a wonderful idea, if I wanted to wait, to be patient, she said. She mentioned the Glastonbury rose from the Christmas legend and said it was best to start them as seedlings. Who was I to argue with a master gardener? So I gave her free rein. To make a very long story short, she got the seeds, nursed them along, as only she could, before they sprouted, and then she planted them three years later according to specifications there, where you see them in bloom. And now starting this season, I am so happy to say Mary will be surrounded all year long by roses, her floral symbol, you know.

"By the way, Beryl, I loved Emil's shot of the other rose arbor in the spring article. It was just the perfect angle," he explained. It made Chris feel good to tell this to Beryl, to compliment her son. He probably had told her so last spring. No harm in repeating it. She liked to hear positive remarks about her special son. He didn't receive very many.

Not that she hadn't listened to Chris's explanation, but the word 'legend' grabbed her. She didn't let it go. "Ah, the legend, yes, the legend of the Christmas rose," she said. "I remember that so fondly."

"I do, too," Chris said with a trace of sadness. "My mother told it to us, to my twin sister Beth and me, when we were little. We were fascinated. Imagine that poor little girl, way back many centuries ago. She was so sad she had no gift for the Christ child that she cried. Then the snow melted where her tears fell, and, in that very spot, the Christmas rose sprang forth. And that became her gift for the baby Jesus. My sister and I couldn't imagine that—a flower in the snow—but our mother asked us if we believed in miracles, and being children, we said of course we did. Well, for us this was another miracle, like the Tooth Fairy, the Easter Bunny and, of course, Santa Claus. That was it. We never forgot that tale."

"Nor should we, Father," Beryl responded. "So your prayer garden has many layers, many phases." She set down her pencil and heaved a sigh. "And winter is not so bleak at all."

"No, hardly. I see it as phases as well," he answered. "I do have to keep the paths cleared when the snows come, but rest assured, I will do just that, as I have in the past. It must be cleared so that I, so that anyone who wants to go there and pray, may do so. The weather will dictate the length of our visits. Remember, the garden belongs to all of us. I also have to keep those feeders full. Our feathered friends, sorry for the cliché, but they need food to survive. I won't disappoint them. "

They both laughed. She closed her notebook.

"The garden is my refuge from a busy, hectic world. Blocking it out, praying there by myself...Remember, I've heard that solitude is often the best society," he said with a wink.

"John Milton," she said grinning, taking pride in her college major.

"Yes, indeed, Milton," he said. "I'm surprised that I remember, after all." He truly was.

"Father Chris, I thank you so much for your time. I can't imagine how busy you must be. It's always a delight to experience what you feel, your passion for the beauty you have brought to that ugly old vacant lot," she said as she crammed her belongings into her tote.

"I thank you, Beryl, and I am sorry for missing our appointment and upsetting your schedule. I look forward to reading the article," he said, getting out of her car.

"Well, you provided all the material," she replied. "Good evening, Father. Send my greetings to dear Father Bernie." She adjusted the rear view mirror, then she yelled out to him, " Remember Emil and me in your prayers, Father." Chris nodded in response. She was already on her way out.

Chris shuddered as she threw the car in reverse and zoomed down the long curved driveway. He prayed that she wouldn't hit anything.

Chapter FOUR

THE EVENING WAS COLD and crisp and invigorating as it should be this time of year. Father Bernie was waiting for Chris to come upstairs to their quarters to dine in their preferred room, the upstairs kitchen overlooking the prayer garden. He had heard the crunch on the gravel and the unmistakable squeak of the pickup's brakes, so he knew Chris was back. As the minutes wore on he went over to his bedroom window where he spotted Beryl Baines' car parked along side the pickup. He could see her and Chris chatting in her car. Ah, yes, the interview. He recalled Chris mentioning the appointment but thought it was for earlier in the day. Regardless, he welcomed more positive publicity for the church. It would benefit St. Aeden's. He figured dinner could wait, and it did. It was next to impossible to keep on a regular schedule Christmas week.

Father Bernard Monahan, aka Father Bernie, hailed from Hartford, the capital city, where he served as a curate in two Roman Catholic churches consecutively in the inner city. He was transferred to St. Aeden's some twenty-five years ago and became a beloved figure in the Wexford Falls community. His piety, wry sense of humor and willingness to lend an ear to anyone in need, Christian or not, endeared him to all. When the elderly pastor in residence succumbed to an aneurysm, it made sense to the bishop to name Father Bernie as interim pastor and administrator of St. Aeden's.

Back then he resided in the first floor quarters. The upstairs, which was hardly used, consisted of several bedrooms, a large den, an office, and an unused kitchen with outdated furniture and an oversized pantry. Arrangements changed only when the title of interim disappeared and he was assigned a new curate who preferred having the privacy of upstairs quarters. Two years later that priest who shall remain nameless left the priesthood much to Father Bernie's dismay. A few more years under the pastor's trusty leadership and tutelage and the young man would have adjusted well enough to the demands of a priest's life. Father Bernie felt responsible in part for the priest's failure. Then it all changed.

Father Christopher Tosi, fresh out of the seminary and newly ordained, was the next young curate assigned to St. Aeden's. Father Bernie knew in his heart that this warm, passionate priest would thrive in the parish, as he did. He also felt he should temper his training to let the priest come into his own. He would mentor him in the best sense of the word. In retrospect, Father Bernie thought maybe he had been too exacting, too imposing on the previous young curate. He had poured out these thoughts, his own shortcomings, to the bishop, who responded with 'Nonsense, he wasn't cut out for the priesthood, that's all.'

This December evening, the two priests sat in silence dining later than the usual hour. Before leaving, Mrs. Hopkins had rewarmed a hearty casserole – one of her many culinary talents – using up whatever remained in the fridge or the pantry in a way no one would ever have dreamed of – at least neither of those two. After the blessing—it was Chris's turn this night—they focused only on the meal. Not that they had nothing to say. They were both tired and morning would be upon them all too soon. Once the dishes were cleared and put into their newest appliance, a dishwasher, they nursed a nightcap, a double shot of extraordinarily fine blackberry brandy to cap off an ordinary, but satisfying meal. The liqueur, warm, sweet, and soothing on the palate, was an early holiday gift from a doting parishioner.

Father Bernie shook his white head in an exaggerated gesture of sheer weariness. Wiry bristles shot out here and there. "What a crazy week this has been, Chris...trying to put all the pieces together, not to mention a slew of hospital visits, two funerals and a trip to state's prison." Father Bernie enumerated the events slowly, one by one, on his gnarled fingers. "It's all that unexpected stuff that puts me in a flurry this time of year."

At first Chris didn't know how to take the older priest. How much was the generation gap going to affect their relationship? But it was their common goals and purpose that bound them together. Chris was eager and willing to learn from an experienced mentor. When Father Bernie gave the OK to clear the vacant lot and create the prayer garden, he learned so much about his curate's focus and dependability.

It didn't take very long for Chris to see that the crusty exterior that Father Bernie exhibited shielded a totally different interior. Father Bernie was personable and often delightful. His experiences provided Chris with what he needed to fulfill his role. And their evening meal was what Chris looked forward to at the end of a long, demanding day. It was their break time, so to speak.

The young curate smiled a slow, knowing smile showing the affection he held for his mentor and pastor. "Unexpected stuff? That's all we have. One thing after another. That's life in all its fullness, its predictable unpredictability. That's what you always say, right?" Bernie only smiled. His mentee was learning well. Chris resumed, "That's why we're here. That's what we do. We listen, we comfort, we do for others. Everything will fall into place. So, Bernie, please calm yourself, won't you? You'll pop a vein." He patted his friend on the hand. "I told you I will handle the prison visits in the future."

"So you think I'm getting too old for that, do you now, Chris?" he snapped, but always in jest, as the two men shared their sacerdotal duties and any and all impositions impinging upon their lives as parish priests. Chris feared at times that he himself too often played the role of mentor, and he reminded himself he shouldn't overstep.

"You, Bernie, never." Chris took a long, slow draught of the liqueur and let it trickle down his throat, soaking in the warmth. "You'll outlive me. You old rascal."

"Oh, so I'm a rascal, am I? Then you're a, uh, a whippersnapper," Bernie volleyed. As a child he had watched enough westerns to take a liking to that old handle. The two roared in laughter. They could relax now. Yes, the evening meal was their time to unwind.

"Touche. Hey, I haven't heard that word 'whippersnapper' in ages and I probably won't ever again. But seriously, if things get too crazy this week, you know we can always call on old Father Wilbur to give us a hand," Chris winked. It was a private joke since calling on old Father Will was indeed a last resort.

Father Bernie raised a bushy eyebrow. "And old Will is just that. Old. We should let him be, unless we are truly strapped, and you know we may very well be."

"Don't rule it out, Bernie. It is always an option." Chris doubted that Bernie would resort to calling on the retired priest although Father Will was thrilled to help out, even if you had to redo things afterward. He watched Bernie catch onto a thought then fish into his shirt pocket to extract a neatly folded sheet of notebook paper. Uh-oh, Chris knew what was coming next.

Bernie unfolded the paper and studied it for a long moment, his reading glasses perched precariously on the bridge of his aquiline nose. Chris called it the eagle pose, though never to his face. You have to draw the line somewhere, he believed.

Bernie had a great sense of Irish humor but...He cleared his throat and began, "Well, Chris, I know how you dislike my lists, you with your self-reputed super memory, but we need to give this a check so we can stay on target for the rest of this week. Very, very important week it is. I don't have to tell you."

"But you just did," Chris barked with a grin. The brandy was loosening them both up.

"Oh, all right," Bernie conceded. "I guess I did and..."

Chris never let him finish. "I know what I have to do and I don't even have to ask you. So don't worry none. I've got everything all set with the floral decorations committee. The poinsettias will not arrive at the last minute, like last year—guaranteed. So, rest at ease in that department. And Barbara's got a good handle on the Christmas pageant. She told me so herself. She knows the drill, and we just have to trust her. So you see I'm there. Right on target. We're where we should be." He watched the tension relax in Bernie's face although Chris wasn't so sure of their being where they should be.

"Guess so. Good, good. Yes, yes, a drill sergeant, she is, that Barbara. She sure is. Good to have people like that. You know, the ones you can always count on to do the job." Bernie nodded, showing some signs of fading.

"And do it right," Chris added brightly. He didn't like to see Bernie get uptight over things before they happened. There was always a way to fix things or prevent disasters from happening. Almost always. All of a sudden his face morphed into a mask of dread for only a brief moment. Thoughts could harm. How well he knew that. He chased them away. "She sure needs to be—a drill sergeant I mean—with all those antsy kids. She's got a baby all lined up, too, to play the infant Jesus. So far, all the children are raring to go, unless they sprain an ankle skating or come down with flu or worse."

"God forbid," Bernie crossed himself. "It is that time of year. Anything could befall the children and us, for that matter..." He paused to study his list. "And the animals? What about the animals?" Bernie was the kind of person who anticipated all things and traversed them in thought. He was a bit of an old worrywart who'd had lots of practice over the years. He figured he inherited that trait from his mother, or from the fact that he was the eldest son of seven children and often got blamed for the mischievous deeds of his siblings. After all, he above the others should know better.

Chris thought for a moment. "Right. We mustn't forget the animals. All the ones from last year and a few new ones. But you know how that can go. Some of those critters are getting on in years and may be arthritic. But as far as I've been able to find out, we should be OK." He watched Bernie react to that word – arthritic. It was always his reason or excuse, the bane of his daily winter existence.

So typical of Bernie, he responded in mocked dismay. "Thanks, Chris. I needed that reminder. I guess I do complain too much." He paused to evaluate Chris's reaction. "Oh, I almost forgot. Did you talk with Dr. Blume about corralling some of the college kids home on break? You know the ones I mean—trumpeters, violinists, flautists? Kind of makes midnight mass so majestic with them aboard, if you know what I mean, adds a bit of flair to the music program. The choir is good enough, but..."

"Uh-oh, not yet, I forgot. I'll do it first chance I get." Chris apologized as Bernie gazed at him with a told-you-so look that said, 'See if you kept a list like me, you'd have remembered.' "Sorry. Last year it was just breath-taking with all the instruments. It backs up the choir and the organ. Gives it what you want to celebrate the birth of Christ. And the congregation just loved it." He said what he thought Bernie would like to hear. How Bernie loved his Christmas music, both popular standards and religious hymns!

The evening meal was just about over when Bernie gestured over toward Chris's glass, "Here you go, son, have a refill. You look like you could use one. Myself too, for that matter." All it took was Chris's frown. Bernie got the message and quickly recapped the bottle.

Chris began to move away from the table. He yawned and stretched his arms wide, nearly knocking off the curtain rod that protruded a little too far from the window. "Oh, no thanks, no more for me. I've had enough. I think I'll get myself situated and relax. First I'll do my Office. Then I'll focus on prioritizing my thoughts, duties, into a, uh, list." He glowed, hoping Bernie would appreciate the positive influence he had on him.

Chris gloated as Bernie smiled a little too condescendingly. It was OK between them. They had become a team. It was always OK. That generation gap, the cultural gap—never mattered much. What did matter was why both were there: to serve, and serve they did – each other and their beloved St. Aeden's. They would gather their forces and resources to make this year's Christmas Eve with its pageant and glorious music program the best ever.

"So a list after all, huh?" The veteran priest mulled over the words, relishing the thought and nodding in approval. He turned and reached over to adjust the curtain rod. Then he stopped all of a sudden, pulled the curtains apart and peered out the window. The panes were steamy. Was there something or someone out there, a shadowy figure, in the garden? He couldn't be sure. He moved gingerly. Then he turned off the kitchen light so as to get a better look.

"Shh, here, Chris, take a look, out there in the garden." He pointed to the far side of the garden. "I see a shadow. Oh, no, look,

I think it's moving, right over there by the bench in front of the bird feeder. Can you see it?"

"Oh, Bernie, take it easy. Don't be so nervous. Remember your blood pressure. It's probably only a cat." Chris called to him from across the kitchen. What would anyone be doing in the garden at this hour in this cold?

Bernie tried not to sound too indignant, but it shone through loud and clear. "Nervous you say? A cat? A pretty big one, I'd say. Come on now, Chris, a cat burglar is more like it. I don't know, with all those break-ins this time of year you hear on the news. Smash and grabs is that new lingo, and you've got your feeders and the statues out there. And what about home invasions? Could be garden or church invasions too. Probably not much to smash though out in the garden, but I don't like the idea of prowlers invading our blessed church, nosiree. And I sure don't relish the idea of anyone grabbing what's not theirs either, if you get my point." He was babbling, as he was prone to do when he was agitated.

Chris walked over to the window, and the two of them breathed onto the glass, fogging it up even more. He wiped it off with the edge of the curtain. "Step aside, won't you, Bernie, so I can get a better look." Bernie shook his head and complied without a word. The kitchen was now in complete darkness, and they didn't want to risk being heard. "Wait a minute... Now I can see better. It's only some kid, looks like a girl, I think, just sitting on the bench, as far as I can make out. Now, Bernie, tell me, what kind of danger could that pose?"

Bernie's respirations were increasing. He repeated, trying to calm himself, "What danger could that pose? What danger you ask calmly and naively? Well I'll tell you...God only knows." His nerves were on edge and his voice quivered. "All right then, Chris, if you don't suspect anything amiss, suppose you go on out there and take a look? See what she wants; see if she needs anything. I'll wait here. Don't need two of us out there. The less I do stairs, the better my legs like it. Remember the old arthritic knees?"

Chris nodded in assent, and as he passed Bernie, he touched the old man's shoulder. He whispered, "I don't know why anyone would be out there at this time of evening. There's nothing to do in that garden this time of year either but pray, but you never know. Maybe pray and freeze. Let me take care of it. I'll be back in a moment, Bernie. You go relax now."

Chapter FIVE

AS CHRIS TROTTED DOWN the back stairs, Bernie yelled in a stage whisper, "You better come back and get the flashlight. It's a pretty decent weapon; you might need it. Girl or no girl." Chris didn't hear him. He slammed the door behind him, and turned on a floodlight illuminating the back yard, which did little good for the garden. All you could see there were shadows from the corner streetlight. He approached the gate as quietly as possible though he thought anyone could hear the crunch on the gravel. He didn't want to startle her. He paused when he got a clearer view of the 'cat burglar'.

A girl, obviously a teen-ager, was seated on the curved concrete bench at the far side of his garden. Chris saw only her silhouette, but what he did see perplexed him. He stopped to observe in silence. She appeared to be methodically ripping up sheets of paper into tiny pieces and tossing them gleefully into the air. He entered the garden and proceeded slowly down the paved path. If she heard him approach, she gave no indication. She was so engrossed in that activity.

Since she didn't appear bent on robbing the place, smashing and grabbing items, or invading anything beyond the garden, as Bernie had feared, Chris made his presence known. He made a rustling noise with his feet on the frozen pavers and cleared his throat before speaking. At that, she turned slightly not quite facing him.

"Hey there, I hope I didn't frighten you," he said. He was already beginning to feel uncomfortable. "Are you OK, Miss?" For a moment she said nothing in reply. Neither did he. He watched as she continued ripping and whirling the scraps about. Then, "What *are* you doing?"

The teen-aged girl responded boldly, "This." She took another sheet of paper and as though she was demonstrating some type of craft, she resumed. "Watch me." She took handfuls of paper pieces and tossed them into the air above her head, shouting and louder. "It's snowing, it's snowing, it's snowing." By then, she was laughing on the verge of hysteria.

Chris was suddenly speechless. He paused a moment to take in the scene, the enormity of the mess the girl was creating. He was stupefied, then he gathered up his forces and said, "Didn't you hear me? I asked you if you were OK, Miss. I would appreciate an answer. What *is* your problem?...You, uh, can't do this on church grounds." He was now speaking to her back. Then, as she made a quarter turn, he spoke to her profile. The girl spoke at last, surveying her handiwork, "No, no, I'm not OK. Not very OK at all. And the problem is so huge I can't put it into simple words. So, you see..." She choked up.

"Then put it into *any* kind of words," he urged, ignoring her distress. "I only want to know why you are here and why you are doing this. So here now, I'm listening." She straightened and pulled herself together, turned slowly and faced him.

The girl began, "Well, good for you. I'm so glad you are. Nobody ever listens to me." Even in the shadowy darkness, the girl could not fail to notice a jolting look come over his face. Was it shock or perhaps recognition? She couldn't tell.

Chris managed to say, "I, uh, hear you." And that was all. He froze.

She retorted boldly, "Doesn't look like you do. You look like you just saw a ghost or something. You're not one of those creepy guys that's into weird kinds of stuff, are you? Should I be afraid of you? Or do *I* just look that creepy to *you?*" One thing she didn't look like was threatened by Chris's appearance.

Chris was astonished at her fearlessness—venturing out alone in the dark to accomplish some bizarre task. Could he actually call it trespassing? Probably not, but littering, yes, definitely, and disrespecting the church grounds, absolutely. He answered the girl. "Oh, no, no, no. And, no, you do not look creepy at all. I'm sorry. You just reminded me...you're the spitting image of someone...I, uh, um, used to know...a long time ago." He was embarrassed as his voice ended in an uncustomary squeak.

"Can't be all that long ago," she said studying his face, the square jaw, the shock of dark wavy hair, the intensity of his eyes. "You're pretty young. Still."

He ignored her backhanded compliment and got down to business. He was annoyed at this intrusion. This was his prayer garden; he designed it, planted it and cared for it lovingly. He couldn't fathom why anyone would create a mess in it in this manner for any legitimate reason. It didn't make any sense to him. He regained his composure and tackled the problem. "So what do you intend to do with that mess you made in the name of falling snow?"

The girl seemed to weigh those words. She hadn't thought about what she would do after. She was simply doing it now. It was how she acted. She wasn't at step two yet. That would come next. She inhaled deeply as she thought aloud. "You wouldn't get it. What do you know, being what you are?"

Chris was getting impatient and chilled. He hadn't stopped to grab a jacket. He simply had to get to the bottom of this. Bernie would be furious. "I know a lot more than you think, young lady," he responded."

"Well, I'm not that young either, and calling me a lady, well, that's pushing it a bit." She smiled, and he recoiled. "Sorry," she said, an empty word devoid of passion.

Chris needed to know what lay beyond the surface of this girl who unnerved him so. But he also needed to be done with this untimely encounter. "Well now, if you want to make snow, just do it somewhere else...please. You're littering my garden, and you have to remember that these are church grounds." He rubbed his hands together. He wished he wasn't shivering. It diminished his authoritative stance.

The girl shrugged in defeat. "Yeah, you're right. I am. Sorry." She bent down and attempted to pick up pieces that had already begun to scatter in the evening breeze. After a short time, he noted the fruitlessness of it. Plus, some shreds had embedded themselves in the shrubbery, beyond her reach. So she shrugged again.

He stood in silence as she scurried about in a futile attempt to clean up the mess. "Never mind that. I'll tackle it in the morning. I just can't understand why this had to happen, and in our garden." He shook his head in desperation.

Once the girl realized that she was wasting her time, she sat back down on the icy bench and said, "Well, if you must know. Those papers I ripped up are holiday newsletters. You know those stupid flyers, like updates that boring people send out as Christmas greetings, the ones people exaggerate to make their family look like family of the year. Like, 'Merry Christmas, our daughter Brie came out at the country club debutant ball. She's a summa cum laude grad of Blah Blah Ivy League University. And Peter Piper our precious prodigy of a son was valedictorian of his class at Ultra Private Academy and is headed to West Point.' Oh, such gross exaggerations, they make you want to puke."

She paused to catch her breath. "And then on one of them there's a photo of the whole damn family staring zombie-like, like a crew of Ralph Lauren models at the edge of the Grand Canyon—caption reads like--the gang taking a little respite on spring break. That's what the idiot called it--respite. Why not a vacation? Duh—a respite. Mother's friends, three of them, her sorority sisters and their stupid newsletters—that's what these are. Oh, they make me sick. Every year they exchange these stupid lies, ugh, Christmas newsletters. And then there's the *coup de grace*. That's a thing my father says a lot. I think it means sorta like the last straw? You can imagine when...my mother's Christmas newsletter to them...my mother, she went and lied about us, my stupid brother and me, humongous lies. The bragging in *her* letter was hysterical but you know, it really hurt me, because first, she made up impossibly good stuff about us, and second, there really wasn't anything good for her to say about us in the first place. Oh, she did tell the truth when she wrote about all those business trips she takes with my father, like the one they're on now, let's see, in Dubai. She paused a moment as if to ponder something. Yeah, they're there now. So what do I do?"

Chris was transfixed. "I don't know. You tell me." He was still uneasy with her. With her looks. Why did she have to look like *that*?

"Duh, you just saw me do what I did. So I'm telling you. I ripped up the bunch of lies, the stupid newsletters, and my mother's stack of phonies that I was supposed to mail out today but I didn't, bunches of them, and I turned them into pure, driven, OK, maybe not, just into fake snow flakes. Oh, how I really wish it *would* snow." She spoke as though her words legitimized the deliberate act of littering on church grounds.

Chris was taking in a deep breath. "Oh, I see," he managed to say, trying to make sense out of her motive. "Well, you made fake snow." The girl simply rolled her eyes upward, a reaction he judged as typical of kids her age. He wasn't sure what move to make next. The girl didn't budge. She sat on the bench and swung her legs back and forth defiantly. He was about to ask her to leave when he spotted Bernie's face pressed flat against the kitchen window.

For a quick moment, Chris was inclined to laugh at the squished image staring out at him, then Father Bernie raised the window and shouted, "Hey, Chris, Father Chris, what in tarnation is going on? You getting everything under control down there?"

The girl stood, trying to make out the face in the window. "No problem, Bernie. All under control. Over and out," Chris shouted, hoping to dismiss his superior. He could handle the situation himself. The girl was harmless, he convinced himself. She was just a kid, venting her frustrations on their property, though in a most unorthodox way, in the dark, alone. But then he was beginning to wonder just how harmless she really was. She could have scattered her 'snow flakes' just about anywhere—in the park, on the town green. What bothered him was why she'd chosen *this* place. He was relieved when he heard the window shut. Good. Bernie would go on to bed and he'd explain the silly incident over breakfast and they'd get a good laugh before Chris would venture out to pick up all those fake snowflakes. And get on with his real duties.

The girl sat back down on the bench, making herself quite at home. "Who's the old dude?" she asked gesturing up at the window.

Chris couldn't help smiling at that. "Dude? He's my, uh, boss, the pastor. Father Bernie Monahan's his name. He's an ex-boxer, and a pretty good one, at that—*was*, that is, back in his day in the city. He had some reputation then, could've gone pro, but..."

The girl smirked. "Is that supposed to scare me off?" she asked, twirling a lock of her long auburn hair. It unnerved Chris who focused anywhere but on her face, that face that took him back to his senior year in high school.

He quickly lightened, explaining, "Well, you *were* trespassing and littering." He wished she'd just get up and go away. He was cold and tired and didn't feel like explaining himself.

She retorted, " So now I'm breaking the law. I don't see any signs anywhere. Oh yeah, that one: '*Open Sunrise to Sundown*', well if you must know it is somewhere in between those times somewhere. Right? Anyhow, I thought church property was public property, sort of, fair game for anyone to pay a visit anytime. All those nice articles in the paper one for each season, the ones with your picture, you standing there, smiling. Well, they said this was a prayer garden for people who wanted to visit and pray. So...I suppose you're going to report me for doing what I did?"

He thought a moment. Then, "No, I'm not. This is a prayer garden but not intended for night visits. The sign is taken to mean here in Wexford Falls. And it is night here, well after sundown. But no, you're OK. I didn't mean to scare you. I just never expected..."

She stood and turned so as to face him squarely in the eyes. Once again, he avoided her. She pleaded, "I'm not really OK. I'm not. Can't you see?"

Chris grew concerned at her insistent tone. Maybe she needed help after all. He began, "All right, you're ticked off at the lies in the Christmas newsletters given out instead of Christmas cards. I get that; I think I do. All that phoniness, in the name of impressing others."

The girl grew animated, indignant. "Yeah, I am ticked off like you say, especially when ours says I'm an honor student in an International Baccalaureate program. Hah! Well, I was but they threw me out in October and I'm in public school now and doing lousy. I could do a lot better, but I'm just not. And furthermore, my idiot brother is a dumb ass and so not a track star with a ton of trophies. He's mental, if you must know. We'd both have police records if our father didn't have, uh, influence, if you know what I mean," she said. Then she turned trying to face him. Her tone became gentler. "You know you could say *pissed* in front of me. I'm not a child."

Chris couldn't hide his embarrassment. "Some people feel the need to boast even if it means stretching the truth some." He only wanted to end this conversation. Maybe if he'd show some compassion, some empathy, she'd leave, but instead she lingered.

She said, "Stretching? How about stretching it to the breaking point, into tiny little pieces. And that's exactly what I did to get rid of it—ripped them all into little pieces. Besides, my mother will never know I didn't do her mailings, and she'll probably think her gal pals stopped sending out the holiday lie letters. Better still, she won't even give it a thought, knowing her."

Chris responded in silence when the girl lowered her voice saying, "I really make you nervous, don't I?"

Chris tried not to squirm, hoping to avoid any signs of discomfort in her presence. "That's not it. A priest has a lot of things on his mind this time of year." The less said the better, he believed. Attempting any further explanation would prolong the encounter and make him more vulnerable, more edgy.

She smiled, "If you say so. I wouldn't know about those things. Stuff a priest has to do. How would I know?" Some times he thought he heard a little girl talking at him, other times she was anything but a little girl.

He had to know. He pressed on in spite of himself. "Well, uh, you're here in my garden for a, uh, reason. Sure—you left your snow flakes here, uh, but really, how can I help you, Miss?"

"Please, not Miss. It's Glory. That's me, my name," she said wearily. "You probably *can't* help me."

What was her game? Glory? He seriously doubted that was her real name. Let it be, he decided. He was perturbed. "OK, here we go again. Tell me—why are you here?" He began to pace. Bernie probably had his ear cocked at the window which was probably open and if Chris didn't get upstairs soon, he'd probably trudge downstairs and into the garden, and that would be it.

She parried. "What do you mean by here? In this town, this garden, this planet, this hemisphere? There—you asked and that's my answer, a question for a question. Get it?"

"So what are you now, some sort of philosopher?" he queried. What is with her?

She laughed heartily. "Hardly. I'm far too young. And who could want be a philosopher in this century? Oh, that would be a big fat waste of time. Spend all your time just thinking and thinking about stuff and giving your opinion like you're so important and like it could really be worth something—your version of truth to some people who actually read that kind of stuff, and think it over in their minds." She paused and changed her tone to a more pleasing, less defensive one. "I like to think I'm a poet, sorta, though not really, but in a way guess I am. I write poem—mostly my thoughts, those kinds of poems. So I guess they're kind of related, the philosopher and the poet. They live in their heads. I guess when you stop to think of it, it is a waste of time, living in your head. Unless you're like the best rappers. Lots of them out there. They come up with poetry, some really good stuff. You should listen to it, really. You'd learn a lot." She was laughing now.

Chris lost track of his mission and continued. He believed she was very much in need of some kind of help, but he wasn't sure which kind. "OK, so you're not a philosopher; you're a poet."

"Yeah, what I just said," she said. "You know, all teen-age girls are poets. Like we think a lot about our lives. Those are our own unique thoughts, no one else's, and then we feel certain ways like adults *can't*. They're so old. They've lost it. And so we spill ourselves out in poems. Some of them sound so dumb we have to throw them away. Some of them I save though—don't know why."

She laughed at herself like she'd just told a private joke. "We're teenagers. Everyone says we are all so misunderstood just because of our age. Like we don't know life? But we sure know hurt and pain and confusion. Stuff like that. But that's where the poems come from—inside us and partly from life on the outside, I guess. Makes sense, right? Now, take our pathetic English teacher, Mr. Garber. We call him Mr. Gobbler 'cause he's always yakking about ideas and stuff—but not to his face though—or if we're really pissed at him, we call him Mr. Garbage, and we're pissed at him most of the time." She stopped to catch her breath. She was on such a roll.

Chris listened, wondering, he asked, "Mad at him?"

"Cool. You're listening," she cooed at him. "Yeah, at *him*. Who else? In class, like he gives us this look." She mimicked a sour expression. "When we don't see the poem his way. He says we don't get the point. Oh, we get it all right. We just don't want him to have the satisfaction. So we fake it—our way. Anyhow he's always so right. And we're always so dumb."

Chris knew he should end this conversation but he was determined to learn more. "So you're a poet. Hmm." He stopped, waiting for her to continue.

"And you don't know what to say about that," she shot back at him. "Sorry—that was mean. Yeah, I try to be a poet. I really do. Also like the lyrics in music. You know I play the violin but somehow the poems I write don't work with my violin music." She laughed and paused. "Anyhow Gobbler doesn't get things the way we do. He just wants it his way."

Chris explained, trying to hide the fact he was shivering. "Most people in life do, especially in his position, I would think."

She went on oblivious to his discomfort. "So now, Mister, can you tell me why *you're* here?"

Her audacity irritated him. What right did she have? She was hardly an equal. She was a kid, a brash, enigmatic teen-age girl who should not be out alone at night. Yet for some strange, inexplicable reason, he couldn't let go. He began to correct her, but stopped short.

She persisted, pouting. "You never answered my question why you're here. So OK, ladies first?"

"Wait a minute now. You cringed when I called you a lady, remember? All right, enough arguing...I'm here because we saw you out here and thought you were maybe a, uh, prowler, and, uh, no one is ever in the garden after dark. No one needs to be."

She ignored his words. They had little impact on her. "Well, why not? It looks like a cool place to chill. A nice quiet garden, safe enough, I thought. And as you know I had to do this thing which you call littering and then chill, like what we're doing now."

"Yeah, exactly," Chris wasn't into to chilling, especially at this hour, in this place and under these circumstances. "You'd chill all right sitting on that cold stone bench this time of year."

She didn't find his remark very funny by the 'duh' expression on her face. "No, I wouldn't. I needed space and some quiet to feel like shit...oops. I mean lousy. Then you showed up. Sorry. When I looked on my mother's desk and saw those newsletters—all that stupid bragging and stuff, and then when I opened up my mother's own phony newsletter too, filled with all those lies, that she actually was sending out to her friends, I wanted to puke on them all."

"And so you came here and made snow of them instead," Chris summed up, trying to understand.

She agreed. "Yeah, that's sorta true. I just had to do something. And I did...It made me feel better, I guess."

"You guess...well, if you must know, this is one of my sanctuaries. I come here to work and pray, meditate—out here. I take care of everything in this garden—the flowers, the birds, the statuary." Chris hoped she'd understand but he knew better.

Up went the eyes again, typically teen. "Oh, man," she seemed to groan.

"I'm at peace here with nature any time of the year," he stated, hoping she would get his point. "This place is, well, almost sacred. At least it is, to me anyhow."

"I'm sure messing things up right now, aren't I?" This time she actually sounded as if she'd heard him.

He was trying to understand her mood swings. She was defensive, then she was contrite, then she was, well, he wasn't sure what she was, what she felt. "Not really. I'll clean things up in the morning. But if you need to talk to one of us..."

"I *am*," she blurted. That was part of her problem, he surmised. She doesn't take time to think; she just talks. Words fly out of her mouth as though they were escaping captivity and were relieved just to be let loose.

"Am what?" he kept up the volley, wishing she would pack up and leave, unless...

She rolled those hazel eyes again. They were like sea glass. It was so automatic of her he assumed she'd had lots of practice. "Talking. Talking to one of you To *you*. Not the old guy."

"So you are," Chris said. " I commend you. 'Guy' is certainly a lot better than dude. I'll bet you didn't expect anyone to come outside here."

She looked perplexed for a moment. "Maybe I did. I don't know. I, uh, didn't know what to expect, or what I would do from here. I, uh, didn't want to be around people—humans that is. I needed to be alone for a while, then..." She turned away, scratching her chin, avoiding him. "Get it?"

Chris wasn't sure if he got it or not. "I think so," he managed, casting a glance at his watch. "If you're doing OK now you probably should be getting back home."

"Don't hafta." She sounded like a third grader in the recess yard. "I can do whatever I want."

Chris grew irritated. "Oh really? And what about your parents? They certainly wouldn't want you to do as you please, would they?" He wondered what kind of parents would allow a girl like her license to come and go as she pleased.

" Oh, them," she laughed at the very insinuation. "They are in Dubai. Like I told you, remember? I wasn't kidding around. Father has business interests there and Mother, well, she tagged along for what she calls a well deserved getaway. Like she really has to get away from her hectic life of clubs and spas and cocktail hours. I guess she just needed to get away from us, from my brother and me, and, yeah, her own mother too. She, uh, lives with us now." She snickered, avoiding his direct question.

"Mothers do a lot more than meets the eye," he snapped back. "I'm sure no matter where your parents may be that they would want some control over what you do or not do." He paused to let that sink in. "You really should get going. Obviously, someone is watching out for you at your house."

"Duh, yeah, Grandmom is," she admitted. "She's pretty ancient and not totally with it, not all the time. I'm sure you know what that means. When I saw those newsletters I freaked. I just had to get out of the house, and do what you saw me doing, ripping up the stuff." She fiddled with her sleeve. "So I told her I was staying at a friend's house, this girl I used to know at the Academy. Grandmom would believe anything I told her."

Since she looked sharply away, he probed, "Wouldn't she check on you—call to say goodnight?"

"She might if she doesn't zonk out first," she explained. "Anyhow I gave her the wrong number of my friend. So if she tries to call, she won't get me. Ha ha."

"That's not very nice of you, or respectful either," he said. This girl was beginning to be more and more of an enigma to him. He wondered how Bernie would have handled this situation had he come down into the garden, instead of himself. Would he have called the police? DCF? Or maybe he would have told her to get out – pronto—and go home where she belonged.

"Oh, I respect her—when I'm with her," she softened. "She's my Grandmom."

"And when you're not?" Chris didn't even have to ask. He knew. She'd just do as the spirit moved her. He feared which spirit.

Glory gazed out into the darkness and began as though declaring a manifesto, "I just do whatever I please, whatever feels right at the moment. Depends on what's going on, like what the situation is."

At the moment, Chris wished he were upstairs in his room with his mind on anyone or anything but this strange girl, this spunky teen who lied to her grandmother and did whatever the spirit moved her to do. He was speechless. Should he try to counsel her? Would she even listen to him?

With hardly a breath, she added, "Besides, she's got my moron of a twin brother to drive her out of her wits. He's loud and very disrespectful—a real mean s.o.b.—and I'm not like any of that, so she trusts me." She smiled triumphantly.

Chris avoided commenting to that remark. Then, "You never told me your name, your last name."

"So you can check on me, follow up on this, maybe report me to the authorities?" she barked. "Am I right?"

Chris didn't know why he kept this up. Did he really care? She was a nuisance. "That's not what I was thinking." He was suddenly calm.

Glory remarked, "Then what *were* you thinking?" She waited a long minute for him to answer. "You know what I think?" She let that sink in before whispering," I think I freak you out or something, right?"

Chris was glad it was dark enough so she couldn't see him redden. He hated it when he blushed, as he did so easily. "No, you don't. You just..." He was unable to express himself.

" I know, I know, I remind you of someone—probably someone you hated or who hated you, but I can't imagine that." Her voice was gentle again. "You seem very nice and also kind of cute for a priest."

Chris dismissed the comment and tried to ignore the fact that he felt himself blushing again. It bothered him to hear that. He inhaled deeply, then, "I asked you politely. What is your name, your last name?"

"Does it really matter?" she asked. "What's yours? I can't remember. It was in the articles with your picture." She was relentless. She tried his patience. Why was he letting this go on and on?

"Well, I assume you don't belong to our parish," he heard himself say. He had never seen her before so he was positive of that.

"Nope, to no parish, no religion," she said briskly. "I see the sign here says Saint Aeden—what a funny sounding name. Well, we do belong to a church, the church of Saint Dinero. Ha ha. My father tells people that. He's got some sense of humor when he wants to." She figured he'd get it, that she was joking.

"I see, very funny," Chris said, thinking quite the opposite. "Well then, let me introduce myself to you." He graciously extended his cold hand. "My name is Father Christopher

Tosi—and not Mister, please. Father Chris is what most people call me." She fist bumped him, ignoring his outstretched hand. For a second he was taken aback, but figured this is how the kids do it today.

"Yeah, sorry. I had forgotten. I didn't know what to call you so I figured Mister would work. Guess not...Hey, Chris. I'm Glory. Truly that is my name. I said so before but I don't think you believed me." He cringed at the omission of his title. What was wrong with her?

"Sure, Glory." He could swear she wasn't telling the truth. "For real?"

"Well, you could say nice to meet you, Glory." She was playing him. What was her game, he wondered.

And how long would it be before Bernie yelled down to him, or worse, appeared in the garden. "Yeah, I could if that was your real name."

"Oh, sadly enough, it is," she said. "Glory Mae Sterling-Baie. Rhymes, huh? So poetic, right? Sterling-Baie's my last name, hyphenated thanks to my mother who wanted her stupid name attached. Takes two, you know." She took a moment to gauge his reaction again. "Now you know. So don't report me, please. My parents have a hissy fit when I get in trouble and they're not home so it falls on Grandmom's hands. And that really pisses them off. She's too old for that kind of stuff."

He ignored her request. The name rang a bell. He remembered that there were Sterling-Baies who lived in the most elegant home in town—extremely affluent. " Not of Sterling-Baie Enterprises?"

"And why not?" she asked haughtily. "I am a Sterling-Baie. Yup, I sure am. So we need a religion, right? We don't go to church. Almost nobody does any more."

Chris had to allow all that to settle in. A Sterling-Baie, one of *those*. Her father is the wealthiest member of the community, with holdings all over the world. But so what? "Ah, now I get the Saint Dinero thing," he said, "but how did you become a Glory? That's an unusual name. I apologize. I thought you were kidding me."

"Simple," she seemed all too happy to explain. He was listening to her. He had her attention. "My father's responsible for my name, so they tell me. He yelled it out, yelled out 'Oh Glory' when he realized there were two of us inside there—like twins, get it? You know where. Inside my mother. Anyhow, it's a weird story. My father was old when we were born, like around 40. Blew his mind."

"And I'll bet your twin's name is Thomas," he remarked. Why did he feel the need to continue this conversation?

Glory looked shocked. "Whoa, you must be psychic," she said, placing her hand on his shoulder. He cringed. She had overstepped. He backed away. "You really truly must be. How could you ever guess? I never told you. You must have super powers with your God, you being a religious guy and all."

Chris retorted, "It's *our* God, Glory, our God, not just mine. But I expect in a way that I do receive some powers from Him. I am a priest, not a 'religious guy', but religious, yes." He thought he'd leave it at that—no need to explain any further.

"Well, my twin brother's actually Glen Thomas. Thomas is his middle name, but he hated Glen. Leave it up to my mother to come up with a name like Glen." She shook her head in disbelief.

"Ah Glen—nice," Chris added. "What that name conjures up for me is a peaceful secluded valley." A better place to be rather than here right now, he thought.

"God, Chris, you're right again. That's exactly what she said. You know, you're very spooky, Chris." Was she truly incorrigible?

He yawned then attempted to stifle it. "I don't think so, and it's Father Christopher to you, if you please."

"Whatever," she yawned back in response. He wasn't sure if it was a reflex or her need to ape him. "It's far too long a name. But hey, Glory Hallelujah—I'm the quiet one, not Glen Thomas, take away the Glen. And he's not so peaceful. He's loud and stormy by nature, so go figure. And he's very obnoxious—plus he's a patha...pathological liar. I think that's the word. That's what he is. He's just so pathetic. So you see, my parents got the name Glen all wrong. Nothing peaceful about him. Oh, do they ever get a lot of stuff wrong. They think they know it all, but they don't, especially my mother."

"Typical," he said, "at your age, that's how a lot of teens regard their parents. And I do get the whole sibling rivalry thing. Oh, I do." What he could remember about siblings put him on edge. How coincidental, he thought, both he and the girl had a fraternal twin. He would have given anything to have his twin back. Sure, they'd bickered now and then, but they'd shared their lives and their friends and interests and formed a cohesive bond begun at birth. They vowed they would always be close, forever. The Tosis were like that.

Glory pretended to pout. "Cut it out, Chris. I was just starting to like you. Oops, sorry, I slipped again. I'm supposed to call you Father Christopher. I keep forgetting."

"I'll let that go this time only, Glory," he said. Permissive, that's what her parents must be, he mused. They'll pay the price.

The rectory kitchen window opened again. They could hear the scraping sound from the garden. Father Bernie's white head was visible. He leaned out and yelled. "What the heck is keeping you out there so long, Chris? What are you doing now, pruning the holly bushes or tending to something else in your precious garden?" He paused a long moment, waiting for a response. Then, concern colored his tone. "Is she, uh, the girl OK?"

Chris sighed wearily. "Yes, Father Bernie, she's fine. She was, uh, just leaving."

"I was?" Glory retorted, swinging from one side to the other on the bench.

Father Bernie, snapped, "Well, she better be. Now, speed it up, Chris. I want to secure everything, lock it up." He lingered at the window. All the lights had been turned on in the kitchen. It was as bright as a shop window displaying its wares.

Chris responded dutifully. "Be right there." And he fully intended to.

Glory did not appreciate the interruption. "You know, I was not just leaving."

"Well, *I* am," Chris said summarily.

Glory needled him. "Got a curfew, huh?"

"No, of course not," he said, hoping it didn't sound defensive. "I need to run along though. Glory, please go on home now, go back to your Grandmother. Give her a hug goodnight. Tell her that you changed your mind. You're not staying at a friend's house tonight. Go write a poem and take out your violin. Play something, a song you really like, one that makes you have happy thoughts. It will take your mind off the newsletters. Promise me," he said urgently. Then he turned abruptly and started to leave.

In slow motion Glory begrudgingly hoisted up her hobo sack devoid of all the newsletters and headed sluggishly for the garden gate. She made it clear to Chris that she did not want to leave, at least not yet. "Oh, I don't know. That's an awful lot to ask. Well, yeah, OK, since you asked me I'll do it."

Outside of the garden, he heard the gate clatter, shudder and finally bang shut. He hoped it had fastened itself securely. Little good it would do. It was never locked.

Chris ran up the stairs, two at a time, as he always did from the time his legs were long enough. The kitchen was now in complete darkness. A night light casting eerie shadows barely illuminated the corridor leading to the bedrooms and there was no light visible beneath Bernie's bedroom door. He assumed that Bernie had trusted him to take care of things, which he did.

Chapter SIX

DEPENDABLE FATHER BERNIE rose at dawn, according to habit, as he was firmly set in his ways. And he rarely deviated from his schedule. It was comfortable, and it worked for him, until, of course, the unexpected arose. Then it was quite another story. On the other hand, Chris could shift his duties easily and not feel discombobulated. The two priests complemented each other in that respect.

This morning Chris was seated at the breakfast table immersed in the daily newspaper when Bernie returned from mass. By then Bernie's early morning grumpiness had dissipated, tempered by the joy of celebrating the holy sacramental service. He was whistling the refrain of the recessional hymn he'd just sung, albeit a bit off key in his upper range, so typical of tenors without formal musical training. He was smiling and ready for their customary chat over breakfast to review the upcoming events of the day and check the progress of Christmas week activities.

Chris raised his head above the sports section and greeted him. "Morning, Bernie. How goes it today?" His last few words were indistinguishable as they were stifled by a cavernous yawn. He shivered for a moment as though the yawn set the quivers in motion.

Bernie poured a cup of coffee and set two slices of raisin bread in the toaster, which was always on the table, "Oh, all right, I suppose. Getting too cold for all of us oldies. Too cold for lots of them to venture out to mass today. Only a handful of regulars there. Arthritis rearing its hideous noggin, I'd say. The old joints swell and stiffen up. Musta dropped well below freezing last night. These knees have sensors. The knees know. Heh heh."

"Probably. Yeah, pretty cold. That's it," Chris said, then he proceeded to leaf through the paper methodically. He had a habit of snapping shut one page then opening up to another. Bernie got used to that. He had his own quirks, but Chris just ignored them, he believed, or else just stewed in silence.

Bernie pretended to feel ignored. "That all you got to say?" Bernie had been in the business too long not to figure out his young associate.

Chris sensed he was probing. He inhaled deeply. "I'm just tired. Exhausted, if you must know. I'm sorry, Bernie. I'm not very sociable this morning." He feared that his mentor was going to interrogate him about the encounter in the garden last night, ask him why he was out there so long that it was past his bedtime to wait up for details. But, no, it was something else.

Always the shrink, or more so the observant parent figure, Bernie looked him in the eye and said authoritatively. "I can only imagine why. My hearing's good and my memory's still keen, you know."

"Oh, I don't doubt that for a moment," Chris admitted; then he sank back into the newspaper, hoping to avert the topic lurking in the air before it was broached.

Bernie wouldn't quit. "You are indeed a man of few words this morning. Cat got your tongue, hmm?" Bernie chuckled. He knew. He always knew. Was it from years of listening intently in the confessional or just life experiences or perhaps just from living with Chris, noting the ups and downs of the young man's life? Not that he himself didn't experience the roller coaster rides of earthly existence, those predictable unpredictables, as they referred to them.

Chris knew too, knew that Bernie knew. He yawned, not as expansively this time, and without the accompanying shivers. He took another sip of coffee. This talk was inevitable. "Right. That old cat again. Don't mind me, Bernie. I'll come around. I always do, don't I?"

Bernie tried to squelch his avuncular grin. He had such a range of grins. He didn't want to appear too softhearted. "Indeed you do...It's the time, if I calculate correctly. Heard you howling like a slew of banshees were chasing after you. Same old nightmare, Chris, isn't it?"

"What else, and what do you know about banshees? And a slew? Maybe a gaggle or a flock, but a slew? Oh, Bernie, come on. Actually it was more like a pair of them, just two this time, or what do they call it: a murder of crows? Maybe that's a more accurate or appropriate term—murder, death."

Bernie became mockingly serious. "Don't make so light of it, Chris. What do I know about banshees? Hmm, well, I, uh, I know for one, they're not men, at least as far as I know." Then he laughed at his remark. No one appreciated his sense of humor more than he did.

Most of the time Chris did, but this was not the time. "OK, OK. What else are they not? I can answer that one myself. They're not good omens, not by a long shot."

"Well, whatever, you howled like a whole shooting match of them were after you, chasing you, gaining on you. 'Bout four a.m., I'd venture to guess. Looked at my alarm clock. Yup, it was fourish. Never went back to sleep after that. You could wake up the dead, you could, with that howling of yours, or was it theirs?" Then his tone changed as he studied Chris's face. "Oh boy, Chris, it is hitting you hard this year."

Chris was somber, reflective, reliving the dream experience in his weary head. "Yup, it sure is hitting me hard. Sorry I woke you."

"That's all right, son. It's OK. Then Christmas comes along as it always does just in the nick of time, and it helps ease your pain, so have faith." Bernie was used to it. It had to run its course.

Chis didn't need to be reminded but he respected Bernie's patience and wisdom. Sometimes he was plainly embarrassed at his inability to end the nagging dream that plagued him only around the anniversary of the tragedy. "You know I do. Sometimes I think you know me better than I know myself. But it's my subconscious doing this to me, this year three nights in a row. It's exhausting."

"Chris," Bernie went into his priestly mode, "I know the power of deep-seated memory and the traces of pain that can come along with it. Reliving it over and over again hurts. But you know from the past that it will subside. Remember your faith. Find your peace within. You know you can conquer it."

Chris shot him a look of desperation "So far, I'm not doing very well, considering the numbers of years that have passed, ten to be exact. I guess it's my cross to bear."

Always the preacher, Bernie said, "Doesn't have to be. Faith and reason will help you erase these ravages. And time, yes, good old trusty time. Trust me, I've been there. With the passage of time comes age naturally, and thankfully, age does bring wisdom, plus you figure by then, why trouble yourself? It's all going to be OK eventually, has to. Yes, age does bring peace and wisdom."

Chris had heard enough. He welcomed the stunning beam of morning light that had just brightened the dim kitchen, flooding it with hope. It lifted his mood. And so he lightened up. "And a ton of other things. Physical complaints. Just consider your knees."

"Let's leave my knees out of this, if you please. The important faculties work. That's what matters." Bernie sensed that Chris had heard him and didn't need any more advice, not at this time.

"Are you hinting that perhaps we should concentrate on our Christmas week?" Yes, it felt good to change the subject. His troubled, recurring dreams could wait. Christmas was coming at an alarming rate and there was so much to occupy their minds and their days.

"Yes, I am, in a way. If it gets you out of this funk, yes," Bernie nodded. Gloom and doom was not for bright sunny days.

But it was not so easy for Chris. "I respect your hindsight, your longevity and all the rest, I do. But allow me one moment. This dream of mine, this nightmare has gotten more realistic, more lucid than ever. It creeps up on me and takes hold. How can I shake it? It's with me when I sleep and then it creeps in and out of my conscious mind for days. Even with all that Christmas has to offer, it weaves in and out at odd moments."

"Well, we won't let it. Chris, it will fade as it always does. For now, we need to move on, bask in the beauty and sanctity of Christmas. We've got lots to do, lots on our mind to displace those awful memories, and then we can look forward to that wonderful meal and good cheer on Christmas evening. Your good mother phoned me yesterday to make sure I knew I was invited, and my sister too. How thoughtful of her. Yes, I am looking forward to it. Molly too, if she is able."

Chris looked pleased. "Oh, good, then you *have* decided to join us for Christmas dinner. I wasn't sure. I thought maybe you'd go to your sister's again. My mother takes great pleasure in preparing the meal with all the trimmings—literally from soup to nuts. Dad likes to get his hand in it, but she lets him know in no uncertain terms that *she* is the chef. She wants him far away from her precious kitchen, especially when she's filling the cannoli. He has a tendency to sample far too much. One time, she had to remake the polenta cakes from scratch, and that's not dessert, you know, or do you? He had eaten them all. She was about ready to divorce him."

"See, you're lightening up already," Bernie said. His blue eyes sparkled in the sunlight. Bernie was aware of how contagious emotions can be.

"When you join us for dinner it's always loads of fun. How Mom loves to show off her culinary skills! I think she goes overboard when she know you're coming. We sure can look forward to a jovial get together. This year it's at 4:30, a little later than usual. I hope that's OK with you. Oh, incidentally, she's invited some other guests, so it will be a larger gathering. But look at it this way—you'll have a bigger audience." Bernie's look said he didn't know what Chris meant. Chris ignored it.

"Oh, very nice, very nice for you, Chris. It's good for you to be around family." Bernie well knew that. His own family, that brood, had been shrinking in number, especially over the last few years. He'd lost siblings, one by one, and his nieces and nephews had opted to attend out of state colleges and universities, often settling in those states. Christmas at his sister's was less well attended, and she wasn't strong enough to host it this year.

"And for you, too, Bernie. The audience, I meant, but don't take it the wrong way, is for your corny jokes." Bernie tolerated Chris's ribbing him for his joke telling. It wouldn't matter; he'd just go on entertaining people as long as they laughed.

"Corny, you say? So now you're a wise guy," he said, aping the voice of one of the three Stooges. He couldn't place which one. Was it Moe or Curly, maybe Larry, and wasn't there another one? Well, wouldn't that make them the four stooges?

Suddenly serious, Chris responded. "If only I were, wise, that is. What I dread is when Mom pulls out the albums after dinner. It pains me to have to look at those photos, but now she has them all arranged in a viewer and displayed onto some screen of sorts, although her shrink says it's therapeutic to embrace the memories and acknowledge her feelings. How long does it take to acknowledge something like that? She will never ever get over the loss of my sister. She still has the hope chest she'd bought for Beth's wedding day, the day that will never come. I think she's moved it to one of the closets. This year, I suspect, she may not pull out the albums, not with the Powers couple present. I sure hope she doesn't. There are so many reminders that she holds onto. She'll never forget. How could she? After all, she *is* a mother. And of course, there's more. You know what I mean."

"I suppose I do...And neither will you forget your sister. You're not meant to. We hold them in our hearts, our lost loved ones, forever. So hold the good times, those precious memories in your heart. They say it helps you to better deal with the losses," Bernie counseled.

"Maybe that works for some. But those banshees are mighty, mighty powerful, too. They haunt me every year at about this time, talk about hanging onto things. They never forget," Chris said sadly with a strange, far away look in his eyes.

"I said you were howling like they were coming after you. Now you're seeing, feeling these banshees on your heels—these omens, these omens of death... Ah, I know them well from Irish myth passed down to us Monahans for generations. Our dearly departed mother used to scare the bejeezus outta me and my brothers when we'd fight up a storm over—whatever. It was her only way to get us to stop, aside from hitting us on the side of the head," he said, realizing the blasphemy that had escaped. He quickly crossed himself, absolving himself for his slip of the tongue.

"All right, Bernie, I'm taking your advice. Enough of that," Chris said and he meant it.

"OK, OK, one last thing though," he insisted. "It might do you some good to go back into therapy earlier, say, around Thanksgiving next year. That'll give some time for it to work. To sink into your subconscious, I mean."

Chris retorted, "I don't need to. I've got you to dump on. Probably wrong word. You're a good shoulder to lean on." Bernie understood Chris on so many levels that he could tell him just about anything.

"Not strong enough obviously. But, yes, a shoulder it is. Now, Chris, be proactive. Strike before the banshees do." He saw Chris do a modified eye roll and a lengthy exhale, a sigh of growing desperation. Chris recalled Glory's same reaction from the night before. Cancel that thought, he counseled himself.

Chris was shaking his head in a gesture of weariness, "Therapy? That hasn't done me much good thus far. You above all people should know that."

Bernie insisted, "Don't be so sure of that. Why do you suppose they have therapy? It's supposed to help, you know. You've got to stick with it and try. Your therapist is trained to give you suggestions, tips to eradicate bad memories and nightmares, help you reprogram things. That's sounds like new fangled thinking, but if it works why should I knock it? How many times have we been through this before? So yes, I'm putting it on the calendar, Chris."

Chris grew even wearier. "Yeah, that should take care of it," he said with a tinge of sarcasm." He watched Bernie shake toast crumbs from his lap, rise with effort and walk over to the wall calendar to make of note of his suggestion. Then he'd have to remember to transfer the memo onto next year's calendar.

Bernie let it go for the moment. There was nowhere else for it to go. It was time to move on. He watched Chris get back to the newspaper as he got up to clear the dishes. This time he'd take Mrs. Loretti's advice. Today he'd wash them by hand in hot soapy water. She'd claimed her mother-in-law swore by it for her arthritis, her achy finger joints, and it helped her so maybe it would help him. No harm in trying, he thought. Besides that fool, newfangled dishwasher could be erratic at times. Often it baked the egg on the plates and you had to chisel them to get them clean. Chris has told him it'd be better if he'd scraped the dishes first but then Bernie would counter him with, 'Well, what's the use of the dishwasher in the first place, to get them clean, right?'

With the air cleared, Bernie thoughts returned to the night before. He was curious to know why Chris had spent so much time in the garden dealing with that incident. Chris could have dismissed the girl in less time than that, he mused. He surely wasn't about to stay up late to get the story. He needed his sleep, plus he was feeling the soporific effects of the brandy. It was telling him, it's bedtime. And he always listened.

Wiping his soapy hands on the dishtowel, he broke the tangible silence that had insinuated itself between them. He turned to look directly into Chris's eyes and said, "I want to know all about that nighttime invader in the garden last night. Who is she? What was she doing out there? And is there any cause for concern?"

"Any cause for concern?" Chris repeated as though he was trying to think if indeed there was one. "Nah, I wouldn't be concerned if I were you, Bernie." But there *was* a trace of concern in Chris's voice that Bernie recognized. It made the flesh on the nape of his neck prickle.

"But you're not me, Chris. So what is it now? Are you or are you not concerned?" Bernie wasn't letting that go.

"No, I shouldn't be. No, not at all, but..." Chris screwed his features into a look of wonderment, a strange look Bernie had rarely seen on his face.

Bernie caught on. "All right, go on. Finish that thought."

Chris hesitated for a long moment. "I wish I knew where to start. To be honest, that girl really threw me."

Bernie frowned. All they needed were more complications at this crucial time of the liturgical year. "Oh dear...meaning?"

"Not so much what she did or didn't do, but her looks..." He had debated with himself whether he should say anything about it or just leave it alone.

"Uh-oh, a looker?" Another frown. "Not good, not good a'tall, Chris. Come on, out with it." Bernie quickly grew tired of people telling him Father Chris was much too handsome to be a priest, as if there were such standards. But the women seemed to be drawn to him. There was no denying that.

Chris was quick to reply. His tone was defensive. "Not in the way you're thinking, not so much." He remembered the shape of her face, her bewitching eyes, the striking resemblance. He wished it hadn't unnerved him so.

" So now you know how I'm thinking," Bernie retorted.

"All right. I'll give it to you straight. Our nighttime visitor is a dead ringer for my..." Chris paled. He couldn't bear to say her name.

"Your Kendra," Bernie finished the sentence. He'd lived long enough to know that when you least suspect it, along comes someone who resembles a certain person from your past. Other times you see look alikes everywhere. And yes, you react, sometimes in ways that you can't control. And yes, it can throw you, absolutely.

"Yes, that's right. I have a hard time saying it. Just the sound of her name saddens me. But Bernie, it was uncanny, so uncanny. You can't imagine. It took me forever to fall asleep last night. There she was, that girl, littering our sacred space with little scraps of paper, my garden, so beautiful even at this barren time of year, and it didn't matter so much to her, what she'd done, that is...I told her I'd clean it up. But I couldn't help it. I was jolted by the resemblance. I surprised myself...the hair style, the flow of her hair, her eyes, the color, the shape of her face. She's a little taller and very thin, almost skinny. But she's a dead ringer nevertheless."

In his mind's eye Chris envisioned his high school sweetheart. Seeing her, remembering her as she looked the last time he spent time with her, thinking how they would grow old together, never even imagining their dreams would end in disaster.

Bernie blurted, "I think I might say 'spitting image'. 'Dead ringer' does not sit right with me in light of those banshees. Heh heh." Bernie could always lighten up a tense situation.

"Oh, Bernie. There you go again. Your mother must have scared the crap out of you boys," Chris said blithely.

"Oh yeah, it worked," he admitted. "But as we got a little older we used it on some of the younger kids in the neighborhood, mostly to give them a good scare. Now you see why becoming a boxer was a good defense against their older brothers. I musta made some enemies in my day. Heh heh. I don't think much about them these days, the banshees. I've erased them from my mind, unless I conjure them up if I need to, and sometimes I do. Heh heh."

"You're a million laughs, Bernie. You'd be a better shrink than my guy, or my mother's for that matter. But this aside, she really spooked me, that girl. Glory Sterling-Baie's her name." He waited for a glimmer of recognition. It went past Bernie. His mind was focused on the event rather than some unfamiliar hyphenated name.

"Hmm," Bernie paused a moment. "A skinny thing, you say. Probably trying to look like some supermodel. Not good for girls today. Tsk tsk. What's she want with you? Why was she out in our garden in the dark?"

"Oh nothing," he answered, hoping that she really didn't want anything from him. "She didn't want a thing."

Chris did not want to entertain the idea that there might be an ulterior motive for Glory's appearance in the garden. She had a mission and she completed it, strange as it seemed to him. Then after a while she was gone. What else could there be? They'd never seen each other before. He only wished that he could have reacted differently to her appearance.

"That was a heck of a long chat you had with her over nothing," Bernie quipped. He figured something was up or Chris would have come upstairs sooner. Actually he didn't know when he did come up. He'd dozed off minutes after saying his Office.

"She didn't want anything from me, that is," he admitted, not clear as to how much he should say. "She was just pissed at the world, in general, so it seemed. Teen-age angst ...*boredom. Ennui.*"

"On what?" he asked.

"*Ennui*—it's a French word for very bored, or such," Chris explained. Maybe he shouldn't have used that word, but it seemed to be exactly what he believed Glory could be feeling, especially with her parents so far away during Christmas week.

"You don't need to floor me with those foreign Frenchy-sounding words. Come out with it plain and simple. Is she depressed or not, suicidal maybe?" Bernie was beginning to think that there could very well be a problem.

" You know, Bernie, I really can't say. I don't know enough about her to say 'yes' or 'no'. I just needed to be away from her. Her looks were so disarming." He was displeased with himself for having had less control over his emotions.

"She's not a parishioner, is she, or her family perhaps?" Bernie asked, although he was pretty sure he knew the answer. He knew the names of those families enrolled in his parish, made a point to do so, unless these were newcomers, or maybe they hadn't registered yet. They could even be church shoppers, a term he used when referring to those who went from church to church until they found one right fit, and then stayed until a favorite cleric was transferred. Then the shopping would resume. Bernie would tsk tsk at the very idea. But more often than not, he did encounter such folks over the years. But those that came to St. Aeden's usually stayed.

Chris reddened. "Absolutely not. She told me they belong to Saint Dinero's." Chris tried not to give it away, wondering if Bernie would get it. He probably shouldn't have tested him.

"What? Are you joshing me, Chris?" Bernie sputtered, his face reddening, but this was due to rising blood pressure. "No such saint in my book. Nor in anyone's else's, I'll bet either."

"Of course not. It's Spanish for saint money. 'Dinero' means money," Chris explained with a sheepish grin.

"Knew I'd heard that word before, but not ever linked with a saint. Imagine, 'dinero'. That's a hoot." Bernie slapped his thigh and laughed. "They must be nuts. That what she told you? So it was all just a waste of your valuable time out there in the cold, was it not?" Bernie asked, hoping it was not more than that.

"Seems so. I didn't relish being disturbed, on both levels. I was all set to curl up with my latest Patterson novel, after Office. I'm lagging behind in my recreational reading thanks to all we have to juggle this week." Keep it light, Chris said to himself. Don't want to worry Bernie needlessly over what amounts to nothing

"Oh, him again," Bernie took the bait. "Small wonder those banshees are chasing after you. You know, I can suggest some good catholic theologians for bedtime reading. Patterson, bah!"

" Oh, cut it out, Bernie. We all need some diversion now and then. Maybe I'll sic Alex Cross on those banshees. He can handle just about anything," Chris quipped. That made Bernie roar which escalated into a fit of coughing. He gestured to Chris that he was fine. Good, Chris thought, he won't press me about the girl in the garden.

"Better not give Patterson any more ideas. You can hardly keep up with all his books, let alone add another one to them. You'll mess up that psyche of yours," he insisted. It was too good to be true. He didn't lose track of the topic at hand after all. "Now, listen, Chris, if you ever see that girl again, you hand her over to me. I'll straighten her out good." And his look of determination said that he certainly would.

"You probably could. You're right. She's just a typical teen—so misunderstood as they say they are...I think," Chris replied with conviction.

" That's what *they* want you to think, but..." Bernie began. His pensive look disturbed Chris.

"So you think she might be looking for attention? Some ulterior motive maybe?" Chris asked, his brow wrinkling.

Bernie cast his all-knowing look straight at Chris, unbalancing him slightly. "Well, look where you found her. She hardly belonged out there at that time in the dark. I'd bet on it."

Chris volleyed, trying again to keep it light. "I think you'd place a bet on almost anything."

"Adds spice to life, my boy. Heh heh." Bernie couldn't resist wagering on anything. And he had great confidence in his powers.

"I guess we all need diversions of some sort," Chris agreed. "We most definitely do. You know mine, and I know yours, as different from one another as ours may be."

"So they are. So they are," he said, but then he wouldn't let go. "Anyhow, I'm still trying to figure out why a young teen would sit outside in the cold at that hour? To pray, I suppose." He snickered half in jest.

"No, if truth be known, she was just letting off some steam," he said. Then he smacked his forehead in recollection. "Ooh, I'd better get out there quick before they blow all over creation." He got up suddenly, folded the newspaper, and grabbed his jacket from the hook outside the kitchen. He hoped he'd have time to do the task.

"What in tarnation are you talking about, Chris?" Bernie growled. "You picked up the last of the leaves and all sorts of twigs and debris weeks ago. Don't be so darn fussy about your garden. We've got more important things to do right now."

"No, it's not that. It's, uh..." Chris all of a sudden felt very uncomfortable. He hoped the conversation would end. The situation was over. Why beat a dead horse?

"Oh, I get it," Bernie exclaimed with an all too familiar look and a tone that said otherwise. "It's part of the nothing you two were talking about all that time."

There was no way out. Chris relented. "Oh, all right, if you must know...she was letting off steam, uh, in the form of shredding Christmas newsletters and throwing the pieces all about." He didn't like the way his voice would squeak when he was very uncomfortable.

"Oh, them, those awful brag sheets," he said nodding. "Can't stand them myself. Half the time they're gross exaggerations. But at least the senders keep in touch at holiday time, right? Can't knock them altogether. But wait a minute, you said, throwing the pieces...littering our beautiful garden"?

"So now it's ours, not mine?" Chris was trying to avoid the seriousness of the deed. Here goes... "Anyhow she was making, uh, snow flakes out of the, uh, shreds." This time he was able to control his voice, make it sound more matter of fact.

Bernie grabbed at it. "Lordy. I hope you chastised her, maybe even scared her a little. That's what I'da done." Bernie clenched his fists for emphasis.

" You mean with some banshee stuff?" Anything was worth a try.

" Nah, not to a girl, Chris. Well, come on, what'd you say to her?" Chris was hoping that Bernie remembered he had a commitment in just minutes so he could end this interrogation.

"Oh, Bernie, I can't remember exactly. Only that I'd pick them up in the morning light, the scraps of paper, that is." That should ignite a firestorm, Chris feared. He was braced for it.

"In the meantime the night wind takes care of it and blows them all to kingdom come, like all over the front steps of St. Aeden. Tsk tsk. Once things like these blow about, no telling where they can wind up. No stopping them either—like bad rumors, they are. Yup, just like bad rumors. Not at all like you a t'all, Chris," Bernie said in a harsh tone of voice.

"I'm going right out there. I'll do what I can, scoop up as many as I can find. That's about all I can do," Chris admitted with a shrug. "It wasn't possible last night. It was too dark and windy. She did try though."

"Try, you say. Harrumph! Well, I say next time she invades our sacred garden, and I sure hope there is no next time, I'll deal with her, and you can bet your life she won't look like anybody I know. That's a guarantee. We've probably seen the last of her though—if you scolded her good and proper, and I sure hope you did," Bernie said, annoyance marring his usual cheery countenance. "You know I should get her out here to do the job herself, clean up her own mess...No, no, I don't want her here—unless maybe she needs us for a very good reason. After all, we are here to counsel, if need be, but then, well, why court disaster?" He was rambling. Chris decided it was prudent to remain silent.

Chapter SEVEN

FATHER CHRIS SET OUT to complete the daunting chore of retrieving the shreds from the night's artificial snow burst. He would have cursed Glory for her misdeed if he had not been a priest. He should banish the thought, but it was hard to deny it. He was clearly peeved, and rightfully so.

And so he figured he had better start somewhere—at the source, his garden. Lowering himself onto his knees on the frozen ground, he recalled Kipling's reference to the gardener as one who spends a good amount of time in that position as part of the labor. However, Chris was sure this was not at all what Kipling had had in mind. But he needed to be on his hands and knees to dig in and pry loose the paper fragments that were caught in the shrubs, those that were not taken aloft by the night winds. It was chilly and frosty there with little cooperation from the early morning sun to warm him.

When he first created the garden he had decided not to install trash barrels, as he could not imagine anyone needing them in a prayer garden. After all, it wasn't a picnic ground. It was to remain pristine; people would respect it.

He recalled the time when Father Bernie told of a van of senior citizens stopping by the rectory to see when the garden tours might be taking place. They must have gotten hold of one of the newspaper articles touting its beauty. Mrs. Hopkins interrupted her chore and stood by the door dumfounded, wiping her wet, soapy hands on her apron. She let Father Bernie do the talking. He merely pointed to the direction of the garden and said, 'Help yourselves. No tours.'

Later that day he told Chris that the group wandered for a short time in the garden, then left to pursue other interests that Wexford Falls had to offer, to include local fast food joints. Evidence of the town's modernization was found as Chris did his daily sundown inspection of the garden. A balled up big Mac wrapper had missed its target, intended for somewhere outside of the garden, and landed in a spirea bush. Nearby was a lipstick stained styrofoam coffee cup with a stream of sugary residue spilling out onto the decorator stones. He doubted that that particular one was a miss, just carelessness. People should know better, he mused.

Glory should have known better as well. But since the garden was the scene of the crime it made sense to scour it for more remnants that could drift off in flight and settle outside the churchyard limits, as he feared many of them already had. He plucked them out of his beloved holly bushes, scratching his hand, his wrist, on the prickly leaves as he stretched his arm inside the branches. Some scraps were deeply embedded; others had settled on the statuary, secured in place by the morning frost, ready to soar in flight once the sun rose a little higher and defrosted them. There were quite a few so maybe fewer got outside of the garden than he anticipated.

As he worked, it bothered him that he was obsessed with that girl known as Glory. He felt it would have been so easy to settle the situation quicker had she not been a Kendra look-alike. His Kendra was stunning in her naturalness, and Glory could have been her twin sister, although a slightly younger version and several years removed. He couldn't believe how many years had passed since the tragedy. Could it really be ten already? Some days it felt like only yesterday. Other days it felt so far back in the past that he could hardly imagine himself at eighteen.

Chris recalled that memory alters an event over time, and subsequent recollections of that event render it less and less true to the original. Chris thought that perhaps the same applied to facial recognition. It too could become less reliable. So if it were even remotely possible for his Kendra to materialize before his very eyes and stand next to Glory, he should be able to point out so many differences in their appearance, that the resemblance would be less apparent and his reactions the night before could easily be erased. The whole thing would be put to rest.

Then if he were to see Glory another time, she would be just another person, not necessarily a Kendra look-alike and he could go on his merry way. Sure, he jolted himself back to reality, how likely is that? She's still in my active mind—a spitting image, altered or not. And there was no doubt that his reaction had affected Glory. She picked up on it too. He noticed it, but shuddered at what it could mean, what it could lead to.

It bothered him to be plagued with these thoughts as he checked out the immediate neighborhood, sack in hand, picking up what he hoped were the remnants of Glory's frustration and not simply ordinary litter. Finally it became next to impossible to distinguish between Glory's handiwork and plain old trash. Discards were simply discards, dampened and soiled over night. The futility of it all made him feel foolish.

"What'cha doing there, Father Chris?" came a familiar voice from Swenson's Hardware Store located diagonally across the street from St Aeden's. It rang out to Chris as he was stooped over in her driveway, deciding to pack it up. That sing-songy voice could belong to none other than Mrs. Swenson, Eva, who along with her husband operated the store for decades. "Did'ja lose something? Want me to help ya find it?" She was always jovial and knew all their customers by name. People came to their store rather than to the big box stores. It was like visiting an old friend.

Chris was hoping that no one would spot him searching for remnants of the newsletters but it was too late. "No, Mrs. Swenson," he called back to her, straightening his vestments. "It's too complicated, but thanks anyway. Have a good day." He nodded politely, opting to avoid conversation. There's no way he would succeed in explaining this to anyone other than Bernie. Even then, that hadn't turned out so well.

All he needed on top of his seasonal nightmares was another layer of concern and distress. Come on now, he ordered himself, get with the holiday spirit. Plus he did have to scurry. He was due at St. Joseph Church in half an hour to concelebrate a funeral mass, a request from a college buddy whose mother had died unexpectedly. Something connected with a medication she was taking, he was told. He shivered just thinking about it. His own mother, Marie, ever since the tragedy, had been on tranquilizers. As needed, she always said, and now he had reason to worry that she could accidentally...

He banished the thought and substituted prayer for fear and worry as he always did. How could he let himself be so vulnerable? He was a priest, having received a divine calling. He should handle himself better, tap the resources available to him. Since he didn't have a hair shirt handy, he rummaged around in his pickup's glove box for a stray Hallowe'en treat. A flattened Reese cup should do it. Ah yes.

One glance at his friend, Marty Tisdale, and Chris could tell how devastated he was at the loss of his mother. Marty's father had passed while he and Chris were sophomores in college, though Marty was a few years older. After high school he had worked side by side in his father's manufacturing company until he decided to move on, to become an English teacher, a career he had dreamed about and felt the time was right to make it a reality. Chris and Marty really didn't know each other but they were in two or three classes together. When Marty failed to show up for class one full week, Chris inquired to see if anyone knew why he had been absent. Finally it was the prof who'd told him that Marty's father had died of a heart attack, suddenly. He added that it was while shoveling snow.

When Marty returned to class, Chris offered him his notes and learned that Marty was blaming himself for his father's heart attack. If he'd stayed in the business, he'd explained, he would have been the one to shovel the parking lot, not his father. Chris himself knew all about tragedy. He told Marty you can't change the past and blaming yourself does you no good. Chris knew that it was easier to give advice than to take it.

Their mutual tragedies drew the two young men closer. They became fast friends. But as both were commuter students they saw each other mostly when their schedules were similar. They would have lunch at the Student Center now and then. Weekends they might attend a sports event together with their dates, but as the years went on, Chris had no serious romances and eventually dated less and less, then not at all. He had something else in mind whereas Marty began to date a foreign student. She was the one, he told Chris. The couple married right out of college. Chris was his best man.

It was a blessing Marty had such a wonderful wife whom his mother adored. It helped her cope with the loss of her husband. When Sylvie became pregnant Marty's mother was jubilant. Then she sank into a depression after Sylvie's miscarriage. A second miscarriage followed only months later. Then finally a miracle! All was proceeding well as Marty and Sylvie were expecting their first child in the spring. Chris had hoped the anticipation of fatherhood would soothe the pain of Marty's loss. Chris vowed he'd be in touch with Marty more often—as often as time allowed. And yes, he'd be honored to confer the sacrament of Baptism on the new baby. But no, he had other duties to perform today so he couldn't join the family for brunch after the blessing at the cemetery. It was there that he spotted his mother among the mourners. How thoughtful of her to pay her respects to Marty and Sylvie. After a brief visit to his twin sister's grave just over the hillside, he gave his mother a hug, and their private little wave and headed out. She knew well that his time had already been spoken for.

BERNIE SAT FOR A FEW minutes watching Chris perform the thankless chore of picking up the mess in the garden that that girl had made. Then he saw Chris cross the street to continue searching for more paper fragments. Enough, he said to himself, shaking his head in desperation.

Just as he was about to say his morning Office, he heard the phone ring. Mrs. Hopkins called up to him the same time as he noticed the red light blinking on the call button. Just what he needed, a visit from the bishop, today, and, in only one hour. Yes, sure, he could be available. You don't say 'no' to his Excellency, friend or not. So really he was in the neighborhood and thought he'd pay a visit? Yeah, sure, Bernie said to himself after he'd hung up the phone. Something's up, and true to form, it won't be good news. He yelled down to Mrs. Hopkins to put on a pot of fresh coffee and defrost a few of her cranberry orange muffins. Take out the butter too. It had to be soft enough.

Sure enough, Bishop Gregory Miles appeared at the front door of the rectory with his ever present smile, which could presage just about anything. He was a large framed man, at least six-four, with immense hands and feet to match his imposing size. After taking his overcoat, Mrs. Hopkins escorted him into the sitting room where an inviting fire blazed. She offered him an over sized chair, which he graciously accepted. His thinning inky black hair was slicked back in his signature style though his hairline had receded some over the years.

The expandable mahogany coffee table held the spread that Bernie had ordered. Cloth napkins were folded in triangles at each place setting on an over sized square cloth that Mrs. Hopkins herself had embroidered, a gift to her beloved Father Bernie. She mimicked the bishop's behavior, the smile, stretching her lips until Bernie dismissed her. She wondered why it didn't seem to strain His Excellency as it did her face. She too figured that something was up.

Father Bernie entered the room and the bishop rose. His Excellency was first to speak. "Ah, Bernie. so good to see you again. How long has it been?" He extended his hand, then he hugged Bernie as he often did when greeting him.

They'd known each other for more years than they could remember. Bernie appeared to be searching his memory for a plausible answer. "Weeks, I guess." Then Bernie gave him one of his lighter weight grins. He knew something was up. He could sense it. After the usual amenities, the two men sat in their designated chairs. It was time to begin. They tackled the muffins with gusto. The bishop said they were the best he'd ever tasted. Bernie guessed he'd say that to all his hosts, but then maybe not.

Mrs. Hopkins was so talented she could have started her own bakery but remained loyal to St. Aeden's for such a long time that it would be a stretch for her to engage in a new business, a bakery. Wexford Falls already had Abigail Murdock's Bake Shop, which would make for tough competition. It would drive one or the other out of business, for sure. But unbeknownst to Father Bernie and Father Chris, Mrs. Hopkins would sneak over to Murdock's to buy muffins, but only when she was strapped for time. Of course, she would never to admit to that.

The two clerics had known each other since seminary days, Gregory Miles being a year ahead of Bernie. Whereas Bernie was content in his capacity as a parish priest serving his community, Gregory Miles's intention was to rise up in the ranks, which he did, having earned a graduate degree in canon law. The two, however, remained fast friends. But in his position, Miles always held the upper hand. That was just fine with Bernie as long as he was allowed to do his work without too much interference from 'on high', as he often referred to the bishop's power.

"Let's get down to business, Bernie. I'm sure you have a full day and you really didn't need me poking around here this morning," the bishop said in his rich baritone voice as he leaned over to face his old friend.

Bernie thought he'd play dumb as he had not an inkling as to what the bishop would want this week of all weeks, just days away from Christmas. Thoughts ran through his mind, as he waited for whatever boom the bishop was about to lower. Or maybe it was something positive. Sure, don't kid yourself, Bernie said to himself.

The bishop got right to it. The smile became less intense, understandably, as he was working on a muffin. "You know, Bernie, you and I always see eye to eye, do we not?"

"Well, yes, Greg, we usually do. I suppose so. Can I take a guess as to why you're here?" Bernie asked almost sheepishly now. He thought it was a good idea to keep on enjoying the steaming brewed coffee, to relish it as he stalled to come up with a reasonable guess.

"Go right ahead, Bernie. Say it," the bishop responded as he reached out for a second muffin. "May I?" He poured himself more coffee and topped off Bernie's cup. Then he poured cream into his own cup and helped himself to two teaspoons of sugar. He stirred the brew mindlessly, longer than necessary to blend the sugar throughout the liquid.

At last, Bernie ventured, "I think you'd like to say one of our Christmas day masses. That would be lovely."

"I wish I could, Bernie, but I'm already spoken for," he said wiping his chin with the starched napkin. "My masses have been all lined up for weeks now unless something unexpected arises. No, no, that's not it at all. I've come to see you about Christopher Tosi."

Bernie fairly jumped. He set down his coffee cup, spilling a little onto the table covering. He attempted to blot it up. "So, what about Chris?"

"Easy, Bernie," the bishop said smiling. "No problem with Chris. It's all good, I assure you. The fact is I'm thinking of moving him in the spring over to St. Damien's. You know they also have a school there. And I need someone young and dynamic like Chris Tosi. He's got a great reputation. I'm sure you of all people know that."

Bernie was speechless. He let the bishop go on. "My plans are to send Roland Donovan over here to St. Aeden's. You know he goes by Rollo, not Roland. He's not working out quite as well as expected over at St. Martin's. Good man, but not really a good fit, if you know what I mean."

Bernie figured the bishop could tell him whatever he wanted. He hadn't heard anything of that sort in the diocesan rumor mill. As far as he knew, Donovan and St. Martin's was a decent enough fit. At last, Bernie spoke. He realized he had a battle on his hands. And he was always up for a good battle when he thought he had a fighting chance to win. Then out it came, impassioned. "Roland or Rollo, as you say he prefers, could never replace Chris Tosi at St. Aeden's—not in a million years."

"And why not, I ask you?" the bishop retorted, flushing a bit. His smile began to shrink, replaced by an odd quizzical look. It wasn't the answer or the tone of voice the bishop had anticipated.

"Because, Greg," he began, then realized he needed to convince a man who was not easily swayed once he'd made up his mind. He tempered his tone. "Because Rollo Donovan has very bad allergies, yes, that's it. Serious allergies. So bad he can't even be desensitized with those allergy shots, they say. Next time you see him, just take a good look at him. He's always got a wad of Kleenex balled up in his hand. Sniffs and sneezes during every conversation I've ever had with him. He's a good priest, nice enough fellow, I guess. But those allergies..." Bernie shook his head from side to side to stress his point.

"So?" the bishop looked perplexed. He knew full well that Bernie could be a tough adversary, and could offer a sound argument. "Lot of people have allergies and function quite well in the world. So, level with me, Bernie, is that all? Just the allergies thing?"

"Well, that's quite enough for this place, what with the prayer garden and all. And, uh, what if I, uh, get a pet, a dog, like a watch dog, for instance? Rollo would go anaphylactic on me or worse," Bernie said. There was no grin; he was pleading his cause—earnestly.

"A dog now, Bernie?" the bishop's dark eyebrows leapt up. "Aw, come on, since when were you a canine lover?"

"I'll have you know, Greg, I am a true animal lover. I, uh, just haven't gotten around to it, but some day..." Bernie was defending his stance until the bishop cut him short.

"Sure, some fine day," the bishop interjected. "Get real, Bernie, after all these years. I need a better reason than that."

"Very well, then. Do you know the reputation that our magnificent prayer garden has had thanks to Father Chris, and how we've grown in numbers, several new families coming from other towns I might add, generous people, since Chris has been with us? Why, in a day or so the latest article on the garden is coming out," Bernie spoke up enthusiastically. "Personally, I think we should wait a few more years, yes, that's it. Send Rollo Donovan over to St. Damien's instead, why don't you? I hear he used to be a teacher once. He'd be the right one. Much better fit in my humble opinion."

"Ah, yes, Bernie, I guess you're right about that. He was indeed in education. Taught middle school social studies before he entered the priesthood, if I recall correctly. Yes indeed, you're right, Bernie. I'd forgotten and that's not like me at all." The bishop seemed to be relenting.

"Besides, Rollo would not be able to maintain Chris's prayer garden with those awful allergies of his, and I couldn't handle the work either. It's a big job. You can't imagine the daily upkeep. And Chris does it all himself. So how about a special favor for an old friend, Greg, leave Chris be, at least until I retire," Bernie asked. "We're good for each other."

"Retire, old boy?" the bishop lightened. "You've got many more good years ahead of you, as we both do. All right, all right, take it easy, Bernie, I'll take your request under consideration."

"Can you just give me some peace of mind, Greg?" Bernie asked. He opened his mouth to say something more then stopped himself. It was better left unsaid, he decided.

The bishop too paused a long moment, sipping his coffee, contemplating. Bernie hoped he would determine Chris's fate before he left, at least for the near future. And he prayed that the answer would be what he wanted to hear.

"All right, this time you win, Bernie," he said finally with a smile. Capitulation was rare on Bishop Miles's part. "I won't leave you in suspense. I can send Donovan over to St. Damian's in Tosi's place and we can see how that works out. I already have someone in mind to fill Donovan's place. It's a domino effect, you know. Not everybody's happy, but then they knew what they were getting into, right?"

Bernie heaved a sigh of relief. He answered, "Yes, right, Greg, of course. How can I thank you?"

"You really mean that?" the bishop said with the customary smile returning full force. "Well, how about wrapping up a couple of your cook's delicious muffins for me—to go, that is?"

"Here," Bernie said with a huge grin, "Here you go, Greg." Bernie grabbed a clean napkin and set the remaining muffins in and wrapped them up as requested. "Don't worry about returning the napkin. We've got bunches of them."

Then as though the two clerics had not had a contentious discussion, they wished each other a merry Christmas, hugged, and parted. Bernie could hear Bishop Miles complimenting Mrs. Hopkins on her excellent muffins. Bernie wasn't sure he'd even share this with Chris. The very thought of his being considered for an imminent move would not sit well with either of them.

ABOUT TWO O'CLOCK CHRIS had swung by Dunkin Donuts for his usual lunch pick me up, a light coffee and a plain bagel with cream cheese—to go, that is. It was no time to hang around and chat with the manager, Buster Greenleaf, who had a habit of bending his ear with stories, punctuated with 'right?' every few thoughts, or with requests. The snack had gotten Chris through the grueling schedule of the day.

As was customary before the supper hour, Chris stopped inside St. Aeden's to kneel before the statue of the Blessed Virgin Mary and contemplate the day's events. He meditated and prayed. A special prayer was for Matthew Barton, an inmate and parishioner, in his mid-twenties hardly old enough to understand his direction in life. Chris had paid him a visit at the prison, about a 30-plus minute drive through the hills. He actually enjoyed the trip, especially for the scenery, as he drove through the winding hills, their images reflected in glossy frozen lakes. These trips, however, made Bernie weary so Chris gladly took his place as Matt's spiritual advisor.

Matt Barton looked forward to Chris's visit. It broke the monotony of his incarceration, where every day was predictable, and always gave him something to hope for. For a few minutes Matt was able to ignore where he was and why he was there as the two mostly chatted about sports and local news. This proved therapeutic for Matt but only in the short run. Occasionally he'd ask Chris to check in on his fiancée, Ruthie Symond, who lived in Birch Valley. On one day, Matt knew in his heart she'd wait for him, or hoped so at least. On other days, he expressed his fear that she wouldn't. It just wasn't fair, Chris thought—Matt Barton was to be married in a week, and at his stag party on a blustery Friday night, he had insisted he was sober enough to drive home, but a tragic collision proved otherwise.

Two persons were killed in the wreck, a father and his young son returning home from the movies. Chris knew them both and has since comforted the grieving widow. The family had no other children. Matt survived the crash with only minor physical injuries—a few abrasions and contusions; the emotional shock, however, was anything but minor. Chris wondered over and over again how Matt's friends could have allowed him to drive in an apparently impaired condition. Involuntary manslaughter was the charge and with it came a three-year prison sentence. Matt felt nothing but remorse and regret every day of his confinement, interspersed with frequent bouts of depression. Chris knew those feelings too well and how they could gnaw at you. Matt got along much better with Chris than he did with Bernie, although Bernie offered him the needed comfort and support nonetheless. It was more the generation factor.

WELL PAST SUNSET AFTER the daily tour of his garden, Chris bounded up the back stairs through the kitchen into the bathroom and back after washing his hands. Bernie was already nearly done with his dinner, but joined Chris for what would be a second blessing as well as a second helping for himself; it certainly wouldn't hurt any. Chris thought he should be hungry but for some inexplicable reason he wasn't. He took a small serving and picked at it while Bernie ate voraciously. There were usually four dinner rolls in the bread basket in the center of the wobbly formica top table. Two were already missing.

Bernie eyed his young assistant. "What's with you, Chris? You're a bit late aren't you? And, you hardly touched your dinner— and after such a busy day. I would guess you'd be starved. Homemade mac and cheese has always been one of your favorites. Mrs. Hopkins makes it just like my mother used to. Come on, eat up. Try some of this red pepper relish with it." Bernie always had to add some condiment or another –ketchup, relish, whatever struck his fancy or was on a shelf in the fridge. Chris preferred things straight away—no frills. If it was good food, well prepared, why adulterate it with some goo from a jar?

Chris hadn't let go. He thought he had cleared his mind but the thoughts flew back— boomerang like. He was mulling over Matt Barton's sorry situation – the imprisonment, the loneliness, the futility. Ruthie hadn't come to visit him in four or was it five days? Matt was worried. What was with her? Would Chris stop by to see her tomorrow to check on how she's doing? Sure, why not? But when would he have the time to pay a visit? Chris could only try. But on Christmas week, how could he manage to squeeze in anything more?

Chris answered, "I'm not really very hungry tonight, Bernie. I know I should be. It's not the food. It's me, I'm afraid." He pushed aside his plate as Bernie reached for roll number three. Ever observant, Chris gave him the look. Each seemed to have mastered the look to admonish the other, to show distaste or disapproval, and it worked. It was indeed worth it to avoid having words.

Yes, indeed, Bernie was delighted that the bishop had come around to his way of thinking. He was thankful for Rollo Donovan's allergies, and ashamed of himself for thinking that, and for capitalizing on it as an excuse. But how could he let Chris go? It was much too soon for a move.

"I know I shouldn't," he explained, "eat that roll, I mean. Gotta watch my weight and other stuff you don't have to say. You should have the last one." Bernie acknowledged Chris's gesture of refusal and eagerly changed the subject. "I bet the children wore you out at the rehearsal. Heh heh."

"In part," he said. "That and the visit to see Matt Barton." Bernie reacted with a silent, sympathetic nod. He was relieved that Chris wanted to take over the prison visits. He as administrator had best spend his time in his office when not assuming other priestly duties, at least for the busy Christmas season, not that driving in the snowy hills would be a picnic either.

Bernie said with some concern, "Right. It's always difficult. Poor guy. By the way, I got the call. You know the one I mean." Chris didn't. He shrugged. There could have been any number of calls. And Bernie surely wasn't about to mention the bishop's visit and hoped that Mrs. Hopkins would remain mum. He made a mental note to remind her. "Couldn't believe it," Bernie continued. "Who would have thought Barbara would have an emergency the day of such an important rehearsal?"

Chris leaned back in his chair, a habit that worried Bernie. One of these days he'd go ass over teakettle. His mother used that expression. She could say 'ass' but the kids weren't allowed to use that kind of language. When he once told his mother that the word 'ass' appears in the Bible and after all it's only an animal, he got a swat. He said in a matter of fact tone. "Aren't all emergencies untimely?"

"Well yes, most of them," Bernie admitted. "She, Barbara that is, had such an awful attack, pains in her belly and her chest." He indicated by showing him just where on his own person. "She had no choice but to seek medical attention. Hope she doesn't need surgery."

Chris feared the same. "I sure hope not either. Maybe it was just indigestion. We really need her there so bad with just a few days left to get the pageant just right. All that orchestration. She's got wonderful ideas and gets the kids motivated and keeps them on target. You know how they can get so distracted. And... she's so much better equipped to handle rehearsals than I would ever be. Lucky for us, you thought of good old Mrs. Rafferty. Fortunately, she came to the rescue. She said she agreed to come on board to offer some guidance, as she calls it—guidance. It's enough to drive me out of my wits. Plus, she's much too bossy with the kids. She claims she's helped oversee Christmas pageants for the past few years."

Bernie chuckled. "Try 30. The woman's a pain you know where—and a blessing as well. But...you can always count on her, so, Chris, be nice to her in case Barbara's out tomorrow or longer. Heaven forbid."

Chris feigned consternation. "Oh, she can't be. Time is running short. For that matter, Barbara is able to manage humans *and* animals. I'm not too sure about Mrs. Rafferty and myself, for that matter. Those cows can be very testy. And old Ethel, the goose, has a mind of her own, nasty creature. She'll nip us if we're not careful. Ethel will behave though if Mrs. Jones decides to hang around. I hear the Joneses want their llama in the mix too or else Ethel may have another engagement. Can you believe it, bargaining over an animal! What next! So we need to pray hard that Barbara recovers miraculously over night. She's a farmer. Not you or I."

Bernie smiled. "Oh, come now, Chris, just trust in the Lord—and in Mrs. Rafferty—now there's a real farm girl, that one—don't even know her first name. Guess it's just Mrs. Heh heh."

Chris responded with a smile and a nod of agreement. Bernie had a way to calm his nerves. "Fine with me." He yawned and pushed his plate away.

Bernie said, "Chris, why don't you take a little something to make you sleep, maybe banish the banshees—or at least put 'em to sleep, dope 'em up a little." He slapped his thigh laughing.

Chris regained his forces. "Nah, let me at 'em. I'll conquer them some day—or die trying. It's more like the time for some quiet reading."

"Hope it's prayerful. You know I can suggest some good theologians, for reading. Yes, I know. You've heard me say this before," Bernie said resigned. He slapped Chris on the back; then something grabbed his attention outside in the garden.

He rose sending the table rocking. Chris laughed. This happened all the time Bernie sprang and leaned too hard on the end of the table. The jar of relish fell over and rolled on the floor, spewing some of its peppery contents in a long streak. Chris retrieved the jar, wiped up the spill with a napkin, and put the cover back on. He placed it on the counter next to the fridge. Bernie was oblivious to the spill. He was like a wild animal, still and silent, surveying his prey. He walked over to the window.

Chapter EIGHT

"WELL, I'LL BE. A SHADOW," Bernie announced, "out there in the garden, Chris. Don't people know it's after sunset? I guess they can't read the sign. No one should be out there." He stood still scarcely breathing as though the sound could possibly alert the intruder. "Uh-oh, I fear an instant replay of last night if you can imagine that. Looks like that ghost girl again. Drat! Wonder what she's up to now. Some trick up her sleeve or some drama of sorts. What's she got to rip up this time? Her report card? The daily news? Anyone's guess, I suppose. You know, Chris, we could do without this."

Bernie looked infuriated, breathing loudly through his nose. He darkened the kitchen, and peered out the window to get a better perspective on the situation. Then he motioned to Chris to join him. Chris stood silently by the window, keeping out of sight. He was already beginning to feel uneasy. "Yeah, that's her, all right. That's Glory. I can tell." He felt very unsure of himself. He wondered where this was going—two nights in a row. "I'll take care of this," he said to Bernie with a sigh as he went to grab his jacket.

"So you're sure you want to deal with her again? Not a good idea. Why don't you wrap things up here and settle down for the evening? You sure could use a decent night's sleep. Let me handle things."

Chris shot him a look that said 'sure, go for it, good luck.' He figured Bernie would not be in harm's way and could probably get to the bottom of what brought Glory back to the garden. And so Chris relented without hesitation. He didn't want to be in her presence if he could avoid it. "You know you're probably right. You don't mind? She's a challenge—a handful, as you would say." He knew he should feel relieved but he couldn't help feeling that that wasn't the last of her.

Bernie on the other hand was undaunted. He'd get rid of her. "Not at all do I mind. Nosiree! Leave her to me." He grabbed his down parka from the coat rack, put it on, and zipped it up to his neck. The evening had grown cold. He pulled his cap from the shelf above the rack, and set the earflaps in place to protect himself from the icy evening breeze even though it might affect his hearing. He could always raise the one flap to better hear the girl. He figured he didn't need his gloves, despite Chris's admonishing look that screamed—protect your arthritic fingers. He ignored the look and headed down the steps, carefully holding onto the railing, which wobbled a little in spots. He'd need to take care of that—some other time. First things first.

He stepped gingerly across the frozen ground leading to Chris's garden. Even in the bleakness of the winter night, in the dim moonlight there was a glow, a sense of mystical beauty about the garden, a sense of peace and serenity regardless of the season. So what if it was in part illuminated by the street light on the corner.

Father Bernie did nothing to soften the sound of his footfalls as he approached Glory. She was preoccupied scanning the various places in the garden, the shrubs and wilted plantings, the pavers and bowers, and the statuary. When she realized who it was, she looked up. Disappointment marred the prettiness of her face. She cast a look of obvious disdain. Wrong person.

Bernie chose to ignore the look. She was a teenager; they could make those sour faces one minute and show you another in a flash. He could remember when…He nodded slightly and addressed the intruder. "Good evening, Miss. May I ask your name and what we may do for you?"

Glory did manage to change her attitude. She had expected the older priest to chastise her with a deluge of complaints. She was so used to that from adults. Instead he was anything but unfriendly. He even forced a weak smile. So she smiled back at him and said, "Oh hi, you must be the other guy—the boss."

"I suppose you're right about that," he said studying her, trying to fathom what bothered Chris so much about her appearance. Yes, she was very attractive, by anyone's standards. "I'm Father Monahan, but you'd know that if you belonged to my parish, St. Aeden, the grounds of which you are presently standing upon after sunset—that is, after hours." He made sure to emphasize that the garden was closed to visitors and that she had failed to heed what the sign indicated.

Her reaction told him she was unfazed. He hoped he didn't sound overly pompous, but she had no right to be there at this time and he could throw his weight around if warranted. He decided to test her. "But I hear you belong to that, uh, Spanish church, uh, Saint Dino or something like that. Must be out of town. I say that because I've never heard of it."

Glory laughed at what she took for gullibility or naivete, then she immediately felt embarrassed. "Oh no, Saint Dinero, not Dino." All she could picture was Dino the Dinosaur from old reruns of the Flintstones. She settled herself and continued. "Oh, he told you. He remembered. I'm surprised he did. That's so silly. My father jokes around all the time—when it suits him. He tells everyone how religious we are and stuff like that. Says he goes to Saint Dinero's. Most people get it, if they know Spanish that is, and they get a good laugh out of it."

Bernie said, "Yes, Father Tosi told me all about you." He paused and looked her straight in the eye, watching a broad smile brighten her face. Dimples made her even prettier. She was nearly a head taller than he was, in her high-heeled boots.

"Oh, he did? What else did he say?" she seemed almost giddy.

Bernie did not appreciate her gaiety. "If you recall, I'm the one asking the questions around here. What is your name, please? I think you forgot that I asked you."

"No, sorry. I guess Chris forgot to tell you that. I'm Glory Sterling-Baie," she answered. He wondered if she could ever feel genuinely contrite for her rudeness, her actions, or her intrusions. This wasn't the time or the place for her to just come popping up.

Bernie was playing it cool. He was curious to find out what her real motives were. His suspicions were growing. "Very well, Glory. Thank you. And you're here, I presume, to pray in these serene surroundings this joyous time of the year to prepare for the birth of the Savior of the world?"

"Oh, yeah, right," she said. "You mean the manger baby. But I don't see any manger out here. But no, not really, it didn't cross my mind. I didn't think of coming here to pray. I came here to see Chris. I hoped to get his attention." Her candor was a thunderbolt. It was not what he wanted to hear. Chris doesn't need anything else to complicate his life.

"He's Father Tosi to you, if you please," Bernie said sharply. "And if you came to see him, as you said, then how did you plan to make your presence known? Beam thoughts at him, or make a racket to get his attention, maybe cast pebbles at the kitchen window?" He paused and gave her the look his mother always gave him when she was angry at him. "Well, this time, you got mine, young lady."

Glory grew defensive. "He said I could call him Chris. Yeah, Father Chris. I, uh, could see you guys up there at the window and I thought, uh, you'd see me and come out here. It is kinda dark though."

Bernie realized he had to keep his anger in check. He would tread gently, didn't want to cause a ruckus with this one. "So now you come into the garden about the time we have dinner. Hmm."

"Right," she agreed nodding her head as though it was a normal thing to do—wait in the garden until a priest arrived. "I can barely make out your faces though—just a young guy and an old guy. That's what it looks like from here." She twittered nervously, leaning on one foot then, the other.

Indignant, Bernie went on, "You got that right. I'm the old guy, if that isn't so obvious." Glory laughed at his quip. "Funny?" He said. "Didn't your parents teach you to address members of the clergy with respect, using proper titles, I mean, or did you forget that too?"

"Oh no, I respect you." Contrite look again. "Don't get me wrong. I do. I only came here to tell Chris that I kept my promise to him." She looked down at this man with the reddened face, his feet firmly planted in place, authoritatively. One earflap of his winter hat was snapped up and the other down, covering an ear. Fly away strands of white hair flapped in the breeze. She thought he could have looked like her grandfather if he'd been alive, but no, he was the one in charge.

Bernie did not like the way this was panning out. He quickly conceded that titles didn't matter so much. He needed to know what this girl might be up to. Promise, what promise? he wondered.

"Well, he's not very happy with you," he barked. "He had one heck of a time chasing all those little scraps of paper you tossed in his garden, as if he had nothing better to do with his time. You should know he's a busy man. He's a priest, for heaven's sake. That should mean something. You know, he even found some of your mess next door and across the street, all over the place." Bernie gestured in those directions as though she needed help determining to what extent her handiwork had spread.

"Oh, I don't think so. If any pieces of paper went that far then they probably weren't mine," she defended herself, with a wave of her hand, "unless they jumped way, way up over the bushes." She laughed at the very thought of the scraps taking flight and soaring beyond the hollies, which had grown very tall, and gliding to a halt so far away—at least in her mind.

Bernie did a slow sizzle, which was not at all good for his health. "Well, I beg to differ with you. I'll bet they were yours, after all." How could Chris have put up with her last night, with her antics and her attitude, he wondered. He must have nerves of steel, or maybe there was something else...He banished the thought.

Glory insisted, "I was only turning something ugly and dishonest—those phony newsletters—into a thing of beauty –pretty little snow flakes, like I used to make in cutouts back in grade school. I told him so and he seemed to understand. I know he really did." She began to shiver. He interpreted that as meaning she was uncomfortable. This seemed to be getting to her.

Bernie challenged, hands on hips, "Oh, he said so, did he now? Really?"

Glory hesitated a moment. "Well, not exactly, not in so many words. He didn't need to." She looked away from him. His questioning was making her squirm. "But he got me. Yeah, he did."

"That may very well be, but I got you now," he said in the most authoritative tone of voice he could muster. He had had enough of this banter. "Well, you're here, now what can I do for you?"

Glory responded openly, "You can give this to him, um, please. Last night he told me to go home and write a poem. Well, I didn't go right home though, but anyway, here's the poem, it's in this envelope here. Don't you read it. It's for Chris, uh, Father Chris."

Bernie heaved a sigh and took the envelope from her. It was not an ordinary business envelope but rather a lacy perfumed, feminine looking one. As he turned to leave he cast a glance at the far side of the garden; then he did a double take. He espied the statue of the Blessed Virgin Mary, and then he understood why Glory was shivering. It was cold out there and some of her outerwear was elsewhere.

"Well, I'll be," Bernie muttered mostly to himself in amazement, then louder, accusatory. "Whatever did you do to our beautiful statue of Mary, the holy mother of God?"

Glory was dumbfounded. "Me, I didn't do anything *to* her."

Was she serious? Bernie was incredulous. He wasn't fooled. "Well, maybe you bore witness to some spirit or another that outfitted her for winter—wrapped her in a scarf and put earmuffs on her to boot. Can you shed any light on this, young lady?" Bernie could feel his pressure rising.

Glory grinned. "Lots. I guess I would say *I'm* that spirit. But, hey, no one ever called me that before—a spirit. Rad. It's cold out here so I thought I'd give the statue my pashmina. I've got lots of them. I borrow them from my mother's closet. She's got so many she wouldn't notice one missing. And...it's not a scarf like you said. It's much bigger. See?" She stroked it lovingly. "It brightens her up a so much; she's very faded, she would actually would benefit from some paint or makeup. She should be warm now. Plus it looks better on her than on me. Us girls got to stick together. Cool, huh?"

Bernie tried to keep his own cool. Now he wished he'd have let Chris have a go at this. "Oh boy, us girls. And make-up—God forbid! I've heard everything now. A mere mortal teen and a statue personifying the holy immaculate mother of our Savior—in the same breath—and as *allies*. Not cool a'tall, nosiree."

He shook a finger at Glory and took a deep breath. "You're very misguided, you are, Miss Glory Sterling—or whatever your name is. You need that whatchamacallit, that scarf and those earmuffs yourself—look at you now, you're shivering." He gestured at Mary. "She's a statue. She doesn't feel the cold a'tall. People don't go around doing things like that, dressing up statues. What's wrong with you?" Glory recoiled, speechless, as Bernie removed the outer garments from the statue and handed them back to her. His look was searing.

"I meant well," she explained as she wrapped herself in the pashmina. She pocketed the earmuffs. "I really, really did." Bernie wasn't quite sure what to believe. She could sound contrite, but...she wasn't a child; she was a teen-ager. Didn't she know any better?

Bernie had had enough. "I can't figure out *what* you meant. Now run along home to your parents."

Glory said, "You mean to my Grandmom. My parents are in Dubai on a business trip this week. Chris must have told you that too."

Bernie refused to lose his temper. "Oh, sure. He must have. I just don't recall."

Glory reminded the priest of her errand. "Please give the envelope to Father Chris." She stressed the word 'Father'.

"Oh, for sure I will. Most definitely. Now run along. Scoot. This is not a teen-age hangout." He escorted her to the gate.

She proceeded obediently. Then she paused, letting him pass in front of her. "Ciao. I'm on my way." She shut the gate once Father Bernie had headed back to the rectory, but she lingered, gazing up at the kitchen window where she had watched the priests dine earlier. When Bernie put the lights on, she noted the absence of Father Chris. Only then did she leave the church grounds.

A spate of thoughts flooded Bernie's mind. It doesn't all add up, he mused. She had emerged out of the blue. They'd never seen her before last night, but the whole town knew of Sterling-Baie

Enterprises, as if this entitled her to do whatever the spirit moved her to do. She's surely got something brewing, but who knows what? And what about Chris? God only knows where he is on all this. Oh, I'm just ruminating, he reminded himself. Let's hope it will all blow away and vanish like those shreds of paper she scattered all over the garden. Don't really know yet. Bad timing, whatever it is, what with Christmas a few days away and Chris's nights in an uproar.

Chapter NINE

BERNIE STOOD NEARLY frozen in place like a statue in the still darkness of the kitchen, surveying the scene below to ensure that Glory had indeed left the church grounds. She had. He waited there a few minutes longer. Shortly after, Chris emerged from his bedroom. He wore the weariness of the world on his forehead, on his whole face.

"Well, I thought you'd be all nestled in your chamber, Chris. I prove myself wrong," Bernie said with a faint wheeze. Chris reacted with a concerned look, but avoided the topic. It was too late to engage in a battle about Bernie's health, the do's and don't's of it.

"First I was, but I had to eavesdrop," Chris admitted sheepishly.

Bernie snapped. "It's like the North Pole in here. You opened the window, didn't you now?" Bernie was always lecturing him on energy prices, on being careless. It wasn't so much carelessness as not thinking of the consequences. His mother had always closed doors and windows and turned off lights for the whole family. It just wasn't a concern, but it should be, he decided.

"The better to hear you, Bernie," Chris joked, hoping a little levity would help. It didn't. Bernie didn't crack a hint of a smile.

"When you consider the price of heating oil, you might rethink things," he advised, as he removed his jacket and hung it back up on the hook.

"Sorry. I didn't think," Chris said. "I was curious as to why Glory came back. That makes two nights in a row. She must have another problem or something." He hoped she didn't.

Bernie shot back. "Problem or something? Problem, you say? That girl lives in a world of her own. Do you know what she went and did?" Bernie forgot that Chris had eavesdropped.

But Chris knew. "I got most of it. No offense, Bernie, but she is not as loud spoken as you."

"You're right on that," Bernie began. The harshness in his tone was unmistakable. "Plus I was very annoyed at her. She has no right to be in that garden at night. Can you imagine? She dressed up the statue of the Virgin Mary like it was one of her dolls. To keep her warm, she said. Put on some weird gigantic scarf that she called some unpronounceable thing—a pashamajig." He paused to catch his breath. "Is she crazy? And then there she stands shivering in the cold. Remember the old term— 'airhead'? Well, that's what we've got here. She's an airhead, Chris. That's what she is. Plus, she has very limited manners. Non-existent, I might add. Kids these days. I just don't know." He shook his head in disbelief.

"It's Christmas week and her parents are away," Chris explained as if it would compensate for her brashness.

"Well now then, that should explain it all, shouldn't it?" Bernie was growing impatient.

"How could it? We don't know the whole story if indeed there is a story," Chris replied.

Bernie wheezed again. "Well, she better not show her face here again. I've had my fill of her. Oh, I almost forgot. She kept her, uh, promise to you." Chris looked uncomfortable. The word 'promise' scared him.

Bernie's remark put Chris in a tailspin. He blurted, "What in the world are you talking about?"

"This. Right here." He handed the envelope to Chris. "There's a poem inside, a poem for you. I'm not to read it. She said so. Now what do you have to say to that?"

Chris didn't like Bernie's tone at all. He tried to calm himself, but inside he could feel his heart begin to pound. "Well, naturally, I'm a little surprised."

"Oh, only a little?" He looked Chris squarely in the eye. "She said you told her to go home and write a poem. Is that right?"

Chris managed a tight smile. He didn't like to explain himself, especially when he was innocent of any wrongdoing. "A poem, yes, I did, but not *for* me or *to* me. God, how easily things get taken out of context." He recalled what he had suggested for her to do the night before. He had no idea that she would actually follow through.

Bernie began to sound paternal. "Well, would you enlighten me on the context? You know, there shouldn't even be a context, for that matter. She came into the garden after hours, which she shouldn't have, and made a holy show of a mess, and you told her to leave. If there was anything else resembling a context, I'd like to hear about it. You know how rumors get started and where they can end up, and then can they ever be rectified completely?" He didn't wait for an answer. He knew he was right.

" Yes, Bernie, I do," Chris said with a sigh. "But you know I'm not that brusque of a person. We can't or we shouldn't be in our role in the church and the community." He was trained to listen actively. He didn't need to remind his elder, but at that moment, he felt he needed to do so.

"But there's a time and a place, remember?" Bernie said summarily. "People call us for an appointment or drop into the rectory, not emerge out of the blue in the garden at night for some silliness that we're supposed to understand and condone."

"How well I know. Let me continue, please. I asked her questions like 'why' and her answers led to more questions. I did ask her to go home and give her grandmother a hug," Chris said. "She led me to believe she's not very honest with her though."

"She didn't tell me any of that," Bernie was quick to respond. "Impulsive girl, she is. And somehow I don't think for a moment that honesty is her best policy, not a'tall, not this girl."

" Maybe not, but since she told me she likes to write poems," Chris went on, " I guess I told her to go home and write one. I gave her no further details as to what kind of poem or whom she should write it to or for. It would give her something creative and constructive to do instead of wandering around and littering my garden and disturbing our peace. She could have written one about, uh, hypocrisy or disgust about the newsletters, or something along those lines. But I never ever said write one for me. You should know I would never say that. Besides she was such a Kendra look-alike, I felt very uncomfortable, unnerved in her presence, which unfortunately she picked up on. I am not responsible for how she took that. I just needed for her to leave."

"Maybe she interpreted your attention as, uh, you being interested in her," Bernie remarked with no malice aforethought.

However it was intended, Chris stiffened; then he resumed. "Well, I was interested in her as a human being, a kid, a teen-ager who was dealing with stuff, stuff she found hard to deal with. Kids that age detest phonies; they're idealistic for the most part, or is it delusionary? Maybe a little of both."

Bernie was all ears. "And?"

Chris wanted desperately to bring this interrogation to a peaceful end. "And I got rid of her. Period. I didn't think she'd come back, and certainly not with a poem for me."

Bernie quieted down. Then he turned the fragile lacy envelope over and over again, as though through the sense of touch, he could learn its contents. It was translucent. He held it up to the light to see if he could read the poem, but it appeared to have been folded with the lettering on the inside. Finally he spoke, softly, conspiratorially, "Shall we open the envelope?"

Chris was not about to take the suggestion. He could care less what the poem had to say. "Why don't we just rip it up—envelope and all—and be done with it?"

"That we can do." Bernie was acting wily, which Chris did not appreciate at the moment.

"Would you like to do it?" Chris asked. He had no ulterior motive. Get rid of it and it's over and done with.

Bernie huffed. Curiosity was getting the better of him. "You know... maybe we should open it. We can read it together." He smiled his usual impish grin, which didn't make sense to Chris in this situation.

"Both of us? You want both of us to read it together? Why?" Chris asked with raised eyebrows. He did not like that idea at all.

Bernie looked thoughtful. "And why not? Maybe she does have a problem, say, suicidal tendencies and we can, uh, intervene, save her."

Chris stopped him in his tracks. "And maybe she does not. Look, Bernie, you know the sappy drivel these teen-age girls write."

Bernie reflected a moment, gazing at the wall beyond his young associate. "Oh, sure, I do. I was young once and there was this homely girl, at least she was homely in my eyes way back then. Her name was Beatrice Smalley, yeah, that was her name. Strange I can remember that. Anyhow, she obviously had a huge crush on me...wrote me a love poem. It rhymed, too. Imagine, her, of all the girls in the class, writing me a love poem. Needless to say, I was not interested, not in the least, not with those looks of hers. Yes, I know she was one of God's creatures but she was no looker—not back then, nosiree. But, boy oh boy, did she ever blossom into a beauty queen a few years later and when I finally *was* interested in her, she clearly wanted nothing to do with yours truly. End of sad story. Heh heh."

Chris was amused. "Poor you. You got over it."

" Yeah, with cold showers," Bernie admitted with an aside glance that shouted embarrassment.

In this lighter mood, Chris said, "All right, Bernie, this poem, on the other hand, could be rap lyrics, which could be far from sappy. Some of the rap poems today are pretty clever. Kids today are into them, gives them a vehicle to vent. Clever rhyming, too. You should listen to them some time, but I must admit some are a little, uh, harsh. I say we give it a look. You can join me, Bernie. I've got nothing to hide." He gestured in an arms wide open pose.

"Oh Chris, tomorrow's another day. We can deal with the poem thing tomorrow. How about that?" Bernie said with a wide yawn. "I think I'll turn in. You should too. We've had more than enough excitement today. With the fresh morning light comes new ideas."

"Let's hope so," Chris said weakly.

Chapter TEN

CHRIS HAD ONE OF HIS better nights, a well-deserved break from the nocturnal terrors that plague him this time of year. Maybe the banshees found another victim to hound. He laughed to himself at the very idea. Then he convinced himself that they were still lurking in his subconscious but that the recall factor was absent. We don't always remember our dreams, he'd read somewhere. In any event, he was grateful for a sound sleep and the blessed break of day.

Chris's first thoughts turned to the issue of the poem, what it might contain. Maybe Bernie would forget to bring it up. Both had other things on their mind this morning. Chris was seated at the kitchen table, a pensive look gracing his features. He began to review his schedule for the day over a cup of rewarmed coffee. First and foremost, he was determined to polish his Christmas homily days before he would deliver it. He didn't want to run the risk of a last minute rewrite.

Meanwhile Bernie was readying himself to celebrate a funeral mass. Chris could hear his pastor's frustrated groans as he struggled to decipher a hand-written biography of a deceased parishioner. Bernie was expected to deliver it as a eulogy in an hour or so. He glanced up at Chris, his brow furrowed. "Much as I don't prefer typing myself, I sure wish Joe's son had taken the time to type up the bio he sent over last minute. I've got half a mind to give my own thoughts. I knew Joe Biddle well enough to say a few words. Good man, he was. Can't say that about his son though."

"Here, hand it over. Let me give it a try," Chris offered, setting aside his work. He took the wrinkled sheet of paper, shook it out and began to read aloud. Then, after a moment, he looked up at Bernie and asked, "Does that help any?"

The folds on Bernie's forehead began to smooth out. "Sure does. There were a few words here and there I just couldn't make out...thanks." He folded the paper and rose to finish dressing as the phone jangled which at that time of the morning meant something was up, something that would stretch one of their schedules. And it did.

Chris took the call. It was for him. From his bedroom, Bernie could hear him say, "Sure I can, I'll be over some time this morning. See that she stays home. I don't want to miss her."

SEPTUAGENARIAN MURIEL Symond greeted Father Chris with an anguished, slanted smile. It took effort and it was horribly out of sync with her usually cheery countenance. Her dark brown eyes sparkled when she was animated, when she talked to anyone. Today they were lackluster, dull. Her full cheeks often held creases of mirth but not this morning. Today she was not the longtime school secretary that had greeted countless students, teachers and visitors to Birch Valley Middle School daily for decades. No, she was the concerned mother. She was worried, almost frantic, about her daughter Ruthie, age 25. Despite the marked difference in their ages, Muriel having adopted her daughter well in mid-life, the two women were very close, and strangely enough, usually saw eye to eye, but not so much this time. Ruthie wasn't talking. How could she explain herself?

Sure, it was difficult for Muriel to observe her daughter dealing with a fiancé imprisoned for three years, and having to defer their wedding plans indefinitely. Ruthie insisted, who would want to make wedding plans that far off in the future? Anything could happen. But Muriel had learned to cope with Ruthie's periodic bouts of doubt and depression, even occasional outbursts of anger directed at Matt, at herself, at the world. At times Muriel offered soothing words of compassion, other times she took a tougher stance, and told her to just get with it. She'd say, sometimes life was meant to be plowed though, but it all works itself out eventually. Young people are always so much in a hurry for things to happen right away, she'd tell her daughter. Three years in a lifetime was nothing, but to Ruthie and Matt it was an endless, painful eternity. Chris figured this time neither method was working for Muriel. He didn't have much time to ponder any further as a teary, sullen Ruthie flew into the front room after hearing voices in the foyer. When she spotted Father Chris she cast a rueful glance at her mother.

"You had to call out for help, didn't you, Mom? Like everything that happened last night can be fixed and forgotten," Ruthie barked hoarsely to her mother, who only returned a puzzled look. Everything about Ruthie was always straight—her shoulder length chestnut hair, her pert straight nose, and her direct but laid back manner. Any way you looked at it, she was a very likeable young woman. No, today was a crooked day for her, a bent out of shape day—everything in her life was askew. Her jeans and blouse were disheveled and wrinkled as though she'd slept in them, and her face was ruddy and tear-stained in long jagged streaks. Her hair looked matted and her amber eyes were bloodshot, telling Chris that something indeed had transpired, serious enough for Muriel to seek Chris's help. He figured that Ruthie had said very little to her mother, which prompted the desperate call to St. Aeden's, and to Chris specifically. Then to Chris, Ruthie softened her tone, "Father," she began. She cleared her throat. "I'm really sorry Mom had to go and bother you. I'm going to be OK. Really."

But she failed to convince either herself or Chris. By then, Muriel nodded to Chris and left the room quietly. There was a long, awkward moment of silence. Then in an obvious act of desperation Ruthie gestured to Chris to be seated on the sofa as she opted for a straight chair opposite him. He sensed her discomfort. She was struggling with herself and she was clearly pained. She looked nothing like the reserved, polite young woman he'd counseled after the incident that resulted in Matt's jail time.

He tried not to study her too long. He feared the silence could become palpable, uncomfortable for both of them. Prolonging it could unnerve her, so he spoke first. "Ruthie," he said gently, "I'm not going to say a word. It's up to you if you want to speak to me. Yes, your mother asked me to stop by. There was good reason for it, I understand. She's concerned. Let me know how I can help."

"Father, I'm not so sure anyone can help," she said wiping her eyes. "I don't know what I'm doing. I made a big mistake and now I'm terrified. I'm scared for Matt, and it's all my stupid fault. I should have said 'no' and stuck with it."

Chris shot her a puzzled look. But he kept silent. Let her speak if she's willing to. He could see her probing her thoughts, weighing her words. He merely nodded. That seemed to give her courage.

"Well, Father...Here goes. This is why Mom was worried, actually freaked. I'm surprised she didn't call the police instead, have them put out an amber or some kind of color alert for me. I forget which one," she began. Somehow hearing her own words helped her go on. "I, uh, didn't get home till after five this morning, and I guess Mom stayed up all night staring at the clock, wondering if I was dead or alive, or lying helpless in some gutter. She probably phoned the hospital. You know I didn't even ask her that. She was in such a panic. Then I came home finally. And I was in bad shape, just look at me, and, uh, like I said, I made a big mistake." She shifted in her chair. Chris could see how upset she was.

She sighed deeply; then she resumed. "Let me go back to the beginning, Father. I, uh, ran into an old friend, actually an old boyfriend of mine last week. Now that I think of it, I think it was accidentally on purpose on his part. Had to be. And, uh, he asked me to meet him for coffee last night, but we would wind up after that going to, um, a bar. Right off, I should have said 'no' but it seemed innocent enough. Two old friends getting together. What could be wrong with that? He said he just wanted to talk, catch up on each other's lives. Well, after a couple of drinks we wound up at his apartment, and we, uh, talked some more."

Chris listened, nodded, and remained silent. Let her finish. She would continue and she did.

"Father, would you believe it? I found out he's still interested in me after he broke it off with me five years ago, married and divorced some idiot and now he has a two year old son. But now he's kinda free, says so anyhow. Well, I made it very clear to him I was not interested in, you know, a, uh, relationship, not that kind anyhow, not with anyone. After all I am still engaged to be married...some day," she added with a sigh, her last thought for Chris's benefit. She seemed a bit calmer now.

"So, Father, listen, I was really surprised how hot he kept his apartment. Like fuel oil is so expensive, you know. First it felt nice coming in from the cold, but then it was much too hot so I asked him for a drink of water which he got for me out in the kitchen." She swallowed hard and paused. "I was so dry I drank the whole thing down like in one big gulp, and a little later, he, uh...Well, he started, uh, and then I, uh, said 'no' and told him I meant it. Yeah, that's what it led to and for a while he seemed OK enough with that, which kinda surprised me. Guys don't give up that easy, you know." She blushed. "Well, I guess you know. Well, we were, uh, hanging out in his living room, like mellowed out, listening to some CD he had on—country music, his favorite, Garth Brooks it sounded like. Then something came over him, like out of nowhere he came out with, uh, I was too nice and pretty to be saddled for God knows how long with a no good drunken ass felon. That's what he called Matt. Well, Father, I almost hit him. I told him Matt's a decent guy. He was set up. That's what it was, what it had to be. He was innocent and is appealing the sentence, you know, and then he told me I didn't really know old Matty boy. That's what he called him. Like he knows him or something. No way. Father, I remember his exact words. He said to me, 'Your guy is not the choirboy you think he is. You know he's in for trouble in the big house. I got friends in there. He better watch out.' When I asked him, 'watch out for what' he gave me a sneaky sorta grin. That put a real scare into me. So then after a while I was getting woozy and I started to let him, uh, have his way with me, you know? I can't say it, Father. Uh, maybe then his friends would leave Matt alone? Next thing I knew I couldn't make myself talk, like say words and stuff. If he was talking, I couldn't hear him either. I was very drowsy like I was on another planet. Then I guess I must have slept. When I woke up, I was on his bed, my clothes were, uh, well, you know...and he was gone out somewhere. I didn't take the time to look. I grabbed my bag and my car keys, and well here I am. My mom was a wreck and so was I. I'm not sure what really happened or didn't happen, but, uh, I can't say what I'm thinking. That's what's bothering me so much. All that was just a few hours ago, and now I still feel terrible. I feel so bad I could die. At first I thought telling you would help but now all I feel is guilty." She wore a mask of dread. At this point she began to tear up.

Chris stood up and approached her. He sat down beside her and touched her hand. "OK now, Ruthie, don't be so hard on yourself. You're human. You met with a friend, innocently enough, and when things escalated, you were faced with a dilemma. You feared for Matt's safety. Don't blame yourself. By the way, Ruthie, do I know this guy?"

"You might, Father," she answered calmly. "His name is Sonny Gilberto. He has a younger brother named Spike, Spike Gilbert, spells it different. You may have run into him at one time or another."

"Name sounds familiar. I can check for you, check to see if he has a rap sheet," he offered.

"Oh no, please don't, Father," she panicked. "If he finds out, I, uh, don't want anything to happen to Matt."

"Sounds to me like Sonny is bluffing. Sure, if he wanted to rekindle a romance with you he'd want to convince you that Matt is unworthy of you. Do you see what I mean?" He watched her take in his words, and nod.

"Father, I should fess up to Matt, right?" she asked. She looked troubled again.

"I wouldn't," Chris replied without hesitation. "No, let it blow over. Stay on target with Matt. He needs lots of support, and so do you, Ruthie. He needs you now, especially since he's confined there at Christmas time."

"But what if Sonny starts bugging me? What if he wants to date me again? Then what do I do?" she fired at Chris.

"I don't know if this makes sense to you, but forget the 'what if's' for now. Can you just focus on Christmas? It's almost here. You say that Sonny has a two year old. He'll be busy too. You can bet on that. This will buy you time. Tell yourself this will blow over, and please forgive yourself. It's not all your fault. I, uh, assume you called in sick today."

"Well, yeah. I'm in no shape to face anybody. I, uh, think Sonny might have slipped me something, like maybe in my drink of water.

I wouldn't put it past him. Sorry, Father," she said. "But that could explain a lot."

"Hold on, Ruthie. Tell your mother you'll be just fine, but you need to get some sleep. Call me if I can help," he said.

"You've already helped me sort out my feelings, Father. I don't know how to thank you. I was so angry that my Mom went and disturbed you," she said.

"She was worried. You'd do the same if you had a child that was as distressed as you were," he said with a half smile.

"I suppose. If I ever get the chance to have one, with Matt being where he is, and..." she said, wiping her eyes.

"Come on now, lighten up, Ruthie. Go tell your mother you're OK and believe it yourself," he said, "and now I really have to get going. I'm here for you if you need to talk, ever."

"Hey, wait a minute, Father, what if, just what if someone put something in Matt's drink at the stag thing that night? I know him. He'd never drive if he'd had too much to drink and he swore he didn't, but they said he was really impaired at the scene. You don't think...?

"Wait a minute. Was Sonny invited to the stag?" Chris asked eagerly, latching onto a thought.

"Oh, I doubt it," Ruthie responded, "but you never know. He could have been at the bar, which was crowded so they told me, and after last night, he may have...Maybe I'm just being hopeful." Her voice trailed off.

Chris interjected, "You know, Ruthie, that's a thought. If you think that could be even a remote possibility, you might want to get in touch with Matt's lawyer, the one handling the appeal."

"That's Mom's nephew, my cousin Bert," she said. "I suppose it wouldn't hurt to talk to him. But you know how long things take to fall into place. How could there ever be any proof? Look at the time that's passed. I don't want to give Matt false hopes. He's having a hard enough time as it is. I know, I should go see him more often, but he's so depressed that it's really hard for me. I leave there depressed myself." She shrugged her shoulders, but somehow, after talking to Father Chris she felt emboldened.

Ruthie saw Chris to the door and shook his hand. She thanked him for his interest and advice. She stood there by the open door with the icy wind blowing into the foyer until she heard his pickup leave the driveway and head off. The air felt sobering. Maybe I can get over this, she said to herself. Maybe Matt will win the appeal, and maybe everything's going to be all right, we'll go on with the wedding, and, and maybe pigs will actually fly some day. She called out to her mother that she was going upstairs to bed to catch up on some sleep as Muriel charged into the front room with a tray of coffee and donuts, nearly knocking her daughter over.

Chapter ELEVEN

HOW COULD IT BE EVENING already? Father Bernie mused as he set about arranging things for the next day. They would have to deal with that pesky girl's poem another time. Unanticipated events seemed to upset their plans this day. But each priest, in his own way, managed to make steady progress toward the big events scheduled for Christmas Eve. The evening meal was laid even later than ever leaving little time for much of anything else.

And so on the early side, Father Bernie and Father Chris retired to their rooms to settle down and pray. Less than an hour later, Chris, half asleep, staggered into the dark kitchen for a drink. He sat at the old Formica table sipping a glass of milk filled to the brim with ice when his attention was drawn to the window and outside to his garden. Astonished, he feared the worst, and that amounted to more of the same. Impossible. He shuddered at the thought. He wasn't so sure he should alert Bernie or not. But Bernie might hear him go downstairs. Some of the stairs creaked, the bane of old houses—creaks and squeaks—and always at the wrong time.

He didn't have to concern himself after all with waking Bernie. Just then he ambled into the kitchen in his plaid robe and fuzzy boiled wool slippers. He was rubbing sleep from his eyes.

"What's happening, Chris? Is anything wrong? Are you feeling OK?" he asked. "I thought by now you'd be sawing wood." Bernie could fall asleep almost instantly upon hitting the pillow and awaken at the least flutter of movement. Not so much sound as motion would disturb his sleep, and it often did.

"I'm sorry, Bernie. I didn't mean to disturb you. I was dying of thirst, and you know the rest, well almost all the rest," Chris said pointing to his frosty glass. Bernie's look outside told him something was up. "Now take it easy, Bernie. I'm not sure myself. Sit down, please."

"What's the matter, Chris? Something funny going on, right?" Bernie asked hoping that something funny was not going on, or anything for that matter. He was bone tired but he couldn't be fooled.

At this point, Chris could only gesture to the window. Bernie followed the cue and peered out the window. Chris joined him to get a better look. A blinking red light grabbed their attention.

"I wonder if it's coming from the street," Bernie said. "Could be some kind of emergency vehicle out there in the road beyond the garden. Maybe there was an accident."

"I don't think so, Bernie," Chris muttered. "Note the rhythm of the lights. They're tinier and blinking. That's no emergency vehicle. I wonder..."

"Not her again, is it? I sure hope not. If that's *her* up to something again *I'm* going to lose it. I really am," Bernie hissed. These nocturnal tricks were not good for his health.

"What do you suppose the blinking lights mean?" Chris asked innocently.

Bernie was quick to say, "What else? Looks to me she's advertising something now. Oh, Chris, there's something very, very wrong with that girl." He was wringing his hands.

Chris figured there was a logical explanation, there had to be, but he couldn't think of any. He was worried about Bernie's health. "Take it easy, Bernie, or you'll have a stroke. It may not be her after all. You stay put. Let me go down there. I'll check it out. Let me take care of it." It occurred to him just then that the issue of the poem had been tabled.

Bernie stood immobile, hands on his hips, waiting, wondering as Chris went into his room to dress. He returned minutes later in jeans and a heavy duty flannel shirt. This time he grabbed his down jacket all the while his mind was playing tricks on him. If this is Glory's handiwork, will she still be out there? Was it even Glory who's responsible for the red blinking lights? But who else, and why?

Bernie stopped him, saying, "Just get rid of that dang red light, Chris. It's got to be one of her doings. I sure would like to hear *that* explanation. Brash girl." He paused, then, "Maybe we should call the cops."

"Hold on a minute, Bernie. Please. Let's see what it's all about before we do something we may regret. Maybe it's not her at all," Chris said hopefully, but one night after another? He could tell Bernie was at his wit's end, and it scared him.

Bernie headed toward his bedroom door. "Wait, Chris, I'll join you. We'll tell her a thing or two, get her reported to DCF." He was puffing now. "We'll read the riot act to her. You, uh, both of us have been too kind to her."

"Please, let me handle her. Give me a minute. Here, hold onto the poem, the envelope here, I mean. Maybe we *should* read it when I get back if we're not too tired. I'm not sure what the right thing to do is," Chris said wishing the whole thing would vanish into thin air. Bernie frowned and nodded reluctantly.

"OK, well, maybe you're right. You go ahead down. The poem's the least of our concerns right now," he said. What good would it do if the two of them went down there? Besides, he was tired. He heard Chris bound down the stairs and he prayed for the best.

Once in the garden Chris didn't see anyone, but he sensed a presence nevertheless. He walked over to the statue of the stag and shrugged in disbelief. It was bedecked with a string of blinking red Christmas lights looped around it and a large red bulb on the nose. Finally he called out, "OK now, Glory. Where are you hiding? I know it's you, Glory, come on out." The only reply was dead silence. And so he tried again, "Glory, come on now. What is your game? What's that strobe light you've got on our stag? What in the world are you trying to do to us? We're getting tired of this whole thing." Chris seemed to be addressing uninterested molecules of air. He was growing increasingly angry.

Then he heard a rustling over to his right, and Glory popped out of the bushes as though she was spooking a friend. "Boo! How'd you know it was me, Chris?"

But he wasn't spooked at all, just weary and very much annoyed. Was he wasting his breath, his energy? "Father Chris, not Chris. You have a very short memory, Glory. Didn't your parents..."

She stood opposite him. He was glad for the semi-darkness. He couldn't bring himself to look at her. "Yeah, yeah," she answered smugly. "The old guy asked me the same thing. Sorry, I keep forgetting. It's hard to get used to saying 'Father' to someone who isn't not my father especially someone who's only a few years older than me."

Chris may have been too tired to dialog with her, but he wasn't about to let her get away with rudeness and disrespect. "You're talking about Father Bernie, not the old guy. I resent that."

Deep sigh, then, "All right. I get it. Respect. I don't ask you to call me Miss Sterling, do I?" There, she was parrying with him.

Chris jabbed back at her, "No, not at your age. And for your information, respect goes much farther than just using a proper title." Then his eyes were drawn to the blinking lights, the reason he entered the garden in the first place. "Miss Sterling, what have you done to our stag?" He found her insolence and her motives difficult to fathom, or was it ignorance, in the true sense of the word?

Glory acted shocked. "What? A stag? Is that what that creature is? When I saw him first I thought it was a reindeer, like Rudolph, you know. So I decided to make him look like Rudolph—for Christmas—I'm trying to get into the spirit. It doesn't go good though with your Mary statue or the other guy statue either, whoever he is. Get with it, Chris, I mean Father Chris. Those guys could use some holiday dressing up, too."

Chris was indignant. "Those guys! If I weren't half asleep I'd set you straight on who's who and what's what in this garden." As if she really cared who was who and what was what.

Glory retorted, "Well, you look wide awake to me. You're talking to me, right?"

Chris did not expect a wise crack. "Father Bernie and I do not appreciate those red lights on the stag's face, and worse than that, it blinks. It's an attention grabber. This garden does not stand for that kind of attention. I've told you what its purpose is. It's not an amusement park. And then, you've got those red and green sparkly garlands all over his back. What goes?" Chris tried not to sputter, but he was sounding unlike himself.

Glory laughed. Those dimples again. "Well, no matter, I think they look real cute—festive if you know what I mean—get with it, Chris. Tis the season." She frowned when she noticed that Chris was not with her. Then as suddenly as a cloudburst there came the tears. Then a whimper.

It backfired though. It wasn't going to work with Chris. He wouldn't allow it. But he was glad that it was he and not Bernie down here at this moment. He took a harder stance. "Now what? First you laugh then you're sad. What is it with you?"

Glory sniffed into a Kleenex, she cleared her throat, and said huskily, "Well, you would be sad too if your parents called from their fun in the sun spot and said they wouldn't make it home for Christmas. Grandmom told me when I got home from here last night. She got a long distance phone call from them. And, and, uh, worse still, no Christmas tree at our house this year so I, uh, I brought some of our decorations over here for your garden thing to make it festive and jolly, like it should be. We won't need them this year. Some thanks I get." She blotted her eyes. "You're mad at me. And the worst thing of all is that Grandmom didn't ask Mom where she hid all the Christmas presents. So my holiday will suck, suck, suck."

Chris was trying to digest what she'd told him. Could he believe her? Should he? Finally, he managed, "Oh, I see." He wasn't sure that he actually did. She clearly didn't get what a prayer garden was for, or even a prayer for that matter, he suspected.

But she seemed placated for the moment. "Good, then maybe you'll stop yelling at me and say thanks for making your reindeer so nice and bright."

Chris was tired and weary. He said, "OK, I suppose you meant well, Glory, but it's all so confusing, to me and Father Bernie."

Glory directed her comment to her boots in a whisper, "I'm sorry you don't appreciate it. I just wanted..."

Chris feared the water works again. How those teenage girls could turn them on in a flash. So he started to explain, "It's not..."

They both heard the kitchen window push open, then Bernie's voice as he yelled down.

"If that's you know who out there, tell her to get rid of that glitzy junk...now...and get lost—once and for all. I've had it with the likes of her."

Chris was jolted back to reality. He said calmly, "Glory, you heard my boss. It's got to go—the lights and everything else." Bernie was right. He had to tell her in plain and simple language, let her know they won't tolerate such nonsense even if her antics seem to make sense to her. Still her motives left Chris guessing, wondering.

Glory persisted. "Do I have to? Wait, you can at least tell me why you have a reindeer in your garden. That's weird. The Mary statue I get. Everybody knows who she is. She's got to be super special. You should have seen the fit your boss had when I dressed her up. As for that other guy statue, I'm not sure who he is, but I suppose I can take a guess."

Chris would have preferred to be anywhere but here out in the cold but he didn't want to ignore the patron saint of their church. He would tell her even if it prolonged the encounter a minute or so. He inhaled deeply; then resigned, he asked her, "Glory, do you remember the name of this church?" He didn't care at this point if he came across as condescending.

He was so unused to people taking such things so matter-of-factly and irreverently, but that was Glory. He felt there was no excuse.

"Yeah, Eden," she said, "sorta like the garden of, you know the story of the Garden of Eden, right? But you say it kind of funny."

"I guess we do, sort of. It's Aeden, St. Aeden that is, with a long "A". He's a saint from way, way back, many centuries ago in England. And his symbol in religious art is the stag, what you're calling a reindeer, which is why we have one out here, why I sought out that statue."

Glory looked at Chris as though she'd received a shock, followed by a quizzical look that she seemed to exaggerate and prolong. He was starting to understand her expressions, those that were spontaneous and those that she forced in order to intensify the desired effect. "Well, if that isn't the silliest thing I ever heard—sounds more like it belongs in a fairy tale."

He watched her relax, get more comfortable with their discussion, her time with him. Chris would finish what he started. He continued, "I suppose you might think so, but if you knew why, you'd understand."

"He must have been one odd looking dude if he looked like a reindeer or a stag, I mean." She burst into spasms of laughter. "Just think, going into a museum and seeing a painting of a stag and saying, 'Hey, look here. Why it's good ole' St. Aeden.'"

"No, that's not it at all," Chris retorted soberly. He did not dare to share her humor overtly.

And now her game. "You gonna tell me or what? I wanna know. Come on, Chris, Father Chris. There I did it again. Darn. It's hard to remember." More Glory-like petulance.

"All right, OK," he acquiesced, playing into her hands. "To put it simply, as church history tells it, it goes back to when St. Aeden made a stag disappear. Now this was during a hunt and he wanted to spare it from the ravages of a pack of hounds, which would tear him apart if they caught up with him. So poof! He made the stag disappear into thin air and the hounds took off after some other prey."

Exaggerated shock, disbelief. "Wait a minute, you expect me to believe that? What've you been smoking?"

Chris was almost amused at her insinuation. "It's true. That was a miracle. St. Aeden performed this miracle—the transformation that I just mentioned. To be made a saint in the Catholic Church, first, you have to be a holy person and then you must perform two miracles—and there must be proof of them. You don't need to know the other miracle. I'm not so sure I can remember it myself, or if I ever knew it."

Glory mulled that over for a while. All of this was out of her realm of knowledge. Far out. "Hmm," she began, then paused a moment. "I can't imagine what creature you'd have for a symbol if they made you a saint. You could be a robin or maybe a dolphin or whatever. I guess that would depend on how you're doing the miracle, like where you were and what was happening, like whoever you're trying to save, and stuff. You could make some animal or maybe even a human disappear to save the poor creature."

"Don't even try to imagine. It will never happen," he said, wondering what kind of foundation her parents could have provided for her, what code of ethics, what belief system. Was she that naïve? Or was she flirting? If so, she wasn't succeeding that well. He still could not look her squarely in the eye. It was always a side glance, and nothing more.

She wanted more. Curiosity took hold. "Hold on. I was just thinking—shouldn't miracles be on people, and not on critters? Not that I don't like animals; they're cool, most of them, not all are creatures of prey though, or rabid ones, who actually start off nice enough but then they get bitten, and, well, you know the rest. And, uh, like who likes scavengers or crows or buzzards? I can think of a few others, too, uh..."

"Not always," he interrupted what he feared would be a litany of predators. That should end their conversation. He was exhausted and she seemed super charged...as though she could run forever on her battery—the energizer denizen. He was amused at the thought.

This time Chris was relieved to hear the window open. Bernie sounded vaguely hoarse, but his message was loud and clear enough to be heard. He yelled out, "That damn red light is still blinking. People will think we're running a house of ill repute—a goddamn whore house. Get rid of it and I mean—now—or else." Chris could imagine Bernie crossing himself at his blasphemy, but he was so riled.

Glory heard the urgency in Father Bernie's voice and promptly clicked off the red flashing lights and unwound the string of lights and garlands to disrobe the stag. She gathered the unwanted Christmas decorations and shoved them into her sack, with deliberate, exaggerated haste. Spite ignited her hazel eyes. She jerked tight the drawstring and heaved the bag over her shoulder.

Then she sighed and uttered a wistful 'good night' to Chris and strode haltingly, her head downward, toward the gate. Chris stood for a moment, then sighed deeply and secured the gate. He straightened the sign that Glory had chosen to ignore on three occasions and headed for the back entry of the rectory. He could envision the scene when he and Bernie would process this bizarre episode.

Chapter TWELVE

IT WAS A SUN-DRENCHED morning but the temperature belied the blinding brightness. It was as cold as it has ever been on any Christmas week in Wexford Falls due to a front traveling in a southeasterly direction from the Great Lakes into the western hills, presaging lake effect snows at any time, according to the Channel 8 forecaster. Cold as a witch's teat, Celia Drummond, the senior librarian, used to say. And the falls, which is practically a misnomer, is not much of a falls. On a good day, after substantial rains, it's a decent sized trickle spilling from a height of five or so meters over some jagged rocks, into a winding brook that wends its way over pebbles, a few of considerable size, through the west side of town. But the townspeople can and do proudly boast of having a waterfall in their town, unlike their neighbors in surrounding communities. Wexford Falls residents believe that it's the height of the falls rather than the volume of water that makes it a legitimate claim to merit the name 'falls'.

Icicles glistened from the pines that ridged the town green, an odd geometric shape, neither square not trapezoidal, the designated spot for the annual St. Aeden Christmas pageant. Father Chris on off moments supervised the reconstruction of the manger from the odd pile of wood dumped in front of the garages on St. Aeden property. Last year they had dismantled the manger board by board, figuring they could recycle it one more time for this year. They certainly didn't want a manger crafted of fresh, unseasoned wood. The intent was to make it look as authentic as possible. Now with some special prayers and most likely a dose of divine intervention, it miraculously took shape.

Chris had corralled his friend Marty Tisdale, who had taken the whole week off from work to settle his deceased mother's affairs. Marty was only too eager to help out. The physical work would be good for him, he told Chris. Furthermore, he was driving Sylvie crazy, pacing and otherwise getting in the way at home, and plopping this and that from his mother's house into the limited space of their apartment. They hoped to find a larger place after the baby was born. Chris had told him of a large flat not far from St. Aeden's that would be unoccupied in the spring. Marty had told him that he hoped it would still be available when they were ready.

THE SUN CAST ITS HARSH light onto Chris's dark ringed eyes, a tell tale sign of a troubled night's sleep, betraying any comments Chris might have made that he was feeling just fine today. He adjusted his chair away from the light, which minimized the darkness of the shadows under his eyes, and then said to Bernie, "I am starved. I'm so hungry I could eat a horse."

"And good morning to you." Bernie's non sequitur made Chris smile apologetically. "Sorry, Chris. Can't accommodate you on that. None such equine vittles on hand in this house. Hope bacon and eggs will do for a starter."

"Well, I guess I'll have to see Mrs. Hopkins about that," he joked. "Oh no, bacon and eggs are just fine. Great." Chris dug into his breakfast as though he hadn't eaten for days.

Bernie took a bite of his buttered toast, paused, then reached for the jar of orange marmalade and plastered a dollop onto the remaining toast. He poured more coffee into his cup. Then he said, "Not too many folks at mass this morning. I kept it short.

Mini-homily, too. People like that, you know. Word like that gets around and we'll pack the place."

"It's the cold, Bernie," Chris said, mopping the last of his egg yolk with a slice of buttered toast. "Don't count on usual attendance in this weather. You of all people should know that."

"The regulars all got knees like mine," Bernie stated, sighing. "If they're smart they'll stay put where it's warm."

Chris agreed. He continued to sip his coffee. His thoughts seemed to bounce from one place to another. "Hmm, you never know. By the way, how're the old knees faring this morning?"

Bernie was funny. If you inquired about his health, he was fine. He wouldn't take offense or redden. The vein in his forehead wouldn't pulsate but if you chastised him for not watching his sugar or anything else in his diet, then you'd see another side of him. Chris knew his was a safe question, and he anticipated the answer. Bernie was Bernie.

"Well, I'll tell you, since you brought up the subject," Bernie answered, pleased that Chris was coming around socially this morning. He figured it took a good meal to do it. "Worse than usual. Just be glad you're young, Chris. Soak up your youth and your vigor while you can so you can store it up. Then you can tap into it when you need it, like when you're my age, for example. Oh, it's a chore getting older...a nuisance...Uh, Chris, since I've got your attention now, shall we get to it?"

At that moment, Chris much preferred the topic at hand—Bernie's arthritic knees. He knew what Bernie was suggesting, knew only too well. "Get to what? Am I missing something?" he asked feigning ignorance. Bernie could see right through him.

Bernie gave him a look, *the* look, and Chris looked downward as a child harboring guilt might in these circumstances. "Remember the poem, Chris. *Her* poem. Remember what we said last night? That we would look at it with fresh eyes after a good night's sleep? If indeed you did have a good night's sleep." Chris's eyes told a different story. That look of scrutiny cut deep.

Chris figured he'd better face up to it, and he did. "Oh yeah, I did."

"You were strangely quiet last night. No nightmare, I take it?" Bernie inquired.

Chris told him what he wanted to hear. "Oddly enough, no. I did manage to sleep well enough, sort of." The dark shadows mocked him.

"Hmm, well that's good," Bernie said trying to believe the words he'd just heard. "We didn't need any more agitation before bedtime. We sure got our fill of it with all her cockamamie ideas and decorations. Now who does that girl think she is, a window dresser for Macy's? Heh heh."

Chris inhaled deeply and let his breath filter out slowly. He wasn't quite sure what to say. "She said..."

Bernie interrupted him. "I know full well what she said. The whole thing is I think she's, uh, taken with you, Chris. These actions of hers are nothing more then attention-getting antics. That's what they are. And so far they've worked. That's the sad part of it." Bernie looked directly at Chris who cast his eyes downward once more.

It pained Chris to hear those words coming from his mentor and pastor. It's not that he didn't agree with him. But it hurt nevertheless. "Oh, come on Bernie, your knees may be stiff and out of whack, but your head...?"

"My head is still very much intact, I'll have you know. My intuition tells me..." Bernie feared how Chris would take it.

The last person Chris would want to hurt or disappoint was Father Bernie—ever. "Can we settle our speculations and see for ourselves?"

Bernie stepped back and said, "One second. I haven't heard your, uh, thoughts on this."

Chris tried to remain calm and clear headed. He thought for a moment. "It's, uh, hard for me to say. I told you her appearance still unnerves me. I can't help it. It colors my, uh, speculation. Well, here goes...or, maybe I should handle this myself."

Bernie produced the perfume-scented envelope. The exterior itself hinted at what was inside. "No, Chris, you won't. I've seen too much; I know too much. I'm with you here. Now read, please."

He handed the envelope to Chris who ran his fingers over it. Such delicate, fragile paper. He hesitated. He wondered if the stationery actually belonged to Glory, more likely to her mother. Maybe Bernie should be the one to open it and read it, but his own name was written on it in bold letters and with a flourish. The dot over the "i" was a tiny heart, so typical of teenage girls' writing. It doesn't mean anything, he hoped, but then feared that it might. He opened it slowly, fearing a Pandora's box of toxic ills.

Bernie was growing anxious. "Come on, come on, Chris. We haven't got all day, you know. You should be down on the green making sure everything is set for the pageant. *Tempus fugit.*"

Chris didn't need reminding. Yes, time *was* flying and he had indeed been stalling. Finally he opened it. It was easy to break the seal. He removed the single sheet of paper from the envelope, also lacy and fragile, and touched it, then retracted his fingers as though it was a burning ember. He placed it on the table in front of him. Fearful of what it might contain, he pushed it aside as though it had destructive powers. Bernie was eyeing Chris. At last, he picked it up held it in his hands. It hardly weighed anything—a butterfly's wing, perhaps.

"Now go ahead, read, please. I'm listening," Bernie ordered in a no-nonsense tone of voice. Enough procrastination. Chris complied.

First they're here and then they're not.
They say they love me; they love me not.
He's right here; I have no fear.
I'll be back; he'll never go.
I scare him so; I sure can to tell.
If he loves me, he'll go to hell.
I'm not so sure what I will do.
I'm so confused and he is too.
So I can live or I can die.
And who will know the reason why?

Chris was as silent as a stone. He felt a weight pressing on his chest. The lacy paper in his hand quivered. He was clearly embarrassed, shaken. He realized that the poem could very well be about him. He recalled asking Glory to go home where she should have been and write a poem, and that she did. She fulfilled a promise. He figured it would be cathartic for her after the upsetting newsletters. But the poem was addressed to *him*. The envelope said so, but the poem did not have to be *about* him. Denial—an effective defense mechanism in cases such as these. Bernie thought that Chris might be rereading it silently, thinking and wondering. He detected a faint blush on Chris's face. Chris was first to speak, "Hmm." That was it—nothing more.

All Chris could hear from Bernie was an echo, "Hmm," followed by more silence and another, "Hmm." Then, "So much for rap lyrics." That comment stung Chris.

Finally, impatience overtook Chris and so he blurted, "Hmm. What?" He really needed more time to think, to analyze her motive, to figure out where to go from here. "She's probably blabbing on about her boyfriend, or someone she has a crush on."

Bernie's eyes grew owl like, "Someone?" He grimaced, "Someone like you. Chris, you need to admit that it could very well be."

"Could be," Chris echoed softly, mobilizing his forces to remain calm and resolute. He had nothing to be ashamed about. He had not led her on. They'd only talked, but she seemed to relish the moments that they spent talking—about anything, just talking. "But I sure hope not. So what do we do?"

Bernie held onto the table pushing himself up to a standing position, and the table did its usual wobble. One of the givens in the old Victorian rectory—not that they couldn't afford a new kitchen set. They were just used to this old one. "Well, we just can't sit here. We have to do something."

Chris was indignant. He too stood up and said, " Like what? You know, we could be making a mountain out of a molehill."

Bernie lightened as he always did when the situation warranted. "Hmm, that's an old one. You could be right, but on the other hand..."

Chris assumed a take charge attitude, and faced the situation head-on. "So what bothers you the most, Bernie? If she does have a crush on me, I certainly will do nothing to encourage her, and..."

Bernie remarked bluntly, "You did tell her to go home and write a poem."

Now Chris found himself on the defense. He measured his words, uttering them slowly and thoughtfully as though reciting a passage from memory. "I told her to go home. Those were not her original plans, I'll have you know. Writing a poem was something I told her to do since that is what she likes to do. She told me so. I never implied that she was to write one to, for or about me. Just to write a poem. It would give her something constructive to do. It would give her a vehicle to express her feelings about the newsletters. Another one, I mean. She already did the fake snow thing. What *does* concern me, however, is a hint at what I see as suicide, or is that too far fetched an idea?"

Bernie went into his deep thinking mode, scratched his chin, and faced Chris squarely. "No, not at all. I'm inclined to agree with you, Chris. I guess we need to notify someone."

"Whom do you suggest?" Chris asked, wishing the whole thing would just go away, that the poem would disintegrate and vanish, leaving behind no trace. Phooey on Pandora. He never took that nonsense to heart. His thoughts turned to good St. Aeden and how he had made the stag disappear to save the animal from the ravages of the hounds. But what could he Father Chris Tosi do in these circumstances? He was no saint, and most likely never would be, and if this called for a miracle, he wasn't sure which way to turn. Save himself? Save Glory? If so, from whom and from what? The poem wasn't going away even if he made it disappear.

"Well, uh, her family, of course," Bernie answered, but wondered what kind of storm that would blow up and who would be the real victim. Understandably, he feared negative publicity. He hoped it wouldn't get to that.

Chris was quick to answer. "Her parents are in Dubai...till after Christmas, from what she told me. If this poem stuff is all nonsense, which I hope it is, we don't want to ignite a firestorm. Her Grandmom, yes, that's what we'll do. We can tell her Grandmom."

Bernie shook his head. "I don't know, Chris. That could backfire too, and put you in a compromising situation. Not good." He had no idea what kind of storm that could stir up.

"Well, you said we have to do something," Chris said laying the responsibility on Bernie's shoulders.

Bernie gave him a hard, inquisitive look and replied, "Yes, but what?" He was pacing now, his hands balled.

"Let me see if I can get in touch with her, with Glory herself," he said, his voice tinged with uncertainty.

Bernie heaved a sign, leaned over, and supporting himself on the table top, said, "Oh, I'm not so sure that's such a good idea. She'll get the wrong impression. I'm thinking any time she spends with you is fueling her thoughts and desires, heaven forbid, and making her think you like her, if you know what I mean."

Chris got the idea. "Then, how about you?" he said, backing away.

Bernie shot him a look of distaste. "She's made it very clear I am *persona non grata* where she's concerned. I spoil her fun, cramp her style, as they say. She sees me as an old fuddy duddy."

Chris smirked at his remark but agreed with him and so he latched onto his original idea "She said she goes to the public high school here. That should be easy enough. I'll catch her after school, accidentally on purpose. Chat her up, in a professional manner, of course, and try to get a sense of her stability," Chris suggested, grasping at proverbial straws. He feared Bernie's response.

Bernie exploded, "Well, that's a hoot. And then, what? You can't even look her straight in the eye in the dark without getting pangs about your Kendra—her looks, you say. How are you going to take it in broad daylight?" He stopped to catch his breath, then, "Wait, Chris, I say we take some time and pray over it. This is a job for St. Jude I think, the saint of the impossible, my dearly departed mother's favorite saint. Oh, she called upon him often with a houseful like ours. We need to have faith in St. Jude's powers and then we should get some divine inspiration one way or the other."

"We'd better," Chris said. "Yes, St. Jude is an excellent choice. But I couldn't live with myself if she attempted suicide over, uh, what she says in her poem. And knowing that we had the opportunity to act and we didn't, we'd be partly to blame."

Bernie glanced over at the wheezy wall clock and huffed. "Oh my, enough of this, it's getting late. We've got our hands full this week. You know what you've got to do. I'll take care of phone calls for now, and you...uh-oh, I see the florist truck pulling up. Better not be a problem with those poinsettias, nosiree. One year, remember, or was it last year? They sent us pink and white plants—said they were short on the red ones. Can you just imagine that—short on red ones in this season? Why, I ordered the red ones for Christmas. They're the proper ones. I guess some people never get it right, do they, Chris?"

Chris breathed a sigh of relief—a change of subject, a change of mood. "Come on now, Bernie, don't fret over it. I'm sure they'll never make that same mistake again after the fuss you made. If they have to go all the way to Mexico for them, they won't short you the red ones again."

The vein on Bernie's forehead began to ease itself, less visible pulsation. "I guess I was a trifle hard on them, wasn't I? Heh heh."

"Only a trifle?" Chris was smiling now, relaxed after a testy conversation. Somehow Glory seemed to be at the center of those lately. "I'll meet you back here for lunch at twelve noon sharp—unless I get waylaid, and don't worry, I'll call if that happens."

"You may not be able to break then," Bernie said amicably. No matter how busy Bernie was, lunchtime was lunchtime, not so for Chris. If he was on a roll, he preferred sticking with whatever he was engaged in until it was finished.

"I will," Chris said, hoping he could. "Things seem to be going on schedule, with the pageant, that is. Oh, I forgot to tell you. Mrs. Hopkins handed me a message about Barbara—very detailed, but that's Mrs. Hopkins for you. She's going to be OK, nothing serious. It was just some nasty gastritis. They gave her what they call the Green Cocktail in the ER, some gooey thing that you drink and it worked like magic. She's back to her old self. Nothing short of a miracle, so we can expect her back today at the pageant rehearsal. Thank the good Lord."

"Well, that's good news indeed, for her and for us, but experience tells me she could lock horns with Mrs. Rafferty. Mrs. R is not going to want to let go entirely and pass the torch back to Barbara without a brawl, a verbal one, that is," Bernie said with a wink. "I've seen those two ladies in action together. To put it mildly, they don't always see eye to eye, which is where you come into play, Chris. You're a fair enough arbiter. You may have to use your, uh, refereeing skills this afternoon. Heh heh."

"Yes, this afternoon, after we've had a good lunch," Chris said, picking up his belongings and heading down the back stairs. He was back in Bernie's good graces, and hoped he could stay there.

FATHER BERNIE ENTERED his office on the first floor and began reviewing his duties for the day. Moments later he was interrupted by the insistent buzzing of the front door bell. The sound always perturbed him, but he had not taken the time to change the mechanism and replace it with a less bothersome sound, say, like bells or a musical motif. He always liked the NBC tones. But there were so many other things to tend to, more important matters.

He heard Mrs. Hopkins directing someone to his office, which was adjacent to the rectory kitchen. She escorted in a very tall, thin teen-aged boy, neatly attired.

Bernie looked up from his desk calendar, rose slightly and extended his hand, "Good day, young man, ah, you must be with the florist. You didn't have to bother to come inside. Mrs. Hopkins should have directed you to the side lot over there." He pointed in that direction. "The other van should be over there by now I should imagine. Go on out where they're unloading the first van.

They can use an extra pair of hands." Bernie nodded at the boy, then he resumed his previous task. He thought he had dismissed him.

But the boy stood there, a confused look on his face. "Uh, no, sir, you've got it all wrong." As he began to speak again, Father Bernie adjusted his glasses and interrupted him.

"Oh. Then you must be here about the animals, ah yes, from the farm. I certainly hope there's no hitches. We must have the animals. Absolutely. Can't have a pageant scene without them. Remember, there were animals present at Christ's birth in a stable back then. All kinds of farm critters."

The boy seemed totally perplexed, but he asked patiently and politely, "The animals? Me? You're mistaken, sir."

Bernie seemed not to hear the boy's protest, "For the manger. Can you envision the Nativity without animals?

"Gee, uh, no I can't, but..." he answered, still patient. Still he remained standing there silently by Bernie's desk.

Father Bernie gave the young man full attention by this point. "Then who are you, pray tell?"

He answered, "I'm Glen Thomas Sterling-Baie, reverend. I think I should call you reverend, right?" He extended his hand. Father Bernie was impressed at the young man's firm grasp, proper eye contact, and engaging smile.

Bernie returned the smile. The gracious side of him shone through. "That I am. Reverend Father Bernard Monahan, at your service. Now what can I do for you, young man, uh, Glen, you said?" Then it came to him. The name's the same, his memory told him, Sterling-Baie. He wondered what that girl's brother could possibly want from him. At least the boy had manners.

Glen responded, "Yes, reverend, I did. I'm Glen. Glen Sterling, Glory's brother, her twin actually. Actually I go by Thomas, or Glen, either is fine." He smiled broadly. Bernie could not help being impressed with such a likeable young man.

"Oh, yes," he said, thinking that something was up. He tried not to imagine what, and it showed on his face, in his expression.

Glen noticed the change. "So I see you've already met her. I can tell actually." He hated being judged by his sister's actions, as was too often the case. But people had the tendency to do that.

"Yes, as a matter of fact, I did, as did my parochial vicar, Father Tosi, Father Chris," Bernie said, not wishing to reveal anything further.

Glen stated promptly, "Yes, I know. She's mentioned both of you." He paused, waiting for Father Bernie to react any further.

Bernie bit his lip in contemplation. Should he or should he not reveal anything. Then he asked with some hesitation, "She has told you what she's been up to?"

Glen answered, "Well, sort of, yes, she told me a few things, her version of course—sounds so much like Glory. Nothing she did would surprise or shock me." The all-knowing look on his face sealed it.

Bernie wondered just how much he should reveal to Glen. If anything, let the brother do the talking, but... "Really? She had a few choice things to say about you. I heard through Father Chris, Father Tosi, that is. She didn't paint a very pretty picture, made you sound like a juvenile delinquent of sorts. Ah yes, sibling rivalry, how well I can remember it in a houseful like ours. Heh heh."

Glen laughed at that. "Well, it's best not to believe her actually. She's uh, got problems, big ones."

Bernie tried not to get unraveled. "Oh? She does, does she now?" Let him continue, he told himself, and he wanted to know what those problems might be. The poem she'd written loomed large in his thoughts. Its implications worried him.

Glen answered quietly, almost apologetically, "I wouldn't lie to you, reverend. She, on the other hand, is a path..." He struggled with the word but Bernie knew what he meant. Glory could pose a real danger.

He spoke faster than he should have, then he regretted it. "A pathological liar, I'll bet. She claims you are just that yourself, among other things."

Glen seemed unnerved by that, remark. He frowned. "Reverend..." Bernie didn't let him finish.

"You know, son, I prefer Father Bernie. That's what people call me, and you seem like a nice enough man, polite and respectful," he said and meant every word of it.

Glen composed himself and said, "OK, Father Bernie it is. Well, anyhow, as I was saying..." He paused, anxiety taking over; he broke eye contact and studied his shoes. One lace was coming undone.

"Yes, you need to tell me why you've come to see me," Bernie said, fearing what Glen might be about to reveal.

Glen said, "Actually, it was the other, uh, reverend I wanted to talk to, but you seem to know a lot about Glory yourself."

Bernie smirked, then he tempered his reaction. "I saw her in action and I did speak to her on one occasion, as well." He paused to let that sink in, both for Glen's sake and for his own. "And Father Chris, yes, oh, he's tied up right now, won't be available until later in the day. You see, we're getting ready for our Christmas pageant." Then out it came with little warning. " I, uh, do you happen to know anything about a poem your sister wrote the other day?"

Glen laughed riotously as though Bernie had told him a joke. "Not a poem? Oh, no." He smacked his forehead in a gesture of exasperation. "No, not another one. Who was it for this time?"

Bernie was so glad Glen came along at just the right time. He would shed light on the whole poem caper, he hoped, and perhaps on what to do next. "Certainly not for me, Glen." Bernie made a dumbfounded gesture. "It was...well, I might as well tell you since

I don't know how to reach your Grandmother or your parents, for that matter."

Glen sensed a repeat performance. Had his sister done it again, and so soon? He shuddered. "Oh, no, not one of those poems. They can only spell trouble with a capital T."

Glen grew silent. He recalled just months ago when his sister took a fancy to an older man. It cost their father a fortune to make amends for all the damage she caused, and some of it was irreparable. But this time a priest! He hoped it wouldn't be a replay of last summer. Or, of the incident last fall at the Academy which led to her expulsion and more.

No, Bernie was not about to let Glen read the poem. Bernie decided he would play along. Let Glen provide the information. "How so, young man? Should we be concerned?"

Glen pondered, then looked upward from one side to another trying to decide what he should or could disclose. "I can't really say in this case, but she does have a history. OK, let me give you an example and you can judge for yourself."

"Hold on, I probably should send for Father Chris, since it kind of involves him," Bernie said. He felt the hairs on his neck rise.

Glen said, "No, that's OK, you said he's busy. No, Father Bernie, not yet, please. Hear me first." He had warmed up to the older priest enough to trust him, and so he shared what others in the community probably already knew about Glory.

Bernie acquiesced. "Very well." Until that moment he could not have anticipated the enormity of Glory's transgression.

Glen was kind. He could have been blunt and harsh, but he stuck with the facts alone, dispassionately.

It grew very still in the room. Bernie could hear the fire crackling in the fireplace, supporting an air of intimacy and comfort. He hoped the door buzzer would not sound. He didn't need any interruptions, as was so often the case, especially this time of year. People would buy friends and family religious articles for Christmas—crosses, rosaries, and medals commemorating their special saint or the crucifixion—and would stop by at their convenience to get them blessed. And what could he say? He was a good priest and these were his parishioners, many of whom he'd known personally for years and years. And these included the local butcher, the baker, and yes, a real in the flesh candlestick maker. Really. He loved to tell people that. And so any moment Mrs. Hopkins could appear at the door escorting someone in with a jewelry case in hand and a supplicating look on their face, proffering apologies for interrupting their good pastor. And he would say, 'Why certainly...what a lovely cross,' and begin a personalized blessing. Yes, Bernie always accommodated his parishioners.

Glen seemed to understand. He respected the silence that had insinuated itself between them. At last he began as though telling a tale, rather than revealing his twin sister's indiscretion, "You see, uh, Father Bernie, Glory has this thing for boys, uh, as most girls her age do, but with her it's big boys, I mean *men*. When she finds one that she really likes, for whatever reason, only she can tell you, she obsesses, gets in their face, writes them poems, and puts them, I guess you might say, uh, at risk for whatever. Not that she tries to, it just happens, I think. It's not good. And she's a pretty girl so most boys, er, men are flattered. You may not know but she is in therapy, our parents insist on that, but she skips out on her appointments whenever she doesn't feel like going, which is not a good thing. She, uh, well, uh, it seems like she just does what she does. Oh, she's clever enough. She'll use whatever means to try to get the guy to like her, not thinking ahead about what could happen. This whole thing—it consumes her. She gets totally obsessed over it, like I said. I'm a little embarrassed to tell you this, reverend."

He hesitated, then at Bernie's signal continued, "OK, here goes. Um, over the summer, we had this guy, nice guy, a young mail carrier. He, uh, smiled at my sister when she came to the door to get the mail, and he chatted her up—bad mistake on his part. That's all he had to do, actually. Well, she'd invite him in for Grandmom's homemade cookies when our mother was out. Then there were other things she'd cook up to get him inside for one reason or another. All he had to do was give her attention, and she took it to mean...you know. We don't know all the details, or else they kept them from me. Anyhow, Glory went and wrote him a poem like usual, rhymes and stuff, saying that she'd die without his declaration of love. And then it got, well, you can figure it out..."

He stopped to assess Bernie's reaction. The priest paled. Glen continued, "Oh, there's a lot more to it too. Well, the poor guy who was a newly wed, he freaked out, and refused to bring mail to our house. He nearly lost his job. Meanwhile, his wife found out and blamed her husband, not knowing what Glory is really like. Anyhow she threatened Glory—the whole thing nearly wrecked their marriage. It was all a big fat mess. Money talks, they say. Well, my father took care of things, as he always does. Cost him a bundle, too. The guy and his wife moved out of town and it didn't cost them a penny. And, oh yeah, he was able to get a job right away. I guess my father must have had a hand in that, too."

The phone rang bringing Glen's account to an abrupt end. Bernie made a gesture signaling to Glen that he should wait, while he took the call. Glen paced around the room rather than appear interested in the phone conversation. Then he stopped and warmed himself in front of the fire.

Bernie held his hand over the mouthpiece and excused himself. Glen, however, did get the gist of the conversation.

"Oh, yes, hello, Dr. Blume." Bernie began in his priestly telephone voice. "How are you, busy I assume especially this week...What's that you said?...Oh, you did. I'm sure he got the message. He's...Oh dear, yes, the flu...Well, I guess we have to keep on trying...Yes, if I hear of anyone, I'll be sure to let you know...When, what time did you say...Oh, OK...I will...You too. Good-bye, Dr. Blume." He hung up the receiver and directed his attention to Glen once more.

Glen jumped in immediately. "Um, Father Bernie, I really should talk to Father Chris, but that's not the real reason I came here. I know Glory has been a nuisance—she told me so herself—but she wants to do a favor for you. She'd like to, uh, make amends. I think you might say. Seems that way anyhow. I, uh, didn't mean to eavesdrop, but I think I know what your conversation with Dr. Blume was about. He's short on musicians for your special service, right?"

Bernie responded, "Yes, indeed, I'm sorry to say. Midnight mass on Christmas Eve, the time we need them most. We must have musicians. Brass, strings, you know. The people in our congregation expect that. At this late time, we're in a dither."

Glen wasn't sure what a dither was, but he could guess. He noticed the vein pulsating on Bernie's forehead, and read it as a sure sign of distress. "I can imagine. Well, Dr. Blume, as you know, he also teaches music at the Academy that I go to, so I know what he's planned for the music part of your church program, your special service, I mean. He tells us students a lot about his music programs actually. He's a neat guy. We like him a lot. So did Glory, that is, when she went to the Academy. I also know your violinist has the flu..."

Just then, Father Chris burst in, breathless. Without little regard to Bernie's visitor, he blurted, "Bernie, guess what? You're not going want to hear this."

Bernie gave him the look. He was in no mood for guessing games. "Then you better tell me."

"I am," Chris said sheepishly, realizing he had interrupted something. "Dr. Blume..."

Bernie smiled, putting Chris at ease. "Yes, Chris, calm yourself. We just found out. Looks like we'll have to work miracles. The instrumental part of the program must be in tact. We need a good violinist, but at this short notice..."

Glen interjected, "Excuse me, reverends. That's the real reason why I came here, Father Bernie."

Chris looked confused. "Who's he?" he asked Bernie. He then realized his manners were lacking. "Uh excuse, me, you are?"

"Glen Thomas Sterling-Baie, Reverend," he said, introducing himself for the second time in this office. "Oh...so you're Father Tosi, glad to meet you."

"Are you...?" The tall slender build, the thick shock of auburn hair. Chris couldn't imagine why *her* brother could be here.

"Yes, I'm Glory's brother, her twin actually," Glen admitted with a pleasing smile, hoping the young priest wouldn't prejudge him based on his sister's machinations.

Chris smiled, "Ah yes, I can see the resemblance." Anyhow this one has manners, Chris thought.

Glen looked up at Chris's face, took in his overall appearance and knew why Glory could be attracted to him. Chris fit the clichéd description of tall, dark haired, and handsome—to a T. "We may look alike, just a little though, but it ends there. If you get my drift."

Bernie couldn't wait to fill in Chris as to what had transpired. Chris's arrival seemed to bring a sense of calmness to him. "I think Glory's been telling us a pack of lies about her brother. If I'm not mistaken, it looks like he's about to offer his services as a violinist for midnight mass."

Chris sighed, "Oh, what a relief that would be. That would solve our problem. Our pastor here, Father Bernie, absolutely must have strings at Christmas Eve, and good ones at that. It's tradition here at St. Aeden's."

Bernie added, "And Dr. Blume is also his music teacher at the Academy. Imagine that. Busy man, choir director and music teacher on top of that, or is it music teacher and choir director on top. Oh, you know what I mean." Bernie couldn't resist the opportunity to be playful—whatever was needed to break any tension.

Chris asked Glen with a frankness that surprised Bernie and Glen, as well, "So you didn't get thrown out after all?"

"You mean me, get thrown out like Glory?" he seemed shocked at Chris's insinuation. That always happened. Glen always tried to keep his individuality. Glory certainly kept hers, fortunately for him. "No, of course not. Why should I get thrown out? I follow the rules. She doesn't. She got the boot, not me. Besides, it would kill my parents. My father is paying big bucks so I can get a good education there. They had a fit when Glory got thrown out. Actually the school had considered pressing charges. But, well, that's another story. You two have jumped to a wrong conclusion. I'm not the violinist. My musical talent is very limited. Glory has all the talent for both of us."

"And?" Chris was half curious and half fearful at what Glen might be suggesting. He recalled that she played the violin but not...

Glen could tell that both Chris and Bernie were skeptical. They could do without anything more Glory had to offer. Her history preceded her. But was that Christian to prejudge others?

"Please," Glen entreated, "she wants to save face. It's like she's apologizing for her intrusions and her antics, which she insisted were well intended, though very much unappreciated." Then most unexpectedly he chose to add, "Anyhow, she likes you, Father Chris..."

Bernie cast a hardened look at no one in particular. He heard Chris say, "According to that poem, it could be more than that."

Glen said calmly, "Well, maybe not. Glory is like that. Father Bernie can explain to you. I should go. You're busy. I hear someone at the front door."

Chris said, "That I am, busy, and so is he—with Christmas almost upon us. But Glory, she sent you here to present her offer to play the violin. I don't know what to say."

Glen said politely, "I think I would say 'yes' if I was in your place. Knowing Glory as I do, she'd be destroyed if you didn't accept her offer. It's her peace offering. She's really very good on the violin—a real prodigy. Dr. Blume will tell you. And she's a quick learn."

Chris considered the offer. Only to play the violin—that's all. To save our music. Make Bernie happy. Nothing more. What harm could it do? And so he asked Glen, "And the two of you would be able to get to midnight mass, even with your parents in Dubai, as I understand?"

Glen laughed at that. "Dubai? Is that what she told you? Yeah, yes, if you give me the time and place, I'll have our driver take her, I mean us, to a rehearsal and to the midnight service. She'll go. She wants so much to do this for you. She says you're very nice."

Chris thought the better of saying, 'that's what I'm afraid of.' He said to Glen, "All right, then tell her that we accept her offer." He feared second thoughts.

Bernie wasn't so sure of that. He cautioned, "Wait a minute, Chris. Are you sure you want to do that?"

"Why not? She's volunteering to get us out of a bind," Chris replied to Bernie, then, "Glen, we thank you for coming. It was nice meeting you."

Glen smiled and said, "Me too. Bye, Father Bernie. Thank you. She won't disappoint you, I promise."

Chapter THIRTEEN
(Christmas Eve)

IT WAS AN HOUR BEFORE dusk and heavy clouds were hovering overhead, blocking the last feeble glint of the sun's dying rays. The police had already cordoned off the streets a block in all directions from the town green. A hush came over Wexford Falls. Even the trickle of the falls had stopped—frozen solid so there was no flow. The brook below was coated with a thin layer of ice. A hint of a flurry threatened, although most thought it would be fitting for Christmas Eve.

The scurrying of last minute preparations belied the stillness of the green. The lighting team could be heard arguing over where in the tallest elm to affix the gigantic star fashioned from glitter sprayed oaktag. Crew members were setting up spotlights at various locations around the reconstructed manger, which was strung with blue-white lights on the eaves. Meanwhile, the sound system engineers were busy at work testing, blasting sound bytes hoping to provide the right balance in the accompaniment for the hymns and carols. Dr. Blume's annual composition—a new Christmas carol—was to be aired about mid-way through the event. Understandably, only a select few were allowed to sing it.

It had to be perfect, they said. They being Mrs. Rafferty the head honcho, who had unseated Barbara, whose one-day absence had dethroned her as leader. The two butted heads to the extent that Chris wondered if the whole thing would ever come together. But by nothing short of a miracle, it seemed very likely, however, with Barbara as second in command. Just add people and animals and hope that every creature great and small, human and animal, blends in perfect harmony and you have it: a truly unforgettable Christmas pageant. But then, each year they said this one would be the best ever. Chris said he would settle for just a *good* pageant since this year he was the overseer.

Parishioners and community members of various denominations were beginning to gather. They carried folding chairs and blankets; some undoubtedly hid flasks in the pockets of their parkas. Soon after, the 'actors' began to arrive in period costume, many with turtlenecks, ski pants and wool socks under their angel outfits or shepherd robes. A live baby was expected to portray the baby Jesus, weather depending. In that case, his stand-in, a life size rubber doll of indeterminate vintage uncovered from Mrs. Rafferty's attic, was wrapped near the manger ready to go. How they were going to execute the transfer had yet to be determined. Chris decided that was not his problem, but he was concerned for the well being of the human baby. The weather certainly was not going to get any warmer, not this time of year.

And for the well being of all the spectators and actors out there in the cold, the two ladies, Rafferty and Barbara, had agreed on one thing—the pageant from start to finish would not exceed one hour—sixty minutes firm. They held their ground on that. And the pageant would begin promptly at four p.m.; they conceded that a delay might be inevitable. But everyone needed time to go home, have a good supper and rest up for Santa or Midnight Mass, or both.

The participants lined up at their designated spots on the green, readying themselves to approach from various corners. Beryl

Baines had been the unanimous choice for the narrator. When the spotlight trained on her, resplendent in a long flowing robe of Kelly green, she announced that one and all would begin singing in unison "O Come All Ye Faithful." At that moment the sound system let forth a deafening belch not unlike a fire breathing dragon, before settling into a less turbulent accompaniment. This was fortunate because some of the animals leapt in shock, as did Beryl Baines.

Chris and Bernie sat together in what one would call the front row, though the seating configuration was more or less willy-nilly—rows and aisles blended into one scatterplot on the frozen grass. Chris was concerned that Bernie was shivering. He placed his own woolen scarf around Bernie's neck and, surprisingly, Bernie did not resist. He was engrossed in what he would later call an amazing pageant. As long as Chris had known him, it was always the same comment regardless of the pageant. And as Chris knew from experience, some were clearly better than others. The success of the pageant hinged upon the number and types of hitches encountered. The talent of the participants factored into it as well.

Chris could get a good look at the animals from his vantage point. Julie Jones in her role as a shepherdess was strategically placed near her own animals, which was a proactive stratagem. Thus far, the animals seemed to be minding their own business, which is what you'd want them to do. Let the sound system go awry again and who could tell what chaos could ensue? It could be too daunting a task even for Mrs. Jones.

He noticed that the Joneses got their way over the protests of both women leaders. Lorenzo, their prized llama, got into the act. It was the only way Julie would allow Ethel the goose to participate, which was a smart move because old Ethel would take a nip at you if she were so inclined. But the two Jones creatures got along, being stable mates. One kept the other in check. But a llama in a

Christmas pageant? Mrs. Jones, an avid animal lover and farmer's farmer, said, 'So who cares? You wanted animals, you got animals'. The children said it was 'cool.' To the women leaders of the pageant, she retorted, 'I'd worry more about the children than the animals.'

Chris took a close look at the baby Jesus, who in his aged rubberiness was stiff and unnaturally posed, his swaddling clothes hideously askew, which was not a major concern for the moment. The Mary actor spotted that and corrected it after a few minutes. Chris was relieved that the live baby had apparently been scooted off unobtrusively to a less chilly location, warmed by a battery operated heater.

As the angels gathered to surround the manger, Beryl announced that everyone will join them in singing the final hymn, "Angels we have heard on high." It would have been perfect if not once again the loud belch issued forth from the sound system. This time a goat got rambunctious and butted the nearest cow, which slammed into the side support beam of the manger, threatening its stability. The onlookers gasped, but oblivious to the incident, Beryl prevailed, inviting all to sing, 'sing with all your heart'. Apparently the goat too got the message as he settled down and got into the final act of the pageant, as he should.

Chris hadn't noticed as he sang the final 'Gloria' with gusto but Father Bernie had drifted off, his head in an awkward position, and was snoring softly, more like an intermittent purr. He awoke with a start as the applause spread around him. The spectators stood and continued to applaud until it became clear that the animals did not appreciate the clamor, although they deserved recognition as well. After the 'curtain call' the actors rushed out to grab the coats that their parents or friends were holding for them. In minutes nearly all had scattered save for the lighting, stage and sound crews. Both Mrs. Rafferty and Barbara accepted the kudos graciously, beaming and bowing. Mrs. Rafferty gestured to the crews and to Father

Chris, and those who had not yet dispersed cheered even louder. The women leaders approached the two priests to get reviews from them; those were the ones that really mattered to them.

CHRISTMAS MORNING AROUND three a.m. Chris lay awake, wide-eyed, replaying midnight mass in his head. The service was solemn and majestic, celebratory and jubilant. It was the sum of all things beautiful that he felt in his heart and in his mind. Father Bernie's little nap during the pageant took the edge off the day's end weariness and he emerged bright and well focused, as he should in concelebrating the high mass. Chris believed that the service enriched the spirits of all those who attended. The choir was harmoniously uplifting and finely tuned under Dr. Blume's expert direction. Blume himself did a solo that turned heads, his velvety baritone voice right on target for "Jesu Bambino". And he was accompanied by none other than the guest violinist Glory Sterling-Baie, who then performed a one verse solo, which brought tears to one's eyes, as congregants expressed to Chris after mass. They wanted to know where he found such an accomplished violinist.

Why is he always perplexed when it concerns Glory? How could someone so mysterious and conniving be so gifted musically? He guessed they were not necessarily mutually exclusive. But what bothered him—and nothing should have bothered him as he stared at the clock ticking away—was what he espied affixed to Glory's red velvet dress. It was apparent only as she exited the church, her violin case in tow. She beamed proudly as people approached her and praised her musicality. Her smile was disarming. Chris too was surrounded by church-goers gushing with holiday wishes as they exited the church. He nodded over to Glen Thomas, who was shaking Father Bernie's hand, and to a

distinguished looking couple who must have been Glen and
Glory's parents, since they were with him. They were escorting an
elderly woman in a luxurious full length fur coat that Chris figured
had to be Grandmom. They were carried along with the throngs of
people, many of whom come to church, spilling out into the aisles,
only on high holidays, so he never had the opportunity to meet the
Sterlings.

The corsage was strategically fastened to Glory's dress near the
right shoulder so as not to interfere with the placement of her
violin—simple white blossoms tinged with pink, a small cluster
with a few scant green leaves. Chris could have sworn they were
his Christmas roses, the cherished ones, which had only come to
life weeks earlier this year after being nurtured for three plus years.
The corsage was held together with a sparkly gold ribbon. As Chris
tossed in bed, he wondered if he could be mistaken. Would she
have had the audacity to pluck them from his garden? He mulled
over the idea. He could go out to check, but he didn't dare; sleep
was eluding him and it wouldn't serve either of them well to disturb
the household to verify his suspicion. But he would do so after his
noon mass. And what if it were true? How could he handle it?
So now add that conundrum to the issue of Glory's poem. As he
grasped for solutions he gradually fell into a welcome sleep, until
about five a.m. when he was roused by the sound of his own voice.
Talking in his sleep? What was he saying?

"Kendra," he heard himself say in an alpha state, somewhere
between wakefulness and sleep, "Kendra, why did you steal my
Christmas roses? They belong in my prayer garden, not on your
dress. Kendra, why...why did you?"

All of a sudden he woke sufficiently to understand what he had
said. "Am I losing my mind?" he said audibly. Then he realized
that he could disturb Bernie if he didn't control himself. Bernie

would be saying the first Christmas day mass and would surely need precious sleep especially after his marathon day.

Finally Chris reasoned that the prospect of seeing Ada and Jack Powers, Kendra's parents, later at Christmas dinner conjured up thoughts of their daughter, Kendra, his beloved Kendra. And so it made sense, he reasoned, that his agitation with Glory was intertwined with thoughts of Kendra. The resemblance that Glory bore to her continued to unnerve him.

Chapter FOURTEEN

BACK IN SEPTEMBER 1985 when Marie and 'Fred' Tosi were newlyweds, they wished upon their favorite star, which was the brightest star they could discern with the naked eye: it was to have one boy and one girl some day, and then their family would be complete. It was always some day, which back then seemed like light years away. 'Fred', a nickname he preferred to his foreign sounding name, and Marie had their wish come true a month shy of their first wedding anniversary. They never expected that the blessed event would fulfill their dreams at the same time: fraternal twins, a boy and a girl. Fred's father loaned them money to purchase a starter home, which after a while became too small for them, but it was all they could afford until Fred's carpentry business took off, which it did after a bumpy start.

The Tosis flourished in the small town of Birch Valley, but when the children started elementary school, they found a roomier, delightful Dutch cape several blocks away. As young children, Chris and Beth got along surprisingly well for siblings and remained very close throughout high school although their interests diverged. Beth was more introspective, an avid reader, and Chris was the outgoing athlete, though both participated in sports and Chris was not at all averse to picking up a good book now and then, especially mysteries, which as an adult still comprise his recreational reading.

"You better pick one or the other," his mother commanded after his freshman year. "Basketball or football. Which is it? You choose, Christopher." He recalled presenting a convincing case for sticking with both sports, but his mother, supported by his father, prevailed. And so he chose basketball. "A wise choice," they told him. And they were right.

But it was OK for Beth to do both field hockey and track, he noted, but kept silent. Beth would always win over her father, and of course his mother would acquiesce. Beth was his little girl. And it was her father that approved of his twins' taking skiing lessons way back in third grade. Over the years both Tosi twins became accomplished skiers, and each winter they would spend as much time as possible on the slopes.

TEN YEARS LATER, DECEMBER 2004, just days before Christmas break, the ski resorts were up and running. More snow was predicted for the weekend. Beth and Chris had planned an evening at Mohawk Mountain with their friends. Anton Drubec, a foreign exchange student whom Beth was tutoring in English, was coming along. He was not really a date, Beth insisted, only a good friend. That was fine with Chris, since he and Anton had become best friends not long after he arrived from Croatia to spend senior year in the United States. He would then return to continue his education at university. Anton and Chris were the two best players on the Birch Valley High School Basketball Team. Chris forgave Anton for coming along and robbing him of his position as the team's center. But Anton had the skill, the wingspan and the height advantage, being close to three inches taller than Chris, and a full year older. As it was, the addition of the Croatian athlete was a boon in their team's success.

Chris, of course, was taking along his date, his special girl, Kendra Powers. He was head over heels in love with her. Even though Kendra and Beth were classmates they really weren't what one would call 'friends' but that changed since Chris began dating Kendra the summer after a brief but stormy relationship with Kendra's younger sister Aleks. He found Kendra a refreshing change from Aleks who after a few weeks had proved to be domineering as well as a gossip monger. Aleks , who liked to be the one in charge, wanted to get back at Chris for dropping her and taking up with her older sister so she threw herself at the school's popular star quarterback who did not hesitate to accept her advances. By then Aleks had gained quite a "reputation." Chris cringes when he recalls his liaison with her.

The two couples, Beth and Anton, and Chris and Kendra, hung out together at school events that fall. They'd go to movies and dances and matches. And now that winter had arrived right on schedule, it was time for skiing. Anton couldn't wait to hit the slopes. None of them could. The ski event at Mohawk Mountain had been planned ever since it was announced that there would be a half-day of school for teacher in-service meetings that winter week. The teens would fit in the ski trip along with Christmas shopping for presents, decorating and, of course, last minute studying before the holiday break. They had submitted college applications so there would be no slackening off. They didn't want their grades to slide, and potential acceptances to be withdrawn.

The girls were anxious to model their new ski outfits that they had ordered from LL Bean. Maybe not very sexy, but functional and warm. They were counting the hours until their trip. The Tosis, Chris included, were becoming concerned that Beth was getting a little too interested in Anton, who would be returning home to Croatia in June after graduation. It would be ages before she might be able to see him again—if ever. But as for Chris, he knew in his heart, that he and Kendra were bound to each other forever.

School was being dismissed at 11:30, giving the two couples more than enough time to have a quick lunch, pull their gear together, and head out for the slopes. They would have several hours of skiing and then supper at the lodge before heading back at a respectable time in the later evening. They could sleep in the next morning. Five minutes before dismissal time, Chris heard the all too familiar voice booming over the P.A. System. Little could Chris have anticipated how a shift in the basketball practice schedule would change the course of his life forever.

"All varsity and J.V. basketball players must report to the gym immediately for an important meeting regarding a mandatory practice today. Failure to do so will result in your being replaced." The tone was unmistakable. The coach did not kid around—not on matters such as these.

Anton shrugged—such was life. He was so grateful to be in the U.S. playing basketball in an American high school, and on such a successful, winning team that he took the disappointment in stride. The Birch Valley team was expected to defend last year's championship. With the addition of Anton, Coach believed they would. The boys could go skiing another time, he said, knowing that several of the players had such plans for the evening. Chris winced when he heard the announcement. There was no choice. The practice would have to take precedence over skiing. He had looked forward to gliding down the slopes with Kendra, showing her a few moves and techniques, and sharing a hot chocolate at the ski lodge, sharing precious moments with her.

Aleks was smug. Good, she said to herself when she learned her sister would not be going skiing with Chris that evening. Who needs Chris any way? Kendra will get by without him, she convinced herself. Since the summer Aleks had taken on a brittle edge. Ted, her cherished quarry, the quarterback, had dumped her just days before the start of school. She was a short-lived trophy girl. Soon after, she noticed he had been cozy with a sophomore cheer leader. Aleks couldn't imagine what he saw in her. She found the girl rather ordinary looking.

Beth was disappointed that the boys couldn't join them for the evening, but only momentarily until she concocted a plan—a stratagem. This she hoped would work with her father. It usually did. And if so, her mother would go along with him, she was sure of that.

Resigned to Coach's demands, Chris and Anton pulled together their gear, and lumbered home for lunch. Yes, they would report to the gym later in the day for practice. There was no other way. There would be no practice the next morning instead, as the team members had requested, practically pleaded. Coach himself had other plans, and he was the one in charge not them, he reminded them. They needed the extra practice, he reminded the team members, if they wanted to stay on top.

As Beth had predicted, her dad did relent. At eighteen, Beth had been driving for two years and could take a passenger along. She had shown herself to be very responsible. The two girls could go skiing together. Her mother gave Mrs. Powers a call to see how she felt about the girls going skiing without the boys as long as they kept a reasonable curfew yet to be determined. And of course, weather was always a consideration, especially wintertime in the Litchfield hills.

And so after a hot lunch Kendra and Beth set out for the slopes in the early afternoon, about a 40-minute drive. The weather was cold, crisp and clear. Curfew was set for 11:30 since there was no school the following day. If a storm threatened, then the girls would head out earlier, they had promised. Snow was not expected to begin, however, until dawn at the earliest, according to the latest weather forecast. You could never tell. Mother Nature, however, had a mind of her own...

Chapter FIFTEEN
(December 2014, Christmas afternoon)

BERNIE WAS PACING ABOUT in the kitchen bedecked in his best suit, new burgundy and gray striped tie and camel hair overcoat. He kept eyeing the table where the cellophane wrapped coffee cake that Mrs. Hopkins had left them sat in plain view, beckoning him to sneak a sliver. With a single piece missing, he could tell at a glance it was her apple cinnamon walnut prize winning recipe. What a nice snack it would make before the late afternoon Christmas dinner in Birch Valley at the Tosis. Just a little sliver, he mused, couldn't hurt that much. Chris could read his thoughts.

"It will ruin your appetite, Bernie," Chris admonished. Words were often unnecessary. The look said it all, but Chris chose to be emphatic.

"What are you talking about?" Bernie retorted, as if he didn't know. Both were about two feet from the prized target.

" I've eaten next to nothing today. If you don't bring your full appetite, my mother will be offended," he answered. "She pours everything she's got into that Christmas meal. Course after course, you'll see. You won't be able to budge. She won't cook like that the rest of the year."

"I know, I know," he said sheepishly. And then one of Bernie's subject changes. "So what time should we be heading out?"

Chris estimated that if they left at 4:00 they would be there just on time. He wasn't about to arrive too early. His mother liked to work solo in the kitchen and he wasn't sure what mood his father would be in. Christmas reopened the wound of the loss of his little girl, and he expressed it differently than his wife did. Marie complained to Chris that he practically lived in his basement workshop, although he was engaged in his favorite activity, woodworking. Marie viewed that as hiding from the world but she wouldn't dare express that thought to her husband. At least it kept him from hitting the bottle too often. His hands were constantly busy. She was grateful for that.

Chris suggested to Bernie that they go downstairs for a while to the sitting room to receive any visitors who might happen to stop by. After all, it was Christmas Day. As in previous years all kinds of homemade goodies arrived, and that was just fine with Bernie.

Bernie noticed that Chris seemed ill at ease, fidgety, he called it, as they were sitting sipping a glass of wine, which should have relaxed him. A Christmas recording of Bing Crosby, one of Bernie's all time favorites, could be heard crooning in the background. Actually no one came to pay the priests a visit, which was fine as long as Chris was concerned. He was wrapped in his thoughts.

Finally Bernie spoke, "All right, Chris, what's eating you? You're wriggling all around like you got ants in your pants. Heh heh. Not even the wine is soothing you and you're not getting any more since you're driving this afternoon." He cast his paternal glance at Chris.

Chris said, "All right." He hesitated longer than Bernie could wait.

"All right, what? Come out with it, Father Tosi," he said with a quirky little grin. Temper anything with humor and it helps, or should anyhow, was one of Bernie's philosophies.

"All right then, Father Bernie, come with me outside to the garden," he said. Then he added, "Please. I know it's a little cold."

Bernie gave him a strange look. "Are you nuts? When I could be here like this now, why should I want to go out there?"

Without further ado, Chris got to the point, and told him of his suspicions, about Glory's corsage. Bernie pooh-poohed the idea, and if so...

"I'm going to stay calm until I see for myself. You can come along with me. I'd really like you to, but..." Chris stopped for a moment, hearing what he just said, hoping he was being rational, hoping against hope. He was pretty sure of what he had seen. He had gotten a good look at Glory as she was leaving the church. She hadn't yet put on her coat, and there it was, as plain as the nose on your face, as Bernie would say—the corsage of Christmas roses staring him right in his face. His precious Christmas roses—painstakingly nurtured until their recent bloom, which should have been in their designated place gracing his statue of the Virgin Mary in the prayer garden, where they belonged undisturbed. And not plucked and pilfered to adorn a red velvet dress for whatever reason she had in mind. Oh, he hoped he was wrong.

Bernie gulped the last of the wine, placed the goblet on the coffee table and rose with some effort. He fastened the buttons of his overcoat and gestured to Chris to follow him outside. He would humor Chris.

The garden was serene, frozen as though it were a tableau, which in winter for the most part it was. They stopped at the gate to take in what Beryl Baines would have masterfully portrayed in her article and photo spread. Everything was dormant and still except for a few brave sparrows at the feeders and his precious Christmas roses, which so brazenly defy the laws of nature.

There was no need to examine the Christmas rose plantings. The proof of his suspicions was right there in front of them—one bush was devoid of blossoms, which had been there a day ago. In its place was a sizeable poinsettia pot whose blooms strangely mimicked those of the Christmas rose. Had someone painted the edge of the petals in shades of pink? Would someone have even thought of doing that? And why? he wondered, or maybe it's just the species. He thoughts were tangled, but one emotion prevailed—indignation. How could she?

Strange, neither of the two priests had heard the purr of the Sterling's limousine pull up to the garden entrance when they were in the sitting room awaiting visitors. Had they not discovered the poinsettia plant then and there in the garden, unlike the Christmas roses, it would have frozen and perished in the cold.

Bernie cast a sympathetic glance at Chris, "You're jumping to conclusions, Chris. An animal, some rodent or another, a hungry squirrel could have eaten your flowers."

"Sure, an animal with high heeled boots and dark auburn hair, an animal who knows her way around this garden, who will do anything to serve her own selfish needs, for attention," an anguished Chris replied. His sculpted jaw was set in anger.

"I suppose you're right about that. Take a look down here, around the foil wrap, see here, on the ribbon. There's, uh, an object of sorts hanging from it. Let's see," he said, bending down to fetch it.

Chris intervened. "Let me, Bernie." Bernie obeyed, straightening up and rubbing his lower spine. "It's an ornament, I think, a Christmas tree ornament." Chris unfastened it and held it high for Bernie to see.

"Well, I'll be," he gasped. "It's a violin, tiny glitzy little thing, it is."

"And hitched on with the same ribbon adorning Glory's corsage. What a coincidence," Chris said, visibly shaken. Too many steps backward, he thought.

"How true to form. She always tries to make amends for what she's done," Bernie blurted without really thinking through the essence of it all. "Strange girl, that one."

"It's far more complicated than that, Bernie," Chris heaved a sigh. "Remember, we haven't dealt with the poem yet."

"I know," Bernie agreed. "You know, Chris, it's got to be close to 4:00. Why don't we think of heading out to your folks' house before I attack that coffee cake upstairs?" The poem, the violin ornament, and anything else that has to do with Glory Sterling can wait, as far as Bernie was concerned. It was Christmas Day. He could already taste Marie's holiday meal.

Good old Bernie to the rescue. Chris checked his watch and said, "Right. Let me run upstairs to get the gifts. Oops, I almost forgot. I locked them in the pickup yesterday."

"Let's take my Chrysler. It's Christmas. Don't need to be chugging up in your old pickup. Just remember to move the gifts, now will you, Chris?" Bernie said.

Ever the pragmatist, Chris asked him, "How's the tank? Got enough gas?"

"Enough to get to Birch Valley and back, I should think, two, three times over," he said with a wink. Bernie, as a rule, never let his tank run below half in the cold Litchfield hills—never, nor in any season for that matter.

Chapter SIXTEEN

CHRIS EASED FATHER Bernie's trusty old Chrysler Cordoba into the spot on the side of the driveway his father had always set aside for his son when Bernie accompanied him. Fred Tosi had been raised to always treat the clergy with the utmost of deference. The roomy sedan was sparkling inside and out from a top of the line detailing, which was an early Christmas gift from Chris. Bernie too was shining from head to toe, decked out in his holiday best. A new Burberry scarf was draped jauntily around his neck; it diverted attention from his overcoat, which probably saw as many birthdays as Chris did. Chris told him with a smile that his winter coat was a little démodé, old fashioned, as Chris explained the expression to him. At that, Bernie performed one of his inimitable facial groans, not unlike a grown up eye roll, as he had such an aversion to foreign words—but only those he hadn't learned. However, his Latin and Greek were still very much up to par, even excelling his associate in that department. As for Bernie's hair, Chris advised him to tame the rambunctious wiry strands with some gel so as not to look Einsteinian in the follicle department. Bernie held back his laughter. He wanted to tell him to mind his own beeswax, but he figured he was going to Chris's parents on this special day. So he'd better hold his peace.

All in all, Bernie did look quite dapper. Chris, on the other hand, could have looked perkier. Weariness had made its mark on his young face. He had endured the many challenges of the week, the one weighing heaviest on him was acting as supervisor of the pageant. He drew highly positive comments on his prayer garden, winter season, which had reemerged in the minds of the parishioners, a credit to Beryl Baines's timely article. It surprised Chris that so many of his parishioners told him they'd never heard of the legend of the Christmas rose. Many said they'd pay a visit to the garden once Christmas season was over to see the Glastonbury rose in bloom despite the harsh winter weather. But connected with the garden as well was the Glory conundrum, and it showed no signs of resolving itself—just not yet. That nagged at him and eroded his peace of mind.

He was, however, filled the with joy and hope and, yes, more often than not, the sense of peace that comes with the Savior's birth, that he infused in the joyous homilies of his Christmas masses. And so with a little help from above, he smiled radiantly, ready to celebrate the holiday dinner at his family home. He hoped his mother wouldn't notice the tell tale signs of distress etched on his face through the joy he was doing his best to project. But he knew in his heart that mothers know. They always do— especially in his case, since they shared the same loss.

Chris recognized a few cars parked on the street near his parents' home. A few he did not. One of them belonged to Penny Mullins—he didn't know her married name. Chris waved to her as her brood was being tucked into an oversized SUV. She was only a year behind him in school. He was incredulous as he counted—one, two, three children. Mrs. Mullins stood, coatless, her ruffled apron fluttering in the breeze, waving furiously and blowing kisses. As Penny waved and turned to get into the van, he could see she was pregnant again. He was happy for her, for them, for the life choices they had made.

Ah, the choices we make, he said to himself contentedly, as he escorted Bernie up the flagstone walk to the front stoop. Bernie had opted to be the bearer of the gifts, a small package and a considerably larger one. Bernie had forgotten what Chris had found for him. He had given him the money and left the rest to Chris, whose judgment he trusted. Something for the house, he figured. Marie loved to cook, and Fred was a craftsman, so it would be easy for Chris to choose just the right gifts.

The two priests were greeted with warm embraces and kisses first by Marie who ran out from the kitchen, then by Fred who accepted the packages and then disappeared. Marie had decided that Chris could assume his father's duty of bringing coats upstairs to the guestroom. Fred, in turn, would be the entertainer, which to Marie entailed directing guests into the living room, taking drink orders, and making small talk. He also had the responsibility to keep the hors d'oeuvres coming, as needed.

Since Marie was running the show this day, Chris obediently brought his and Bernie's coats upstairs as directed. He didn't, however, go straight to the guestroom. Rather, he paused with uncertainty in front of a closed door—the one to Beth's room that was always kept closed. He dared to peek inside just for a moment. He'd stayed away from her room since that fateful day. Gingerly, he opened the door a crack, then a little wider. He entered. It was a girlie girl's room—a cotton candy confection of shades of pink—with posters covering much of the wall space—her favorite celebrities of the day. The dollhouse that their father had made for her one Christmas years ago was anchored in the same place as always. He bet his mother still dusted the miniature furniture with a toothbrush as she set about on her weekly dusting brigade. The same starched pink and white striped curtains, refreshed each season, he imagined, still graced the two side windows. And the fluffy pink rug looked pristine, unmarred by foot footfalls or other indentations—though like everything else in the room—was dated, unused. He stood there frozen in time—realizing that he, her twin brother, was the only anachronism in that room.

He stopped short, however. One addition caught his attention at the foot of the bed—it was a patchwork quilt, which did not match the rosy décor. A closer look revealed squares and other geometric shapes of fabric, remnants of familiar pieces of clothing, Beth's. His mother would always hang onto their old clothes, unless someone really needed them. Then she would pass them on. He recognized a piece or two of Beth's field hockey skirt, bits of old pajamas with dancing clowns grinning, a polka dot blouse which matched the one that his mother had worn, a pair of floral shorts that she'd worn on their last family vacation to the beach...

He recalled that last family vacation. That third week in August. Beth practically lived in those shorts. She'd put them on over her swimsuit. They stayed in, what his mother described as 'rustic', a cabin on the bayside of Cape Cod, Massachusetts. He and Beth complained. They found it lacking in modern conveniences and their father told them they didn't have to stay inside all day to lament what was lacking, but to get outside and enjoy all that the Cape had to offer. But that week it was possible for only a few days. Rains drenched the northeast for the rest of the week, forcing the Tosis to find indoor activities, which, in retrospect, they all decided, wasn't half bad. The twins were turning eighteen that week and somehow Marie was able to make the wettest day of the week a memorable birthday celebration—regrettably their last as twins, and as an intact family. They vowed to return each year to the same place the same week every year no matter where they were living—even when the twins were married with children. They would all be there together. Sadly, that vow was broken.

Chris stood there studying the quilt, such an intimate connection with Beth. He touched it lovingly, stroking it. As his eyes clouded over, he told himself that he shouldn't be in there. Not now. It felt like he'd been in there forever; he was an intruder. This museum belonged to his parents, not to him.

His mother's voice brought a halt to his musing and a relief to his sense of loss. "Christopher, what are you doing? Come on down. You're leaving Father Bernie sitting all alone in the living room." Chris was jolted back to the present, calling back to her, 'Coming' then he tamped his eyes with a tissue he found on the upstairs hall table in a box decorated with Christmas wrapping paper. He was glad his mother was decorating, getting more into the holiday spirit. Dutifully, he strode into the guest room where he spotted some familiar wraps already piled on the guest bed. Beryl Baines' long car coat and Emil's worn brown leather jacket protruded from under others. He was curious as to why Beryl and Emil Baines were invited. He didn't know that his parents even knew them. And where were they now? He didn't see any other guests when he and Bernie arrived. But he thought that was Ruthie Symond's green jacket and her mother's fur collared coat there on the bed. He was quite sure of the owners since he had spent time with Ruthie throughout her fiance's trial and sentencing. The poor girl was coping with so much, but where were the Symonds now? He hadn't spotted them in the living room.

Seeing Beth's room set him thinking about any shrine the Powers family might have had to Kendra. He didn't know if there was one since over the years the Tosis had drifted apart from the Poweres. So, he was quite surprised to learn that they were coning to Christmas dinner. He didn't even know where they were currently living. Oh well, he said to himself, there will be enough guests present to take the edge off any uncomfortable moments that might occur. And there was quite an array of persons, but it was his mother's prerogative to invite whomever she wanted. He hoped that the old saying 'the more the merrier' would turn out to be true. This was so good for his mother, for both his parents. For him though, he wasn't so sure.

As he was galloping down the stairs, he heard the doorbell and raced to answer it. His mother certainly knew how to take care of persons in need. Marty and Sylvie Tisdale, radiant in her fifth or was it sixth month, filled the doorway. Greetings and another trip upstairs with coats left Chris running. This time he went right into the living room to join his friends. By then, his father and Father Bernie were chatting amiably and the Tisdales were noshing on hors d'oeuvres and sipping non-alcoholic punch. He stopped for a full ten seconds to ensure that his father was managing the guests and then headed off to the kitchen.

He buttonholed his mother as she scooted from the dining room to the kitchen to ask her why the Baineses were here and where were they, by the way. Before she could say a word, he told her that he should probably take an educated guess. Where else would someone like Emil be? His guess was confirmed as he heard the cellar door thrust open and saw him emerge with his mother in tow. The lure had to be the old Lionel train set, yes, of course. His father had kept it up and running forever, and was often seen watching the rail cars in their continuous travels; he was mesmerized. Chris imagined that it soothed his father in certain moments—certainly a more salubrious alternative than alcohol. Fred missed his little girl and grieved in a way only known to him personally. As for the Baines duo, they greeted Chris warmly and were directed to join the others in the living room. It didn't matter to him why they were here. He was just glad that the single mother and her special needs son had a place to go on Christmas Day.

Chris thought of his mother, bending over a hot oven, beads of perspiration forming on her forehead. All burners, crock pots and warmers were turned on, synchronized to ensure that everything would be done and not overdone or underdone. Everything was boiling, broiling, simmering or roasting, all as scheduled, which baffled Chris. How was it possible? He couldn't imagine how much time and effort went into the preparation and orchestration of each dish. But it was so good for Marie. She'd been heard saying on more than one occasion, ' Food is God's love made edible.' Embracing that thought must have contributed to her success in the kitchen, and opening her home to those in need of good company cinched it. Everything would be perfect, he said to himself, mostly to convince himself. After all, the guests did their share as well, coming with quick breads, gingerbread confections, favorite dishes, but when all was said and done, it was Marie the master chef who accomplished miracles in the culinary and social departments.

Chris offered to set the table and Marie accepted his offer, one less chore for her. She showed her son just how the place settings should be, all 12 of them. She warned him not to even think of touching the *anti-pasti* platters that she'd placed at either end of the table until all were seated. Meanwhile she was concerned that Fred had made too many trips to the kitchen to replenish trays of hors d'oeuvres. She feared they would spoil the guests' appetites, and took him aside and told him so. He merely responded with a shrug, and removed a few canapes from the trays.

Beryl and Emil Baines arrived in the dining room just in time to correct some placement errors Chris had made. She gave Emil the job of putting on the napkin rings, which would take him forever, they hoped. Define the task clearly and let him go forth was Beryl's philosophy where Emil was concerned, but hang around and make sure he's on the right track. Emil was eyeing the stuffed olives, so Chris handed him one and helped himself to one as well. Beryl pretended not to notice—and as all know so well—she doesn't miss a trick. Reporters are astute observers. The job dictates it.

A jangling of the kitchen phone interrupted his chore. Chris dashed to grab it for his mother, but she had already taken the call. She yelled out to his father that it was Ada Powers and that she and Jack sent their apologies; they'd be a little late. They didn't elaborate—only that a surprise was somehow involved. They said to go ahead with the first course. They'd catch up later. Of course, Marie wouldn't hear of that, at least not at first.

Chris was surveying the transformation of the dining room table to accommodate the guests. It occupied almost the entire length of the room. His father had put in the two extensions, but they were short on straight back chairs. He would have to scoff up two more. He remembered there being a few stacked in the den closet. As he opened the den door he came face to face with Ruthie Symond and her mother Muriel, a stellar example of a success story despite all the challenges associated with raising a child half a century her junior. It was a kind and loving relationship, which proved to be beneficial to Ruthie especially in these trying times. The two women had been watching television, a pastime that Ruthie engaged in lately almost to the exclusion of others, according to Muriel.

Muriel greeted Chris warmly, then exited the room but not before signaling to him to remain behind for Ruthie, if she needed to talk. He took the hint and closed the door behind her. Ruthie smiled at Chris. It lit up her face. She looked stronger than the last time he'd seen her. "Father, I don't know how to thank you," she said softly. "It wasn't so much what you said or did, but how you made me feel."

"You were feeling very low," he responded. "I'm glad things are better now and that I was able to help you in some way." He wondered if she'd been over to visit Matt, to face him after her night with Sonny Gilberto. He'd let her bring that up if she cared to.

"Father, I saw Matt. I brought over his Christmas present. I know it was a little early. I have something else for him too for the next time I visit," she explained.

"I'm sure that made him very happy," Chris offered.

"Oh, it did," she replied. "He wasn't as depressed like usual." Then she added in a half whisper, "We talked a little about the appeal but I didn't say a word about me seeing the lawyer with my, uh, thoughts about, well, someone slipping something into a drink. If it happened to me at Sonny's like I think, well, it could have happened to him too. Kind of explains things a little, I hope. I'll wait till after the holidays."

"Good idea," Chris agreed. "You know, you can call if you want to continue our conversation, Ruthie."

"Oh, right, thanks. I guess I'm keeping you from what you have to do." She said, realizing Chris was needed elsewhere at this time. "But, one more thing, Father. I got Matt a daily journal, you know, one with an inspiring thought on the top of each page. No issue with that, bringing it inside either. He loved it, the whole idea. Maybe writing in it will make him hopeful."

Chris nodded in assent. He said to himself that she should do likewise, write in a journal to express her thoughts, to cope with her bouts of depression and anxiety. He was well aware that Ruthie had had the proposed wedding date tattooed on the inside of her left wrist. If she thought anyone was looking at it, she would conceal it with her other hand. It embarrassed her when anyone asked her about it. Muriel would often tell her it was OK, that she could have the year redone later on. Her eyes said it all, 'Who knows when or even if?'

Once the requisite number of chairs at the table matched the anticipated number of guests, Marie emerged from a steamy kitchen, drying her hands on her apron. She announced, "Everyone to the table, please. Dinner is about to be served." No one needed a repeat call.

Chris gestured to her that the Powerses hadn't arrived yet. She told him that they could catch up. She had changed her mind. She would serve the soup course and that he should invite all to partake of the *anti-pasti*. She added that they should take their time, dine leisurely. It was Christmas. She was concerned that the Powerses could be quite late, but there was no need to hold up the guests who had arrived on time. After all, it was already after five.

Marie placed an industrial sized tureen of *pasta e fagioli* soup on a tea-cart that she could wheel from one place to another as she served. Chris had never seen the cart before. He figured his father had made it for such occasions. Upon further scrutiny, he believed it bore the hallmark of his father's craft. Yes, no doubt.

After Father Bernie's blessing, the Tosis and their guests enjoyed a leisurely first course. Homemade garlic knots complemented the dish. Chris looked around the table and was not at all surprised to find each pair of guests chatting quietly with the other member of the pair—the Tisdales, the Symonds, the Baineses, his parents when they were seated, and he and Bernie. Normally his parents sat at either end of the table but for this meal they were seated side by side to facilitate fetching and serving. Give everyone time, he said to himself hopefully, and the conversation among all will develop naturally. Just as a lull in all conversations became obvious, but not uncomfortable, a knock was heard at the kitchen door. It was Ada and Jack Powers entering from the breezeway entrance, gushing with apologies. Ada Powers handed Marie a bakery box that she placed on a space on the kitchen table. Fred took coats and the Powerses joined the other guests at the table and consumed their first course remarkably fast as the other guests took another shot at the remnants of *anti-pasti*. Soon there were no more garlic knots. Marie knew they would be a hit. They always were, and they seemed to complement any dish.

Beryl addressed Chris between bites, "Uh, Father, did you get to see the article in The Hillside Journal yesterday?" She didn't wait for him to answer. She had the answer herself. "Oh, you probably didn't with all you had to do with the pageant and the masses and all that was going on yesterday."

Chris, his mouth full at that moment, raised his hand, and indicated 'no.' It was the farthest thing from his mind.

Marie chimed in as she cleared away the soup bowls, "Oh, Christopher, you absolutely must see that article. It's just beautiful. Why Beryl made a special trip here yesterday to hand deliver a copy to us."

Chris smiled and nodded in recognition. He was sure she'd done a fine job writing about the winter season in the garden series, which would mean a nice boon for the parish, as in the past.

At that, Beryl announced to all at the table, "That was when Mrs. Tosi, uh, Marie asked me what I was doing Christmas Day." She paused to smile at Marie. "And I told her we, that's Emil and I—we'd be sharing his favorite holiday meal—roasted chicken, cranberry chutney—I make it myself—peas and pearl onions, but Emil picks out the onions, and mashed potatoes, but I don't let him watch how I do it. And, oh yes, homemade apple pie a la mode. So when Marie asked if I'd be alone at Christmas, I told her, no, I'd be with my Emil. That's when she asked us if we'd like to join her family and friends for Christmas dinner later in the day. Well, of course, I said 'yes, we'd be delighted'; and here we are. Imagine that. Two Christmas dinners in one day! Are we ever blessed, aren't we, Emil?" Emil just looked at his mother, trying to figure it out. To him 'blessed' was more of a visual thing—something someone does to you, like when Father Bernie does the sign of the cross and you cross yourself, a holy thing.

Marie told everyone she'd pass around the article after dinner, but Beryl interjected that it wasn't necessary. She'd brought along extras if people wanted their own copy. Chris reddened. He didn't need all the attention, but he recognized that Beryl had a warm heart, and was a darned good reporter, and Emil's photos were amazing. He had a keen eye for capturing scenes just right, and from the best angle.

Marie told the guests that she was really moved reading about the legend of the Christmas rose that she'd told to the twins year after year when they were little. And so it logically followed that Chris's prayer garden would be the focus of the moment, with Bernie adding his own touches to the conversation.

It was obvious that Marie was becoming impatient. She addressed the Powerses, "Ada, Jack, I'm waiting for your surprise."

"Yes, Marie, so are we," Ada Powers replied matter-of-factly. She was not one to wear her heart on her sleeve by any means. Actually it was her husband Jack looking as though he'd burst from holding in the surprise yet to be delivered.

Up to this point, the Powerses hadn't revealed much of anything about themselves. Both reticent by nature, they spoke when spoken to, which did not serve to keep a conversation flowing. After the accident, they'd kept much to themselves, moving out of Birch Valley only when Aleks went off to State University. They were staying at nearby Clover Hollis's Bed and Breakfast Inn for a few days since Ada had an appointment with her specialist in Wexford Falls. She told them emphatically she wasn't about to change doctors, not if she could help it. She traveled to the area once a year, and this year, it was the right time. So when Marie invited them to Christmas dinner the timing was perfect. They said they might stay on a little longer, depending...but they didn't say depending on what, and Marie wasn't about to pry. In Chris's mind, they were Aleks and Kendra's parents whom he'd seen only now and then ten years ago, and to interact with them any way but superficially could cause him anxiety, maybe even pain.

He couldn't imagine how Aleks ever got into State. She was not much of a scholar in high school. He had no idea how long she stayed at State or if she even managed to graduate. And seeing the Powerses again was reopening a chapter he'd done his best to close.

The best ways of moving the conversation along, he noticed, were compliments on Marie's gourmet cuisine and requests for her family recipes. Beryl and Sylvie had asked for copies. Muriel Symond chimed in, claiming she couldn't cook anything unless it was from a package. Ruthie had often joked about it. "Mom's so right. She can work miracles with Hamburger Helper and stuff like that, but it begins and ends there." Sylvie offered to give some lessons on the nouvelle cuisine, but the consensus was that French cuisine was much too complex to master unless you've studied at one of those blue ribbon culinary institutes. Sylvie simply smiled in response, punctuating it with an inimitable shrug as only the French can do. Jack Powers entered the conversation saying they solve the problem easily enough by dining out, or buying meal fixings through Blue Apron. Emil looked to his mother for an explanation of that, which never came. The arrival of the entremets course ended all conversation.

Marie entered cheerily balancing an ornate silver tray bearing small cut glass bowls. "And now for the palate cleanser." She could hear Emil ask Beryl what a 'palate' cleanser was, and she told him that he should give it a try; he'd like it very much as he had a sweet tooth, and just think, it wasn't even time for dessert. He was confused. To him, a palette was what you used when you painted, to put the different colors on. You could mix them on it too and make pretty new colors, as he was used to doing. He remembered the name. And a cleanser, wasn't that something his mother used, yeah, Comet, that greenish powder to clean the out the bathtub when it had a scum ring? Guests seated near Emil held back their laughter as Emil asked his mother about those words. Regardless, he dug into the palate cleanser with delight.

All twelve were relishing the melon ball sized scoops of lemon raspberry sherbet when a rapping was heard at the side door. Ada Powers, so uncharacteristic of herself, turned sharply, shouting, "Our surprise is here. She's here." She nearly knocked over her crystal goblet with her elbow. As it were, a few drops of Chianti spilled onto Marie's heirloom tablecloth. "Our dear Aleks is here, fresh off the plane from jolly old England."

Chapter SEVENTEEN

CHRIS DID A DOUBLE take. To him surprises were supposed to bring delight, a wish come true, things of that nature. This one was anything but, in his opinion. First, she sashayed in as though she was a celebrity. On top of that, she was late, very late, and uninvited as a guest for a sit down dinner, and on Christmas Day, to boot. Had Marie known in advance in might be different. Aleks's 'I'm so happy to see everyone' smile seemed anything but sincere, but that was Aleks, the old Aleks who could always put on airs. She embraced both her parents, whipped off her designer coat and slung it over her arm. Fred was about to get up and take it but she declined, saying said she'd run it upstairs since she had to use the powder room. Chris excused himself to get another chair from the den closet while Marie scurried to pull together a makeshift place setting. At this point she wasn't concerned that it wouldn't match the others. Then she and Chris rearranged a few seats at one end of the table to make room for Aleks.

By then the sherbet balls had pooled into a rosy goo since everyone had ignored the entremets when the 'surprise' walked in. They'd set down their spoons and looked up to take everything in. Then they inundated the Powerses with questions, some talking all at once: What did their daughter do for a living? What had brought her to England? Have you been there to visit her? Is she married? The Powerses had hardly expected all the attention. They were just thrilled to have their daughter with them if only for a short time, and at such a special time – Christmas Day.

When Aleks noticed an additional place setting, she called out to no one in particular. "Oh no, I didn't mean to drop in for dinner, I mean for a meal. I didn't. And I'm not really hungry; I'm just so very, very jet-lagged. When I found out where my parents would be, I just had to see them." She scanned the table then she said in a dulcet tone, " It's so nice to see everyone even though I don't really know everybody. It's Christmas, so, uh, merry Christmas one and all." The response was polite smiles, nods and a chorus of well wishes.

Fred was given the privilege of making introductions, and Aleks respectfully nodded to each person, although it was unlikely she'd remember all the names, or even cared to. Would she ever see them again? Marie's entrance with a platter of stuffed shells broke the awkwardness of the moment for Chris. She cautioned her guests not to fill up on the pasta dish since it was not the main course. Although this was one of Chris's favorites, he'd suddenly lost his appetite. He fidgeted with his cutlery, steering one shell from one side of his plate to the other. He alternated that activity with frequent sips from his water glass. When he couldn't take the anxiety any longer, he excused himself to go help his mother in the kitchen. His father gave him a look, but seemed to understand the situation.

Chris said to no one in particular, "I'm sure Mom could use some help with the roast, slicing it, I mean. If you'll please excuse me." He rose and sought temporary refuge in the kitchen.

Away from the dining room, he began to whisper to his mother. The dinner conversation and the Christmas music in the background should have been sufficient to block out any communication in the adjacent room, but he persisted, asking if he could help with anything.

"Christopher," his mother asked, her fork raised in the air, "What is it? You know I can handle the roast myself. Your father stopped carving the meat for me years ago. Go on now. Spend time with the guests."

When she saw him just standing there, she knew. "OK, it's the Powerses, right? I was afraid you might feel a little uncomfortable with them here at first, but I sense it's not so much them but Aleks. I am right, aren't I?"

"Yeah, her. That was some surprise. Mom, you're always right," he admitted. She could tell right away he wasn't himself after Aleks had arrived. "We haven't seen them in ages, and it brings back, uh, well you know." Oh, she knew only too well. Her response to that was her easiest and most available defense mechanism—the smile, but a patient, loving smile and then silence, and as need dictated, back to business. She returned to her slicing.

They didn't need to speak any further. Each could read each other's thoughts. Neither one of them was sufficiently healed, but she would not be able to fully comprehend Chris's annoyance at seeing Aleks. That was a private matter best left unsaid.

Before returning to the dining room, Chris hesitated. He needed to ask his mother if she knew anything about Aleks. Marie sighed deeply. After a long moment she explained that when she'd phoned Ada, she inquired about her daughter and had learned that Aleks had gone off to England after leaving State University without graduating. She'd filled a position for a nanny to two small children. Their father was a man of means. Marie checked the stove top, peered into the oven and summarized quickly, telling him that Aleks had broken up the children's parents' marriage and the father had subsequently married her, but they've since divorced. She heard Aleks wanted to return soon for the children's sake, claiming that they miss her. Who knows? Marie added.

"Well, she certainly didn't have to show up here," he protested as Marie finished slicing the pork roast. "She could have visited her parents later on, say, after dinner over at the Inn." There was something more to Chris's annoyance other than her presence there, but Marie figured it was not the time to probe.

"Well, she didn't." Marie said, handing the platter to him. She needed him to focus on something else, anything else. "Here, Christopher, take this, will you dear? Be careful, it's hot and very heavy. Put it down, yes, right there. Good." She indicated a spot on the counter. "Now, I have to tend to the gravy. You go and finish your pasta. I don't want this to get cold."

Still, he lingered. Hands on her hips, Marie said gently, "Put on a smile. It's only a dinner. Be sociable. There's enough guests for Aleks to talk with. You might go out there and see if anyone needs anything."

"Will do, Mom," he said feeling less fidgety. "If you're sure you can handle the rest yourself." Her look said it all. She shooed him away.

And so he returned to the dinner table saying, "She's got everything under control. What a supermom she is."

A chorus of 'here-here's' followed. If the main dish was all set to go, he figured he'd keep busy. He set about to collect the pasta dishes. His mother wouldn't know which was his as not everyone had finished theirs either. Despite his mother's cheerleading, he was still trying to cope with Aleks's invasion. He prayed for the peace, hope and joy of Christmas to fill him entirely, without allowing intruding thoughts, but her very presence unnerved him still after all these years. Perhaps because Aleks was Aleks as he knew her to be—conniving, lacking empathy, and vengeful. He wondered if she had possibly mollified her harsh ways over time. She had been a step-mother for a few years, bonding with the children, but he sensed she was the same as before. She had never forgiven him and she'd let him know it, he feared, but hopefully not in front of all the guests, not at his parents' table, not at Christmas.

The table was buzzing with conversations. Beryl felt it was the right time to enlighten the surprise visitor with the article she'd written about Chris's prayer garden. "You really should come see it for yourself," she said, her voice tinged with pride. After all, through her journalistic acumen, she had brought the prayer garden to the forefront once again. She didn't notice Chris cringing. He didn't want Aleks of all people in his garden.

"At this time of year?" Aleks retorted, unconvinced. "It's winter in case no one has noticed. An article about a garden in the winter? How can you make something out of nothing? What's alive in winter?"

Beryl looked peeved. How dare this woman challenge her capabilities or her credibility as a journalist? Beryl sat upright, gave her a searing look and volleyed, "Well, why don't you read the article? You'll see. And check out Emil's photos. They'll show you." She patted Emil on his shoulder and he beamed.

Now all eyes were on Aleks, not so much that she seemed nonplussed over the garden article, not having seen it yet, but that she was holding center stage, getting exactly the attention she always seemed to crave. No, she hadn't changed.

In the quiet that followed, Aleks stared over at Ruthie's forearm, beyond the time one would consider unintentional. Not getting any overt reaction from Ruthie, who was always reserved in company, Aleks cleared her throat and addressed her, "Say, uh, Ruth, right? Um, I thought I'd got your name right. I'm curious. Pardon me for staring, but, uh, tell me, what does your tattoo mean?"

Ruthie gulped and paled. She'd hiked up her sleeve a little too far since it had grown warmer in the dining room and failed to realize that she'd exposed what she wanted to remain hidden. She didn't want to discuss that topic, not in the presence of a tableful of people, some of whom she didn't know. It would be far too painful. She obliged, however, searching Chris's eyes for help. "It's, um, a date." She made it sound as though that would suffice. No more information was needed, she felt.

Aleks, not to be left in the dark said, "Well, yes, I can see that. It's got to be an important date to have it inked on your skin forever."

Chris wished for an interruption—any kind of interruption. Muriel searched her daughter's eyes before offering a response to Aleks. "Well now, that's her secret and she wishes to leave it that way." Then she smiled as politely as she could so as not to be rude to Aleks.

"Cool," Aleks said not entirely begrudgingly. "Speaking of secrets, I suppose we all have our little secrets, don't we?" She glared knowingly at Chris who responded only by ignoring her.

"And if we tell them, then they're no longer secrets," Ruthie remarked, gaining some degree of courage. Her mother's little nod told her she'd handled it well.

Emil, who was loath to participating in conversations unless he was asked a question, directed his comment to his mother. "Secrets. I'm not very good at keeping secrets, I'm not, unless the person makes me say, 'Cross my heart and hope to die.' I don't want to die so I have to keep those secrets. I do." He nodded at Beryl for approval.

Beryl gave him a warm maternal smile and a loving pat on his shoulder. "Emil, listen, I'm going to share a secret with you."

He looked perplexed. Finally he spoke, "But everyone will hear it unless you whisper in my ear, but, uh, you always tell me it's not polite in front of other people to do that."

Beryl agreed with her son, "You're so right, dear, yes indeed, I have told you that on more than one occasion." Then she announced out of the blue for all to hear, "I'll bet no one can guess my real occupation."

The guests looked bewildered. Then a chorus rang out saying "Reporter! Journalist! Writer!" It was obvious. She had written for The Hillside Journal. Everyone knew that. When Beryl's response was nothing more than a poker face, they whispered among themselves. Then Beryl smiled broadly. She was the cat who'd eaten not just *one* canary but a whole bellyful of them. When she told the secret she'd held onto for many years, they gasped.

"Well, I'll be," Father Bernie said, his brows reaching a height not seen before. "Who'd have thunk? You, Beryl Baines, our local observer and chronicler of local facts and real events? Nah, not possible."

Aleks continued the bombardment. "Wow! The only thing I can say to that is that you must have had a string of lovers."

"You don't have to, to write about them. It's all just a formula, and, a good imagination," she explained with a sheepish grin. Her eyes said more. She allowed them to travel, expressing her inner racy thoughts.

This seemed to intrigue Aleks to no end. "Then I would guess you've been married and divorced. So how many times? And I would imagine you'd have to have, uh, experiences." Then she wondered aloud, "Are they steamy, your novels, I mean?"

"Sizzling, red hot," a different sounding Beryl purred. Raising and lowering her eyebrows provocatively, she fed that one's curiosity. She expected the conversation would go above Emil's head. Why, not, shell it out. It was what Aleks wanted to hear. She hoped the rest of the group would not think any the less of her for the genre she'd chosen to put food on the table for herself and Emil.

Emil had hung onto the thought of his mother being married and so he was drawn into the conversation. "Mom is married. She's married to Billy Baines. That's my dad."

"And Billy Baines has been, uh, absent since..." Beryl saw fit to explain but was interrupted, gratefully.

"Last year, since last year, Mom. Billy Baines comes around one time a year, to see me," Emil interjected, "and you; he comes to see you, too". He began to count on his fingers. He looked down at his hands, embarrassed. "But, um, he always brings a nice friend with him, sometimes it's the same pretty girl, sometimes not. They're my friends." Beryl looked away. Silent.

"I'd love to read one of those romance novels but I'm not sure I'd recognize your pseudonym," Aleks said feigning interest. Chris was relieved, however, that she focused on someone other than herself—or on him.

"Now that is truly my secret, and it's going to stay that way," she added glibly with a sly grin.

With that said, the topic changed and Aleks yawned, a loud pretentious one, nearly exposing her uvula. "Sorry," she complained once her jaws had relaxed. "It's not the company. It's that darn time difference. I just got here yesterday, and you know it takes a few days to go away entirely."

Ada Powers sat bolt upright in her chair. "I thought you just landed, um, a few hours ago. Whatever do you mean, Aleks?"

"Well," Aleks began her defense in a lackadaisical tone of voice. "I flew in to JKF and I, uh, crashed at Becky's loft in Manhattan. You remember Becky Samuelson, from school, don't you?"

First Ada shrugged then she nodded affirmatively but her eyes said otherwise. It's was easier to agree. The name did not ring a bell for her; she was obviously peeved at her daughter.

"College pal, Mom," Aleks said taking a long draught of wine. "We did Christmas Eve together, just us two. Poor kid, she's fresh off a real lousy break-up, like yours truly, and so we, uh, commiserated and then we partied...Well, it was a long night, but here I am, and I'm so glad I was able to find out where you'd be today. Imagine, back in Birch Valley."

Ada wouldn't let go. "But I thought you just got here today." She sighed. Jack Powers figured he'd stay out of it. Let his wife beef. She was good at it. He helped himself to more wine.

"Today, yesterday, hey, the thing is I'm here today with you and Dad for Christmas," she protested. "And I'll be staying in the area for a few more days."

Emil began to twirl a bread stick so vigorously that it flew out of control and boinged Father Bernie's glass causing a pinging sound. Bernie only gave him a sneaky aside smile and whipped it back to Emil. Beryl placed her hand over the missile, which told Emil, 'Enough.' Bernie accepted a refill on his wine from Jack who had placed the decanter directly in front of him. Chris wondered how long it would take his dear pastor before the corny joke telling would begin. Not that a little comic relief would be unwelcome.

But no, not yet. Aleks grabbed still another opportunity to run the show. Her next assault began with asking how she should address Chris. "So Chris, tell me, is it Father Tosi, Reverend Tosi, or whatever? What do we call you?" she asked in a playful tone, which irritated Chris. Her body language told him she was flirting.

Pretending not to care, Chris answered, "Father Chris is what I go by, but to my friends I'm Chris, as always." He hoped the guests didn't notice how uncomfortable he was with Aleks, despite the mess he was making ripping apart a dinner roll.

"Oh, Chris, we were so much more than friends," she cooed with a killer smile, intending for all to get the message.

"I like to think we're all friends here at our table." He tried to deflect her blows. "Aleks, you should remember Marty Tisdale, the guy right next to you. We were in the same class at State."

Marty to the rescue. "Right and I remember you there, too." Sylvie shot him a suspicious look.

Then Aleks announced to the guests, "And our good friend Chris took off like a locomotive and finished his degree in record time." She went on, "Oh, Chris, I admire you so much. A real scholar you were." Chris prayed it would end there.

"That wasn't it at all," he said wearily. "I just wanted to be done with it, and graduate early. There were other things on my mind that I needed to explore, and I'm so glad that I did."

"Oh, yes, and now you're a priest." She was smug, nodding at him, looking through him. "Who would have guessed, you of all people, Chris? Surely not I."

Oh, if only the next course would arrive, Chris hoped. Anything to take the focus off Aleks and him. Fortunately, Sylvie rose to stretch, drawing attention to her condition. She apologized for distracting the others as she caught the table leg causing her dishes and glasses to rattle. Chris could have hugged her though. Now it was her turn to answer questions: How far along was she? Was the baby's kicking uncomfortable during the long meal? What names had they picked out?

She said to Aleks, "The baby, it only flitters from time to time, that's all." Occasionally, she had to think of the correct English word and it embarrassed her when she was mistaken.

Marty said, "Sylvie, I think you mean flutter, not flitter." The affection in his voice made any corrections he might make acceptable to her. She'd always insisted that she wanted to speak correct English.

"Oh, your English language, so many words, so many like the others. OK, I feel flutter," she said with a nervous laugh, as she sat back down.

Out of the blue came Aleks again, "Say, Chris, I mean Father Chris. Sorry, I just have to try that out. Does it ever sound weird to me, calling you Father." She glanced at the mess he'd made with the roll. She gave him a knowing look and tapped his toe under the table, which drew a knee jerk reaction and a wincing that he hoped he'd squelched before it became obvious to the others.

He said nothing. He'd let her say what was on her mind.

"Remember the last time we saw each other?" She asked pointedly.

"Uh, not really," he said trying to be casual, but figured he'd better say something innocuous, whatever came to mind that would put an end to her attention getting behavior, her attention directed to him. "I guess it was high school." He had now stacked the roll remnants into a neat little pile. Emil began to do the same thing. Conversation often bored him.

Aleks could see Chris begin to unravel. "No, wrong," she blurted triumphantly. "It was at the Student Center at State." She paused waiting for him to speak. He didn't. He sipped more water. "You and another guy—kind of a cute one if I remember correctly—you were all sitting with a bunch of girls. They were hanging all over you guys. It looked like you were studying, going over notes, or something."

"Probably were," he said, rising to a standing position. Fred gestured to Chris to be seated as he himself went into the kitchen to help. He returned in a flash, a shy grin on his face. No, Marie didn't need his help.

"That woman, she's got everything under control," Fred announced. Chris thought, 'I only wish I did.' To him, it was an eternity between the last course and the next.

Aleks could keep it up forever. She seemed to be enjoying watching Chris squirm. Chris explained to her that he, Marty and some girls in his class were filling in gaps in their notes, studying together for a European literature exam. He recalled that she came up behind him and ran her fingers through his dark wavy hair, whispering seductively 'Guess who, Sweetie?' However, he wouldn't give her the satisfaction of revealing that detail, or of guessing who it was back then. Not here at the Christmas dinner table in front of all the guests.

Marty, he told her, was that other cute guy. He watched Sylvie give her husband a loving look. If Chris hadn't invited Aleks to join them back then, which obviously upset her, it was because they needed to focus on the notes for the exam. She would be bored, he told her.

"No, I wouldn't be bored, not at all. I would've enjoyed the company. Maybe I'd have taken the course next semester," Aleks protested. "Now I remember it all. You, Chris, put your arm around the girl sitting next to you, saying you two had a date right after the review session. And you, Marty, gave the redhead a glance and said pretty much the same thing. So that meant I'd be left with the others—all of them girls. I got the message and so I just left. I was pretty put out, I'll have you know."

By that point Chris was feeling dizzy with all the attention focused on his end of the table with Aleks always vying for center stage. Who really cared when they last saw each other? Certainly not the other guests, but they were listening nevertheless. He wished they weren't.

"So you guys were Lit majors?" she assumed, as though she really cared.

"Yup, I was," Marty said with pride in his voice. "And now I teach English at Birch Valley High, all levels, Advanced Placement included." He was proud to be asked to teach the premier English course for bright seniors and utilize what he had learned in his studies to enrich their experience, to demonstrate the value of the liberal arts, which he professed would serve them well in whatever path of life or career they ultimately chose to follow. Marty spared the guests any defense he would make for his work. He could only imagine how Aleks would react to it. He was about to get a taste of it.

"Oh, I'm so sorry for you," she feigned sympathy. "You have my condolences. Teen-age brats! You poor thing. And English—of all subjects—yuck! What a waste."

Sylvie chimed in. "Well, he loves it, and he does it well. For him it is his passion." Sylvie felt she needed to defend his career choice. Her own mother was, still is, a professor in Paris at the Sorbonne.

Marty couldn't resist putting Aleks in her place. "Well, it's just one of my passions. Come into my class if you dare, then you'll be forced to rethink your judgment. The kids are great. And I'll have you know my other passion is my Sylvie."

"Oh, *mon cher*," Sylvie gushed. She touched his arm and gave him a smile that could melt ice.

"Father," Aleks exaggerated the word, refocusing her attention on Chris. "Father Chris, I suppose you were an English major too."

"You suppose wrong, Aleks," he said resolutely. "I wasn't." He turned away from her, hoping it would end her inquisition. Why should she even care? The door to the dining room swung open just in the nick of time. He thought he might have upbraided Aleks a moment ago if she'd kept on. For someone who wasn't even going to eat, she eyed the main dishes like a bird of prey as Marie wheeled in the tea cart. Thankfully, the delectable aromas seemed to clear the air and release the tension that he imagined was obvious to others.

"Enjoy," Marie said proudly. "Savor each bite, but don't forget to save room for desserts. More good old family recipes." Then she remembered that Ada had left another dessert on the kitchen table. She figured that it would be a slight not to serve it as well. What's wrong with guests having a sampler?

Finally, Marie herself sat at the dining room table. She hoped no one heard her little sigh. It felt good, relaxing, to finally join the others. She was especially pleased that Father Bernie seemed to be enjoying her cuisine and the company. He'd been unusually reserved, listening to the others.

"Best cooking I've had in a long time, Marie Tosi," he said. "I'm savoring every morsel of every course. Different from the kind of cooking I'm used to. That's not to say that Mrs. Hopkins isn't good, but yours is still the best in the world."

"Maybe not the world, Father, but certainly the best in the house. I'll take credit for that," she said beaming. Fred showed her his exaggerated frown. He couldn't fry an egg or boil water successfully. But then again, he never had to. "Oh, Father," she said as though she'd just remembered something. "I was sorry to get the call the other day about your sister. It would've been so nice if she could make it."

He stopped chewing a moment to respond. "Oh, you mean Molly. Yeah, so sorry it was last minute. She's got some health problems, you know. She's getting on in years, well, like all of us. I'll be spending a few days with her to keep her company and cheer her up a little. Gotta prepare her for what she won't want to hear. I've been named the designated person to tell her that she's, uh, going to assisted living. Me, her only surviving brother. Tell you the truth, I'm not looking forward to that, nosiree. You'd think her useless son would do the honors. Nah, not him, so that leaves yours truly."

Chris brightened and smiled when he addressed his pastor. "I'm sure you'll cheer her up all right with your corny jokes."

"Hey, wait a minute. If they're so corny why would people laugh at them?" he asked half seriously.

"At *them*?" Chris chided.

"Well, of course at them, what else? Laugh at me?" Bernie was being lured into a trap.

Marie took charge at this point. "How about if I make up a nice plate for Molly and you can take it to her when you visit?"

Bernie told her it would be very nice. He thanked her. But he wasn't through with Chris; he'd show him for ridiculing his joke telling.

"Well, now since we're talking about Molly and assisted living and all, let me tell you about the last time Molly was driving some of her lady friends to lunch. Yup, I've just got to tell you what happened to dear old Molly."

He poised to begin; first a wistful look appeared on his face, then dead pan. His customary raconteur mode set in and would prevail. It had to do with the element of surprise, he calculated, but would never reveal it to his audience until the end. Bernie paused until he had everyone's attention. Silence. All eyes and ears were focused on him.

"WELL, MY SISTER GOES out in her old Chevy with three of her cronies, uh, lady friends, in the back seat. No room in the front passenger seat. Got all sorts of stuff all over so no one can sit there. That's Molly for you. She's not the most organized. Well, anyhow she's driving along, so she tells me, when she hears a siren. And she can't tell where it was coming from. Hard to tell, you know? She figures she's OK, abiding by the law, no broken taillights or such. She's sure she's following the speed limit so she just keeps on driving along. The posted speed limit on that stretch of the road was 45 miles per hour.

"Then she sees those flashing lights come up right up close behind her. She goes, 'Uh-oh, a cop. I better pull over.' The police officer pulls over as well. He motions for her to roll down her window, which the good woman does. Then she fishes in her big old purse for her driver's license, and she pokes around in the glove box for her registration in her typical style—slo mo. By that time, her hands are shaking so bad she drops the cards. The officer must've been a saint; he waited so long for her to hunt and dig them out of the mess on her seat. Uh-oh, one had fallen down somewhere on the floor, which had all kinds of papers all over. Well, anyhow the conversation went something like this, so she tells me if I've got it right.

Officer: Where you going ma'am?

Molly: Taking my friends to Welch's Deli.

Office: Are you in a hurry? They're open all day, you know.

(He poked his head into the back seat and saw that the three passengers there were huddled together, pale as ghosts and shaking like leaves in a nor'easter.)

Molly: No, sir. No hurry.

Officer: Do you know the speed limit here?

Molly: Sure do, Officer, sign says 91.

Officer: What?! Lady, that's not the speed limit. It's the route number.

Molly: Oh dear, sorry, Officer, I must've got the signs mixed up.

Officer: Those ladies back there are white with fright. Why do you suppose that is?

Molly: Oh dear, I wonder if that's because we just came off of route 110; were on it for maybe 15 minutes or so."

EVERYONE AT THE TABLE roared, from snooty Aleks to her prim mother. Beryl almost choked on a piece of pork. After she caught her breath she had to explain the humor to Emil, who finally got it and burst out laughing, a guffaw they'd never heard from him before.

Marie pondered a moment, then she had to ask him, "Now Father, be honest, did that really happen to Molly?"

"Heavens, no," he admitted. "But since we were talking about her, I figured, why not make her the lady in my joke? And Molly was fair game, the way we always teased each other and our dearly departed brothers, too. But, no, she hasn't driven in years. Bad eyes."

Guests then told Chris he was too hard on Bernie, that if this was a sample of his humor it wasn't at all corny. They wanted more, but Bernie graciously declined when he met Chris's eyes.

As the main course was finishing up, Fred informed the guests that he needed a little fresh air. He suggested that the guys join him out in the sun room for a cigar break while Marie made coffee and trayed up the desserts. When he asked if there were any takers, all the men except Emil and Chris got up from the table.

"I can open up my box of new Cuban cigars—Cohibas," he said proudly displaying the contents of the box he'd received as a gift from one of the neighbors for whom he'd done restoration work on a breakfront.

"And another thing you can open up are the windows out there since you'll be stinking up the sun room," Marie said feigning exasperation. She wasn't at all thrilled at the idea of cigars, but once in a while it was OK, she conceded, and it was Christmas, after all.

"Yes, dear," he said with a sly smile. She wouldn't be as conciliatory if company wasn't present. Chris gave Bernie a look but Bernie only gave him a 'What the heck' look in return. Then Fred motioned to Marty to come upstairs with him to grab the coats. Chris seized the moment to intervene again in the kitchen to help his mother cut the cake and fill the cannoli. With the two of them working together, it would speed up the smoke break, he hoped.

It was more the aroma of espresso and dark roast coffee brewing that lured the men in sooner rather than later. Plus, with the windows open out there, the breeze was blowing the ashes about. They were glad to come in and warm up. Fred told them to drape their coats over the chair backs, which Marie usually frowned upon but dinner was almost over so she relented.

Marie's tiramisu was a hit. Chris told his mother that her mini cannoli were the best she'd ever made. She credited him with putting on the finishing touches—candied fruit on some, shaved dark chocolate on others. Marie said she'd be happy to put on an Italian dessert demonstration for anyone interested if they could all find a compatible date. Chris doubted that it would happen. He knew the women too well. Marie ended the holiday meal bringing out an array of cordials that she'd kept hidden from Fred for what she said was 'ages'. Most passed, but Aleks asked if she could sample a few before deciding. She gulped down a shot glass of Bailey's Irish Cream only minutes before announcing that she really should think of running along and catch up on her sleep. After all, she had to take her mother to the doctor's early in the morning, and oh, that jet lag. You don't get over it in one day, she reminded everyone a second time.

"But not till ten, Aleks dear. I don't see Dr. Glassman all that early," Ada called out. "You know it's not like me to make early morning appointments."

Aleks saw fit to inform her mother that she had been nursing a splitting headache for the last several minutes and should really be going.

As the day came to a close, guests began to leave in pairs, as they had arrived. Marie gave each guest a goodie box. She packed a large case for Molly with enough food for a good three days. Father Bernie said he'd be much obliged to help her out during his visit. Once the guests had left, the Tosis and Father Bernie exchanged gifts.

As Chris was getting ready to leave he felt a prick from a sharp object in his coat pocket—the violin ornament from the poinsettia plant they'd found in the garden. He handed it to Marie and told her to put it somewhere on the Christmas tree. He didn't need it. She reminded him that all decorations including the tree were being taken down first thing tomorrow and stored away for another year. To her Christmas was over until next year. She'd done her part for the holiday. She saw no need to prolong it. So she handed it back to him. He hoped he didn't show the disappointment he was feeling. Maybe he'd put it back on the poinsettia plant. Its new home would be the first floor sitting room where Bernie received guests. He'd try to avoid that room but Bernie wouldn't even give it a thought.

Chapter EIGHTEEN
(The following morning)

FATHER BERNIE RETURNED from early morning mass humming the refrain from the recessional hymn, "Joy to the World" as he entered the kitchen. He broke into the lyrics "And heav'n and nature sing" singing with gusto. Then he saw Chris, slouched at the breakfast table, head in hands. Only when Chris looked up did Bernie notice how disheveled he was. Ignoring the obvious, Bernie offered his usual pleasantries with a smile, hoping to bring good cheer to his sleepy associate. Chris returned a groggy grin. And then Bernie knew it was one of those nightmares. All he had to do was look at Chris. Usually the yelling disturbs Bernie's sleep, but not Christmas night.

Chris admitted it was a rough night. When it was those dreaded banshees, ranting and raving during the chase scene, he always woke up sweating. This time it was more lucid, like frames in a film moving through their sequence, a little more awful than usual. There were three of them, ragged and hag-like, in flight pursuing a speeding vehicle. Their long, stringy hair flapped maniacally propelled by the night winds. There was something that was clouding the air, obscuring his vision—snow crystals, sleet particles, some type of icy precipitation. He couldn't tell. But he could make out faces this time clearly enough—at first, not alien but familiar. At the forefront were two of the creatures—one with his basketball buddy Anton Drobec's face, the other with his very own, but it was an older haggard version of himself. Behind them was a scrawny banshee equally haggard in appearance. He recognized it as a wizened version of Aleks Powers. She was yanking the two men, pulling them in the opposite direction away from the vehicle. Chris didn't need a psychiatrist to interpret this latest nightmare of the accident scene. He was horrified at its implications.

"Are you OK?" Bernie asked Chris, pouring him more coffee and a cup for himself, too. Chris's response was ambiguous, a single shoulder hike that defied interpretation. He was still reeling from the shock of the nightmare. He nodded reluctantly, slowly, affirmatively.

Bernie figured he would stress the positive. "Ah, what a glorious day, Christmas was," he said hoping to jolt Chris back to the real world. "Everything went perfectly, from midnight mass to that feast at your parents' home. Pleasant company, too, well for the most part. You know what I mean. Boy, if I ate your mother's cooking every day I'd be as big as an elephant."

Chris chuckled, trying to imagine a Bernie avatar in a fat suit. "Right you are about that. If I may be so bold, you were well fueled yesterday, no wonder you slept so soundly."

"Well, I did have a designated driver for which I have to say, thank you," Bernie said, bowing slightly as he cleared the table. Chris only nodded, managing a weak smile. He was still drained.

"All right. OK. But how about no Monday morning quarterbacking, Chris? Deal?" Bernie requested, half in jest. "You were the one who brought it up first with that fueling nonsense."

"Yeah, I guess I did. I'm very, very beat this morning. Sorry. I'm just feeling the effects, or rather the after effects of everything,'" Chris explained. "Too many shockers, that's what it was."

"I think we were all shocked that that Glory girl actually showed up at midnight mass and played so beautifully. But that was a good kind of shock, if that's the right word. Oh, she did just fine on that violin of hers. So surprising, considering," Bernie said thoughtfully. He remembered how obnoxious she had been that night he encountered her in the garden, and then there was that poem...and what it could lead to, an issue waiting to be dealt with and resolved.

"Well, I didn't expect to see that kind of corsage on her," Chris said, looking crestfallen. "I'll bet my life she was the one that stole my precious Christmas roses and then left a replacement token in their place—that weird looking poinsettia. I swear she must've painted the edges of the petals to match the roses, and then there was that little violin thing attached. That sure smacks of Glory."

"Yeah," Bernie agreed. He seemed almost amused at her antics. "That little violin thing. It must be her calling card. Heh heh."

"Oh, come on, Bernie," Chris retorted. "Let's hope she doesn't call on either of us any time soon. There's no need for her to intrude upon us. Christmas is over. We don't need her and she doesn't need us."

"I'm not worried about her coming to see me. She doesn't like me, for sure," Bernie stated with conviction. "But you, on the other hand...I'm sure you haven't seen the last of her. I trust her brother's appraisal of her rather than her appraisal of him." He recalled what Glen Thomas had revealed to him in his office.

"Never mind me." Chris needed to drop the subject. He too feared the consequences associated with the poem. "The shocker that really got me was Aleks, not only her presence at my parents' house but those insinuations. You saw how she kept jabbing at me.

She's nasty. Her parents I could have taken, but her, too much of the past comes to mind," he said grimacing, shaking his head.

"Yeah, she could use a few lessons in propriety," Bernie said, pursing his lips. That look of his reminded Chris of his ninth grade English teacher Mrs. Finley when she wanted to stress a point. At times Chris felt like laughing at the similarity, but he didn't want to insult Bernie who certainly meant well and could resent any such comparison.

Chris wasn't so sure he was comfortable sharing the latest variation on his nightmare, but he couldn't resist the one detail that shocked him the most. "I saw her. She's one of the banshees, Bernie. I saw Aleks's face. How can she be involved in my dream?" he blurted in spite of himself. "She was there and I can't stand being in her presence, in any state of mind, awake or asleep."

"That was pretty evident at the table," Bernie said. He hoped Chris would tell him more about the nightmare that left him in such a state of mind. He could wait though—if and when Chris was ready. "Oh, Chris, I must say I was surprised to see, uh, Kendra's parents at your folks' house."

"Her parents?" he repeated absentmindedly. "Not really. Remember, they used to live in our neighborhood, only a few blocks away. I don't believe my mother has kept in touch with them very much since the accident, but, Aleks, as I said, seeing her at my house was overwhelming."

Bernie said nothing. He simply nodded, figuring Chris would go on, which he did.

"She'd married some wealthy English guy. It was quite a scandal over there, we heard. She'd dropped out of State University to 'find herself' so she'd told everyone and went abroad. After some time she got a job as an au pair, and what she did find was that the children she cared for were not enough. Their father, though, was. Knowing Aleks and how she goes after a guy, the father took a fancy to her, divorced his wife and married her. She'd been in England until, from what I gathered, just recently. I could be wrong. I really don't know when they split or do I care. I had a chance to get my mother alone in the kitchen for a few minutes, and she filled me in in part. Long story short, Aleks is recently divorced and, I assume, looking for herself once more. Or worse, looking for someone."

"Let's hope that someone isn't you. After yesterday, I wouldn't be too surprised, " Bernie said. Then he felt ashamed for uttering those words. "Let's hope she finds herself. Sounds to me like a lost soul."

"In more ways than one," Chris remarked. He was relieved that she'd be leaving for England in a few days. If he could just get her out of his head, he'd be OK.

Bernie persisted, "You know, I found it strange the way she focused on you. Couldn't take her eyes off you." Chris did not need to be reminded of that.

"Yeah, I noticed. I'd be blind if I didn't. But I tried to avoid eye contact with her hoping it would divert her attention." Chris paused, then he avoided eye contact with Bernie. Get the focus back on Bernie, he thought. He'd had it with references to Aleks. "And you, you hit the sauce a few more times and got caught up in a silly tale of yours."

"No matter, they were a rapt audience. How they all loved the Molly story. Heh heh. Hey, if I recall, you agreed to no more Monday morning quarterbacking," he said striking back at Chris. Bernie knew Chris would come around. He always did.

"Did I say that? Well, I must have been in the fog..." Chris said, trying to get his wits about him. Once he'd had his second cup of coffee he was revived and the effects of the nightmare lessened so he could undertake his daily responsibilities clear headed.

"You know you did. Don't take this the wrong way now, Chris, but did you ever have any interest in, uh, Kendra's sister Aleks once upon a time?" he asked. "I sense you must have at one time or another, judging from the way she looked at you. She certainly implied...you know what I mean."

"Oh, Bernie, I take it back about your speculations. You're right on the money," Chris admitted sheepishly. "Well, yeah, I did, and man do I regret it. She was sore; I guess you'd say downright vindictive when I started dating her older sister. They were only one year or so apart in age. Aleks did all she could to try to break us up—spread rumors and stuff. Kendra just ignored them. She knew her sister."

Bernie asked, "Being so close in age, were the sisters close at all?"

Chris looked upward to one side, trying to recall what he hadn't repressed or forgotten. "It was so long ago. I'm going to say 'no.'" He paused. "I adored Kendra from the time we starting dating, and I was so glad to get rid of Aleks. She was such a phony. I think, though, they may possibly have shared some things. Girls do. Plus, they shared a room, so there couldn't have been too many secrets. Hard to hide anything in such close quarters. But I wouldn't put it past Aleks to sneak around or eavesdrop. She would have gone to just about any measures to break us up. I think she always figured she still had a chance with me."

Bernie thought maybe he could help if he knew more about Chris's situation. Chris would only reveal so much. Thus far, Chris hadn't achieved much success with counseling. At best it was nothing more than a Band-aid. As the anniversary of the tragedy approached, very little helped. Only prayer kept him afloat during the most stressful moments.

Bernie said sympathetically, "You'll never get over your loss." He himself had lost brother after brother, a few sisters-in-law, too, but not tragically and not in their teen age years.

"Losses, Bernie," Chris said sadly. "I lost my twin sister Beth, my only sibling, which was in effect losing part of me. That's what it felt like, sometimes, still does. And my parents lost me in a sense. Sure, I come by as often as possible to visit, but they'll never have grand-children. They have no legacy in that regard. They go on sailing through life doing their daily chores as best they can, but in their private moments, I can only imagine, as in my own private moments...I lost my Kendra and Kendra lost her future, our future together."

Bernie ignored the reference to his girl friend. " Oh, pooh. What do you mean about your parents? Look what they have in you? They must be so proud."

Chris was pacing in the corridor. He needed to end this conversation, but at times Bernie could get in a talkative mood. He only wanted to help, if Chris was willing to open up.

"Oh, I guess they are proud, that is...Oh, Bernie, I can't help it. I relive that scenario over and over again in mind. The two girls in their new ski outfits, the ski date that we couldn't keep, that extra basketball practice for a special game that I never even got to play...How could I?"

He paused. Bernie heard him sigh. Chris spoke slowly, remembering, reliving the pain and loss of those days. It was as though he had rehearsed these lines over and over like for a scene in a play; they were engrained in his memory, replete with the emotional effect. "I'm sure I've told you this before, Bernie. I wound up giving up basketball altogether. My life just went to pieces. I don't how I made it through the rest of the school year. I gave up my basketball scholarship to Providence College, lived at home, and commuted to State —for my parents' sake mostly—but

I felt I just didn't know where else to go, what to do with my life – it was the same all throughout my college years. That car crash...If only we'd been there, Anton and I, we might have handled the car differently and swerved out of harm's way. Saved the girls. Saved lives, and gone on with our plans for the future."

Bernie listened intently and Chris stopped pacing. "Now, Chris, you don't know that," Bernie argued. "All four of you might have been killed."

"No, I don't know that, and I never will," Chris said resolutely. He took a deep breath and continued, "There's one more thing you don't know, Bernie, and it's hard for me to admit this. I'm not sure if Aleks knew—I hope she didn't—but there were three deaths that night. And that haunts me in ways you can't imagine. I've never told this to anyone. I could never say it, but here goes...Kendra was nine weeks pregnant." He turned away from Bernie. "There, I said it."

Bernie did not do a good job of covering his shock. But with his age and experience, he thought he'd heard it all. And he knew all could be forgiven. "Oh, my. I am really sorry. That explains a lot. The nightmares...the banshees, especially now that you've seen them with faces, I think. It even explains why you're so unnerved in Glory's presence. She could very well be a reminder of what could have been...had, you know...had a, uh, daughter...the resemblance and all to Kendra."

"Hmm...you know, I never thought of it that way, consciously that is, but the subconscious can be a pretty powerful force; I guess it can color one's perception and...fuel one's fears." Chris was ruminating. He knew what dreams were made of.

"And...it can also play tricks on you. Dreams are not always what you think they mean. And they're certainly not logical or coherent. But they can surely dominate your thoughts, haunt you," Bernie added, having seen enough evidence of it in his own household. "Fairly impossible to maneuver when you're sleeping. But don't let your dreams drive you. You don't want to lose control, Chris."

Chris was troubled, and Bernie was there for him, Bernie with no graduate degree in clinical psychology, but gifted with a sixth sense and spiritual awareness sweetened with a healthy dose of common sense.

But all it took for Chris was seeing Aleks again and dodging her insinuations and tell-tale glances. He would have rather that she'd just come out and said things instead of tormenting him. Finally Chris spoke. "Aleks knew," he said, then he hesitated a long moment. "I think, she did that, uh, Kendra was... I don't think Kendra would have told her that early on, but I strongly suspect that Aleks found out some way or another. That would have incensed her because then she knew that Kendra and I would be bound together for a lifetime as a family."

---------❦---------

THAT LAST NIGHT HE was with Kendra will forever be etched in his mind. It was mid-week, a few days before the tragedy. Beth had just left to drive Anton back to his host parents' home so Chris found himself alone with Kendra in the Tosi family's room where the four friends had gathered to watch the first half of a college basketball game on TV. The third quarter had not yet begun. Chris was bursting with excitement and couldn't contain himself any longer. This was the time to show her the letter that had arrived earlier that day. His parents already knew but were sworn to secrecy until after he'd told the news to Kendra. He expected her to be thrilled for him. She too was relieved that they finally had the opportunity to talk in private. She had held a secret inside her for weeks now. She decided this was the time to reveal to him what he had not suspected. He went first. Not only had he'd earned early admission to Providence College but he had received a basketball scholarship and full tuition. He studied her for a reaction, hoping she would share the same joy as he did. Instead, Kendra blanched at what that could mean for her, for them, for their future. When Chris heard the news that she was pregnant it hit him like a sucker punch. They both looked stricken.

BERNIE JUMPED IN. "That Aleks found out that her sister was pregnant, maybe so, but maybe not. But don't dwell on that after all these years. What good will it do you now?" Now it was Bernie's turn to end this conversation.

Chris sighed. "I'd like to think I have no idea why she chose to come to our house for Christmas dinner. But knowing her, I think I do. She could have gone to see her parents later in the evening. After all, she didn't even bother to see them Christmas Eve. Did she really have to spend that time in New York with her friend instead of family? No, but that's Aleks for you. She does what she wants when she wants...thinks only of herself. Her own parents lost a child, and what does she do? She runs off to Europe on an adventure, no, not right away, but she could have stuck around for the sake of her parents. Oh no, she and I did not part on good terms, and she had to know I'd be there at my parents' house for Christmas dinner. You know, I couldn't really bring myself to speak to her after the accident. She went to all kinds of measures to reconnect with me, but I didn't want anything to do with her. I paid my condolences to her and her family and that was it. I avoided her as best I could that last semester I was in high school. She did come up to me at my graduation after her parents and mine received diplomas for Beth and Kendra. The whole event was more than I could bear. And, uh, the only other time I saw her was that encounter in the Student Center, and, I must admit, I was hardly civil. She still resents my avoiding her. I snubbed her, you might say. Long time to hold a grudge."

Bernie thought a minute. A long pregnant pause. "Oh, Chris, come on now, she wanted to be with her parents at Christmas. That's why she came to your house. Probably figured she'd just endure your presence, easy enough to do with so many guests there, but we both saw that she couldn't. Now Chris, let the passage of time and your prayers blunt those negative feelings, your anguish, and your suspicions, too."

"Such sensible advice, Bernie, and I should follow it. But all of a sudden I bring up the pregnancy, and it's no longer a thought I can release. It doesn't fly into thin air. No, it becomes tangible, so real to me, another loss I sustained...but I swear...I'd never mentioned to anyone...never uttered the word—pregnancy." Chris was shaking. The very word had the ability to wound. He watched Bernie cogitating, measuring what he would say next.

Bernie nodded as much to say, 'I hear you.' But a thought came to him and he was as hesitant as Chris was in verbalizing it. "Were you, uh, um, ever intimate with Aleks at one time or another, if I may be so bold as to ask?" There, he said it. It might help him better understand Chris's stance on Aleks. It had to be more than meets the eye.

Chris looked at him long and hard. He wasn't sure how he felt—mostly confused, befuddled as to where this would lead, and he was tiring of this exploration into his past. He took a deep breath and let it out slowly. "Nothing else to hide," he said with a shrug. "I suppose there's no harm in telling at this time, but yes, I was. I'm ashamed to admit." Then a faraway look overtook him. "After much flirting on her part she thought she'd won me over that spring, and she sort of did. She was so sexy and outgoing, the way she dressed, the way she smelled, the way she moved, you know the kind, always seeking and getting attention. And there I was, a vulnerable hormone-charged adolescent. Long story short, I, uh, lost my virginity to Aleks one night. It only happened once, I swear. It didn't take very long to see what kind of a person she was, definitely not my type. What did I know at that age? Then over the summer before senior year, I started dating her sister—a much nicer girl.

"When Kendra found out she was pregnant, things changed. They had to. My plans were still to go on to college, but I would marry her first. I told her I would do the right thing. We'd have to finish high school and face our parents and friends and...Aleks. I guess I was afraid of the whole thing. Oh, it wouldn't have been easy, not at all, but we'd have managed somehow, at least I think we would've. I was young and in love and then, by some cruel hand of fate, we were robbed of our future together, however that would have played out, and now here I am as you see me." Chris was spent. Then he relaxed and said, "Don't get me wrong, Bernie, I am so blessed to be here."

They were both silent for a time. Bernie broke the silence. "Yes, you've picked up the pieces and reshaped them beautifully into a meaningful spiritual life. You are a devout and beloved priest, a good person who does so much good for others."

Surprisingly, after Chris bared his soul, he felt a sense of relief. "Thanks, Bernie, much thanks to you in shaping me. I needed to hear that. I'm sorry, sorry, sorry. Yes, I've redirected my life and my goals."

"You certainly have, Chris. However, my suggestion for you to resume therapy is now a strong recommendation. Though I can't force you to do so against your will." Bernie was right but Chris wasn't ready at this time. Each year after Christmas, with the start of the new year, he usually lightened up and the nightmares vanished, but right on target with the anniversary of the accident night, they reemerged, banshees and all.

Not wanting to make a commitment at this time, Chris whispered, "We'll see. I'll think about it."

Bernie could read him like a book. "Ah, my dearly departed mother's favorite stall phrase. And yes, we will see. But listen, I may have thrown a monkey wrench into your healing process. I don't know if you'd heard me, but I opened my mouth to Aleks and her parents to, uh, come make a visit to your beautiful garden. After reading Beryl's article I figured they might be intrigued and come check it out for themselves."

" I wouldn't be concerned about that. They must have seen that by then you were three sheets to the wind and that the offer was at best lukewarm. I mean, why would Aleks want to come and visit my garden? No offense. Only if she had a reason, would she come, but I see no reason at all for her to come here. I think I made my thoughts very plain to her."

"Oh, come on, I was only being friendly to them," Bernie said. "Besides the idea of a prayer garden might do Aleks some good."

Chris's expression told Bernie he was out of his mind, not very priestly of him. "You don't know Aleks. There's always a motive. She sets her sights on something or someone and there she goes—right after it. No, she'll probably just head back to England; there's not much around here for her."

"One last thing, then I'll drop any comments about Aleks. I have to ask you: does she look very much like your Kendra?" Bernie asked. The method to his madness was clear to Chris.

"I really couldn't stand to look at her Christmas day, but the funny thing is that years ago it was hard to tell they were sisters. But on Christmas, I think she had done her darnedest to copy Kendra as she remembered her, from her hairstyle to her mannerisms. She'd even changed her hair color," Chris said, hoping he wasn't imagining it.

"After all this time, how can you be so sure? Girls that age are always experimenting with their looks. I shouldn't have even asked you. I'm sorry. Let's drop the whole thing and move on. How about coming outside with me for a few minutes and take a little stroll in your garden? Fresh air will do you good. Then I've got to get ready."

Chris was quick to reply. "Maybe good advice for me, but not for you. You'll get a chill and your knees will know it, and then I'll hear about it."

Bernie retorted, "I know, I know, my knees will stiffen up and ache. Just wait till you're old. You'll see. To blazes with my knees. You and I both need some fresh air. It'll wake you up and brighten your spirits. Maybe we'll spot a cardinal out there. Love to see that color in winter. The feeders should be full unless the squirrels overindulged at Christmas dinner like us. Heh heh."

"Quite possibly," Chris agreed.

"Let's go check out your holly bushes. I find those nice red berries a bright bonus these bleak winter months, too," Bernie said quickening his step.

"You and what creatures?" Chris said. Bernie smiled. He could see Chris coming around. Even referring to nature did wonders for Chris. If the power of nature could elevate his mood, then he was off to a good start. All the fears and anguish he harbored inside would diminish, so Bernie hoped and prayed. Bernie held a lot inside for Chris's sake. He wanted nothing more than to help his young associate to shed his fears.

Chapter NINETEEN

BERNIE SPOTTED NOT one but a pair of cardinals—a rare sight, he believed—perched on a branch in the denuded crab apple tree in the far corner of the garden. He tapped Chris on the shoulder and pointed as he let out a little squeal and clapped his hands in delight. The two priests kept their distance, and the clapping sound was thankfully muted by his gloves; so, undisturbed, the birds kept on doing what birds do. Then Bernie went over to check the feeders. To his dismay he noticed that they'd been raided, most likely by creatures other than birds, treating themselves to their own holiday leftovers. He tsk tsked, whereas Chris only shrugged, commenting that all creatures need nourishment wherever they can get it. It was a primary need for survival.

Chris then realized how hungry he himself should be. He'd only picked at Christmas dinner and bowed out of breakfast this morning. He was too numb to enjoy anything edible after that horrifying nightmare. Not even Mrs. Hopkins' delectable coffee cake still there on the kitchen table could tempt him. Maybe later, he said to himself. After the cardinals flew off, the priests surveyed the bank of hollies bordering two sides of the garden. They'd grown considerably over the last few years. Chris was pleased that Bernie seemed as interested in the flora and fauna as much as he was, though his pastor spent far less time there, especially in the winter months. He also realized that Bernie was trying to distract him from his anguish by getting him out in the garden. Chris checked out the one side of the Christmas rose bush that was devoid of its first year blossoms. He said nothing, but Bernie could sense his sadness. He reminded Chris that the flowers would return next year. And that inevitably caused Chris's thoughts to return to Glory.

Bernie espied her first, clad in a winter white cashmere coat, a brightly colored silk scarf gracing her long neck. She was hatless and her long flowing hair swirled in the light breeze. Her chunky heeled boots made a clunkety clunk on the walkway. An oversize designer sack was slung over one shoulder. She strutted about in search of a sign of life.

"Speak of the devil, Chris. Will you give a look over there, heading this way?" Bernie said to Chris in a half whisper. He feared Chris's reaction. He himself never thought she'd take him up on his offer.

Out of earshot and partially out of sight, Chris whispered back, "I can't believe my eyes. Geez, I need to get out of here...fast, but..."

"Not possible. Too late," Bernie said. "She's already spotted you. Now be polite. You'd best treat your enemy with kindness. I'm not saying 'turn the other cheek' but relax. She won't stay forever. I'm confident you'll handle her well. Now I'd better leave you two alone. Anyhow, I'm not quite ready for my little vacation to Molly's, still have to pull a few things together. My good for nothing nephew Peter will be picking me up in a few, so Molly told me when she called. He doesn't like to be kept waiting, like he's got more important things to do, lazy thing that he is. Oh, how my sister spoiled him. It's a wonder she got him to come get me in the first place." Bernie said in a tone of mock desperation. Then he turned to escape the temptress.

Chris pleaded softly, "No, Bernie, please don't leave yet. Peter can wait. I can get rid of her a lot faster if you're here with me.

Maybe you can tell her a funny story, even if it's corny; make it a long one, and then she'll get restless and leave."

Bernie said, " Thanks. But nah, I'll leave you to set her straight. Maybe you can help her find herself. Give her some priestly advice. Heh heh. I've really got to get going, Chris. Peter may take off if I'm not ready. I'm not fooling you now. And I'm looking forward to spending a few days with dear Molly—not too thrilled about being the one to break the news to her though. You do remember that assisted living thing. Good luck to you on all fronts." And off he went.

As Father Bernie was leaving the garden he greeted Aleks with a cheery hello and a wave and then he headed for the rectory, whistling an unrecognizable tune.

Aleks let herself into the garden and was taking in the surroundings when she addressed Chris with his back to her. He turned when he heard her voice. "Well, well, Chris, nice place you've got here. If you must know I did read that article that everyone was gushing over at dinner yesterday, the one that that romance novelist wrote. Imagine that! Yep, there is some charm to this place, I must admit, winter or not. Very interesting statues you've got and some charming stone walkways." She looked all around, as more birds glided in, some lighting on the branches of the crab apple tree, others digging into the feeders.

"Very nice. You've got some flighty visitors here too, in addition to myself." She laughed at what she hoped would be amusing to him, pointing to more birds descending above the tree. It wasn't at all amusing to Chris. He remained stone faced. "It must be quite beautiful here in the springtime, with all the flowers and the birds and butterflies flitting about. This must be a veritable fairyland of flora and fauna, so I've heard. And you did this all by yourself. Amazing. Very different activity from the Chris I used to know, if you get my drift. Some garden. So sublime, Chris. Yes, sublime." Her effort may have been a full court press, but he was immutable.

After a moment, he spoke. His words came out weak to his chagrin, but deliberate. "I've never heard anyone describe it quite that way before. Sublime." Just play back what she's dishing out. Don't challenge her. Don't give her any fuel. Lay back; let her lead. She'll tire of herself getting nowhere. Chris was determined to rid himself of her and save face.

Aleks persisted, "Sublime, Chris...sublimation. Hmm, so this is what you do in your spare time?" He knew what she was insinuating. It wasn't kind. Play dumb, he told himself.

And Chris did continue to play it cool. "I'm very surprised to see you here." No greeting, no amenities. Very much not like him at all, but then this was Aleks before him in his prayer garden. She wanted to see *him*, not his garden.

Aleks twirled the ends of her scarf and let them loose, creating a kaleidoscopic effect and then leaned toward him. He stepped back, feigning interest in one of his bushes. "I should well imagine. You just saw me yesterday. Or rather *I* saw *you*. You hardly looked at me at all. I guess I still have that kind of effect on you."

Chris didn't flinch. "Oh? I wasn't aware of that." He occupied himself plucking off a few dead twigs. He stepped back and surveyed his work.

"I'm sure you weren't." Aleks shot back at him. "You made eye contact with all the others, but not with me. Strange, isn't it, don't you think, Chris, don't you? That's got to mean something."

"What is it, Aleks? I'm sure you're not here to reprimand me for my communication skills or lack thereof." Chris was becoming exasperated. He hoped he wasn't falling into her hands.

She replied more amiably. "Well, no, I'm not. Actually, Father Bernie, dear man, isn't he? He invited Mum and me to pay a visit."

"So now she's Mum; how very British of you. And you took him up on his offer. So where is your Mum?" Hold your tongue, Chris, he said to himself. Don't be a wise guy. She wants to keep you talking to her.

Aleks went on to explain. "Oh, her, I dropped her off at the doctor's office, some specialist she sees once a year for God knows what. It's just down the road from here; you know that professional building across from the strip mall? Remember she told us at dinner yesterday that she had this appointment and that I was taking her, so I figured since I was in the neighborhood I'd stop by, pay a visit to the garden. I wasn't even sure you'd be there. My good luck." She didn't seem to notice the sour face Chris made.

"Besides it's depressing to be around her very long," she went on as though he might be interested in anything she had to say. "They don't really do very much, my parents, that is...so nice of your mother to invite the folks to your Christmas fete. I've never seen such food—never ending, course upon course, and very gourmet. It's a wonder you guys aren't as fat as, uh, hippos." She paused to laugh at her attempt at humor. Chris didn't. "As you can well imagine, Mum started to go downhill after the, uh, accident. She lost part of her life when she lost Kendra. And all she's got left now is me, and Dad, poor soul. We hardly ever talk about anything meaningful any more, plus I've been abroad for so long. You kind of drift apart, you know. Distance can do things to you. Really, Chris, I have no idea where Kendra ever got her warm fuzzies. Certainly not from our Mum."

Her comment hurt Chris. That was her very own mother she was talking about who had suffered a terrible tragedy. He fired back. "It's likely they ran out of that stuff after Kendra was born." He knew that remark would sting Aleks, but he couldn't hold it back.

"Ouch," she over dramatized. "I'll forgive you, Chris, since we're on your hallowed church grounds. And, if I might add, you look very priestly today. You look even better than I remember. Anyhow, I told Mum I was going to visit an old friend. She didn't even ask who. I told her I'd pick her up later." She was becoming playful, which annoyed Chris.

"Is that what I am to you? An old friend? Really?" Chris grew animated. Why was he keeping this going? Don't give her anything to respond to.

Aleks looked intently at him, her eyes trying to reach a place deep inside him where she could connect with him. "Well, you were, and so much more than that, but..." She lowered her eye lashes, tilted her head.

"Aleks, come on, what is your real reason for coming here?" Chris could not be amiable or hospitable with her. "It's certainly not Father Bernie's invitation, and it's not the article that Beryl Baines wrote."

She thought a second then blurted out. "I just had to see with my own two eyes what you've become since..."

"Since what?" he interrupted, looking away from her. Somehow she'd taken that as a cue to make herself at home, seating herself on a concrete bench, her luxurious coat spilling onto the cold earth. He'd been taken in by her once. She would never succeed again despite her gargantuan efforts.

"No, Chris, since when," she said, recalling her brief encounter with him.

"Since I fell in love with Kendra or since I entered the seminary or since I was ordained a priest?"

"Maybe since yesterday, Christmas dinner at your parents' home. Remember the festivities?" She was working it for all she was worth.

"That's preposterous. I'm the same person I was yesterday," he said. He was trying with all his might not to play into her hands.

"Didn't seeing me do something to you? Anything?" she prodded. She was hugging herself to keep warm. He ignored that.

"Should it?" he asked, ignoring her ploy. He wasn't going to allow her to triumph.

"I don't know. You tell me. Should it?" Aleks fired back. She loved how the wind blew his wavy hair into his hazel eyes, how he raked it with his fingers, pushing it back in place. It kindled a flame inside her. To her he was the most handsome man she'd ever known.

"Will you stop playing games with me, Aleks," he pleaded, holding his stance firmly.

Aleks sighed. "You know, Aleks, Aleks, Aleks, I'm tired of the name Aleks, the name you knew me as. I know you don't believe me but I tried to change, to reinvent myself and create a new Aleks. And I really have changed whether you think so or not. I think living in Britain did it. I was Aleksandra there, and I got used to it. Actually I prefer it. The children tried to say Aleksandra but they came out with Xan. Cute, right? But eventually they learned to call me Aleksandra, as their father did. So much more proper, don't you agree?"

"Very interesting Aleks, but you lost track of what I said. In case you've forgotten, I said no games." Chris was losing patience with her. He had a full schedule for the day, and with Bernie away, he'd be more pressed for time than ever. And he had no time or patience to banter with the likes of her.

"Of course not, just honesty," Aleks said, realizing she was getting nowhere. "I'll be blunt if that's what you want."

At this point Chris decided to be truthful, knowing it would hurt her feelings or thwart her intentions. "I really don't want or need anything from you, Aleks, honestly. So you might as well leave. Period."

Aleks stood. She looked stricken. Then out it came. "You know, Chris, I knew a lot more than you think I did. Kendra and I were very, very close. We had no secrets between us."

Chris was dumbfounded at Aleks's comment. Close? Not in your life! Although close in age, the two girls were so unalike they could have come from two different planets. Aleks was flashy in appearance, brash and outspoken whereas Kendra was pretty in a natural looking way and sweet with a disposition to match. Whenever it served her purpose, Aleks used her wiles and sex appeal to snag a guy. Kendra didn't have to. Aleks drove her peers away with her egocentric ways, so unlike Kendra who drew people to her by her kindness. Immediate gratification seemed to be Aleks's motto. Kendra, however, was focused on her future plans, to become a registered nurse or even a nurse practitioner, that is, if she and Chris wanted to postpone marriage until after graduation from college, but circumstances dictated a change in the path she would take.

Aleks must have deluded herself into thinking that she and her sister were close, but Chris seriously doubted that. They were anything but close. Yes, it was true that Aleks tried to hang out with Kendra and Beth but only to push her way into their lives for the sole purpose of winning back Chris's affections. She was openly hostile at times towards Kendra for dating Chris and was quick to express her doubts of Chris's intentions, and Kendra knew that Aleks was one girl who did not like to lose—especially when it involved a guy she'd set her sights on. To say the two Powers sisters had no secrets from each other could not be further from the truth.

"Meaning?" He should have bitten his tongue. He was setting himself up for an attack.

"Meaning," she began, then hesitated, brushing off the bottom of her coat. She'd let him stew a while. "I knew the, uh, situation." She said the word 'situation' in such a way that it was loaded with meaning. Now was the time to play her trump card.

"Situation, what situation?" he said trying to quell the emotional maelstrom swelling inside him. Oh, he knew too well the situation. How could he not? He hoped that Aleks didn't, but he feared she could have found out. "I have no clue what you're talking about, Aleks. Can't you just let Kendra and Beth rest in peace—as I have spent years trying to do?"

"Wait a minute, Chris," she snapped, disregarding his request. "What about me? I'm trying to achieve peace with my own self before I head back to England. I have two beautiful step-children who miss me very much. I'm going back for their sake. And I have no idea for how long. I have no idea how things will turn out there. If things don't work out, I'm not sure which way my life will go." She heaved a sigh, seeking sympathy.

"Well then, I wish you and the children well," he said, hoping she'd dropped the whole situation idea, and leave—now.

"How sweet of you, Chris," she said switching to a dulcet tone.

"No, I mean it," he said. He watched her sit down again purposefully. He hoped she didn't notice his reaction.

She lowered her voice. "Tell me, Chris, didn't you know?"

"Didn't I know what?" he said. Uh-oh. He wished there was a way out of this.

"Look who the game player is now," she said. "You know, about Kendra?" She looked right at him, through him. He was shivering. He was unraveling against his will.

He managed to say, "Didn't I know about Kendra?" He stopped to refocus. "Enough of your riddles, Aleks. All I'm going to say right now is that I lost someone I loved very much and hoped to marry. That's the end of it. No more discussion. You need to end any foolish speculation you might be conjuring up."

"Oh, no, I'm not speculating, or conjuring up, as you say," she threw at him. "I *knew*. I knew everything."

"There was nothing to know," he said at an attempt to defend his stance. "That was the past and it's gone—forever." He watched her, trying to read her. "Do you feel it's important to bait me like this? Taunt me for your own self-satisfaction?"

"I feel it is important for you to know that I knew she was pregnant." She waited, and was about to speak again when she heard him say something under his breath.

He sighed. "Can we not go there?" What good would it do anyone to bring that up? "You know, Aleks, you're unbelievable. I'm not interested in what you know or what you think you might know. What purpose does what you're saying—your speculations or your reputed knowledge—what does it serve here and now, for you and for me, for anyone, for that matter?"

Aleks swung right back at him, relishing his vulnerability. "Well, you tell me, Father Tosi."

"I think your intention is to hurt me, maybe a payback for me choosing Kendra over you, for which I have zero regrets." At this point, Chris decided to be as open and honest as he could. Then he added, "Or maybe something to occupy your mind since your divorce. It must have been his idea, I take it." He was angry, breaking his silent vow not to fuel her.

"Now, that is cruel, Chris. If you must know..." Aleks's eyes were blazing with fury.

He cut her off. "I could care less. Now please...please leave. I have work to do and I can't spend any more time out here."

"Chris, you've got to believe me," she persisted. "She, uh, Kendra, did not want the baby. She told me that herself. Yeah, that's right. She was an emotional mess—hormonally fueled obviously.

Pregnancy can do that, you know. But you probably didn't notice that. You were so wrapped up in your basketball back then. But she did not want a baby. Period. Said it would ruin her future. Said it..." She paused to catch her breath. She observed him looking away from her, pacing. "I found her diary. She hid it under her mattress, but I only found it months after the accident, then I burned it so my parents wouldn't see it. I couldn't do that to them. They've suffered enough. She was planning to... well, you can guess."

Chris was furious. "I don't believe you. That's a bold faced lie, Aleks. There was no diary. Kendra would have told me. She told me everything. And trust me, she'd never..." Chris did indeed know Kendra kept a diary but not at her house. There was no way Aleks could ever have gotten her hands on it. Never.

"So you think, do you, Father Chris? How do you know she didn't commit suicide and murder too? Remember how Beth used to get awful migraines. I know that for a fact and so do you. After all, she lived in your house, under your roof. What if she'd gotten one that night out there on the slopes. You know a storm was coming and Beth was very sensitive to changes in atmospheric pressure. It gave her blinding headaches, and maybe, just maybe, Kendra had to drive home."

She paused, observing the effect it was having on Chris. Her words were striking him like jabs in a fistfight. His jaw was set. Even then she found him devastatingly handsome. "The police report said it was such a charred tangled mess they couldn't tell who was driving. What if Kendra was in a frame of mind, her being pregnant and all, and didn't give a damn because she figured her future was ruined, and was speeding and, uh, got into that accident? It would get rid of all her problems...You know, Chris, she really didn't think you'd marry her if she got pregnant. She figured you'd change your mind. Your parents would talk you out of it, and her future would be ruined, her future not yours. You had so much to lose, she said to me."

"Enough, Aleks," Chris shrieked. He could only defend himself with words, the right ones, surprising himself at the intensity of his response. "How can you be so cruel and heartless? Lies, those are all lies. I can't believe you could stoop so low to make up all these hideous stories about your sister. That's monstrous. You're accusing your very own sister. I don't believe a word you said." He was trembling with anger. It was one thing to have lost in love but quite another to harbor an arsenal of evil thoughts and fling them like weapons capable of inflicting injury.

"Well, you should because I know more of the truth than you do," she argued. "I lived with her."

He took deep breaths, forcing himself to regain his composure. "I can't say it was nice to see you again after all these years, but...just know in my heart and in my mind that I chose the better one."

Aleks reddened. "So you think...She was not at all who you thought she was."

"You don't hear me very well, Aleks. I have moved on and you would do well to do the same. The past is past. It can destroy you if you let it take control. It can be a vise. It can squeeze the life out of you and leave you a cracked shell of yourself, limping through a senseless existence of meaningless experiences, on the brink of crumbling and falling apart." He was trembling.

Aleks fought back. "Maybe so in some cases, but the past shapes our lives, doesn't it, Chris? I hear you've had a rough time with that."

"Well, your source is mistaken. I'm just fine. I've found my true calling in life and I couldn't be any happier," he said, again trying to regain his equanimity, to counteract her hurtful words.

"You know I almost sent you the quilt," she said, softly, as though she hadn't devalued her sister and angered Chris. She was baiting him again. "You know, the quilt, I mean. The Kendra quilt."

He gave her a quizzical look in return. The quilt? Could she be talking about a Kendra memory quilt? He didn't know if Mrs. Powers had ever made one. Back then it was enough for him to plod through his daily existence and finish high school. He'd had no communication with the Powerses after the services, not so much by choice. There was no need. That's just the way it was.

"Yeah, the Kendra memory quilt. You know, the one our mothers made after the grief counseling sessions. They went there together. I saw Beth's on her old bed. That's where your mother keeps it, right?"

He wasn't about to protest. He knew Aleks knew it was there, in Beth's room, where she had no business being. She'd gone upstairs to the powder room and surely she'd peeked in. That's what Aleks was—sneaky. Marie Tosi would keep the quilt on Beth's bed forever. It was made of those little scraps of Beth's life sewn together into one precious coverlet. She could caress it, hold it up to her face, inhale its scent and feel the presence of her daughter if for only a moment. Then, after so long, the comfort would wane and the tears would be released. But if there was a Kendra memory quilt, if only...

"Well, in one of my softer moments when I was the whole world to two beautiful children and one wealthy guy, one Mr. Reginald Whitford, Esquire, I thought of mailing the quilt to you for a souvenir, say, a peace offering. Why not? I thought you'd like a little piece of Kendra to keep next to you, to cuddle up with at night, but then I guess life got in the way and I forgot. So I let the kids have it or rather they took it off my boudoir chair. They thought it would make a nice blanket for their new puppy's bed. Well, if you must know, the puppy, being what puppies are, made short work of it, so now it's gone—poof, forever. Oh, God forbid, I never told Mum about it. She believes I still have it. She'd kill me if she knew. Now you know how close Kendra and I really were. Do you think our mother would have entrusted the memory quilt to me if we weren't, huh, Chris?" She looked smug.

Chris couldn't respond to any of what she'd just said. He was frozen. He only managed to say, "Take my advice, Aleks." He tried to formulate words that might erase what he'd just heard: horrible accusations about Kendra and heartlessness on Aleks's part. How much of her was human? How much of her was demonic? Finally, all he could say was, "You came to see the garden, you've seen it, now you should plan to leave. You said your mother is at the doctor's. You really should be with her."

She was about to protest but was interrupted by the looming presence of another visitor.

Chapter TWENTY

CHRIS TURNED AROUND and to his astonishment, he noticed Glory crouched over one end of the garden, likely within earshot of his conversation with Aleks. He wondered how long she had been sequestered there. Despite school vacation she was smartly attired in stylish clothing and her signature high-heeled boots. She like Aleks was hatless. For a moment it was almost like seeing the two Powers sisters together. He shuddered at the thought. Heedless of whether she was intruding or not Glory emerged and spoke first as she approached the other two.

"Hey, Chris, oops I mean Father Chris." She made a 'duh' expression at her blunder. "How was your Christmas?...Oh, sorry. I see you're busy," she chirped in an unusually cheerful tone as she glared at Aleks, studying her from head to toe. "Uh-oh, looks like I interrupted something."

Aleks too checked out the teen-age girl for a long moment before responding in a sultry tone. "*Au contraire*. I was just leaving. He's all yours now." She smiled beguilingly. At that, Chris flinched.

Chris said, "We, uh, were just catching up. Aleks is, uh..."

"Just an old friend," she jumped in, smiling lovingly at Chris. She continued to stare at Glory.

"Hey, Chris, she's very pretty," Glory said as though Aleks wasn't even there. She then noticed Chris's typical reaction at being addressing improperly. He was about to speak but not fast enough.

"You know, Father Chris," Aleks interrupted, stressing the word 'Father'. "You wear your title like a loose cloak." Was she reprimanding him for not correcting Glory, or was she trying to impress him with poetic language?

"Duh, whatever is that supposed to mean?" Glory now addressed her question to Aleks.

"Why don't you ask Father Chris?" Aleks was playing her Miss Superiority role. "He's the English major. So he digs flowery lingo. You know—imagery and that kind of stuff, where you try to picture it in your mind."

"Oh, I don't think so; he's not an English person," Glory responded with conviction, studying Aleks.

"Oh, so you think?" Aleks retorted. She wondered, 'Who *is* this girl? And what's really with Chris?'

Chris jumped in. "Aleks, that was Marty Tisdale if you remember our conversation from Christmas dinner. I also got your take on English as a major, as did everyone else at the table. Not much respect for the liberal arts or for what those studies do for you," Chris said. "You have to forgive Glory for slipping. She's not Catholic. She's not used to calling me 'Father' either. And rest assured, my cloak is firmly fastened. Be aware of it. It doesn't slip, and I don't have to be an English major to appreciate your simile."

Glory piped in, "Right, yeah, he's more of a philosophy sort of guy."

"Uh-oh, I see, a man of big ideas," Aleks said, enjoying the slant of this conversation.

Chris would set her in her place, and it wouldn't hurt Glory to listen either, and so he took a chance to capitalize on Glory's appraisal. "As a matter of fact, I like to combine the two—the literary and the philosophical domains. They go hand in hand."

Aleks rolled her eyes and Glory only stared at the woman's unexpected reaction. Glory asked Chris, "Huh, can you give me an example? I don't get it. Even if you explain it I probably won't get it either, but would you anyhow?"

"Well, now I think I'd bore you both," Chris said. He needed both of them to leave, but he was torn. Then he thought they could benefit from what he felt the need to say, so why not? "I may not have been a literature major but I loved European literature. The one quote I find myself recalling at times is from the Russian writer, Dostoyevsky, from his diary, that is. It deals with there being a single supreme idea on earth." He slowed his delivery to ensure that they were hearing what he said. Their eyes were fixed on him.

"Hold on, Chris, oops, I mean Father Chris," Glory interrupted. Aleks flinched, noting the loosening of the cloak again. "How can there be just one supreme idea? There's got to be a whole mess of, uh, supreme ideas out there in the universe."

He observed Aleks mimicking the cloak slipping, using her scarf to demonstrate. Rather than let disgust overtake him, he pushed on. "That single supreme idea is, now listen carefully, 'the concept of immortality of the human soul.'" Chris uttered those last words as though each was a precious gem to be valued, enunciating them for maximum effect.. "Yes, immortality of the human soul, I said. It would do you both good to keep that in mind. There's so much more I can say about that but not here and now. I've got too much to do today—right now."

"That's OK for now, Father Chris," Glory said. "You'll tell me that I'm too young to understand everything you do. You can explain it to me another time. I don't really understand much of what you know, but I do know you have some super powers."

"Really now?" Aleks was rapt. "Come on. What do you know that I don't know about, uh, Father Chris?"

Chris was shaking his head. He signaled 'Enough.'

Glory persisted, " Well, he's sorta psychic." She watched Aleks raise her eyebrows in disbelief.

"As she said, she was just leaving—for England," Chris interjected. Aleks looked surprised.

"Well, not right away," she told Glory. She was enjoying this. She wanted to know more.

"You're probably wondering who I am. Well," she paused a moment, her eyes glued on Aleks. "I'm a new friend of Father Chris." Glory saw fit to explain, turning to face Chris who was looking up into the crab apple tree at a bird about to light.

Ignoring Aleks, Chris directed his attention to Glory. "You asked me earlier how my Christmas was and we were, uh, distracted. My Christmas was blessed. You heard my homily at midnight mass. I hope I didn't bore you. And as for the Christmas dinner, my mother's a great cook. And how was yours?"

"Full of surprises. Guess who showed up?" she told Chris. Aleks watched the two of them interact. Glory was shifting her weight from one leg to the other and Chris was picking mindlessly at a nearby shrub. It was obvious to Aleks that the teen had a crush on him.

"Your parents," he responded with a hint of a grin. He'd seen them at midnight mass. He should stop this conversation, he told himself. Neither of the visitors belonged in his garden, not for whatever purpose each had in mind.

"What did I tell you?" she said to Aleks. She obviously knew he'd seen them. "I think he's psychic, or has special powers, or else he has a direct pipeline to God, or something."

Aleks grew impatient. "You probably don't know this if you're a new friend of his, but I would never go that far to say that about Chris. Though special he certainly is. He used to be one heck of a chick magnet back when..." She smiled knowingly at him and winked.

That took Glory by surprise. "Huh? He does know a lot of things that it's impossible to know."

"Oh, I don't doubt that. Not for a minute," Aleks was being her old self once again. "He knows what he loves and he loves what he knows." The more she could fire at Chris the better, she thought. He had angered her with his sense of superiority. But she did not get the reaction she'd hoped for.

"Aleksandra, say hello to your, uh, Mum for me and have a jolly good trip across the pond. Maybe a reconciliation with Mr. Whitford? Now wouldn't that be nice?" Chris was giving all he had to rid himself of her presence.

"A reconciliation! That's something you can't even imagine, Chris," she said arranging her scarf. She poised herself to leave then suddenly turned back toward him. She took him off guard, grabbed him in a bear hug and kissed him hard and long. He teetered then he righted himself, embarrassed that Glory bore witness to this act of brashness.

"Good-bye, Aleks," he managed to say, shocked and reeling from that unwelcome kiss. Then he looked away from her, and there was Glory waving at Aleks, saying 'Bye' to her.

Chapter TWENTY-ONE

CHRIS WAS SO RELIEVED to see Aleks leave the garden that he thought he could even tolerate a visit from Glory, which surprised him. But why was she there this time? He'd soon find out. He'd get rid of her as soon as he could. He was aware that the day was passing and he had a list a mile long, as Bernie liked to say, including some of Bernie's duties that lay ahead of him. But he still felt the sting of Aleks's kiss in his mouth, on his lips. What was she thinking of? How dare she do that? And with Glory as witness to the deed.

Glory seemed to be taken aback as well. Chris stood deathly still as she approached the statue of Mary. She examined the bush in the morning light, focusing on the denuded side of the bower where she'd removed the Christmas rose blossoms to make a corsage for her dress for Midnight mass. Then she looked sheepishly at Chris hoping to avoid that topic of conversation but realized it was inevitable. She'd thought that leaving the poinsettia with the painted petals would compensate for her act. Plus she'd left the tiny violin ornament for him as well, a souvenir of her glorious instrumental offering.

"She's gone," Glory sighed once she believed she had Chris's attention. "Good. You know, I really didn't like her very much. There was something about her. Snooty, I guess. Phony, maybe?"

She waited for any reaction from Chris. He looked the other way. Then, "Hey, I have to tell what my parents gave me."

"I see they made their way back from Dubai," Chris said, without much emotion.

"No, it wasn't Dubai. I just told you that because, well, I told you that. It was the first thing that came to mind. It was Sacramento, Sacramento, California," she admitted, again waiting for Chris's reaction. Was he going to reprimand her for blatantly lying to him the other night? No response from him. She went on. "They had to go to a funeral there and stayed on a few days longer with my mother's cousin. They bought her a tree and decorated it for her. They made her celebrate Christmas a day early even though her husband, that's the cousin's husband, well, he had just died. But they made it back here for Christmas Eve. Your service. Grandmom too. They went to hear me play the violin." Glory lit up when she spoke about her parents.

"Why didn't you introduce them to me?" Chris asked since it seemed like the polite question to ask.

"Well, I, uh, didn't know they were there actually. Not at first. Then I spotted them standing on the side aisle. It was so crowded. Some guy got up and gave Grandmom a seat. She could never stand so long in one place. Her feet would get numb. I really wanted you to meet my parents after, but you were surrounded by tons of people, shaking your hand, hugging you, telling you how beautiful your service was, and stuff. I'm glad I got you out of a mess, me playing the violin, since your regular person was sick," she said.

"It was much appreciated. You're quite accomplished. Everyone complimented Dr. Blume on his program," he said. Keep the responses short. She needs to be on her way, too. He could focus only on where he should be at this time and it was not in his garden.

Glory couldn't resist telling him. "He's a pretty cool guy for an old man."

Chris couldn't help laughing. "He's hardly that old. He's just gray."

Glory smiled in return. "He looks like Santa."

"Yeah, I guess the beard does it," Chris agreed, then he told himself to get moving. Any more conversation with Glory could be construed as encouragement.

"I wish he'd shave it off and dye his hair. He'd be kind of cute," Glory added.

"Please don't tell him that," Chris warned, and he found himself laughing along with her.

Then he remembered the trouble Glory had caused with the young mail carrier, and how it changed his life. No, he shouldn't prolong the conversation. She could easily interpret it as his being interested in her, returning her affection. He reminded himself to be wary, cautious. She always had some ulterior motive, and hoped against hope it wasn't what he feared it could be.

"Oh, I'll probably never see Dr. Blume again. He's over at Glen's school, the Academy, my old school," she said, adding, "I'm not welcome there." She paused a minute then shifted her thoughts to Aleks. "Hey, Chris, was that pretty lady an old girl friend of yours before you decided not to have girl friends any more? She called you a chick magnet. Wow! Imagine that."

Chris wished that she'd forgotten Aleks, but how likely was that? He hoped he wasn't turning a tell-tale color. "Peuh! And why would you want to know?"

"Because she's so pretty, she dresses like a super model and she's into you. Still. I can tell, the way she looks at you, and stuff, you know," Glory said, watching for a reaction from Chris.

Chris did not provide her with one. Straight faced, he said, "That was way back in high school. We do things in high school that we would like to forget, and fortunately we do. It's healthier. When you're an adult..." He was cut short.

Glory jumped in before Chris could complete his thought. "I'll be the same when I'm an adult. I'm not going to change that much. I sure don't want to be like my parents, especially my mother." Chris could understand her teen-age way of seeing things—at least on that subject.

"You were going to tell me what your parents got you for Christmas," Chris said. He should be reminding himself to end this and get on with the day.

"A European adventure," she said, twirling around.

"That's quite a gift," he said, then he wondered aloud. "All right, Glory, are you telling me the truth this time?"

"Of course, why would I lie about that?" she asked, conveying surprise at his inquiry.

"Well, Sacramento is not Dubai," he retorted. At that she was speechless. She smiled at him.

Chris began to walk away from her, signaling the end of their conversation. "I hope you'll be more truthful. I don't know why you told me your parents were in Dubai in the first place." He turned and noticed that she was following him.

Glory shrugged. "To make them sound more exciting, I guess. I don't really know. I just did. That's all."

"Didn't you know they were going to make it back for Christmas?" he asked, figuring another lie was coming.

"I suppose I sort of did. Yeah, I did," she admitted, looking at her boots. Was she really ashamed?

"Then you were not always truthful to me," he probed. He was trying to understand this enigma of a teen-ager.

Glory shot him a cocky look. "Well, what difference does it make now?"

"Don't you want to be regarded as honest and trustworthy?" It was time for Chris to play the wise cleric.

Glory sighed, one of her affected ones. "Well, I didn't burn the house down or hurt anyone while my parents were away, although I was tempted to kill my brother a few times. He's such a twit."

Chris did not appreciate her playing the defensive act. "That's not quite what I meant. Trustworthy. You need to be trustworthy. Truthful." Back to his cleric role.

"Hey, I'm curious about that big idea you were talking about before." Glory stopped in her tracks. What was it with women, Chris mused, were they all so adept at a quick change of topic? His mother was. But with Glory, no, it was a stall tactic, and it was working. "The one you said that Offski dude wrote that you liked a lot. You made a big deal about it to me and to Aleks, like we needed to know it. Like it was so important in life."

"Offski?" Chris had to think a moment.

"Yeah, you know the one, Offski. His first name was Dusty, I think," she said earnestly.

"Dusty Offski." Chris's mulled it over. Then a broad smile revealed all his laugh lines, making him even more handsome. He couldn't hold it back. He laughed out loud. "That's a good one, Glory. I think you mean Dostoyevsky."

"Yeah, that's right, that's him," she agreed. "Maybe if you're too busy I can ask Mr. Garber about him but I bet he never heard of the guy. But you know this soul stuff gets me thinking but then I don't really understand souls and stuff, like I told you. I know I'm supposed to have one, a soul that is. But remember, we don't go to church."

Chris nodded knowingly. Enough.

But Glory wasn't finished. She capitalized on it. "Guess what?" She didn't wait for an answer. "I'm learning Catholic. I had to come here to the garden, and there you were! I couldn't wait to tell you that. I thought that would make you very happy—happy like a friend should be for a friend."

"Oh, really? Since when?" he asked, fearful of her answer if there was any truth to it.

"Well, that should be obvious, but what I'm going to tell you is—since the midnight service. I liked it. I liked what you had to say. The rest of it was kinda mysterious." She looked about as sincere as he'd ever seen her, though she could be crafty.

"Well, that's nice, I glad you liked it," Chris said, hoping it didn't mean a steady diet of Glory in the future. They only had violinists at holiday masses.

"Aren't you happy to hear that, that I'm learning Catholic?" she asked. She wanted so much to please him.

"I might be if I knew exactly how you were going about it, and if you were truly sincere," he answered. "No joking around?"

Glory looked at him strangely. "Oh, no, just the truth. I might like to go to your church, to St. Aeden's if I learn Catholic but I'm not so sure that other father would like having me there."

Ignoring that reference to Bernie, Chris stated emphatically, "You don't just learn Catholic; it's not like taking school subjects like French or geometry or history. I think what you mean is learning to *become* a Catholic. And that, Glory, is a life changing process."

"Yeah, something like that, if you say so," she remarked casually as if in her uninitiated mind it was just another thing you took up.

This was a lot for Chris to digest. He didn't know how to take that revelation. "What do your parents think about that?"

Glory said boldly, "Oh, them, they don't know yet. I just started—yesterday, after Christmas dinner. They were all mellowed out from after dinner drinks, cordials, my mother calls them. And they do make you cordial," she said with a giggle. "Anyhow, they won't care as long as what I'm learning keeps me out of trouble.

They have their hands full with Glen Thomas. I'm sure you could see that for yourself." Chris couldn't imagine that. By all indications, the young man seemed very much the opposite of his sister.

"So you're the good twin?" he half stated.

Glory was fit to correct him. "The better twin. You'll see."

"So where are you getting your instructions and from whom?" he asked. He knew no one was available for instruction at such short notice especially during the holidays. Not any of his staff anyhow.

Glory shouted, amused at his proper grammar. "From whom? Mr. Garber would love that. Well, my Grandmom is the 'whom' that is teaching me." Another giggle. "She used to be Catholic once, she told me. She even has her own Catholic textbook, a raggedy old yellowed thing—some funny name, ball—, bald—like. I can't remember exactly."

Now it was Chris's time to be amused. "You don't mean the Baltimore catechism?" He wondered if his mother still saved a copy. Most likely not, or he would have seen it among her old books in the basement.

"Yeah, I think that's it. But, no, she's not telling my parents about it either," Glory said. "No way. My mother loves it when Grandmom and I spend time together. That means she doesn't have to. I guess the generation gap is there for oldies too."

Chris chose to ignore that. "So you really have begun?" Chris said trying to convince himself that she might be telling him the truth.

"Right, but we're not going to go in order in the book," she explained. "That's too boring. That's my idea and Grandmom says she doesn't care how we do it."

Chris acknowledged her with a nod. Then, "OK." He wasn't prepared with what came next. He could never imagine what he was about to hear.

This is how the first lesson went. "I throw that old book in the air and if it lands face down on a page, then we talk about it—whatever's on the page," she said as though it made sense. "Makes it like a game. And games are a good way to learn stuff, especially stuff that's hard to learn and sorta weird. But if that's learning Catholic, then it's cool. I'll put it all together when I have to, but with Grandmom's help, I guess."

Chris needed time to take it all in. "That's a strange way to go about it. You know there are more modern books for instruction. And more effective means, I mean lessons, and other teachers in our parish who could make it easier to understand." He didn't want to insult the integrity of Glory's Grandmom, but he was leery of her method and lackadaisical approach.

Glory was just pleased to inform Chris. "This is going to work out fine. Plus Grandmom likes the attention. She knows me. She figures I'll get tired of it before long. Who knows? Maybe I will, maybe I won't."

Aha, Chris said to himself, sounds like a whim. He questioned her sincerity, her real motive, but he really didn't have to. He knew the answers.

"Do you mean, am I serious?" she sounded indignant. "I am. Dead serious. I want to learn Catholic."

Chris wished she didn't remind him so much of Kendra. Every interaction smacked of her—at least as far as her looks were concerned, certainly not her personality or anything else. He had to remind himself that Glory was nothing at all like Kendra in reality and maybe, just maybe, there was a remote possibility she did want to convert to Catholicism, or as she said 'learn Catholic', though he seriously doubted it. What the poem suggested told him so. This could be just another step in some master plan of hers. He was learning of her history. It frightened him to envision what could happen.

Glory went on. "I really do, but, um, it kinda depends on a lot of things. Like the subjects, you know, the topics. Some of them are way out—like I said—weird."

"Probably because you don't quite understand them," Chris said. "It's too soon—takes time for it all to sink in, for you to really get it."

Glory argued, "But what matters is that Grandmom does, doesn't it? She had to memorize everything so I guess that means she understands it. Then she teaches it to me, and if I think it makes good enough sense, I learn it. Pretty simple."

Chris wasn't about to argue with her. It was anything but simple. It might have been easier if he'd expounded on Dostoyevsky's quote. "Well, good luck, but if you really are serious about becoming a Catholic, I can direct you better than your Grandmom can."

Glory was thrilled to hear that. "But would you? It would be so much more fun with you, Chris."

"Father, Chris, remember?" Then he shuddered, remembering Aleks's icy imagery, maybe not so sloppy but uncalled for. A loose cloak, of all things. How could she? Was she really intimating what he thought she was?

Glory said, "Yes, I do, but I keep forgetting. All along, you don't seem like anybody's father, just a good friend."

"Wait, Glory, don't get me wrong. What I'm saying is that I can refer you to one of our religious instructors. Mrs. Rafferty, for example, she's been doing this for years. She'd be a good one to explain everything to you so it makes sense," Chris said earnestly.

Glory made a face of disgust and practically shouted, "Oh, God, *her*? That ancient old relic? The kids told me I should've seen her at the pageant, ordering everyone around, even bossing the adults. Can you believe that? She's lucky one of the animals didn't attack her. She teed off everyone. It had to be exactly her way. Even Dr. Blume was laughing at her, they said. No, I guess I'll stick with Grandmom although she's probably even older than Mrs. Rafferty. At least Grandmom is patient and she's hard of hearing, that's what she calls it. She doesn't like the word 'deaf'. But I still wish you were the one teaching me." Chris was amazed how easily Glory slipped from one mood to another.

"Well, Glory, I'm afraid that's not possible," Chris said firmly. Even if it were it could be explosive, he said to himself.

Glory entreated, "But if it was, would you, would you then?" Now she was a whiny little child.

"Not a good idea," Chris said emphatically. " I'm too busy. Parish priests don't have time for that. We have staff that instruct in religion."

"I don't think that's the reason at all. I think it's because I look too much like...you know who, and it bothers you, and even now that I know you better, you still can't look me in the face," Glory fired back. She wasn't entirely off base.

Chris felt it was better unspoken, what he needed to say. "Glory, I'm sorry, but I really do have business waiting for me."

"But I'm sort of like business, right?" she persisted. "I'm talking to you about Catholic, right? That's your business."

"Enough for now, really. Some other time, Glory. I really must be going." Once more, he started to leave.

"Like what other time, Chris?" she was whining again. "Wait up, I have to ask you about, um, about your, uh, bushes, those over there by the reindeer statue, I mean the stag."

"What in the world are you talking about now?" He was becoming exasperated, but tried to hold it in check. Glory was motioning for him to follow her over to the bushes that bordered the side street.

"I, uh, have a question for you." She paused, buying time. "You see these shiny bushes with the sharp edges? These over here are loaded with red berries. See? But this one is over here is picked clean. No berries on it. Birds I guess got them, right?"

"Come on, Glory. These right here are my holly bushes. You've seen them a lot of times before. So why this interest now?" he feared another Glory ploy.

"Well, I've only been here at night, don't you remember? And it's daylight now and I just really noticed them. So I'm wondering why the birds only ate this guy's berries. They must be very picky. The other bushes are loaded. Look. Check these out." Anything for the stall.

Her question seemed innocent enough, but she should've known the real answer. Chris explained wearily, "Because this guy's a male. He doesn't get berries. But because he's near enough to them, the females are able to produce berries. He does not even touch the females." That should do it for her, he believed.

Glory feigned sadness, overdone for effect. "Poor guy, he's all alone, but it's a good thing he's here. Otherwise the females wouldn't..."

"Wouldn't get berries," he finished her reasoning. She was wasting his time.

Glory kept on, "How sad. So the female needs a male. And a male..." Oh, Chris got it all right.

He kept it very matter of fact and responded before she could finish, "Right you are, in the case of the hollies, and...I've got to get going, Glory."

He started to leave and stopped by the gate when she circled in front of him, nearly tripping him. She caught him off guard and grabbed him the same way Aleks had. She started with a hug, and then tilted her head back just far enough to plant a long, hard kiss on his lips, which were still smarting from Aleks's vengeful kiss.

All he could manage after he caught his breath was a weak, "Glory. What...? How could you? What's wrong with you?"

Glory breathed heavily, then relaxed. "Your old high school friend that you don't really like can do it, so why can't I? And you like me, I know. So it's different." Chris now had no doubt of Glory's true intentions. He dreaded where it could go from here.

"I, uh, need to go. I have so much to do," Chris muttered as he heard a car turn abruptly and grind away up the gravel driveway. Anger fueled his departure—anger and frustration, and trepidation.

"Me too," Glory said. She could see the effect her act had on Chris.

What he didn't know was that Ada Powers had asked Aleks to drive her over to St. Aeden's to see the prayer garden before heading back to the inn where she and her husband were staying. Rather than park on the street, Aleks decided to spare her mother the walk so she pulled into the driveway around the bend to a turn-about, near the garden entrance. Whatever noise her car made on the gravel must have blended in with the traffic sounds at the intersection where St. Aeden's was located. Her timing could not have been worse.

Chapter TWENTY-TWO

CHRIS SPENT THE REST of the day trying to forget the stinging on his lips, a foul taste in his mouth, and the pain in his heart. Or was it his soul? What was it all about? Was he at all to blame, and if so to what extent? He searched and searched his mind. It led him nowhere. How could those two think of doing such a thing? In his spare moments, he prayed to ease his troubled mind and alleviate the pain that tugged at his insides. Was it fear, guilt, shame? No, it was indefinable. It was more than that.

Meanwhile dear Mrs. Hopkins would keep the household running smoothly and Chris well fed in Bernie's absence. He marveled at her—such a dynamo of energy. She'd said to him, it was about time her pastor got to spend a few days away from the rectory. He deserved a break, although she didn't envy what he was charged to do over at his sister's.

Inevitably, old Father Wilbur would be called upon if needed. Chris told her he would relent and call upon him only when he was about to go over the edge. Then Mrs. Hopkins would laugh, a little tinkle of a giggle, which did not seem to fit her imposing persona. He did notice, however, that she was looking pale today and that she was coughing intermittently. He hoped she'd get some rest when her day's work was done. He knew her husband Carl to be an easy-going guy but suspected when Mrs. Hopkins got home from the rectory that part two of her workday was just beginning.

She'd often referred to Carl affectionately as a couch potato, but Chris could take a guess at what that implied.

After saying his evening Office and praying for guidance after his morning experiences in the garden, Chris opened up his Alex Cross novel to the dog eared page, always a Patterson novel, a long entrenched habit, and continued reading where he had left off before the frenetic pace of Christmas duties usurped his time. He dozed off fully clothed with his reading light on. Just hours later, he awoke with a start before the dream was over, still thinking he was part of it, half awake, in an alpha state. Something had disturbed his sleep. A noise from the street, perhaps? The dream could not be categorized as a nightmare; it wasn't particularly scary or horrifying to him but it was bizarre and even a little amusing. How curious it materialized in Chris's subconscious mind less than twenty-four hours after Aleks and Glory had met in the garden, after those forbidden kisses.

He remembered the dream all too clearly. Aleks played a central role as she was wont to do in real life. Amazon-like in stature she wore a crooked crown and a long white robe with a multi-colored flowing cloak. Her eyes were blood red, laser-like in intensity. She gave the appearance of an evil goddess, though not like one he could recall from any mythology he'd ever studied. She was more like an underworld figure, resurrected from the bowels of Hades. She was making long strides up and down the paved walkways in his prayer garden, which was interspersed with weeds and hideous overgrowth. Chris was only a spectator, hidden away in the hollies, plucking the berries, fingering them, something he would never do. What she was doing intrigued him. Little pests—iguana like—would crawl one by one into the garden parade like and she would squish them as fast as they came into sight. She would dash here and there stomping on them, trying to keep up with the increasing number. Those she couldn't reach, she neutralized with a lethal stare. She worked frenetically, crazed. The amazing part was that every single pest had Glory's face.

He lay there a moment contemplating. He wasn't shaking or even perspiring. All was quiet. Nothing resolved, he simply rolled over, still clothed, and fell into a deep restorative sleep. Maybe everything would be all right after all, he thought. He overslept, nearly late for the eight o'clock mass. This was a time when he wouldn't have minded old Father Wilbur taking over. Then the office phone rang. It was Mr. Hopkins. Mrs. Hopkins would not be in for a few days, most likely the rest of the week, he told Chris. He could tell her husband was upset. She was down with a nasty bout of the flu. Came on like gangbusters, he'd said. Without further ado Chris dialed Father Wilbur's residence. Yes, he would definitely need another hand, and as always the older priest was willing and ready to lend a hand. One hand only—as it would take two Father Wilburs to take the place of one Father Bernie.

But Father Wilbur did surprise Chris this time. He sat in for Bernie at two diocesan meetings and took notes, and said two funeral masses the days Bernie was at his sister's. Tragically a seventh grade girl had died in a snow mobile accident on a trail up in the hills. They'd hit a tree—massive head trauma—she didn't have a chance. Her older brother had been navigating the sport vehicle, and was now in the hospital with a broken femur as well a broken spirit. His distraught mother was keeping a post surgical vigil at his bedside. Chris felt he should stop by the next day to console the family when he could fit in a visit. He could only imagine the pain and grief the girl's brother was dealing with, losing his sister that way. Father Wilbur had paid a visit during what would have been his lunch break today.

Muriel Symond had phoned asking Chris to pay a 'social call' to Ruthie. 'Just tell her you were passing by,' she confided. 'Keep me out of this. She wouldn't appreciate me interfering again.' She was concerned that Ruthie was having second thoughts about marrying Matt. Some days, his prison sentence seemed like an eternity stretching out before her. She wasn't sure she could wait that long. She told her mother she'd decided not to visit him for a while to sort things out in her mind. Uh-oh, Chris thought, then he'd be called upon to visit Matt at State prison. Matt thrived on Ruthie's visits and held onto the thought that they'd be married as soon as he was released. If his appeal of the sentence went through, then it would be sooner. Hope. It was what kept him going although his frequent bouts of depression concerned his loved ones as well as Chris, who'd been a long time friend of the Symond family. Chris wondered what had happened since the last time he counseled Ruthie. She had so much faith in the journal process for Matt and for her. Too bad it wasn't working, as she had hoped.

———— ⟨⟩ ————

"ARE YOU SURE IT WASN'T just a dream?" Chris asked a disturbed Mrs. Swenson. She'd settled for him when she learned that her dear Father Bernie was away. Now she was not a member of St. Aeden parish. She wasn't even Catholic for that matter, but she and Bernie had developed a close friendship over the years with her co-owning the hardware store across the street from St. Aeden, and Bernie being a frequent customer rarely called on a handy man to do odd jobs. He was Mr. Fixit himself and he always needed something or another, and she was always there to help him find exactly what he needed. So it made good sense to her to go to the older priest for advice.

"Oh dear, Father Chris," she whimpered. "I don't know what I'm going to do. My Swen's acting so strange these days. He has, uh, visions of people, long lost relatives—cousins, uncles—dead ones at last, and as far I can tell, uh, he believes they're real, I mean alive, and that they're right there in the room with him, not all the time though, thank goodness for that. But I do hear him, uh, talking to them. Just him. They don't answer back," she explained with a half smile and a nervous laugh. "Oh my, Father, I think he's coming down with dementia. I don't know what I'm going to do with him. I can't run the store alone. It would be too much for me without my Swen." Well, Chris too wasn't sure what to do with either of them. It wasn't really his place to do so.

He decided that the best way to deal with her at the moment was to invite her to take a little stroll with him in his garden, expecting that it would divert her attention from her problem and refocus her attention on anything else. And it did to some extent. She observed the birds at the feeder and offered him some advice as to attracting different types of birds. He listened intently, nodding silently. He assured her Bernie would be back in a few days and he would be more than willing to chat with her then. He also mentioned she might phone their primary doctor, but he never expected the reaction he got. It nearly threw Mrs. Swenson into a fit. Well, how was he to know that Mr. Swenson didn't trust 'that breed'?

With Mrs. Hopkins out, there was no hot meal waiting for Chris at the rectory that day. Weary of fast food restaurants, he took a side trip over to his parents' home. Father Wilbur was holding down the fort, as he used to say. Chris would be sure to bring home a plate for him. Marie would see to that.

"OH, CHRISTOPHER, I'M so happy to see you, glad you could make the time today, with Father Bernie out of town and all," Marie gushed, hugging her son and rubbing and kissing his frozen cheek. "Oh, my, frigid out there, isn't it?" He had phoned her earlier and she had a sandwich and hot soup waiting for him.

Chris agreed. He flung his coat, gloves and knitted cap onto a kitchen chair, which was fine if no guests were present. His mother never took her eyes off him. Something was amiss. He broke the silence by asking where his father was. Marie told him he was downstairs restoring a piece of furniture he'd picked up at a tag sale. He'd join them after. But Chris explained to her that there wouldn't be time for 'after.' He yelled 'hello' downstairs to his father who said he'd be up in a minute or three, one of his common expressions, which could mean any number of minutes. And Chris didn't have extra time. His mother said she had lots of news for him which she always said, and she often did. He would eat and listen, if she didn't mind. He'd let her talk.

She seemed atypically ill at ease. The first news she had was that Marty Tisdale had called. Chris looked up from his plate to show her he was listening. She went on to tell him Marty didn't want to bother him. He knew Chris was busy and that they'd get together soon. Chris learned that Sylvie was put on bed rest the day after Christmas. Marie said she hoped the Christmas dinner wasn't the cause, punctuating her comment with a smile. She said she couldn't remember exactly why, other than that Sylvie needed to obey doctor's orders to carry the child closer to full term. She said they must have feared a premature birth with Sylvie's history of miscarriages and they needed to be cautious, proactive, she stressed. Marie told him that she'd made several meals for them for the week. Chris was glad that Marty was on Christmas break from school so he could cater to Sylvie. Marie said she'd stop by each day to make sure Sylvie was OK. But that was Marie. Chris was grateful that Marie had the young couple as friends.

He looked up from his lunch when he heard his mother mention Ada Powers. He was surprised to hear that she'd dropped by the day after Christmas. That made two visits in two days, and after so many years, but he was more surprised at what she'd told

Marie. He put the remains of his sandwich aside and began to fidget. Ada had stated point blank that Aleks and she too believed Chris wasn't suited to be a priest. They'd paid a visit to St. Aeden's and, uh, didn't like what they saw. Ada didn't elaborate. Marie told her she was shocked at that cruel comment about her son and angry too that Ada came to tell her what couldn't possibly to true. She almost refused the cookbook Ada shamelessly presented her with, one she'd heard about on the Food Channel. Ada told her it was a belated Christmas gift that she'd forgotten to bring Christmas Day. Marie wondered, was it really a Christmas gift, or was it just an offering to cushion the shock she would undoubtedly experience? She told Chris how she had blanched when she heard that ridiculous insinuation, and she assured Ada that she was clearly mistaken. She wouldn't have seen anything that would indict her son. That was impossible. She couldn't imagine anyone making that accusation, and then refusing to comment further. That wasn't fair. In reality, it was heartless.

Not in a million years would her son be unfit. He was special. He had a calling and he answered it willingly, fully aware of all the responsibilities that went with it. Then he was ordained, that unforgettable solemn service with the powers it conferred on him, and Marie knew in her heart and mind that he'd be a priest forever in the true sense of the word. She would stake her life on it. Marie was too polite a person to take umbrage very long at a visitor. When she asked Ada what evidence they had since they were together only at Christmas dinner in the presence of several guests, she told her that Aleks had paid a visit to Chris to see his garden while she was at the doctor's. Later, after the appointment she herself and Aleks were right there just outside the garden intending to visit when...but then she stopped short. She froze and said she had to leave, just like that.

Chris thought for a moment. Then he recalled he might have heard the crunch of gravel as a car approached the parking area by the garden entrance that morning, but figured it was most likely street noise outside the garden. When a car veered around the corner, you could hear the tires on the sandy surface as the roads were well treated this time of the year. Oh, no, it could have been Ada and Aleks. They must have seen the kiss, when Glory virtually attacked him. He'd had his arms at Glory's waist, but only to repel her attack, to push her away from him. It must have been Aleks and Ada who'd pulled up and seen what no one should have seen, what should not have happened, what could be construed as…He was horrified.

Marie watched her son panic. So they did see something after all. There had to be some truth to what she and her daughter had seen, or thought they'd seen, but why did she feel the need to go to the Tosi home and upset Marie and then run off and leave her wondering? His mother was standing near him, unsettled, wringing her hands. She needed to know more. There had to be a logical explanation. Chris was visibly shaken over what was obviously misinterpreted, and Marie felt nauseated.

At that moment he didn't know what to tell his mother. He froze, at a loss of words. He would have to retell the whole Glory situation to explain and he wasn't about to do that, not at this time. Fortunately for him, he was saved by the bell—the dring dring of his cell phone. It was Father Bernie's sister Molly, the very one who was to be going to assisted living just days from now. Had he broken the news to her yet, Chris wondered, or was he waiting until just before he was to head back to the rectory? But it wasn't Molly with the health problem; it was Bernie. Molly jumbled all her words together she was speaking so fast. He could tell she was very upset.

"What do you have him doing?" Chris asked, relieved for the timely distraction, but concerned nevertheless. Chris feared Molly had her brother packing boxes and hauling them somewhere, in preparation for her move, overexerting himself when her nephew, many years younger than Bernie and in much better shape, could do the work. Chris could feel his mother's eyes fixed on him, listening intently for tell tale signs in his voice. He was visibly shaken, and experience told him, mothers know, at least his mother had a way of knowing. But he prayed she didn't know. He could thank Ada for that, at the very least. But did she really have to tell Marie that her son, the priest, was 'unfit'? It wasn't for her to make that determination, but then what she'd seen...

Molly told Chris that it took all the courage Bernie could muster to broach the topic of assisted living, touting all the obvious benefits, but he never mentioned the drawbacks. Chris heard the familiar little 'heh heh' that he thought must be in the Monahan genetic makeup. She told Chris she feared he was leading up to telling her that he was the one going into that type of living arrangement, and retiring from his priestly duties at St. Aeden. But how could that be, she wondered? He had many good years left to serve his parish and community. Whatever would he do in assisted living, this brother of hers who had to be in the midst of everything? When he was forced to admit it, that it was not he but she who would be leaving her home, he began to mix up his words, as she explained. He got dizzy and claimed that one side of his head felt 'funny.' Chris became upset. He told her he'd arrange to have Bernie come back to the rectory as soon as possible, and he'd see that Bernie was checked out.

The day was becoming unbearable for Chris. Before Marie could put together a plate for Father Wilbur, Chris was gathering his outer garments and preparing to leave. He told her he really had to get going immediately and he'd pick up something at

McDonald's. Father Wilbur wouldn't mind. Chris needed to tend to Bernie—right away. He checked his schedule for the rest of the day. Then he phoned Father Wilbur to ask him to cover for him until he got back.

The brother of the girl killed in the snow mobile accident could benefit from more counseling, as could the boy's father who had replaced the mother at his bedside. Chris felt bad he himself couldn't be there, but Father Wilbur's age and experience, not to mention his sincerity and compassionate ways, should be very helpful, as it had been the previous day.

Molly lived in Hartford, the capital city, about a 40 plus minute drive from Wexford Falls. Chris called back and told Molly to have Bernie gather his belongings, no arguing about it, and to expect Chris to pick him up on the double. He told her not to mention doctors to Bernie who was of the same ilk as Mr. Swenson. She told him not to break any speed records, that Bernie would survive. He was a tough Monahan. So were his brothers—now deceased, Chris remembered. He was shaking.

Marie understood the urgency of Chris's rapid departure, but she was still pained with Ada's biting comment and no real explanation to lend credence to it. She'd always respected her former neighbor. But there was obviously more to it. There had to be. People you respect don't go around saying such defaming things like that for no reason. She saw how it affected Chris. Maybe he'd open up to her another time. In the meantime she figured she'd be of greater help to the Tisdales as she put together enough of her chicken cacciatore to last the couple for two or three days. She included a box of pasta that she knew Marty could boil up according to the directions on the box. A container of her homemade Marinara sauce would complete their meal. Why not a few more cannoli? She'd stuff them right away, and stop by early enough for their dinner. Then she looked over at the side counter and espied the cookbook, the one Ada had gifted her. She opened the cover to see if it was inscribed. Fortunately it was not. Perhaps Marty could use a cookbook. Why not? She wanted nothing more to do with the Powerses. Her dear son, she knew in her heart of hearts, was above reproach. They'd have a talk soon...to clear the air. She tried to understand why he ran off without an explanation for the subject she'd broached. But he had his priorities, and Father Bernie's situation was more pressing, in her estimation.

Chapter TWENTY-THREE

BERNIE DID NOT ACCEPT Chris's explanation that he was in the neighborhood and thought he'd stop by to pay a visit. He could only imagine how overscheduled Chris was, even with Father Wilbur as co-pilot. That Chris missed seeing Molly at Christmas dinner didn't cut it either. Bernie was too swift to buy that. Then he noticed Molly had his bags over by the door. Once he realized the reason for Chris's 'visit' he was less than pleased. He saw no reason for Chris to intervene. He told Chris he was not like the proverbial fish; he wasn't at Molly's three full days so as to stink, and of course, he punctuated that with his 'heh heh.' No, he felt just fine, despite tell tale shadows ringing his eyes and a little twitch at one corner of his mouth. He was enjoying a few days off with his sister. A little more time to perfect his salesmanship and he'd have sold Molly on the assisted living deal. She would even have a choice of residences, none of which held any appeal to her. Clinching the deal wasn't going to work this time around. Leaving her home was just that; she wasn't about to settle for a substitute home—at least not yet.

When Molly described Bernie's little fugue of sorts, he was embarrassed. He scratched his head sending wiry tendrils of hair in all directions, and studied Molly's faded braided rug, mercilessly unbraiding a loop with the toe of his shoe. But Molly insisted that he go back to the rectory with Chris. What's a day or so less? Thankfully, there was no mention of a doctor. Had there been, Bernie would have balked like a mule. So the issue was left unspoken. Bernie picked up his bag in slow motion letting Chris know exactly how he felt about cutting short his visit on the word of his budinsky sister. Molly relented. She assured him she would consider the alternate living arrangement—some day—only to appease him. Bernie knew what that meant.

But there was one condition left unsaid at the moment. It hinged on Molly's staying put. And that involved a friendly canine named Paddy. Molly, with a sheepish grin illuminating her deeply lined face, presented Chris with a bagful of bulky contents. She asked him to open it and look things over which he did exaggerating a quizzical expression. He looked from one Monahan to the other. A hand made wooden sign slid out when he tipped the bag—***BEWARE OF THE DOG***—it said in bold lettering. Something was definitely up.

"Does this mean what I think it means?" he asked feigning ignorance. He thought pets might not be allowed where Molly could eventually be going some day but occasional visits were permitted. He also learned that she couldn't really afford the dog walker any longer. So changes were to be made, sooner rather later, and this one affected both Bernie and Chris, and Mrs. Hopkins and whoever else happened to be staying at the rectory.

BACK AT THE RECTORY at breakfast the next morning, Chris broached the topic of a little health check up, just to be on the safe side, reminding Bernie that it was timely. Bernie huffed and rose to pour more coffee. He dumped in a hefty portion of real cream, not customary for him. He'd pilfered it from the downstairs fridge, the cream intended for visitors. Fat free was in the upstairs fridge in consideration of Bernie's health. Chris suspected Bernie was delivering some kind of message, or was he simply rebelling?

He was ignoring his elevated cholesterol, and he knew better. There was nothing wrong with him, Bernie insisted, maybe a little fatigue arising from a change of beds. That's all. Chris only gave him a look that said, 'Yeah, sure.'

"Well, Bernie, how did it feel to have a few days off?" Bernie would know Chris was building up to the forbidden question. Silently Chris mused, 'Can I call the doctor to stop by for a look see, not today of course, but maybe within the week? We can put it on the calendar. You know, the same way you get me to see the therapist—sooner rather than later.'

Bernie was suspicious. "Well, about my little vacation—what do you think? I'd like to say it was good, but I can't really. There were good parts and not so good ones."

"I'll bet your sister was happy you made a visit; she could wait on you hand and foot," Chris eased into the key topic. He could only imagine.

"You'll have to ask her. She talked to you behind my back and I see you've been listening to her—Mrs. Know-it-all. She's an old fuss budget. Two nights there and at times I was ready to go anywhere else. Other times, it was really nice, catching up on old times. Us two, being the oldest, we always took the heat, got blamed for all the mischief our little brothers got into." He paused, smiling to himself. "I must admit Molly's a decent cook, plain stuff, though, but good enough. Sloppy housekeeper, I might add, stuff out of place, fuzz balls under foot, crumbs here and there, and, oh yes, Paddy's feeding station could be a lot neater. Can't really blame her though. It's probably her eyes—can't see all the dust and stuff. I really worry about her tripping and falling, but she's stubborn, thinks she can do anything like she used to. "

"Aw, Bernie," Chris said. "You've got to complain about something. Poor Molly. "

"I suppose. With me and Molly, you've got to understand, it's nothing more than a game. We're always poking fun at each other but with my nephew Peter, that's something else. She ignores me when I light into her about him. Doesn't come around enough like he should. Wouldn't kill him to. So why shouldn't I complain about dear old Molly? She complains about me all the time. Goes back to childhood as you can well imagine. Can't live with her, can't live without her. We're always one-upping each other. Heh heh."

"Right," Chris agreed, then, "Be glad you still have one, a sister, I mean." Chris could have bitten his tongue. He didn't want it to come out that way.

"Ah, Chris, all this talk about my sister. I've struck a nerve," Bernie said sadly. He touched Chris's shoulder. "I'm sorry. I didn't mean to. By the way you're not sore that I brought home our new housemate, old Paddy, are you? Molly really can't manage him any more. She can't see well enough to walk him. She'd probably break a hip or something. But, oh, how she'll miss his company. She sure will, and now you'll enjoy having company out there in the garden. Nice safe place for him to exercise. And he is just a big sweetie pie—bark's worse than his bite. Heh heh."

Of course it would be OK. It set Molly's mind at ease and a canine buddy would be good for the two of them. Chris wasn't so sure about Mrs. Hopkins though. He hoped she would accept him as one of the household.

"Oh, no, not at all," Chris said in response to Bernie's concern. "It'll be great company for us and a good enough watch dog, which we could really use around here. Got a nice snappy bark but I can see he's a lamb. No, actually, I'm glad you brought him here and you did a favor for Molly. We can bring him over to visit her once in a while. Sure, she'll miss him but he'll be in good hands. I'll have to train him to behave in my garden and go only where I allow him."

"Oh, good. I was leery about asking you first—you might have said no," Bernie admitted but he knew Chris would be accommodating. "But no one else could take him, not Peter, oh no, not in his house, so what was I to do? I, uh, kind of offered. And in a way, I could tell, Molly was relieved. She hates to admit she's not like she used to be, but neither am I."

Chris ignored that. "No problem, he'll be a good friend. I promise you." Paddy curled up at Chris's feet, taking in the conversation with one eye open. Paddy, in dog years, could best be described as middle aged, and of dubious parentage. Molly had gotten him at the pound in a rebound a few days after her beloved hound Alfie was run over by a passing car.

Paddy was very playful and alternated his time between the two priests, getting acquainted one by one with the rectory inhabitants. They had no idea when Mrs. Hopkins would be strong enough to return to work so they invited Father Wilbur to stay on. Now Father Wilbur was another story. He was, as he put it, 'slightly allergic to furry animals.' And as luck would have it, whom did Paddy prefer from the outset but Father Wilbur, who took his breakfast in the downstairs kitchen and kept his bedroom door shut. Father Bernie thought that was a lot of malarkey, that old Will was just skittish around animals that he didn't know, but he'd let it go at that.

Assuming Father Wilbur was still downstairs and probably didn't have his hearing aids in yet, Bernie asked, "Tell me, Chris, how did Father Will really do in my place?"

Chris decided to tell Bernie what he wanted to hear. "Dear Father Will. Better than I anticipated. Plus, no complaints. I guess he's accepted old age. But of course, he could never take your place."

"I suppose I should take a lesson from him, me and all my beefing about the old knees," Bernie joked.

"Nah, it just makes you more human. Old Will is kind of slow, almost robotic, I would say, and very set in his ways." Chris hoped he was saying what Bernie wanted to hear.

"And you and I aren't? Especially you, and you're such a young one," Bernie offered.

Chris hoped to deflect that. "I try to put one foot in front of the other and go where the good Lord wants me to go." More than ever he wished that, recalling the episodes in the garden and his mother's confusion and distress, trying to unravel the knot in her after Ada Powers's visit.

"Well, if that's not a new slant, coming from you," Bernie said. "So what's happening? By the way, did you wake old Will with your howling? Or were you blessed with no nightmares the last few nights?" Bernie asked.

"That's hard for me to answer. Dreams? Oh, yes, but not as bad. Old Will wouldn't have heard a thing though," Chris said hoping to end the discussion. "Pretty quiet around here this time of year."

Bernie agreed. "Right, it's like a graveyard around here, especially with snow and all, kinda muffles sounds and such unless that blasted girl spook comes around stirring up things. She's always able to make her presence known some way or another. You know, I never could get it that Nero fiddled when Rome burned. Now that's something I could see that Glory girl doing with that violin of hers in the wake of whatever havoc she'd have created. Heh heh."

Chris failed to emote at Bernie's attempt at humor, whether applicable or not. More so, he hoped that Bernie would not mention Glory, but then he decided he'd be as honest as he cared to be. Bernie would understand, but only to a certain degree. "Oh her, Glory. I don't know which was worse, Glory or Aleks, you know, Aleks Powers, I mean Whitford. She still bears her ex's surname. You had your fill of her Christmas day at dinner. Remember the day you left for Molly's, you were just heading out when Aleks showed up, and at your invitation, I might add." Chris grimaced so Bernie would get the message. "Well, later on, Glory popped out from behind one of the holly bushes. She must have heard my conversation with Aleks, which was anything but amicable, I can assure you. Nasty, nasty woman and so vindictive, too. Both of those two I could do without." He prayed that Bernie had no interest whatsoever in that encounter.

"So sorry I wasn't there," Bernie said sardonically. He was poised waiting to hear more.

"Me too." Chris felt everything would have been so different had Bernie stayed on a few minutes longer. Chris wasn't sure how much to reveal to Bernie if he pushed. "Oh yeah, the slant of the conversations would have been a lot different."

"You can bet on that," Bernie agreed. "But that Glory girl again, harrumph. Helped us out with the music though. Gotta give her some credit for that." But it was clear how much Bernie disliked her despite her stellar performance at midnight mass. One had only to observe his reaction at the mention of her name. Then suddenly, "I thought we were done with that one."

"Don't be so sure of that," Chris said frowning. "Listen to this. She's learning Catholic. That's what she calls it."

"Oh dear me." Bernie was incredulous. "Learning Catholic. I can't imagine why. Knowing the likes of her, there must be a reason for that, one of her cockamamie reasons, I'll bet."

"Ditto. I can't imagine where that will lead," Chris responded. It could lead to anything, he feared. Over a short period of time Glory had insinuated herself into his life. Then it came back to him—-the poem, oh yes, the poem—-why had they shoved that prickly matter under the rug? Because it was easier, because of the impending holiday, because, because...Shouldn't it be out in the open and dealt with? Far too much procrastination. Now with Christmas behind them there was no reason for a delay.

Bernie interrupted Chris's thoughts. "Next thing you know she'll be announcing she's entering the convent. She'll show up with a habit. Heh heh."

"Well, she's become a habit around here, and a bad one at that. I guess it's best to ignore her...if we can," Chris said. Let it go and it will go away, he hoped.

"Not much else to do," Bernie agreed. "By the way, I do feel responsible for that Powers woman showing up here the other day. Yes, I invited her to come see your garden. A lukewarm invite at best, mind you. Hardly thought she'd ever take me up on that." Bernie made a distasteful face.

"Me either, and I have you to thank for that, again," Chris quipped. "Although she may have come of her own choosing regardless. She was working at it at the dinner. I think she was on a mission. She's mean and from all appearances still jealous, and most probably a bold-faced liar. At least, I hope she was lying—even if it was only to hurt me." Chris set himself up unwittingly; now he had to do some explaining.

"That's quite a mouthful." Bernie took the bait. "Whatever do you mean by that, Chris?"

Chris sighed deeply, bent down to pet Paddy, and looked up. "I won't beat around the bush, Bernie. Aleks said she was very close to her sister, to Kendra. Aside from sharing a room with her they were not close. Believe me. Contrary to what I admitted to Aleks, Kendra did keep a diary. Though she had kept it well hidden—out of the house. She would never risk her sister finding it. Never. Aleks didn't say how she found out but said she knew about Kendra's pregnancy, and then she said that her sister did not want the baby, and she implied all kinds of hurtful stuff to Kendra's memory and to me." Chris couldn't go on. He held his head in his hands. Paddy looked up at him with his soulful eyes and leapt onto his lap. Chris stroked his silky head.

"How cruel of her. After all these years she blurts out things like that to you." Although Bernie tried to be sympathetic, he was still feeling somewhat responsible for inviting her to see the garden. But then he convinced himself that if she wanted to see him again she would have found a way. Women like her do not give up that easily.

Chris omitted some of Aleks' tirade in the name of privacy. "I'm not sure what else she implied—I can only guess—but if I didn't stop her I'm afraid to think what she would have said. Lies, I'm sure. They would have to be."

"I was defenseless then and there. I was on the spot. What could I do? Did she really mean that Kendra was going to get rid of the baby? I don't know what she was driving at, but I think she wanted to show herself to be superior, to crush me like a bug if she couldn't have me. And now I don't know what to think, and it troubles me." Chris had already revealed more than he was comfortable with.

Bernie could sense the intensity of Chris's pain. "Listen, Chris, does it matter now? You said it—she was trying to hurt you and it looks like she succeeded. Now you must do what you can to get over it. Just do it."

Chris persisted. "She wanted me to think that my precious Kendra was a monster—only to raise herself up so I would see her as more deserving of my love. She was jilted—if that term could apply to a teen age dalliance."

"Hold on a minute," Bernie jumped up. Paddy did as well. "You're getting off track. She doesn't really want you. You're a priest. After what she said, does she think you're going to leave the priesthood and come crawling to her? Come on now, Chris, she knows you're not. She probably came just to make sure. She had to see for herself, and rest assured that she did."

"That could be. I don't know." Chris hoped Bernie was right. "She's returning to England to visit her step-children, says they miss her, if I can believe that. I gathered the ex-husband is out of the picture."

Bernie was quick to say, "And gratefully so are you especially since she's going back there. Let it go, Chris. Refocus." Little did he know the anguish Chris still felt from her brash embrace and provocative kiss.

"I've been trying. Believe me. I've buried myself in reading, and of course, prayer, and running the parish," Chris said with a tinge of desperation causing his voice to tremble. Bring it around to the mundane, he thought.

Chris was relieved when Bernie caught it. "More Patterson, I'll bet."

"Don't have to bet. It's Patterson all right. It helps occupy my mind. Takes me to another place," Chris admitted. As did prayer and celebrating mass, of course Then he remembered. "Oh, Bernie, I almost forgot—if you're up to it, Mrs. Swenson needs to talk to you."

Bernie was surprised. "Eva Swenson? Why does she want to talk to me? Couldn't you handle it? Hmm, I didn't order anything from the hardware, or did I? Can't remember. Wonder what she wants."

"One of these days, run across the street when you have a chance, but get her aside. She won't want her husband to hear what she wants to tell you," Chris said conspiratorially, though no one was within earshot. He was so relieved to change the subject. Just retelling the garden incident brought back that nagging, indescribable pulling at the back of his throat.

"That's strange," Bernie searched his mind. "She couldn't tell you what she wanted?"

"Well, yeah, she did, sort of," Chris obliged him. "But I told her to wait and talk to you, that you'd have an answer. I'm not trying to be mysterious, but you know, the two of you have been friends forever. It seemed to quiet her down."

"Guess so, we have at that; she's a good woman," Bernie said with a smile. Then after a moment, "Hmm, let me see. Swen goes out for coffee," Bernie checked his watch, "around ten like clockwork. Pretty close to that time now. I can run over and see what's up with her. Good woman she is, yesiree."

"Or she can come by when she knows you're back and settled in," Chris said, not wanting to get Bernie back full swing into business too soon. He wanted to see for himself how Bernie was really feeling or if Molly was exaggerating things to get him out of the house. According to Bernie, she was good at that. Maybe she was getting weary of her house guest and what he was selling, and get Chris to believe her and run right over, which he did. If it was a ploy at Bernie's expense, it worked.

Chapter TWENTY-FOUR

CHRIS KEPT A VIGILANT eye on Bernie like a mother hen protecting her delicate eggs. If Bernie sensed it, he kept silent. Chris advised Bernie on his diet, which had suffered in the absence of Mrs. Hopkins, and got harrumphs in return. He told Chris he was no baby and didn't need a sitter, thank you very much. Chris was careful not to inform his mother of their culinary situation. They were eating meals from freezer to micro that Mrs. Hopkins had prepared for such times, which was extremely rare. Had Marie gotten wind of this situation, she would have filled in at the rectory and continued to provide dinners for the Tisdales.

One morning conveniently a little after ten a.m. Bernie ventured over to Swenson's Hardware in search of a more versatile ice scraper, one with a brush doodad, or so he told Eva Swenson. As they chatted about the weather and other everyday matters, she seized the opportunity to grab Bernie's ear. He could tell by the quiver in her voice how serious it could be. Embarrassed to broach the subject head on, she merely reiterated what she'd shared with Chris, though in greater detail as Chris had learned later.

Bernie told her point blank without any cogitating that it was very simple. There was nothing at all wrong with Swen, he declared without even observing the man. There was no problem, only a solution. Bernie assured her that Swen was in desperate need of a change of environment, and it wasn't the annual trip to see relatives in Sweden that would do it. An escape from cold weather and the effects of the early winter rush for snowplows and other weather related equipment was the answer. He suggested a few weeks in warm sunshine and tropical breezes say, south Florida. Maybe some of the relatives could come over and run the store in his absence, as they'd often done in the past. And when he'd get back from wherever, the place was still standing. Of course, Bernie stressed to Eva, she would accompany him. This would not be a solo trip, Bernie impressed upon her, patting her hand. Her husband would come back a new, refreshed man. That seemed to quiet her immediate concerns. If she had any lingering doubts, she kept them to herself.

Bernie told her to check with a young employee of theirs who was computer savvy to secure plane tickets at a decent price but first find a condo or hotel with special rates so they could head off soon. She should book tickets for one of the relatives who would agree to fill in at the store. And by all means, keep it a surprise for Swen. She was delighted with the idea and said she would act upon it as soon as possible, and yes, behind his unsuspecting back. After a hearty chuckle, Eva Swenson hugged her friend and ally, the Catholic priest, and he patted her back and smiled with a sigh of relief. He was sure Chris wanted him to suggest a doctor to run exhaustive tests on the poor guy, maybe attach wires to his head and get a spiky printout, and all the other rigamarole that went along with tests, and in the end all this fuss and bother would amount to zilch. He knew people after all these years. Swen was just overworked, nothing more than that. In Bernie's humble opinion, that is.

------ ⟨∞⟩ ------

NO, THE ADAGE THAT guests like fish smell after three days certainly had not applied to Bernie's stay at Molly's, but it more than applied to Father Wilbur—was it day four or day five? Chris wasn't counting. The kindly old cleric was beginning to annoy Bernie who should have been used to him after all these years. Father Will complained about Paddy, who as luck would have it grew fonder each day to him, following him up and down stairs, even into the bathroom, which he'd always said should be one's sanctuary. He even made a silly laugh sound akin to Bernie's 'heh heh.' Chris conjectured that it was how the older generation laughed, a sign of their period of socialization. Anyhow, Father Will had to go, until the next time he was desperately needed. However, Bernie brought up a new name, Father Donovan, as a stand-in. Chris made a face of disapproval at that. Bernie assured him that he doubted that would happen any time soon. Father Wilbur could continue to make hospital visits but he would return to the retired priests' home—away from Paddy.

Later in the day Chris wasn't too surprised to get a call from Marty Tisdale. They'd get together once in a while to watch a basketball game or other sports event on TV. It so happened that Chris and Bernie rooted for different teams so it was preferable that they watch the events on different sets in distant parts of the rectory. Chris explained to Bernie that he didn't want to bear witness to a massive stroke when Bernie shouted and screamed, reacting to unsatisfactory scores or a referee's bad call. So, every now and then he and Marty would take in a game on TV in the rectory so as not to disturb Sylvie in their apartment, especially with her on bed rest. Chris figured that was why Marty wanted to come by. He wasn't sure who was playing or even when the game began, but Marty would tell him soon enough.

Chapter TWENTY-FIVE

IT WASN'T CUSTOMARY but Chris and Marty met this time in Bernie's sitting room where he received special guests, most notably the bishop. There was no TV set in there. Marty explained that Marie had brought dinner over to his house and the three of them had eaten in silence. She told the couple that Fred was working on restoring an antique cradle for the baby and that he'd warm up his dinner at an appropriate time for a break. He wanted to finish the sanding job first. Whenever Marie was antsy, as Fred described her jangled nerves, he would bury himself in his work downstairs. But she just figured he liked to finish what he started, which was in effect the truth. She always rationalized that it was better than drowning one's troubles in alcohol.

Marty couldn't imagine the reason for Marie's skittish behavior. She couldn't sit still. She seemed to be preoccupied and didn't answer right away when spoken to. She'd ask them to repeat what they'd said, which was uncharacteristic of her. Even Sylvie noticed that Marie seemed out of sorts. Marie, at last, opened up, suggesting that Marty go spend some time with her son. Normally after school, he would bring his papers to grade by Sylvie's bedside so that they could be together. As it turned out there was a collusion of sorts. Marie needed to learn more about Ada's so-called evidence, if indeed there was any, and if she could get

Marty to visit Chris while she agreed to hang out with Sylvie, that could work.

"Can I get you a drink, old buddy?" Chris asked. "Wine, bourbon, a beer—whatever?"

Marty responded with a head shake—negative. Then, after a minute, "Well, maybe, just a sip of wine, red, if you've got any open."

Chris poured an ounce or two for Marty and gave himself a full glass of claret from a decanter on the antique buffet, probably well aged judging from the amount of time it might have been sitting there. Bernie only kept it there for those who were so inclined. Mrs. Hopkins was instructed to refill it once it fell to a certain level.

Chris sensed something was bothering Marty but the two college friends talked of school and upcoming mid-term exams, which was Marty's focus after Christmas break. They made tentative plans to watch the Super Bowl together, hopefully at Marty's. It was Sylvie's idea. Then Chris's attention was diverted to the other end of the room where he spotted the poinsettia plant Glory had left at Mary's statue after helping herself to the Christmas roses. The plant had shed many of its petals and the leaves curled and drooped. It had been neglected in Mrs. Hopkins's absence. He'd have to remember to water it. The tell tale violin ornament was still affixed to the ribbon that encircled the planter. It was more visible with much of the foliage shriveled up on the floor. Glory, he thought, and then he shuddered.

After a while Marty noticed that Chris was not himself either. He was fidgety like his mother, and Chris was fairly sure Marty came to visit because he had an agenda—this was not purely a social call. If there was a game on TV, this time Marty would pass—he had other things on his mind. Chris sipped his wine, distracted by his wandering thoughts, as Marty searched for the right words to broach his concern.

Then out of the blue, Marty turned to Chris and said, "You know, Chris, you remind me of your mother."

Chris was taken aback. He didn't expect that from Marty. "I have no idea what you mean, pal, but I think you're going to tell me. So please don't keep me guessing." Chris released a nervous laugh.

"I don't know if you've noticed but your mother hasn't been herself for a few days, and I just noticed you're acting like her in the same way." Marty said. "What's with it, Chris?"

"Well, we may very well have similar mannerisms. After all, we *are* related," Chris said. Keep it light, he told himself, but he suspected Marty knew something. He looked serious.

"I'm sorry, I don't want to beat around the bush, Chris, but if truth be known, your mother asked me to stop by," he admitted, still uncomfortable with what could come next. "She looks troubled and worried, and she's, well, she's been like another mother to us, to Sylvie and me. You know I lost my own mother because..." The two friends, anchors for each other since their college days, could read each other, and neither was willing or able to take off their masks yet and spill out what the issue was that was building a wall between them.

"I get it, Marty. I'm sorry," Chris said before Marty could go on. Carmen Tisdale had overdosed accidentally on a tranquilizer, interacting with another drug and his own mother, taking the same drug as well when things got tough...well, he surely didn't want that to happen to her. "OK, I'm listening," Chris said. He knew now. Could his mother have spilled out what Ada Powers had told her, that he was unfit to be a priest? He doubted that, but then...He shuddered a second time, this time interpreted by Marty as fear. He'd have to disclose again—first to Bernie, then to his friend next to him on the sofa.

Chris cringed when Marty quoted Marie who had told him what Ada had revealed the day she'd brought her the cookbook.

That was the part Chris had deliberately left out when he'd spoken to Bernie. So he decided to spill everything to Marty whom he would swear to secrecy, even from Sylvie. He and Marty would mutually agree upon what to reveal to Marie for her sanity's sake. And his father shouldn't be told anything, Chris said. He knew his mother would comply. Once Marie calmed down, if that was possible under the circumstances, then his father would relax, experience told him.

Chris provided every detail he could remember, though he was embarrassed reliving the whole ordeal. Marty assured him. "Hey, Chris, you know nothing that I can tell is your fault. You were just a victim of, uh, circumstances, I would say, or..."

Chris's stare burned through to Marty. He hesitated as though there was more to add. Marty looked right through him. "Or was it? Sorry, Chris, I have to ask."

"I had that coming, I guess." Chris's countenance softened. "You know me too well. No, of course it's not my fault. At least none of this since I've been a priest. I take my vows seriously. It's still my past that haunts me, I'm afraid."

Marty just sat and waited. Chris poured him another draught of wine. "All right. Tell me about it, if it helps."

"OK, I'll try," Chris began softly, after hesitating a moment. Aleks is just a rueful reminder of poor decisions, painful learning experiences and, as you know, tragedy. Not much more, though I got the impression she'd like it to be different. The problem now is Glory, but it's not totally her fault, but then it could be. The first time I saw her in the garden it was like I was seeing a ghost. She looked so much like my Kendra." Chris caught Marty's surprised reaction. "She looks like her, I mean it, so I couldn't look her in the eye. Well, she picked up on it, and uh, well, I think she thinks I, uh, like her. You know what I mean."

Marty nodded. Oh, he knew full well about crushes that high schoolers had on favorite teachers, many only a few years older than their students. "Sure do, Chris. Most don't amount to anything. They fizzle out once the kids move on to another teacher or graduate, at least you hope they do. You know how impressionable and hormonally charged kids are at that age. And I'm sure you did everything you could to discourage her."

"Well, Marty, what do you think? Of course I did," Chris said, beginning to feel some relief. But then he recalled that Bernie had told him about his subconscious, imagining Glory as the daughter he and Kendra might have had had she lived, because of the resemblance, but then she'd only be about ten years old. "But she's always one step ahead of me. She's conniving, clever. And oh, Marty, you won't believe this, I almost forgot to tell you about the poem."

"Poem, what poem?" Marty asked. He wondered how much more there was to this. He was thinking how to set Marie's mind at ease without revealing certain things she didn't need to know.

"Let me run and get it. I'll be back in a moment," he said to Marty as he left the room.

Marty had a few minutes to mull over what Chris had told him. He wondered if anyone other than Ada Powers and Aleks might have seen Glory and Chris in that uncompromising situation. Was there any chance Mrs. Hopkins had witnessed it? She'd have to be at which window? He asked himself, trying to remember which rooms faced the garden. Uh-oh, he recalled, the main kitchen has a large bay window over the sink facing the entrance. What were the odds she'd be there at that very moment? They couldn't tell since she'd left with flu soon after. He'd keep quiet about that. Chris was encumbered enough without having to dissect that in his mind.

———⟨∾⟩———

MINUTES LATER CHRIS burst into the room, hastily opening the envelope. He unfolded the poem and watched Marty read it, raise his brows, exhale loudly and then read it a second time. Then he paused to take it in before speaking, "Chris, if a student had written this for me, with the, uh, implications, as you well know, I would be obligated legally, that is, to report it."

"Yeah, I know. Sounds a little suicidal, doesn't it?" Chris asked, hoping for an answer that wouldn't upset him. He already felt guilty for not turning it over right away to someone—her parents, for example, but they were away.

"Could definitely be," Marty said deep in thought. He was concerned for his good friend and how this could mushroom into what he tried to erase from his mind. "How along ago did she write this?"

Chris thought a minute. "I guess the first night after she met me, few days before Christmas. Yeah, that was it. Not that long ago."

"You didn't know her before?" Marty asked. He wondered how this could have happened.

"No," Chris answered. "How would I? She's not in our parish. I never saw her before. She'd seen my picture in the Journal for those seasons' articles. That's probably it. I did find her in the garden at night, which would surely lure one of us out to check. No one should be there after dark. There's a sign posted. Bernie went out the second night, and they did not hit it off, oh no, not at all, not that I would expect them to under those circumstances."

"And you say she played violin for your Christmas Eve mass to get you out of a bind?" Marty was puzzled. He rubbed the stubble on his chin in contemplation. "I don't get it."

"She's a toughie to get," Chris admitted. "Her kiss, as I told you, was only her aping what she saw Aleks do, hard and heavy, but I'm sure now her motive wasn't the same, no matter what she told me. She said something about our being good friends. That's what worries me. I don't need her for a friend. It feels wrong. She does things that no one would think of doing; then she tries to undo the trouble by doing something to make up for it. And I'm caught in the middle of it all."

Marty kept silent, taking it all in. Then Chris interjected, "You know I'm the one who should be supporting you, with Sylvie being like she is—on bed rest and all. How's she doing?"

"She'll be fine if she listens to her doctor, which so far she has been. She knows better. She's disappointed that Clotilde, her mother, can't be with her when the baby comes. Being a grandmother should bring the two closer together, even though they are an ocean apart. We heard not long ago that she'd recently remarried. That was a big surprise for Sylvie. We haven't met him yet, though we wished them well by phone. We only know he was an exchange professor from Morocco. As you know, she's a professor at the Sorbonne, so she can't really get away until later in the spring. In the meantime your mother has been like a second mother to her, and a lifesaver to both of us. We owe her so much. But it was really your mother that I was worried about. Now I know what was bothering her, and I'm sure I can reassure her, set her mind at ease. I'll be cautious as to how I phrase things. I can ask her not to bring this up with you once she is assured you're not 'unfit.' No sense dredging it up. I guess we can say 'case closed.'"

"Whew, that's a good idea," Chris said, the muscles in his face relaxing. "Let's hope the case *is* closed. Thanks, Marty. You're a true friend." That took a load off his mind but there was still Marty's concern about the poem and its ramifications. "So, Marty, the poem, you really think I should do something about it?"

"Most definitely I do, and asap. What if you or even Father Bernie invited the girl's parents to meet with him to, uh, discuss the situation? You did tell me she handed the envelope to him, right?"

"Correct, she did. But I suppose either of us could do it," Chris said under his breath. He hoped it would be Bernie.

"Do it, and then it's done," Marty said. "Just the poem thing. Make little of it, just a FYI sort of thing. Leave out the kiss. You said it was spontaneous, not to condone it, but the poem, well that was deliberate, and it was to be given to you. That should mean something."

"Right, that's what I'm afraid of. We'll find a way," Chris said, not so sure that he would, or that he could even imagine the outcome.

"And now that everything is all settled, or sort of, I have two favors to ask you." Marty smiled and to Chris's relief, he returned the smile. Good, the odious stuff was over, Chris thought.

"Shoot," Chris said as he poured himself more wine. Marty declined a refill. He had a 30-minute drive home on slippery winter roads.

"You know how I asked if you would baptize our baby?" Marty asked. Chris sensed another agenda item.

"I do, and I said 'yes.'" Chris looked at Marty expecting to hear he had decided to go with his own parish priest instead. "Is there, uh, a change of heart?"

"Heavens no, well sort of, yes." He paused; then he smiled warmly. "Sylvie and I would like you to be the godfather instead if you would. We haven't selected a god mother yet."

"Hey, I'd be honored, you know that, actually thrilled, Marty. Thank you, both of you," Chris said. "I hope the next favor is as good."

"Well now, yes and no. That depends on how you look at it." Marty set his wine glass onto the coffee table, careful to place it on a coaster. "OK, here goes. You know the ski club trip that I've been chaperoning the last few years? That's the one with your housekeeper's daughter-in-law. There's always two of us, one for the boys and one for the girls?"

Chris knew of no other ski trip Marty was involved in. He was waiting. He could tell what was coming next. "Yeah, sure I do. You guys have a blast, so you tell me. And Jodie Hopkins is an ace skier, keeps the girls in line too. But I'm not so sure about your skills on the slopes."

"Hey, not so bad, Chris, but I'm not Jodie's caliber, not by a long shot." Again Marty paused. He was watching Chris figure things out.

"I get it," Chris said in a drawl. "Sure, Marty, and you're looking for a sub. How many others have turned you down for one reason or another? So you've run out of prospects, which leaves your old friend." He waited but Marty kept quiet. "I know you can't leave Sylvie alone for a long week-end, can you? And you're getting the courage to ask me if I can fill in for you."

"Right-o." Marty's face muscles relaxed a little. "Can you get me out of a bind? I really have tried, Chris, but..."

"But yeah, you know I love being with the kids, but I haven't been on the slopes since..." Marty knew why Chris couldn't go on.

"Yes, since before the accident," he said. " I know you've been busy so it might do you some good to get away from it all and help me out at the same time before all the spring events are upon you—weddings, Confirmation, your parish festival and all the rest. All you really have to do is be there for the kids, especially during the non-ski time, like at night when they could get into all kinds of things. Jodie can take charge on the slopes. There's only eight or nine kids total from our two parishes. Remember, we opened it only to parishioners in good standing, which means ski club members with dues

paid and all—no outsiders. It's a doable number, Chris, and they're all super nice kids."

"Any couples, if you know what I mean?" Chris knew Marty knew what he meant. He didn't want to deal with teen-age romances away from parental supervision.

"No, not at our end, as far as I know. You can check with Jodie at your end." Marty said. It was almost a deal.

"Oh, you can bet I will. But first, Marty, let me sleep on it, if you can wait a day for an answer. Also I've got to check with Bernie. He'll have his buddy Father Wilbur as a cohort, and, oh, he may not be too thrilled about that. Hey, you haven't met our latest house guest, I mean permanent resident. Name's Paddy."

A few minutes later, Marty had the opportunity as the mutt ker-plunked down the stairs and leapt onto Chris's lap for a cuddle. Then he looked over to Marty, sizing him up. Paddy was followed at much slower pace by Bernie.

Bernie made the introductions and Paddy went over to Marty and offered him a paw. There seemed to be some mutual admiration. Chris decided he wasn't going to wait. He knew Bernie would find it harder to object with Marty right there. So Chris lowered the boom about the ski trip and watched Bernie let it sink in.

"Do ya good, Chris. It's about time you got back on the slopes," Bernie said. Besides he felt it would give him a welcome break from Chris scrutinizing him for signs and symptoms so he could convince him that they really needed to check in with the doctor. No doctor's going to run tests on me, he told himself. Marty looked pleased and Chris wondered why Bernie was eager to let him go. Could his pastor stand more time with Father Wilbur so soon? "Tell me, gentlemen, I lost all track of time when I was at my sister's. When's that big week-end trip?"

"Week-end after next," Marty said. He looked delighted. He thought he'd have to do a hard sell. It wasn't long before Paddy who had returned to Chris's lap ambled over to Marty to lick his hand

and for Marty to head back home, pleased that his visit had been an all around success.

Chapter TWENTY-SIX

THE TWO PRIESTS WERE making headway. It was finally decided after much discussion and haggling, weighing the plusses and the minuses, and all the what if's. Initially Bernie thought Chris should do it since the poem was written to or for him. To Chris it was still a gray area, but it was more black and white to Bernie. And Chris wanted Bernie do it to keep the matter as impersonal and dispassionate as possible. Only one of the Glory's parents should be present, not two, which would avoid undue stress, differences of opinions and multiple interpretations—not to mention action to be taken, or not. They'd ruled out Grandmom at the onset. She'd probably say something about the innocent crushes of a young girl on some father figure of sorts, and pooh pooh the whole thing. Glory's mother would tsk tsk in disgust, saying, 'Not again. Look what it cost us the last time. What's wrong with her anyway?' How they decided upon inviting Glory's father to the rectory remains unclear, most likely by process of elimination although Bernie himself would take the credit and the responsibility of confronting him.

Bernie phoned the Sterling-Baie offices and asked to speak to the president and CEO of the firm, none other than Mr. Douglas Sterling himself. As anticipated, Mr. Sterling was unavailable at the moment, but when Agatha O'Toole his administrative assistant realized she was speaking to the pastor of St. Aeden Church, Father

Bernard Monahan, her tone became more cordial, the same as when she was speaking to a moneyed client they were courting. ' Oh, yes, Father', he heard her say, 'Mr. Sterling will get back to you as soon as he returns from, uh, his work site down town.' She wished him a good day, and he wished her the same. That was step one. Where it would go from there was a crapshoot. But Bernie was a gambling man.

Douglas Sterling phoned back later in the day, and agreed to meet at the rectory early the next evening. Bernie knew this location, his home grounds, gave him the advantage, the upper hand if indeed it was needed. Bernie, however, did not disclose the reason for the meeting, nor did Mr. Sterling ask. It was better left unsaid until Bernie could devise a stratagem or a viable plan of attack. He wasn't sure how he was going to broach the topic, maybe delicately, showing concern for Sterling's daughter's welfare. Then Chris advised him to rethink the issue and be blunt, direct. Get it out in the open. That was all it took for Bernie to tell Chris maybe he should deal with Mr. Sterling himself if he had all the right plays or ploys in mind. Bernie insisted that the man-to-man discussion with Sterling would work just fine and there'd be no more trouble with Glory again—ever. Let Sterling take it upon himself to be concerned if his daughter was suicidal or not. Take the onus off Chris. Chris still felt uncomfortable, but he agreed to just let Bernie do it his way. After all, his pastor outranked him. Chris would be conspicuously absent from the scene. He more he thought about it, the better it would be that way, just one on one. And it would be just about the right time for Paddy's nightly walk—a stroll into the garden for a starter, up and down the five paths.

Chris had bought Paddy a new leash, the retractable kind, so he'd have control of him in the garden and elsewhere. Paddy would have to learn his limits there and run only on the pathways.

Overall, Paddy took a liking to his new surroundings and proved to be a welcome addition to the rectory, though at times his yapping could be distracting. Mrs. Hopkins, recovered from the flu, warmed up to Paddy and walked him up and down the driveway from the church past the rectory and by the garden when the priests were busy. She said it gave her a chance when she had some rare downtime to burn extra calories and trim off some of her post-menopausal flabbiness, as she facetiously referred to her weight gain. More brisk walking was one of her new year's resolutions of which she had several. She also found Paddy to be a fan of her leftover meat dishes. She didn't, however, show much warmth toward Chris, which was uncharacteristic of her. Her curtness became obvious to both priests. Bernie figured she was just weary from her bout of the flu, but Chris had reason to suspect otherwise not that he would broach that uncomfortable topic in case he was mistaken.

As Paddy gamboled about in the garden, Chris heard the crunch of Mr. Sterling's Mercedes easing into the driveway. Minutes later, he spotted the tall, gray haired man entering the rectory. The rest was up to Bernie. Unwelcome visits and intimations of suicide would be the topics and then fade into history, so the pastor hoped. Chris needed to hear how Bernie would handle Mr. Sterling. He was ashamed of himself for even thinking it as he entered through the rear of the rectory stealthily, with a plan, although with Paddy in tow it was a challenge. But Paddy settled down to his dinner topped with a few treats and Chris tiptoed into the front room, which served multi purposes, and now still another.

For the first time Chris was grateful for the rectory's archaic heating system. The register above Bernie's sitting room opened with a little flick of his finger and he could hear the conversation if he put his ear to the floor, which he did. The well-bred part of him did not want to eavesdrop, fearful of what would transpire, without his being there to intervene if he thought it was necessary. But he didn't listen to that part of him. He stretched out on the wood floor, leaning on an elbow, and lay dead still, daring to breathe. He prayed that all would turn out for the best. He really didn't want to hurt Glory since he could also see the good in her, but Marty's advice was to confront the issue or else...

Chris imagined the scenario below. After shaking hands, Bernie would take Mr. Sterling's overcoat and hang it up in the vestibule closet. He heard Sterling decline to accept wine from Bernie's decanter and any other refreshments Bernie offered, said he didn't have much time but was happy to accommodate the good man in his wishes and stop by. Dinner awaited him at home, he told Bernie, and he looked forward to spending time with his family after a long day's work. After the customary amenities Bernie took the lead.

"Well, now, Mr. Sterling, thank you for coming, I'm sure..." he began, but was interrupted as Bernie was asked to call his visitor Doug, at which time Bernie cleared his throat, complied and graciously began a second time.

Chris heard Bernie's preamble, which could have been less verbose, because Sterling excused himself and asked if their meeting entailed discussing terms for a job his company could do for the church, say, a new driveway, modernization of the parish hall, or something else. It was evident that much of what Sterling had noticed passing by the property would benefit from updating, which he indicated was one of his many specialties. When Bernie told him that the reason for this meeting was a personal matter, Sterling coughed, an uncomfortable reaction to the word 'personal', which rarely factored into his business dealings. Personal and business were mutually exclusive, he believed, confounding even the best of intentions and undoing many an almost done deal if both were intertwined.

Bernie didn't mince words. "Mr. Sterling, Doug, I didn't want to bother you and your wife over the Christmas holiday but I feel it is my duty to share with you, a, uh, poem that your daughter Glory wrote to or for our younger priest, my associate, Father Christopher Tosi."

Chris wished he could have seen Sterling's expression as Bernie produced the poem. All he could hear was a weak, "Oh."

Bernie was playing it close to the vest. He'd paused and let Sterling take it in. Chris imagined Bernie producing the envelope and opening it slowly. He would unfold the delicate sheet of paper and reread it to himself slowly, then place it in Sterling's hands for him to peruse. It was quiet for what seemed like much too long.

Then, "Oh, my," Sterling said. Then more silence. "Ah, the young priest that did your service at midnight, the time my daughter played the violin." His eyes would have traveled across the room to the poinsettia plant. "Hmm, and by the way, Father Monahan, I see one of her, uh, miniature violins over there on that plant. She obviously gifted it to you or the other priest. Hmm, that's surprising. I find that hard to believe. I can't imagine Glory parting with one of them. She's got, let's see, seven or eight of them. They're like Olympic gold medals to her. She earned these awards, one for each annual violin competition. She always took the highest honors. Hmm. She must hold you or the young priest in very high esteem." He paused a moment, his eyes likely fixed on the gold ornament. " Ah, I see. I see now."

Chris could only imagine what Mr. Sterling was seeing at that time. Which way would it go? He wondered. Was it time for Bernie to counteract with the garden invasions, or not?

"Well then, Mr. Sterling, uh, Doug, we were, Father Chris and I both, uh, worried that your daughter was, I mean, could possibly be suicidal. If you would reread that line again, please." Chris figured that Sterling was reviewing the poem, weighing the words, the intent.

Then Sterling released a strained, unnatural semblance of a laugh. "You know, Father Monahan, that's Glory for you. If she likes you, then she loves you. If you don't love her back, she's, oh, dear, what should I say, distraught. Yes, uh, I think that's the word. Been through that before, unfortunately. Teen anguish or something like that, you might say. She's an impressionable teen-ager. Oh yes indeed, a little different from her twin brother, a lot different." Silence for a long moment. "We've, uh, had her in therapy, at least she goes when it's convenient for her, that is when she chooses to." He snickered. "You know, her mother should enforce it better. As for me, I'm tied up at the office often until all hours, or I may be away at sites. I travel a lot with the business. I'm abroad sometimes for weeks at a time, you know. Well, I'm sorry this caused you concern, and, uh, I do appreciate you bringing it to my attention." He cleared his throat, then he paused a few seconds and resumed in a more relaxed tone, "I can only say that Glory is fairly predictable but then, uh, sometimes she can be unpredictable. I'm sorry, I don't mean to confuse you. She's a teenager, impressionable, if you know what I mean. But, Father Monahan, if I were you, I wouldn't spend my valuable time worrying about this, uh, matter. You've got much more important things to do, I'm sure, as does your other priest."

Chris figured that Sterling must have stood up to signal the end of the conversation, but Bernie interjected, "Mr. Sterling, Doug, would you please tell Glory of our concern? I don't want this to be just between the two of us. She really should know."

Chris heard him say, "I think you must mean the three of us, to include Father Tosi, who apparently could not be present at this, uh, meeting. Too bad. I shall assume you have spoken for both of you?"

"Well, yes of course, don't need two of us to do it. He has other responsibilities, you know." Sterling did not respond to that. Chris could only imagine what was going on his mind.

"Well, Father Monahan, if you ever need any work done around here, I'll give you an unbeatable price. Incidentally, I could redo that stone work in your, uh, garden out there, make it higher quality than what you've got since the place has become so popular. Your local reporter did it proud—four times around. Lots of good publicity, I'd say. No wonder Glory was attracted to it. She does have an eye for beauty. Smart girl, much older than her years, but her downfall as well. Oh well, if you had kids of your own, Father, you'd know what I mean. Never know what she's up to next. When I see her I'll let her know you were worried about her. The other priest too."

Chris could visualize Bernie trying to digest all that. Maybe the whole Glory problem was over and done with in one short meeting. Thank you, Father Bernie.

No mention of Glory's Catholic lessons with her Grandmom. Chris bet her father knows nothing about that. He had to credit Bernie for knowing where and when to truncate the conversation, to only stick to the problem at hand. Don't hit him with both barrels. But does this wealthy developer really know his own daughter's mind? Chris wondered as he closed the register after hearing Sterling shut the front door. Only then did he head back to the kitchen for a romp with Paddy and a replay with Bernie.

Chapter TWENTY-SEVEN

SHE SHOULD HAVE RETURNED from school hours earlier but true to form, her insolence got her an after school detention. Her teacher would have preferred a suspension, but the vice principal said a detention would do for now. If her behavioral antics escalated, then she'd have a one or two day vacation.

She'd told Mr. Garber to 'fuck off' when the newly sensitive topic of poetry came up. It was a sore subject to Glory after the upbraiding she'd got from her father about the poem she'd written for Chris. She couldn't believe that Father Monahan had gone to the trouble of calling a meeting with her father, and where was Father Chris during this whole thing? She'd heard he wasn't there. After all, the poem was for him not Father Monahan.

When Mr. Garber was expounding on the essence of truth, beauty and other supreme ideas in poetry of merit, as he referred to it, he was moved to validate his claim with a personal example of his own. He puffed himself up to his full five feet, five inches, and announced to the class that he'd like to share how he wooed his wife in verse with a poem he'd written to her. Most of the kids groaned at the very idea of him courting any unsuspecting victim. No way, they were not interested. A few made gagging sounds. If ever that one class could rankle him, *they* would.

Then Glory made a snide remark under her breath. He thought he'd heard what was not intended for his ears and addressed her as 'Gloria' again, which annoyed her immeasurably. You'd think after being in his class since Hallowe'en, he'd get it right, but 'no,' she'd said to herself. It made her dislike him even more than his pompousness.

She spoke out to him in her rudest tone, "My name is Glory, Mr. Garber. Get it right next time, will you?"

Garber did not appreciate a chorus of 'Glory, Glory, Halleluia, her ass goes marching on.' Glory only smirked at the kids at the back of the room, such juveniles as she referred to them, but Garber reddened. He paused seemingly to decide what rebuke he should make to the chanters but then wound up saying nothing. He was focused solely on the main offender.

"Well," Glory spoke, still ignoring the sexist lyrics, "OK, Mr. Garber, will you? They just, uh, reinforced my name, you know."

He disregarded her request. "What did I hear you say, uh, under your breath about, uh, poetry of merit? Did I hear you right?"

"I don't know. Did you?" she volleyed. He asked her to repeat her comment and she asked him if he was a fan of Dostoyevsky.

"I do not believe that is in any way pertinent to our discussion," he barked. "What if I said 'yes,' that Dostoyevsky was indubitably a very good writer, but isn't our topic poetry, and the realm of, uh, ideas and ideals?" he went on. Glory seriously doubted that Mr. Garber had any idea of the Russian writer's 'one supreme idea' that Chris had mentioned in the garden when his old friend Aleks was there. He certainly was no match for Chris, in her opinion.

Meanwhile the class grew more unruly with a few more 'Glory, Glory' choristers joining in. Garber and Glory both ignored the chants.

Glory spoke over the din, "Well, Mr. Garber, shouldn't that one supreme idea of his, the immortality of the human soul, um, show up in poetry of merit or in the poem you wrote for Mrs. Garber?"

Garber didn't quite know how to take it. Was it another of her jabs or was she really interested in the supreme idea postulated by the Russian author? Or in poetry of merit, for that matter? They could undertake that discussion another time if she weren't so testy.

"I don't know what you're talking about, Gloria," he spurted. At this point, he tried to quell the chants by raising and lowering his hand to the class in a 'quiet down' gesture. Glory too was tired of hearing them. She seemed to shoo them away as though they were a swarm of gnats.

"You may have forgotten but I haven't. I had asked you what you said under your breath, remember?" Garber persisted, accentuating each word, which Glory interpreted as badgering.

"Well yes, I said it under my breath so I'm going to answer you under my breath," she said softly, then in a well calculated stage whisper. When he looked increasingly peeved at her insolence, she then continued in a bellowing voice. "I figured you wouldn't get it. I knew you wouldn't even know the one supreme idea. To you, those ideas are all over the place, not one any more supreme than the other. Some teacher you are. You know, just get out of my face. So why don't you just go and fuck off, Garber."

That did it. He could not have anticipated where she was going with her Dostoyevsky stuff and ideas in poetry. But her response wounded him, not only because it was inappropriate but unfounded, in his esteemed opinion.

She didn't let up yelling, 'fuck off' over the chants of 'Glory, Glory' until Garber phoned the office and she was escorted to the vice principal in charge of discipline. But as her teachers in the public high school well knew, Glory was Glory. Even the administrators threw up their hands in desperation, wishing she'd go back to the private school where her parents had paid dearly for her education. But even they couldn't put up with her. Poor little rich girl, they all said—for lack of anything else. A problem in the flesh with no viable solution.

———— ·◈· ————

THAT MORNING BEFORE school Glory, still steaming from the lecture she got from her father, dug into her mother's mad money and pulled out a wad of bills. Once released from the detention room, she dashed over to the corner Walgreen's and bought herself enough make-up and junk to fill a void in her backpack. Then she stopped at the Dunkin Donuts for a latte and two chocolate donuts to wallow in her misery tinged with a hefty dose of anger. Minutes later one of her detention mates, Spike Gilbert, slid into the booth next to her. He'd had a crush on her since she was expelled from the Academy and wound up in his English class. She, however, found him to be a bore like most of the boys her age but he came in handy when she needed weed, which she did at the moment. The money she pilfered would get her enough for a while. So when he slid a little too close to her, she managed to smile at him.

"You sure did a number on old Garbage face," he said to her. She didn't respond. "You know after you left he gave us a quiet study, told us to read poems but they were in the wrong chapter and he told us to do the questions, too. I guess you threw the asshole way off course." Still no reaction from Glory. Spike went on. "You know, Glor, I wasn't one of the guys singing out. I'd never do that to you. It was those jerkoffs in the back of the room." More silence. "I just want you to know I'm on your side, Babe."

"Wanna bite?" she asked with her mouth full of chocolate. She'd heard him but why give him the satisfaction? But it was good; she wanted him on her side.

"Yeah, sure, Glor, I'll take a bite of anything you have to offer," he said in the special tone of voice he reserved for her. It was known that he found Glory to be the girl of his dreams, but what kind of dreams? His buddies could guess.

Nor wanting him to touch her second donut, she broke off a small piece and crammed it into his mouth. "Mmm. Thanks, Glor." He scarfed it down and put his hand out for more. She slapped it and smiled. He looked into her eyes and asked, "Where'd you go after they let us out? I was looking for you."

"I couldn't wait to get my ass outta there. My ass just went marching on, like the song. Ha ha. I just ran out and took a walk, till, well, you know, like here we are. Whatcha do, follow me? What are you some kind of a stalker?" He laughed then joined her in what to him wasn't all that funny. He only wanted her to like him—a lot.

He may have been her supplier, but he was used to her lingo and put up with whatever she thrust at him. He thought it made her even more appealing. They had sort of become friends, in his estimation, but it was a symbiotic relationship at best. He would like to be known as Glory's boy friend but he realized that wasn't very likely. He held onto his hopes any way. Glory had him in her pocket. And both of them knew it.

Today she needed a sounding board. Her father had lost it yesterday after dinner, she told Spike to earn his sympathy. She wouldn't tell him why. She did tell him her father's looking into some ritzy boarding school in Switzerland for her. Spike just about fainted, or so he pretended to. He may have been making money off her and her Academy friends, but he also really wanted to be with her right there in Wexford Falls, not a whole ocean apart. Glory may have been rich, but she was different, the kind of different he liked.

She bought him a latte, which she shared with him. He could hardly contain his delight at the intimacy, though he would have preferred another type of closeness. He always hoped. Sure, it was fine with him. They'd take a little walk before she faced what she called round two of the firing squad at home. She told him she was on everybody's shit list except for her Grandmom who was still grinding away at the Catholic lessons with her spirited grand-daughter. That seemed to be the right way for Glory to stay on her Grandmom's side, her one true ally. Spike didn't ask her about Catholic stuff. Another time, maybe. He could care less. Who needed religion?

"Let's walk down the street over by St. Aeden's, OK?" she asked zipping up her parka. She put on her white angora earmuffs and mittens to match. He opened the door for her and they left. Spike took hold of her furry hand as they walked.

"What's there for you, Glor? Why St. Aeden's?" he asked. "We can walk anywhere we want around here, like on the green, or over by the falls."

"No, I know what I want," she answered with conviction. He wouldn't ask her again. He always let her take the lead, and he'd follow.

When they approached the prayer garden, she looked up at the rectory kitchen window, the one on the second floor where the priests took their meals. It was in total darkness, as was the entire rectory save for a faint glow in the downstairs front room. Night light, she assumed.

Good, she thought, they're out, all of them. The couple approached the garden gate where the 'Open Sunrise to Sunset' sign had been removed. In its place was a new one. She read it aloud, slowly, as though each word had a special meaning of its own. It hit her like a sucker punch—the sign, a home-fashioned slab of wood bearing the warning: ***BEWARE OF THE DOG***. It wasn't there a day or so ago. So why now today? It threw her into a frenzy. She could sense where it came from, and why it was there.

"No freakin' way. A goddamn dog he's got now. A watch dog?" Her anger intensified. "Oh, I guess the mutt's quiet now, not doing a very good job. Or maybe he's out too. Well, that makes a lot of sense. You get a watch dog and you take him away. So what's next, an armed guard? I suppose whatever it takes to keep me away?" she stomped her feet in anger into a pile of snow.

"Whoa," Spike said. He couldn't begin to understand why that sign would set her off like that. "Hey, what's up, Glor? It's only a freakin' sign. Don't let it get you. You think some Cujo's gonna come out an eat you all up?" By then he was laughing at the very thought.

His attempt at humor eluded her. She glared at him. "How could they? I had no idea they were so pissed at me." Consumed with anger, she yanked off a mitten and tore the sign off the post. "Gimme your lighter. Now, Spike."

Spike would give her anything she wanted. He dug into his jeans pocket and handed her the shiny object. She flicked it and directed the flame to burn off the letters, not very successfully though. She swore. Then she tore the sign from the post and tried to crack it. No success there either. That was it: they'd smash it to pieces. It was made of thin wood. When she couldn't get it to crack, using her hands, Spike put it under foot and got it to split again and again. Glory picked up the pieces and put them in a heap there at the garden entrance.

"There," she said triumphantly, "I'll show them." She could spit fire. Instead her breath came out in a stream of frosty air.

"Hey, Spike, come in here with me," she ordered. "Over here." She indicated a spot out of sight by the hollies and flung her body flat on her back onto the bushes, bending a large bush with her weight. She motioned for Spike to join her. He needed no coaxing. She could feel the branches bending, some snapping under the combined weight.

"Hey Spike," she whispered. She didn't want any passers-by to hear them.

"Yeah, Babe, what up?" he asked, hopefully. The close contact was heating him up.

"You wanna hear something about holly bushes?" she cooed. She was so tight to him he could almost taste her chocolate breath.

"You know, Glor Babe, you've got the most beautiful eyes I ever saw?" He was in heaven at that moment, just waiting for something wonderful to happen, hoping.

She ignored his remark. "I said..."

"Yeah, I heard. Sorry. Holly bushes, well, uh, not really, not what I had in mind, but I'll bet you're gonna tell me all about them. You know, I got better ideas." He shifted his weight. More branches cracked.

"OK," she said repositioning herself. "I'll tell you."

Then he said softly, "I'll listen to the bush thing if it keeps you looking at me with those eyes. I like watching your lips move when you talk to me. You can say anything you want to me."

Glory grabbed his attention when she told him the holly thing was sexual. He figured it was going to be a joke of some kind or another. He told her he could never remember punch lines, but to go ahead anyhow.

She adjusted her weight and leaned into him and began the lesson. "No joke, it's for real, they say. Who am I to question? So, the holly bushes, the male bush makes the female bush get berries, you see these little red things, without even touching her. Imagine that. No contact and she makes berries. Weird, huh?"

A little deflated, he answered, "Sound like pollination to me. That's not very sexual. I really don't see it with plants, not in your life. And I don't feel it. Sounds like you haven't had a bio course yet. But, hey, you made me a little smarter today. So, good lesson, Glor. He inched closer to her."

The two allies smoked a joint, saying little, which was fine with Spike. He just wanted to be close to her. Then all of a sudden she shifted her weight and fished into her backpack for her pocketknife, which she'd kept well hidden in case of emergencies. This was no emergency but it would come in handy for what she thought about doing. She turned away from Spike and looked over at the Christmas roses by the Mary statue, the ones that remained after she'd plucked the others on the opposite side. She thought a minute then refocused her attention. She opened the knife and clipped off a few slender holly branches before closing it, although the act seemed like an after thought. Spike sighed with relief. He had no idea what Glory wanted to cut.

By now Spike was in a sitting position, taking in his surroundings. He caught sight of the stag statue. "Hey, Glor, what the heck's a reindeer statue doing in a holy garden?"

"Oh, him, yeah, it's a long story. I forget, some silly tale the priest told me. It has to do with that moldy old saint over there. See that statue. Aeden's his name. You say it with a long 'A' so you don't mix it up with Eden. Like the garden of, you know. Aeden—that's the church's name, too. That stag, uh, it's Aeden's, um, alter ego or something...I think, I don't remember. Not important anyhow. Hey, come on, Spike, let's get outta here," she whispered in his ear, blowing gently. It left him tingling. Then all of a sudden as though an idea struck her, she put out the joint in the snow, reached over and put it in his pocket. "It looks like there's no one over there." She gestured at the rectory. "And the priests and the watch dog are out. Perfect. You and I are gonna have a snowball fight." Then she rattled off the rules, her rules for the game.

Spike was feeling too relaxed for that kind of action, he was hoping for another kind of action, but whatever Glory wanted, he'd go along. The more they did together, the higher his hopes, and he believed he was gaining ground. He'd even agree to mount the stag, or whoever's alter ego it was, if Glory wanted him to.

Glory had the wits about her to select an area where they wouldn't be seen from the street. There the two teens chased each other and pelted one another and hit some unintended targets with snow balls, at least that's what Spike thought. Glory had suggested they put some nice little rocks inside them like she and her brother used to do. Spike wasn't sure that was such a good idea, they could get hurt, but...

They hoped no one had heard the glass break. Not one but three window panels were shattered when Spike said they should end their game. Glory gave him a look and shrugged. The two held their breath for what felt like hours to Spike. When they heard nothing—no sirens or anyone approach—Spike said in a tiny voice, "Glor, hey, I guess we better split."

He had managed to stay beneath the radar with all his dealings and did not want to risk getting arrested for something like vandalism or anything, and from what he could sense, Glory didn't seem at all concerned.

"Yeah, you better run," she said as though nothing had happened. "I'll text someone at home and tell them I was held up." She laughed at the probable impact of her words. "I mean delayed. She laughed but this time it was a more of a nervous chuckle. I'll say, 'I, uh, stopped to grab a bite and saw a friend and we started yakking and, ooh, am I freezing.' They'll send someone to come get me and they'll want me to eat dinner with them and I'll scoot upstairs and tell them I've got my period or something and they'll feel sorry for me and let me alone. Grandmom will come up with something like soup and stuff."

"Cool, see ya, Glor. Later." Spike said. It was all he could manage after the damage they'd caused. He took off in the opposite direction, chilled from their romping and shivering as the temperature plummeted. He didn't need a ride home. His mother's apartment was only a few blocks from the center of town, a neighborhood the Sterling-Baies would deem 'undesirable', and his mother probably wasn't home anyhow. And his older brother, who knows? He could be just about anywhere.

Chapter TWENTY-EIGHT

CHRIS'S CELL WAS VIBRATING inside his jacket, an annoying buzzing against his chest. His first thought was to let it go. He'd check it later back at the rectory. He and Bernie were at his parents' house only for a brief visit, so he thought, but when he told Marie they were coming and bringing a guest for her to meet, she went all out. Baked lasagna, a mixed green salad with homemade vinaigrette, and crispy rolls were laid out and waiting for them. Dessert was a new recipe she was trying out on them. Fred had already given it his seal of approval. How could he disappoint his mother or Bernie, for that matter?

The purpose of the visit was to introduce Paddy to his parents who hadn't had a dog since he and Beth were in eighth grade. His parents offered to dog sit when Chris was on the ski trip. Bernie eagerly accepted the offer, recalling Father Will's discomfort with Paddy, and the cleric's hesitation about taking Chris's place for that weekend. They left it at that—he'd call later with his decision. If Father Will couldn't do it, then next in line would be Father Donovan whose allergy to flowers wouldn't be an issue in the dead of winter, but he wasn't Bernie's first choice. Truth be known, they didn't get along the way he and Chris did. Donovan's personality was such that he would take issue with much of what anyone had to say, Bernie included, whereas Chris and Bernie would always discuss civilly, Chris always deferring to the elder, well most of the time. Simply put, Rollo Donovan was confrontational, liked to argue a point, any point, and he liked being right. That's just how he was. And Bernie wasn't up for that type of deal. He could feel his systolic numbers rise when Donovan just came into the room, ready to spar verbally.

The cell began to buzz again. Chris ignored it a second time. He checked to see who the caller was. He decided he could wait another hour. Sergeant Robert Smith was probably looking for a donation for the Boys Club. Chris donated on a regular basis but with all his Christmas responsibilities, he supposed he'd forgotten. It was a favorite charity of his. He felt like an honorary member since he went to the club when he had free time in the evening and played basketball with the kids. He'd return the call later.

Paddy hit it off better than expected with Chris's parents, but they learned right off to keep the cellar door closed. Paddy for an inexplicable reason to Chris and Bernie began to run up and down the stairs and all around the basement over and over until Marie shut the door and gave Paddy a treat that Chris had brought for him.

He laughed when his mother yelled down to his father. "Fred, what in the world are you doing to that poor dog?" His answer was typical—'nothing', Fred being a man of few words.

He may have been doing nothing all right, but he did have a three-ring circus going on downstairs. Fred had Chris's old Lionel train set in full motion, his boom box playing his favorite classic rock tunes and his electric sander grinding away on the cradle that he was refinishing for the Tisdale baby. That was enough to excite Paddy.

To save his mother a trip, Chris agreed to drop off dinner for Marty and Sylvie on the way back to the rectory. Marty had a meeting at the school, which was in the opposite direction of the Tosis. Sylvie in robe and slippers met him at the door. Chris went in and set up the meal for her. She hugged him and told him she was delighted he'd agreed to be the baby's godfather. The long days alone in bed made her starved for company, he assumed. She expressed displeasure that her mother had remarried so quickly, especially since she'd not had the opportunity to meet the man who'd be her step-father. She also learned she now had a new step-brother nearly half her age. His name was Amir, like his father's. What did Chris think of that, she asked him. He didn't know what to say, so he shrugged and smiled, adding something to the effect that she was very lucky to have a sibling even if he's so much younger and lives so far away. At that moment he heard Bernie honk the horn on the pickup, a reminder that they'd better get going. He promised her they'd catch up at a later time. She hugged him good-by and he left.

He became concerned when the phoned buzzed a third time on his way to the truck. This time he swiped the green circle on his iPhone and heard an agitated Sergeant Smith at the other end saying, "Reverend Father Christopher Tosi, old buddy, where the heck have you been? Don't you know enough to answer the damn phone when you get a call from a cop. What's the matter with you?" Chris's response was equally irreverent. "And why the hell should you give a damn, Smitty?"

That's how the two old friends were. Both had played on the Birch Valley Basketball Team their junior year. Senior year the team went undefeated even with Chris out of commission after the tragedy and Anton so bereaved he couldn't play for over a week. Somehow his teammates pulled together and triumphed in Chris's absence. When Smitty got hired by the Wexford Falls Police Department, Chris was sure his town and St. Aeden's would be well protected. And for the most part they have been.

Bernie honked a second time as he watched Chris chat and laugh, and then look very serious, too serious, almost alarmed.

Something was up, Bernie feared. Chris agreed to meet Smitty in half an hour. He'd tell Bernie they were going for coffee at Dunkin Donuts to do some catching up. Paddy had had a sufficient dose of exercise on the stairs so Chris would forego the nightly walk, and take him downstairs to do his duty. He didn't want Bernie to think anything was amiss, not tonight anyhow. Tomorrow was another day. He was still concerned with Bernie's health since getting that phone call from Molly. Bernie seemed OK enough but he wasn't really one hundred percent, in Chris's estimation. Bernie was clever. He could fake it, but Chris could see beyond the façade.

After settling Paddy upstairs Chris walked over to his garden. At first he noticed the absence of Bernie's new sign by the gate. He didn't have to look much farther. He nearly tripped over a stack of wooden fragments. Vandals, he said to himself, shaking his head in disbelief. A stupid sign, of all things! He was almost afraid to venture into the garden. What if his treasured plantings were uprooted or his statues desecrated? If someone could smash a sign then maybe they would hack away at a statue. He shuddered at the thought. Then he took a deep breath and entered, training his flashlight here and there, his eyes darting down one path and another. The Christmas roses were intact. He said a prayer of gratitude for that. But a holly at one end was bent and a few branches were snapped off clean. "Darn, darn, darn," he said aloud as he heard Smitty's cruiser drive around to the garden entrance. Thankfully, no lights or sirens, as Chris had requested...

The two former athletes and buddies greeted each other as they used to in high school. Smitty suggested they take a walk around the grounds. Chris didn't want to do anything that would make Bernie suspicious of the police officer's visit. So he pretended to take Smitty on a casual walk through the garden first. Chris figured if Bernie was watching he'd think the two were just passing time. Smitty took notes as he examined the bent hollies. Definite evidence of wrongdoing. He saw fresh cigarette ashes on the snow. Recent, he thought, otherwise they would have blown away. Evidence of human presence. And oh yes, a few small branches looked like they were cut with a knife—deliberately. Not much else. The sign pieces told him it was an angry intruder with an axe to grind, he told Chris. 'Someone is very pissed at you or your church' were his exact words.

"Can you get me into the church?" Smitty asked, hoping Chris had the key with him. He needed for them to see the source of the breakage.

"You said you got a call?" Chris asked as they walked briskly over to St. Aeden's main entrance. "Did the person ID himself?"

"Yeah, I got a call. I didn't recognize the name, just someone who was in the neighborhood and heard glass breaking, so he did his civic duty, he told me, and he called. Said he was out taking a walk like he did every day after supper, weather permitting, and thought he saw some kids running. That's about it. I was on the desk, covering for a colleague," he said. "So, buddy, that was when I started calling you. Glad you finally decided to answer. But I'm sure as heck *you're* not."

Chris gave him a look. "So you're still on duty right now," Chris figured. Smitty nodded, said he was on till eleven. If Bernie noticed where they were going, he'd not think of it as an investigation. Any time was a good time to stop in for a prayer, Bernie always said, but he made sure the church was locked up tight after dark, because he'd also say, 'You never know.' The many times the Poor box had been raided taught Bernie a painful lesson.

"I think I'll just use the flashlight. We shouldn't be long," Chris said as he genuflected. Smitty imitated the act then rushed up the side aisle toward the altar. Chris followed, feeling a wave of nausea roll over him.

"Here, over here, Chris," Smitty whispered. He wasn't used to using full voice in church regardless of what was or was not going on.

Chris was right behind him. They stood near puddles of what was melting snow and shards of colored glass. Chris feared they could be the original windows. The gaps in the windows' patterns let in the weak evening light of the half moon and the icy January air. "See these rocks," Smitty pointed out as he knelt down checking the area. He was holding several walnut size rocks in his hand. Disgust distorted his regular features into a grimace. "Kids," he huffed half under his breath. He thought of his own two pre-school age sons and wondered whose kids could have committed that wanton act on a church of all places.

"Hard to miss," Chris said sadly, rolling a stone over in his hand. "This makes the snow balls more like weapons." He was getting an awful pulling in the back of his throat, only all too familiar to him. He looked upward to assess the damage. "Oh, God, look at those windows." He let out a sigh and lowered his head. Smitty could not imagine what Chris was feeling at the moment.

"You know, Chris, here's what I'd say from my experience: one hit's an accident, two, uh, well maybe, just maybe a coincidence. I know, that's pushing it a little." He paused, observing Chris's growing distress.

"I get it. Three's...vandalism. Am I right?" Chris said, paling.

Smitty nodded in agreement, saying it was most likely the act of someone with that proverbial axe to grind, especially combined with the smashed sign on the same day. Chris said he would have noticed if the sign was down earlier in the day. He dreaded the next question. He didn't know what he would or could reveal to Smitty. So he avoided the direct confrontation.

"I guess I should contact the insurance company," Chris said, refocusing on the next logical step to take. He couldn't look at Smitty, but the sergeant and friend saw fit to direct him as to what the procedure should be.

"We need to go down to headquarters and fill out a report," Smitty said in his professional policeman tone. Unlike the lay person, he was trained to pick up on nervousness. Chris's vibes told him it was more than a case of the nerves. "Father Bernie believes we're going out for coffee, which we will. The coffee at headquarters isn't half bad. We have real cream too. The Cremora days are long gone, thank God. It shouldn't take too long." He watched Chris soften at that. His face had been frozen in a mask of dread.

They observed protocol, as Smitty was required to do. Chris tried to estimate the burden this vandalism would cause to St. Aeden Church. He'd have to check on the deductible. And would an artisan be able to get the right colored glass to replace the old broken fragments of the leaded glass masterpieces? In the meantime the openings would allow drafts to invade the church and the heating bill would skyrocket. They had to do something. Chris could sense the consequences and it scared him.

Smitty wanted information from Chris. He had an inkling Chris might know who the most logical culprits could be. He tried asking if he had pissed off anyone lately, say, any of the basketball players at the Boys Club. Chris shook his head. Never in a million years would those boys do anything like that. They respected him, he told Smitty. Everyone seemed to have plans over school vacation. And who would ever do anything to harm anything connected with Father Bernie or his church?

Chris tried to convince him that his greatest fear was keeping this from Bernie until the morning, after at least one of them got a good night's sleep. He could wait until after morning mass, but wait a minute, he'd have to tell Bernie that he himself would be celebrating the early mass. Bernie's eyebrows would shoot up in disbelief at the offer. He didn't want Bernie to walk into the church and see the damage. Parishioners too at mass would see the missing panels all covered up. There would be questions. He feared for Bernie's health. St. Aeden's was his life. Smitty bought that excuse, for the time being, but he knew there was more. Chris was hiding something. Since they were such good friends, he decided not to press. He'd continue the investigation the next day.

"Will this make the papers?" Chris asked, pacing. He'd been chewing on a cuticle since they got to headquarters. He'd hardly touched his coffee, even with real cream, which they'd stopped buying for themselves at the rectory. Mrs. Hopkins, a self-proclaimed coffee addict, had made that decision in the name of Bernie's good health.

"Yeah, it should, when they put in the listing from the police blotter. You know, I'm sure you see them in the paper," Smitty said, observing his friend's reaction. "Should that matter?"

"Well, of course, it matters," Chris said, surprised. "St. Aeden's doesn't need that kind of negative publicity." Chris was still pacing.

"Well, what if it helps catch those jerks? It's one thing to break someone's windows by accident but, on purpose, and at a church? Come on now, Chris, get real." Smitty thought it was more than just the publicity. It had to be. Doesn't Chris want the guilty party or parties to get caught and arrested? Chris told Smitty he'd walk back. The fresh air would do him good.

Chapter TWENTY-NINE

NO SOONER HAD CHRIS exited the precinct did Smitty call out after him to 'hold on.' They had a job to do. Where was Chris's head, he asked himself. It wasn't at all like his old friend. Once Chris was summoned back, Smitty asked him if he knew if the hours at Swenson's Hardware were back on regular since the owners were still away and a Swedish relative was minding the store. Cute little thing, he told Chris blushing.

"Oh yeah, that's the little granddaughter Ingrid. And that little thing is college age, I'll have you know, and doing a huge favor for her grandparents," Chris said. "No one else was available back home. She really doesn't know the store very well, I mean the merchandise, but she tries."

"The hours, Chris, are they open now, do you think?" Smitty asked. He wished he hadn't spoken about Ingrid. But she was a cutie.

"Yeah, they're open till nine tonight," Chris answered. He'd seen lights on there each night until then.

"Well, let's you and I get our butts over there so we can take care of the windows for tonight." Smitty was telling him the obvious. "You can't just let the church freeze up like that."

"You're right, buddy. I'm sorry. I don't know where my head is." Smitty kept wondering the same thing.

With her engaging smile and her lilting accent, Ingrid Swenson had gotten over the shock of seeing the team of a policeman and a priest coming into the hardware store. She directed them to the correct aisle and proudly indicated the wares that they needed. Chris noted the rolls of tape came in several different colors so he bought a blue, a red and a yellow, hoping it would blend in and look less like a patch up job.

The two went to work laying heavy duty plastic over the missing panels, affixing the sheeting to the windows with the duct tape. But all the adept taping in the world could not disguise evidence of the damage.

"That should take care of it for now," Smitty said, feeling all around for drafts. He returned the chair he'd been standing on to its rightful place. Chris surveyed their handiwork, which was about one step up from shoddy, accentuated by the different colored strips of tape. But it would have to suffice until repairs could be made.

Paddy gave it away. They heard his excited bark as he spotted Chris up front near the altar. He loped down the aisle and skidded to a stop. He rolled over by Chris for a belly rub. Then he sniffed out Smitty who reached down and patted his head. Paddy's tail was going at record speed. Some watchdog, nice size and all, Smitty thought, but kept it to himself. Not far behind was Father Bernie at a slower pace. When the church was illuminated it took on a glow that startled Smitty, who was used to a more austere, stark setting in his place of worship—when he chose to attend. The sudden brightness burned Chris's eyes. When his eyes met Bernie's for a split second, he sank like a little boy caught in a mischievous deed.

"Officer Smith, good evening, so nice to see you at this hour. Welcome to St. Aeden's," Bernie began. Bernie knew something was up. "So Chris, you thought you could put one over on the old man."

"Bernie, I, uh, was..." Chris said, eyes downcast, but Bernie never let him finish.

"Oh, sure you were going to tell me, I suppose when the time was right." Bernie's eyes flashed. "You are forgetting this is our church, yours and mine, and if there's a problem, it belongs to both of us."

Bernie looked over at the patch job, then at the two men. He nodded, saying it could do for the night until they got someone over in the morning, someone who could make it more airtight until, until...that was the part that brought him almost to tears. Chris was right. Those were the original stained glass windows and they were large panels. Bernie tried to keep his emotions in check. He was taking deep breaths. Chris could see the effort and the strain, and it worried him.

Smitty spoke first. "Father Bernie, this could do the trick for now, what Chris and I did."

Bernie looked up at the patch job and for a moment the other two could sense his gratitude. He nodded then he remained strangely silent for a long minute, which bothered Chris.

Again Smitty spoke. "Father Bernie, we'll find the guys who did this and they'll pay. I'll get things rolling in the morning. Not much more I can do tonight unless you happen to know for sure who the vandals are."

Smitty studied both priests' faces. They had a pretty good idea, he believed, but they're not going to say anything to me tonight. He decided not to press. The shock of the damage was more than enough for them to bear at one time.

"Chris," Bernie began as he walked closer to the windows and looked up. "We can check the insurance policy in the morning. Gotta look at the deductible, for a starter, I guess."

Smitty agreed that it would be a good idea, and to get an insurance adjuster out as soon as possible. Both priests nodded.

They were weary. Nothing like this had ever happened to St. Aeden's, or had it? The church was built over 150 years ago.

They expressed their thanks to Smitty, who left with an uncomfortable feeling in his gut. He told himself it would pass. He also had a feeling that he might not hear from them. But he had to trust they would know what to do.

Chris did not stop Bernie from refilling his shot glass of brandy before retiring for the night. It would help him to sleep after the ordeal. The second shot worked in reverse for Chris. His fitful sleep was peppered with turbulent dreams none of which he could recall. He was grateful for that.

He decided he would join Bernie at morning mass, which was rare. He feared Bernie would break down during his homily when referring to the vandalism, which was the time they planned to mention it to the congregation. Bernie had mastered keeping the morning mass homilies short and to the point, and it worked. Mass was well attended for January mornings. Chris figured it could be a new year's resolution for the retirees who could make it to church.

Bernie spoke a few timely words in line with the liturgy and provided a lesson to take with those who heard him as he always did in simple terms but added that all should keep in mind the gift of the season—love, joy and peace, and to live out the Christmas spirit. He tacked on what he called 'the elephant in the room'—the patched windows. He amended his statement, apologizing for the profane metaphor. He asked the parishioners to check around to see if anyone knew what had happened the previous night. That was it. Chris was relieved.

Smitty had called to say he'd spoken again to the man who'd seen kids running around the church at the time when he heard glass break. He couldn't tell how many there were or whether they were young kids or teenagers. The man blamed it on his vision, but he said there was nothing wrong with his hearing. When Smitty checked for footprints it was next to impossible to determine anything. Any tracks in the snow were indistinguishable. And in the garden, the walks were clean—no trace of snow or ice. Chris didn't want any casualties. His garden paths were cleared year round for those who came there to pray.

---- ⧸◈⧹ ----

AGATHA O'TOOLE HUNG up her coat, scarf and hat on the rack in her office at Sterling-Baie Enterprises. She removed her snow boots, stored them in a cupboard for such items and slipped into a pair of black closed toe pumps in line with her proper office attire. She was the front person. She had to look professional, and she always did. She had been the administrative assistant to Douglas Sterling for twenty years now, and the job always came first. Sterling allowed her to come in a little later since she attended the early morning mass at St. Aeden's once or twice a week. She'd stay on as long as needed after regular hours so it was never a problem, and because of her allegiance to the company he accorded her a little leeway. She was his right hand person and she felt indispensible to the company and to him. And when he opened his office door each day to greet her, she was usually wearing a bright smile on her long face, which actually made her somewhat attractive, in his estimation. But not so today.

"Good morning, Aggie," he said cheerily after he'd checked to see if anyone else was in her office. He'd never call her anything other than Miss O'Toole in the presence of prospective clients or anyone else for that matter. He was a proper man, a decent man by Agatha's standards. Tall, trim and distinguished looking, with a crooked but engaging smile, he was a good looking man by anyone's standards. He'd never made a pass at her, and although she admired him immensely, their relationship was always above board. Both remembered he was married.

"Good morning, Doug," she said blandly trying to mask her feelings as she busied herself getting situated for the day's work. Likewise, he was 'Doug' when no one was present. Finally, she couldn't hold in her feelings any longer. "What a terrible shock I had this morning at mass." She shook her head in disbelief.

"Is it Father Monahan? Is he all right?" Doug asked, remembering his meeting of a few days ago at St. Aeden's. But he had no reason to believe otherwise. The priest seemed fine to Doug after expressing his concern about the poem and what it could imply. Doug agreed to speak to Glory, which was what the priest had asked him to do.

"I would say he's doing remarkably well, considering what happened at St. Aeden's the night before," she said, settling herself into her new swivel chair. Doug Sterling had taken her to an office furniture company to update their furnishings and urged her to select whatever she wanted. Comfort and style, he stressed. She was hesitant when she saw the price tags. But appearance meant a lot to Sterling. He was big on first impressions and he could afford the best.

She spoke as she set up her desk. He was strict about neatness and order so she kept all her accessories out of sight in the desk drawers. "Someone busted up his windows last night," she said. She didn't notice her boss blanch. She was straightening a paperweight and arranging her pens. She continued, after a long pause, "Some stained glass panels in the church..."

She was beginning to lose her composure. Her parents, even her grandparents were married in St. Aeden's Church, and Father Bernie was a fixture in Wexford Falls, knew everyone and trusted them as well. She recalled his message of love and peace that morning at mass. She found it hard to concentrate on the joy of the season, not after looking at the patched windows. She couldn't imagine anyone being so cruel and heartless to such a kind man.

"Are you serious, Aggie?" was all he could muster. He asked her the questions anyone would think to ask and got the only answers Agatha could surmise.

Doug Sterling went through the motions of going about his business, and Agatha did as well, but without her positive attitude. She was hounded by the very idea of it all—malicious damage to church windows, her church. He asked her to cancel his appointments from twelve to two and reschedule them. She'd know what to do. He told her he'd be taking Belinda, his wife, out to lunch. It was a special occasion, he said, not choosing to elaborate. Agnes knew it wasn't their anniversary or anyone in the family's birthday, and she hadn't been asked to do any shopping for him since Christmas. That must have broken the bank, she thought. However, she did recall they had cancelled a planned trip, combination business and pleasure, to Dubai without any explanation last August. Rumor had it that it had something to do with Glory. News circulated fast in their town, and by the time it was told and retold, it gained greater proportions, but people do talk. She'd witnessed the effects of it all too often.

Sterling phoned once about three p.m. He'd be making on-site visits to check the progress on his renovation of an office building, he'd told her. Lunch was great, country club—can you expect anything less? Then he told her it did Belinda well. Did Belinda well—as if she didn't have life wrapped up in a nice neat package. She needed a pretty bow to stick on top of it too? Her only bane was Glory, and Belinda herself was part of the problem. So much was left unsaid. Agatha had her own ideas about Belinda; they too were best left unsaid. She chased away those negative thoughts; she was a Christian woman.

When Doug Sterling returned to the office after five, Agatha was wrapped up in her work. She never idled and did more than required to keep the ship afloat. Doug believed she was the real catalyst in the business's continual success. He let her know it, too.

"Busy day, I gather, Doug," she said, wishing he'd share what was really going on. She was good at reading him. She gestured over at the coffee maker. He wasn't himself after a two or three martini drenched gourmet lunch at the club. Belinda must drive him crazy, she thought, knowing how demanding the woman could be. Kind of explains the daughter too, she thought. But the son was so different; he should be just like his father some day. Decent kid. Doug didn't deserve another disappointment. Glory plus Belinda was more than enough for such a good man to handle and maintain his equilibrium, but somehow he managed.

"You gather correctly. I'm sorry, Aggie. I should have checked in with you more often. Time just flew," he said, frowning. Then he accepted a mug of coffee from her. He reached into his jacket pocket and handed her a gift certificate for lunch at the club as if she could take the time. She thanked him and put in in her top drawer. She joined him, pouring herself a cup of coffee.

"Doug, you didn't have to. This is my job, remember." Aggie could sound matter of fact when she wanted to. He has had enough emotional upheaval in his life to last two lifetimes. Calls came to the office, to her, from the school and they were not social calls. She'd had to deal with them too often and then pass them over to Sterling, the latest being Glory's outburst in her English class and the tirade at the teacher. To Doug's relief, the disposition was only a detention—this time.

Agatha recalled that awful day when a disturbing call came from the Academy. She had never seen her boss so upset. It was last October and school had been in session for less than two months. Since no complaints ever came about Glen she knew the call had to be about Glory. What had she gotten herself into now that the dean of students felt the need to contact Doug at work and so early in the morning? She passed the call to Doug.

Once things settled somewhat, Doug provided Agatha with the details as he knew them so that when the rumor mill started to turn she would have the correct information from him first hand. He shuddered to think how the rumors could distort the truth.

It seems that in the wake of the mail carrier affair, Glory took a fancy to the new music teacher at the Academy. To his regret, he had praised Glory for her great skills as a violinist, telling her she should already be first violist in an orchestra of high repute. He'd never encountered such talent before in anyone her age. Unfortunately it was the lavish praise he bestowed on her plus his youthful charm and good looks that set Glory's lips smacking. This was his first year at Academy, and as luck would have it, his last. Within the first marking period he was relieved of his duties and given a letter, a glowing recommendation. The last anyone heard he was still out of a job. And all Glory had done to expedite his removal was write him a torrid love poem, so it was said, but...

It was never determined which one of them had made the first move, Glory or Mr. Z., as the students called him, but a scandal was brewing. Glory remained mum and Mr. Z. said it was all a big mistake. He didn't elaborate, however. It was easier to rid the Academy of both of them rather than pursue an all out investigation. The dean wanted no part of police involvement. The reputation of the Academy would be at stake. As usual, Doug felt it was up to him to pick up the pieces. And so Glory wound up enrolled at the public high school. Her expulsion resulted in the loss of her place in the International Baccalaureate Program that the Academy offered. The local public high school did not participate in that prestigious and challenging program. Aggie wondered if Doug had any further contact with Mr. Z. He didn't say, and she wasn't about to ask. She wondered what had happened to set Glory off the past several months where men were concerned. Her first two years at he Academy had been uneventful. She wondered what the trigger event could have been. There absolutely had to be something, she told her self.

"I did some checking around this afternoon," Sterling said. "I'll explain later. I have to wrap things up and get moving." He sounded unusually brusque. "Oh, I almost forgot. Next time you go to your church service at St. Aeden's, put this in the collection basket. Don't lose it."

"Would I do that?" she asked lightly. He'd never done this before. He could care less about the Catholic Church, always figured her churchgoing was just an entrenched habit, like brushing your teeth before bedtime. But he was a good man, a man of principles. She wondered about the envelope, about the vandalism, and of course, dear Father Monahan and his church.

Chapter THIRTY

BERNIE WAS BEAMING for the first time in days. Chris couldn't imagine why the abrupt change in attitude after what had happened at the church and whom they suspected as the perpetrator. Estimates to repair the windows differed widely. So many variables were involved in the whole restoration project that Bernie was caught in a perpetual tizzy of facts, figures, and datelines. Meetings with this expert and that artisan were making the two priests weary and confused. Bernie shuddered when he came to the realization that the safest bet would be to call Sterling who had indisputably the best connections and knowledge when it came to restoration.

When Bernie placed the cashier's check in front of Chris's face, all he could see was zeros—it was for ten-thousand smackeroos, in Bernie's terms. Chris examined the envelope, which bore Father Monahan's name in block letters. The note was brief, in block letters as well. 'If this doesn't cut it, more will come your way.'

Chris was speechless. First of all, an anonymous donor, hmm, and a promise of more, if needed, to do the job. Was it Sterling paying for his daughter's act of vandalism? He'd have to be pretty sure of her guilt to dish out that kind of money. But in the past he was always able to buy out those whom his daughter had wronged. But an act of vandalism to St. Aeden's? This was different. Should Bernie accept the check or not, Chris wondered. Then he asked him point blank, not expecting the intensity of Bernie's reaction.

"And why in tarnation should I not accept it? It *is* a cashier's check, for goodness sake." Bernie looked at Chris as though he had three heads. Bernie paled; a vein on his freckled forehead quivered. "It's an act of generosity by some dear member of our parish, a benefactor, and just at the right time before our insurance premiums hike up and before the bishop, well, let's not go there right now, but there will be ramifications, I promise you, and they may not be what you, I mean, approve." Bernie was rambling as he did when he was rattled, but Chris was getting the idea.

"Do you know something that I don't know?" Chris looked concerned when Bernie mentioned the bishop, a kind of big bad wolf veiled threat, he wondered. "He's such a good friend of yours. What would he do?"

"He's the bishop. He can do whatever he thinks is best for the diocese," Bernie said with conviction. He wasn't letting on to anything they had discussed at their last visit, not at this time anyhow.

Chris conceded that Bernie was right. He seemed to think it was in his best interest all around. And so Bernie placed a call to Sterling-Baie Enterprises to get the process going. The less ado about the matter, the better, he thought. As for Glory, he decided he'd just have to hold his breath and hope she didn't have other plans in mind. He vowed he would not give her any reason to as long as they kept their distance. As a wealthy young teen, she must have other more interesting things to do with her time rather than spite a priest. He wondered how long she would last in the community if her father didn't keep on writing checks to avoid the consequences. But he was worried: was she really at risk for suicide as her poem hinted?

─────── ⟨∾⟩ ───────

AGATHA O'TOOLE ANSWERED the office phone sweetly when she saw Father Bernie's number come up on the caller ID. "Why sure, Father," she said. "He'll call you as soon as he's off the other line. He was expecting to hear from you. Actually, if you can hold a minute, he's just about to wrap up his call and..."

Bernie immediately thought the envelope had come from Sterling himself through Agatha O'Toole, a parishioner, whom he'd recognized. She always took the same pew as so many other regulars do. Who else would have put it in the collection basket? Or maybe it wasn't her. It could have been someone else. He couldn't think of anyone off hand though with that much disposable money. But if Glory and God knows which of her friends maliciously broke the windows, shouldn't they be punished? Face the music and pay...should he say something to that effect to Sterling? Maybe not—if his daughter was involved. Blood is thicker than water, as his mother always said. He was in a quandary. That check was now for St. Aeden's, for him to use as he wished, and Sterling-Baie Enterprises could be counted on to do the job, and do it expertly, which was why he was calling. Sterling, after all, had a stake in it. And he always protects his daughter...

------ ⟲ ------

JODIE HOPKINS, MRS. Hopkins's daughter-in-law, phoned Chris to remind him of the ski club meeting coming up two days before the trip. She told him it was mandatory and that since he was a newcomer at the job, Marty would also be there 'to share his wisdom,'" she saw fit to add.

"Gotta get the kids together for the meeting to read the riot act, parents too, Father. They're the ones responsible for what their brats might do, you know. They're the ones that gotta pay, if you know what I mean," she announced.

Chris wasn't too sure. Did she mean for any possible damages incurred in the ski lodge or otherwise? He decided not to ask her. Just let her do the talking.

"They better be there, those parents, one of them anyhow, even if they heard my spiel before. Gotta reinforce it. You know how people are. It won't harm them to give up an hour or so, miss one of their TV shows." Jodie went on and on.

How could she come across so authoritative with that chippy little voice of hers? She was a feather weight with a big mission, but the kids respected her, mostly because she had tried out for the winter Olympic ski team, and made it. Otherwise they found her a little overbearing. Chris decided he would follow her lead. Marty had already told him that that was the best way. Let her lead. Since Chris was the only newcomer in the group, he listened carefully to what Jodie really did call 'the riot act.'

All the kids were juniors or seniors so there were many eye rolls. They'd heard it all before. And in Chris's estimation, the meeting could have been over in 30 minutes, and not drag on for an hour or so. He felt sorry for Marty, Mr. Good Guy, coming to support him as chaperone. Marty could've been home with Sylvie keeping her company and making a dent in his endless stacks of papers—English essays that took him forever to grade using a silly rubric per the district's demands.

Chris believed he could handle the job. He thought getting back on the slopes might do him good. The weekend weather looked promising, perfect for skiing. He was actually feeling a tinge of excitement. Only one of the boys was from Marty's parish and he and his parents seemed fine. On a trip such as this, they'd all wind up fast friends though Chris wasn't so sure about him and Jodie as co-chapersones. She was hard to warm up to, not at all like her mother-in-law, but then they were not related.

———— ⟨∽⟩ ————

PADDY MOVED INTO THE Tosi's the day before the ski trip. Chris thought it would be a good idea for the rectory pet to have a sleep over in case his parents found it too much for them to handle. But then, Chris did not have a Plan B in mind. He advised his father to keep the cellar door closed unless he needed to exercise Paddy. Fred had taken to Paddy in a way that surprised Chris. Marie surprised both Paddy and Chris putting her culinary skills to the test. No, she certainly didn't expect Chris to try the biscuit, but Paddy surely loved it. He chomped at it till it was only a damp, crumbly mess on the kitchen floor.

"So I found a recipe for dog biscuits. What's wrong with that, Christopher?" I have some peanut butter cookies, with little criss-cross fork marks, just the way you like them, for you and Father Bernie right here in this container. Now don't you mix them up. You can take some along on your trip. There's four dozen or so inside." Chris smiled at his mother.

He ran over his checklist to ensure his parents had everything they'd need for the next few days. When he was sure they were all set, he gave Paddy a loving pat and headed for the door. Paddy, a second biscuit in his mouth, had since run off in search of Fred. They had already begun to spoil him.

As Chris was heading out, Marie dashed over to the breezeway door to hand him an unopened envelope from Anton Drobec, his basketball teammate whom Beth had tutored in English back in high school. It was postmarked from Croatia.

"Why didn't you open it, Mom? It's addressed to the Tosi family," he asked wrapping his scarf securely around his neck before his mother did the honors." He smiled, thinking, 'She must think I'm still a little boy.'

"I forgot to give it to you Christmas day and then it, uh, somehow got mixed up with some of my recipes. I found it when I pulled out the cookie recipe, not the dog biscuit one." She laughed.

"That's a new one. I'm sorry you're getting it so late. It's my fault," she explained.

It felt good to Chris to see her lighten up. Sometimes it takes man or woman's best friend to work such wonders. And it seemed she was over the shock she got when Ada Powers dropped the bomb that her son was unfit to be a priest, and then at that—no explanation. Unconscionable. If it hadn't been for Molly's call he would have had to try his best to explain the Glory thing to his mother. He hoped he'd done the right thing. God bless dear Marty. He'd explained everything to Marie that she needed to hear, custom tailoring the explanation so as to ease her troubled mind. He asked her not to bring it up to Chris, that it should be 'case closed.' It seemed to work, though she vowed she wouldn't invite the Powerses to her house any time soon without getting a sincere apology, and maybe not even after that. "Open it up, Chris. I'm looking forward to hearing what Anton has to say. He was like a member of our family that year," she said. Then she faded. That often happened when thoughts of Beth entered her mind, and Anton was so connected with her daughter that it was inevitable.

Chris hadn't planned to open it just then. He figured he'd read it once he got back to the rectory, but he changed his mind when he saw how just the mention of Anton's name had affected his mother.

"It's beautiful, Mom. Here, take a look at the card." He showed her the artistry. The holiday inscription was in Croatian, but Anton's note was written in the best English he could remember after ten years' absence, he later told Chris. He had written to Chris every year at Christmas time. He had never forgotten the Tosi family, not even after becoming a pro basketball player in his country, playing center for the KK Zagreb team. He went on to marry a medical student he'd met in Germany and they had two young children, a boy and a girl. Their most recent nanny was American, which was good for Anton's keeping up with his English. He admitted that she proofed the note in the Christmas card otherwise he'd be embarrassed with all the errors he would've made. He wrote that his wife Ana had a demanding schedule at the city hospital and that he was often on the road with the team. But he was very content with his life and hoped the same was so for me, he said. He indicated that he would be taking a cruise in the eastern Caribbean sometime later in the winter. Might Chris be interested in joining him as Ana was not able to get away at this stage of her residency? He also hoped to be able to stop by Birch Valley to say 'hello' to Chris's parents. He'd have to see if he could take the time. Marie read the note over Chris's shoulder.

"Oh, Christopher, wouldn't that be wonderful?" she said, not indicating whether she meant the cruise or Anton's possible visit to Connecticut, or both.

"Definitely, it would be great to see him after all these years and talk about the different paths our lives have taken," Chris said. He looked at his watch and told his mother he'd better get going. He also told her he would consider the cruise if he could manage to take some time for himself. Then he thought about the ski trip, which was also kind of a vacation, but not really as he had lots of responsibilities in his role as a chaperone.

---❧---

SERGEANT ROBERT SMITH, aka Smitty, had been doing some investigating of his own after hours. He liked to refer to it as that, rather than snooping. Both priests knew something about the vandalism that he didn't know. He'd stake his career on that. He'd been asking in various places of business if they heard anyone bragging about breaking church windows. Kids do talk, he well knew, and he had good ears. People can't hang onto any news good or bad, he believed. For some reason or another they feel compelled to share what they've heard. Like bubbles, they can only last so long and then they have to burst sooner or later. Rarely do they implode and disappear. Gossip mongers, blabber mouths, snitches—all of them need others to know what they know, what they got away with—a sneaky triumph of sorts.

SMITTY'S WIFE PAULETTE, a part time cafeteria employee at the high school, kept her ears and eyes open at her husband's request after he told her of the vandalism at his friend's church. He told her the priests were likely concealing the identity of the culprits and he couldn't imagine why. Maybe she could help him out.

Smitty and Paulette Duclos had met way back in middle school in Birch Valley. She was a little tomboy and the two along with some of the neighborhood kids hung out together in Winston Park. Back then Paulette could shoot baskets better than Smitty even when he tried his hardest, which forced him to work at it until he finally succeeded in making the high school team, but not until his junior year. Although he was not one of the five starters, he was nevertheless living proof that perseverance pays off. By senior year, Smitty and Paulette had become a couple. A month after graduation Smitty surprised her by joining the army. She herself hadn't made any definite plans for the future. She'd hoped they would continue dating and marry some day, which they did after he was discharged. Neither had any regrets of their choices.

Maybe if Paulette checked out who sat with whom at the lunch tables she'd overhear something. And kids talk. What she did hear, she told her husband over dinner that night, was that some rich girl who'd been thrown out of the Academy earlier in the year was heading off to a Swiss boarding school. She didn't say when, but that's big bucks, not Wexford Falls bucks, not by a long shot. A spiky haired kid whom they called Spike told his cohorts that the girl had just herself gotten in big trouble again. What for, he wasn't telling, but Paulette got the impression he knew what for. And so Smitty would find a way to investigate Spike.

His aha moment came when he decided to stop by some of the places where kids frequent after school and show the managers pictures of Spike. Paulette was the driving force. She often got kids to mug for her at the lunch tables, pretending to enjoy the food. Then she'd paste the photos in her scrapbook along with memorabilia of all kinds. She was addicted to that type of craft. Smitty thought it was a silly pastime, but she took great pride in that activity, said she was preserving history in a way. That was no problem for her. She was friendly and outgoing and the kids were happy to accommodate. They posed, some making faces, or smiled with their mouths full, others were more serious. This would not arouse any suspicion and all would remain nameless. And it worked. Smitty got what he wanted, a full face photo of Spike, making a tough face. Smitty would ask if people saw him around and who he might have been with the night of the vandalism at St. Aeden's. Word would get around and something would leak out. Smitty would get to the bottom of it.

BERYL BAINES GOT WIND of the vandalism and tsk tsked her way through a conversation with Father Bernie. He remained mum, telling her he couldn't imagine who would have the gall to do it. He maintained it was probably a gang of hooligans, horsing around, full of the dickens, he added. He told her he had a story for her and proceeded to tell of when he and his brothers had a snowball fight back in Hartford when they were in grammar school, parochial, he added. One of the brothers smashed the display window of the local bakery and the kids fished in and grabbed their share of pastries, and had sugar icing all over their faces, sticky hands too when they were caught. Bernie was smiling in his recollection, saying 'boys will be boys.' Beryl wasn't. She was dead serious, hoping to get a good story out of him. He said their dad tanned their hides 'good and proper' and they couldn't sit for a full week, plus they had to turn over their paper route money, every red cent of it, his father ordered, to Mr. Schiavone, the baker, until the price of the new plate glass was paid.

"Yeah, Beryl," he said, "I was full of the dickens, my brothers too, when we were little. Heh heh." He watched her expression. She was still not amused. She didn't buy it at all. He was making much too light of it. It would be in the wind, she said to herself, and she'd get her story.

IT WASN'T EVERY NIGHT that the entire Sterling-Baie family sat down to dinner together. Schedules made it next to impossible most days, but Doug Sterling had phoned home in the early afternoon and asked Belinda to ensure that dinner was scheduled at a time when all would be home. He told his wife he didn't care what time that would be as long as everyone in the household was present.

Glory was late getting home from school. She dragged herself into the dining room. She was in a particularly foul mood. She tossed her backpack aimlessly on her chair, plopped herself down defiantly, and pouted. She complained that they had to all sit together and have a slow pokey dinner when she needed the time to study for mid-term exams. Why couldn't she eat in her room? She asked her mother who was already in her silent treatment mode. For what? Glory had no idea. No one knew what he was going to spring on them. Belinda didn't want him to be stressed since she intended to inform him that she was planning a weekend shopping trip in New York.

Everything seemed normal enough through what Sterling had called a delightful meal *en famille*. He liked to toss around foreign phrases to show them his worldliness, and he was certainly well traveled in his business. He often used the expression '*savoir faire*.' But no one cared much for that. They'd let him have the floor, say what he had to say. It was as though he was the only one there. Silence seemed to rule. They were ready to listen to what he had to deliver. What choice did they have?

He announced to no one in particular. "I thought we'd bone up on a little French or actually, uh, a little Italian might be a better idea." A cryptic expression blanketed his face.

They all stared at him. Was he planning a European trip for the whole family for summer vacation, Belinda wondered? If so, why was he acting so serious? Glory remembered the promise of a European trip as a gift for her alone and Glen was trying to quell the growing restlessness inside him. He'd scarfed down his meal and waited as his father seemed to savor each morsel of the meal, in slow motion. He would rather be studying for his exams. He cared about his grades. Grandmom was sipping her lukewarm herbal tea. She was all ears. She loved news, any kind of news. And Glory had not entirely come out of the mood she came in with.

"We might be paying a few visits to Glory in Europe," he said as though it was nothing out of the ordinary. He reached for another roll and buttered it. He nodded before taking a bite. He could see that the twins were impatient, ready to go elsewhere and do whatever. But he was the one who called the plays, held the purse strings, and they knew it, as did Belinda.

"Me?" Glory said. Then she perked up. "Am I going somewhere soon? My vacation this summer, you mean."

"Very likely, but not just summer," he answered in an acerbic tone of voice that always caused her concern. By now she was on the edge of her seat. Then she got up abruptly. "I'd like to be excused."

"Permission not granted," he said firmly. He was running this meeting. "Sit down, Glory, please. Let me finish what I started."

Glory looked glum, then defiant. "You know, you can't send me just any old place. I happen to live here."

"Well, where else can I send you to school? You tell me," he said his eyes riveted on her. His slender face was turning red.

"There are private schools all over the place," she said. Tears formed in her hazel eyes. This usually worked with her father. Her mother stayed mum. It was better that way, but for whom?

"I, uh, have sent a deposit to The American School in Switzerland otherwise known as TAMIS. It's only about ten minutes from Lake Lugano—one breathtaking setting, I assure you. That's in the Italian section of Switzerland. I hear their music program is outstanding. And you are headed there, young lady," he said. His eyes were fixed on her, his stance unwavering.

By then hers were soaked. "My Christmas gift was supposed to be a summer vacation in Europe. Not to be *there* for the whole year. So why are you bringing up this boarding school thing?" she pleaded. He admired the way she could look him squarely in the eye and pretend not to know. To her, it was an exile, not the European vacation she was promised.

"Now you may go up to your room and study," he said. "You still have to pass your exams. Your mother can bring up a glass of milk and some cake. He heard her make a gag expression. He ignored her as she bounded up the stairs. Then without effort, he diverted his attention to other matters. He noted the distressed look on his wife's face. She decided then that she'd break the news to him about her shopping trip another time.

"Doug, are you really planning to send Glory to boarding school? I thought you were just making idle threats to get her to shape up." He didn't answer immediately. She paused, observing her husband pour himself a glass of port wine. He gestured to his wife who declined though Grandmom accepted. "Oh, all right, so what's she done this time?" Belinda asked. She really didn't want to know. Last time it cost them a fortune.

"Try asking her yourself, why don't you," he said. He cut himself a generous slice of chocolate mousse cake that he'd picked up at Murdock's, their favorite bakery, and dug his fork into the creamy interior. He'd nurse the port later at his leisure.

"Doug," she entreated after he'd eaten most of his dessert. She had hoped the sweetness would soften him. "I've got an idea," he said. "What if Glory and I spend some quality time together to, uh, re-bond, like, say, a girls' weekend? I need to see for myself what she's going through. Maybe I can help."

"She's not going through anything, I assure you, Belinda," he said, lapping up the last bit of *ganache* on his dessert plate.

"Could you please give it some thought?" she said. She didn't want to overstep. She could see something was brewing inside him, angering him—something he was keeping to himself.

"I'll sleep on it," he said in a tone of voice intended to appease her. She knew she could get him to relent. She'd take Glory somewhere where they could have a real mother and daughter weekend together like they used to when she was younger. It would do them both good. But a boarding school in Switzerland? She wasn't so sure that was such a good idea, given Glory's recent history.

It didn't take long for word to get out that Father Tosi was going to be the other chaperone on the ski week-end. If only she could just see him, be near him, she'd be so happy. After the family dinner, Glory did go upstairs and she did open her textbooks, but her mind was elsewhere. When her mother brought up dessert to her room, she didn't have to plead with her about getting away for the week-end. It would be so good for just the two of them to be together, and Glory knew just the right place, but her mother would never suspect the reason why. She needed her mother as an ally. This was what Belinda wanted as well, but for other unspoken reasons.

Chapter THIRTY-ONE

IT WAS ALL TOO PERFECT to last. The weather was warmer than expected. The wind less blustery, the snow just the way they wanted it to be, and the bus ride more than tolerable for everyone than anticipated—not too far, not too bumpy. The driver was a senior citizen who went by the name of Uncle Mel. He was a friend of Marty Tisdale, whom he referred to as Tiz. Mel worked part time for a tour bus company and got the group a good deal, which saved them enough money to afford upgrades on their rooms. He had as much fun as did the teens. He sang along with them and kept them laughing at his jokes, some of which were off color, but that was OK because they weren't in church or in school, Jodie rationalized. As the senior leader she could and would put the lid on anything she deemed unsuitable. Jodie surprised Chris. She turned out to be more personable than he'd imagined. He guessed she was bossy only when she'd read the riot act to the kids. He hadn't had much opportunity to spend any time with her in other settings, knowing of her only as his housekeeper's daughter-in-law and Marty's cohort on ski trips. But Jodie turned out to be good company, and she herself admitted that for a priest, he was a regular guy, not stuffy, as she thought he could be.

The kids as Jodie always referred to them skied well into the evening and had a late supper in the lodge restaurant. She advised them to turn in early as they had a full day ahead of them and they wanted to maximize their time on the slopes. Jodie did not want them to get over tired and careless. 'Don't want any broken bones around here, not while I'm in charge. Casualties spoil the fun,' she quipped. The kids too were seeing a different side of Jodie although they knew her from previous trips. This time, however, they were trying out a different ski resort, but it was a first for Chris. He hoped it wouldn't be his last.

No one in the group noticed a canary yellow Jaguar glide into the parking lot and ease into a spot, dwarfed among vans, buses and other more practical means of conveyance. Unlike other vehicles stained with salt and snowy residue, the luxury car had been cleaned and polished and shone like the rising sun.

As they headed northward in an easterly direction, Glory kept complaining to her mother that the sun was so bright she couldn't see. Belinda told her to 'clam it and be grateful you're getting away this week-end.' She gestured to the glove box where they kept sunglasses and Glory pulled out a pair. She examined them, tried them on and checked herself in the mirror. Then she frowned and heaved a sigh, mostly to annoy her mother. It didn't take much. There was always a fine line and Glory knew where and how to draw it, and Belinda tolerated more than most mothers of teens would. It was in her best interest to do so.

They didn't talk much while riding, but that was typical. Belinda only half listened when Glory was speaking and when Belinda spoke, Glory turned to another channel in her head. Her mother bored her. Belinda hiked up the volume on the stereo and got into the beat of the music, bobbing her head from side to side. Glory grimaced. She only tolerated any music her mother loved but the ride wouldn't take all that long so she thought she could endure it.

Once they arrived at the resort, it was Belinda's turn to grimace when she surveyed the ski lodge. It was certainly not her caliber.

She couldn't figure out why Glory had chosen this particular one, but she had allowed Glory to make the choice. Teens need to be taught to be responsible and make informed choices, she told herself. She would do just about anything to keep Glory in her corner.

The two registered in mid-morning and were told their suite was ready. They could go up and settle in. An extra few bucks does wonders. Glory complained that they had to share a bedroom but after booking at the last minute they were fortunate to get any room whatsoever, so the manager had said, thinking 'rich snobby bitches.' He forced himself to be patient and polite when he noticed the look of distaste on their faces. He told them that they'd set aside special rooms for company executives, which did nothing at all to placate Belinda. She couldn't imagine spending a night anywhere with a rating of less than five stars, guest management suite or not.

Glory pouted and ran upstairs, dragging her bag behind her, ker-plunking up the stairway. Their suite was at the far end of a long gallery overlooking the lobby, whose ceiling was vaulted with glossy exposed wooden beams. An oversized stone fireplace, accessible from both sides, lent rustic charm to the open sitting area.

Glory hurried to kick off her high-heeled boots and dressed in her ski outfit, her disguise. She was anxious to hit the slopes, so she told her mother. She was sure no one would recognize anyone else with goggles and ski attire. And she would be sure to keep her distance from anyone from Wexford Falls. But if she spotted Chris that might be different and he wouldn't recognize her. Somehow at some time, they'd connect, she hoped, or else why would she have dragged her mother to this place?

But Belinda wasn't so much in a rush. She suggested an early lunch first since they'd skipped breakfast. But Glory was dead set against it. She grumbled about everything from the fact that one room in their suite had two beds in it, although both were queen size, and they didn't need the other room, which was intended as a sitting room, as though she and her mother would be hanging out there. Why wasn't one of the beds in that room instead of stuck only a few feet apart from the other? Glory wondered. Sharing that room was not what she'd expected. She could hang out downstairs by the fireplace if she wanted to chill and get away from her mother.

And no, she did not want any lunch. It was far too early. Breakfast was over, the staff informed her. Belinda prevailed and Glory being her petulant self continued the griping. The food was unappetizing and the service was painfully slow. She would have gone on and on if Belinda hadn't threatened to pack up and leave immediately. So Glory bit her tongue. Belinda reminded her that this resort was *her* choice so she should just enjoy the good parts, like their being together and of course the exercise and fresh air. Belinda was preoccupied with checking her manicured nails. She did not notice Glory's eye roll. Later, Belinda commented that she hadn't felt so energized in years. She credited it to the mountain air. But for a woman in her forties, she was in good shape. She'd frequented health clubs for as long as Glory could remember. Perhaps they could do it again soon, in a much classier place, she told her daughter. Glory only smiled weakly. She didn't dare say what she was thinking. Once would be quite enough, she said to herself.

Still she hadn't caught a glimpse of any of the ski club members. She couldn't stand the ones from St. Aeden's parish who also attended Wexford Falls High School, and she didn't know the other kids. It didn't matter. She figured they were all the same—dorks. She was beginning to think this trip was all a mistake, but it took her mind off the idea of boarding school, of being shipped off to Europe like excess cargo away from all that was familiar to her. If she went to Europe at all it would be on her own terms, she told herself. But after a moment of ruminating, she was jolted back to the present. She remembered the reason why she was at this ski resort in the first place and settled into a resigned frame of mind. She would see Chris somehow, and...She asked her mother to take her out of the dumb ski lodge to a nice restaurant that evening for dinner. Neither was too fond of the home cooking that the lodge boasted about in their website and served tepid family style. Belinda needed no coaxing. Besides, Gloria feared, what if Father Chris noticed her? There was no disguising herself at the lodge restaurant.

—⟨◎⟩—

CHRIS AND JODIE COULD not have had a more ideal day. They had a late dinner at the lodge restaurant and the kids were sent back to their rooms with snacks. Jodie told them to settle in and spend time with each other. In her officious voice she stressed that the curfew was eleven o'clock, adding that it was late enough if they wanted to cram in a half day more of skiing before heading back. Then she added a few caveats. All she heard were groans. She, as a skier, understood their reaction, and Chris was already beginning to ache. He told her he needed to turn in early. Jodie laughed. He couldn't hide it very well. It was apparent. He told her he was going to his room to say his Office, prayers he was required to say twice daily, he explained to her, and then go to sleep. In contrast with the rosiness of all the skiers, he looked unusually pale.

About midnight a call from the front desk came to Jodie's room. An older sounding man with a wheezy voice. Guests had complained about the 'infernal racket' in one of the kids' rooms, her charges. He told her they could hear loud music blaring, and what sounded like furniture being tossed around. Jodie heard nothing of the sort from where her room was located. She couldn't imagine any of their kids guilty of those accusations. They should be exhausted, she thought. She decided to handle it herself and let Father Chris sleep. He didn't look very good at supper and he ate very little as well, she recalled.

She tip-toed down the corridor in her quilted robe and fuzzy slippers and paused at the suspect door. It sounded like a lot more than a dozen kids having a raucous party. Maybe she'd better awaken Chris. She walked a few doors over to his room and knocked. There was no answer after several raps, so she figured he was sound asleep and probably needed it. Why bother him; let him sleep. She banged at the door where all the noise was coming from. Finally, it opened a crack. She could hear a window opening, then closing, furniture being moved and items being stuffed out of sight, apparently. She told them in no uncertain terms to end it now or they'd go back home first thing in the morning. In seconds kids dispersed, some she didn't even recognize, and it became quiet again. Jodie phoned the desk and apologized on behalf of her group. It had to be well after one before she went to bed, weary and exhausted.

Glory had heard the goings on down the hall. She turned over and over in her bed, pounded her pillows into a nest and tried to fall back to sleep. She had Chris on the brain. She wasn't used to sleeping in a room with someone else, let alone her mother who made little noises every few seconds in her sleep. It annoyed Glory as her sleeplessness persisted. So much of what her mother said and did bothered her. It just did for quite a while now.

The two had gotten along fairly well until that awful summer following Glory's sophomore year at the Academy. Her father had been on an extended stay in the Loire Valley, in France, on a collaborative business venture with a French firm that dealt with renovating the interior of small chateaux, which over the centuries had fallen into a state of disrepair. The intent of Sterling-Baie Enterprises was to subdivide them into modern condos but retain their classic exterior appearance. Since the old nobility could no longer afford the colossal upkeep, some chateaux had become property of the government, which was only too glad to be rid of them. The sooner the condos were for sale the better for all those concerned.

That summer Grandmom hadn't moved in with them yet. She was staying at her son's home for another few months in New Jersey. And Glory's twin brother Glen was thankfully out of the household at summer camp for a whole month. She had point blank refused to go. No one was going to tell her when to swim or play tennis or golf at a designated time of the day.

Her father would phone home every day at dinnertime like clockwork even though it was late at night in the historic city of Tours where he was lodged. He didn't want them to miss his call. He was loyal; Belinda was not. And what she did one weekend changed Glory's opinion of her from that moment on. It also sparked an unwelcome change in Glory.

In the spring her mother had hired a new shopper, a handsome young Latin, Manuel something or another, who was attached to a prestigious designer's house, so Belinda boasted. Glory couldn't remember all those details. They didn't matter any to her. Although Manuel was interning in New York, he would stay at Hollis's Bed and Breakfast for weeks at a time but he spent far too much time with Belinda sipping gin coolers on the terrace, swimming in their pool in his red Speedo, and advising her as to what outfit flattered her figure the most for which occasion. He was sociable enough with Glory, and Belinda was pleased with his choice of clothing from casual to eveningwear. He informed her that he was thinking of going rogue and designing his own line. He asked Belinda to try some of his designs and wear them out to luncheons and galas to get his name known in the area. Of course she agreed to accommodate. Why not, there were fringe benefits.

Glory had been spending the week-end at the home of a new friend Nila whom she'd met at the Academy and wasn't due back home until the following day. But Nila's family had special plans for that evening which included the two girls, and Glory insisted she needed a special pair of metallic sandals she'd forgotten to pack. Nila offered the family's driver to take Glory home and wait for her while she got her sandals.

When she got home, she noticed that Manuel's car was in the driveway and there was no sign of either her mother or him in the main living area or poolside. She could hear soft talking in the direction of her parents' suite in the rear wing of the first floor. It sounded like a TV show, a movie or something. She heard heavy breathing. It must have been some movie her mother had rented as she often did. Glory figured she'd dash upstairs first and grab her sandals then yell 'hi' and 'bye' before heading back to Nila's. She didn't want to keep their driver waiting. Upstairs she searched everywhere in her bedroom, under the bed and in her closet but could not find that pair of sandals. Then the thought occurred to her that maybe her mother had borrowed them. They wore the same size shoe. She'd go check it out. As she burst into her mother's suite, she was yelling out a question. She'd always remember that question. It became etched in her mind as was the scene she interrupted, and that was no movie on TV. 'Mother, what did you do with my gold sandals'?

Glory shrieked at the scene playing out before her, and the unlikely actors—Belinda and Manuel—were frozen in tableau before they realized they'd better move fast—exit, or do something to make things appear what were not. Understandably, it failed. Too much was in disarray; clothing and bedding were strewn on the floor, and nothing could erase what Glory had seen. It was sketched in indelible ink in her mind. It seemed Manuel was pleasing her mother who sounded very, very pleased. Without another word, Glory slammed the door shut and fled as though she was airborne. Nila's house would be a temporary refuge while she attempted to sort out things in her mind, if she ever could.

Neither Belinda nor Glory ever mentioned what had happened that day. There was no way Belinda could explain it nor would Glory be able to accept any kind of explanation. The act spoke for itself. Glory loved her father far too much to hurt him. It was clear that Belinda didn't. The rest of the summer trudged on with the memory of that clandestine act buried deep inside both of them. It was one secret that both of them kept, but their relationship was never the same nor would it ever be. And Glory's path from then on was incomprehensible to everyone except Belinda.

CHRIS WOKE UP AFTER thrashing about in a restless sleep. His bedding was tangled, half on the floor. He had no idea of the time, just that it was dark. He pulled himself up and all he could feel was thirst. More than thirst, he was parched. He hunted for a glass in the bathroom, and found one wrapped in paper at the edge of the sink. As he unwrapped it, it fell onto the tile floor and smashed to pieces. He sliced his index finger as he attempted to clean up the mess. He was dizzy and sweaty. Then he remembered that the desk clerk had given Jodie and him a key card to the employees' private lounge, a practice they often did with chaperones. He would go down there and get a cold drink, maybe some juice. His throat was burning and it hurt him to swallow.

Grabbing the side railing, he lumbered down the curved staircase and passed by the night desk clerk. He noticed the man was asleep so he used his card to enter the private lounge. He'd help himself to a drink and head back to his room. Maybe then he could fall back asleep. By then his head was beating a steady rhythm and he was weak and shaky. What Chris didn't notice was that he'd failed to close the lounge door tightly.

Chris opened the counter top fridge, which was packed with yoghurts and other healthy snacks, and pulled out a small carton of organic apple juice. 'That should do it,' he said to himself. He pulled off the mini straw affixed to the side of the carton and drained the cool liquid. He reached in for another one but decided against it as nausea began to set in. He wasn't so sure he could make it upstairs so he staggered over to an overstuffed sofa and sat.

He never planned to stay there more than a minute or so to get his bearings but he laid his head against the loose pillow back and dozed off. He had no idea anyone had seen or heard him. But Glory did, and as she had convinced herself, she only wanted to see him. Her mother was fast asleep at the other end of the room they were sharing, but close enough for Glory to be bothered by the intermittent staccato like snoring that had replaced the little noises. Belinda usually took an Ambien whether she needed it or not, so Glory knew it would be safe to venture out.

She slithered out of bed and waited a second or two; then she tiptoed over to her mother's bed to be doubly sure she was safe to duck out of the suite. She stood half in half out of her room, gazing into the dimly lit hallway. Earlier she'd heard Jodie out in the hallway and others dashing to their rooms. She stood there waiting and watching, and then came her opportunity. From her vantage point at the end of the hallway, she espied Chris leaving his room. She saw him enter the employees' lounge past the sleeping desk clerk. She glimpsed a faint stream of light coming from the lounge and understood that to mean Chris hadn't closed the door tightly. Maybe she could accidentally on purpose run into him. She wondered what he was up to at this time of night, or was it morning? It didn't matter to her. She knew the time would come when she would encounter him alone. They could talk. How she held onto every word he said out in the garden. She tiptoed downstairs past the sleeping desk clerk and paused at the lounge door. She peeked in, opened the door wider and saw that Chris was asleep, his head bent in what looked like an uncomfortable position. She made the choice to sit down next to him on the sofa for only a minute or two, feel herself next to him. That was all. He probably wouldn't wake up when she was there, and if he did...what harm could it do?

Chris had fallen into REM sleep, moving about, but confined by the limitations the sofa imposed on him. His breathing was labored and his forehead was burning hot. He was deep inside his dream, miles away from present reality. He could see the car Beth was driving, speeding, about to crash headlong into the semi on the curve, that fateful place where his sister and his love, Kendra, had lost their lives. He was running towards it hoping to avert the accident altogether, or at the very least to rescue them. His dreams were always so lucid. Often he'd be pulled back by those same creatures, banshees, heralds of doom that peopled his nightmares all too often. The scenario wasn't quite the same. Each time it differed in so many details. Sometimes the banshees' faces were familiar, though caricatured; other times they were alien like, but all were terrifying. This night, though, it was Kendra, clothed in a diaphanous white robe, her sleeves billowing, hair flowing, eyes aglow, fixed on him, supplicating. She seemed strangely alive. She'd flown unscathed out of the wreckage towards him and into his outstretched arms. He called out to her in his delirium, "Kendra, Kendra, you've come back to me." His arms were open wide to receive her, to hold onto to her, to save her.

Glory, who by then had fallen asleep with her head nestled on his shoulder, restricting his movement, heard his voice and awoke. She put her arms out to receive his desperate embrace. 'Karendra' was the name she thought she heard. "I'm not Karenda," she said huskily, feeling the heat of his body.

He hadn't heard her. Once again, he uttered, "Kendra, Kendra, where are you? Where did you go? Come back, come back to me." He sounded desperate. Then he went limp and fell back into a deep sleep. Glory, only half awake, was afraid to budge for fear of waking him. She put her head back on Chris's shoulder and rested in his arms. She was at a loss of what to do. He seemed so sick. Should she go wake up Jodie or the desk clerk? She thought he needed medical attention, but how would she explain herself being there in the lounge with him? He'd be all right in the morning, she assured herself. She'd pry herself loose and steal away to her suite in a few minutes. Right now it felt so good being with him even if he did think she was someone else, someone he really loved.

JODIE WAS ALWAYS AN early riser. It was a glorious time of day for her, watching the sun rise as she sipped a cup of coffee before the rest of the world stirred and the busyness of life intruded. It was her special time of the day. And this day was no different, except she was bone tired. After the ado of the night before she was lucky to get four solid hours of sleep but her body clock worked as though mechanically set. Darned circadian rhythm! She was up, and she wanted to beat the crowds at breakfast. She needed her coffee—now. She'd use her key card and get into the employees' lounge for a Keurig cup—quick and easy—and she'd likely have choices of various flavors. It would hold her over. The restaurant wasn't open yet, and wouldn't be until 6:30, according to the sign. Maybe she'd even treat herself to a second Keurig, relishing the stillness of the early morning, or she might bring it out in front of the stone fireplace and wait until the kids' wakeup call summoned them down for breakfast.

She padded downstairs into the dimly lit lobby past the desk clerk, and walked over to the private lounge. She fumbled in her robe pocket for the entry card. She inserted it into the slot, anticipating the smell and taste of her first cup of morning coffee. Then she opened the door wide, and her eyes even wider at the sight before her. She quickly forgot about the coffee.

She fairly screamed the words, "Father Tosi." She always used his title in the presence of others. "Father Tosi, what is this?"

Chris stirred at the sound of Jodie's voice. At first it sounded muffled, distant, as though he was in the bottom of a pit. He opened his eyes and coughed. Everything hurt, his muscles, his bones. Then he held his head and moaned. What he noticed clinging to him gave him the shock of his life. His voice came out hoarse. "Oh my God, am I seeing things? You're not my Kendra at all." He rubbed his eyes and paused to see Glory awakening by his side. "Glory, Glory, oh no, I can't believe this. What in the world are you doing here? How did you ever manage to get in here?"

Jodie was speechless, frozen. She promptly shut the door behind her. No one else needed to see this, whatever *this* was. She faced Glory sputtering, "You, miss, whoever you are, you need to get out of here—right now. You were never here. Remember that. Now go to wherever your room is and, just go. Get out of here."

Jodie looked at the sleepy young teen in a flimsy pajama top that looked stained with blood, and skin tight pink flowered leotards. She was barefooted. Even uncoiffed, she was strikingly beautiful. Jodie noticed Chris had on creased baggy sweat pants and a soaking wet tee shirt. His index finger had a long gash that had clotted into a mean looking scab and his hair was plastered onto his forehead. It was a far cry from the Reverend Father Christopher Tosi, of St. Aeden's.

She mustered the courage to speak to Chris, the priest. Nothing felt right about anything. She was afraid of what she thought she had seen, and how to possibly make any sense of it. She had to breathe deeply and calm herself to speak deferentially. "Oh, Father, Father Chris, tell me what's wrong. What happened here? Are you OK?" She could see that he wasn't. She hoped there was a logical explanation for what she'd just seen. She wondered what that could be, what could have gone on during the night. It certainly didn't look very good.

He looked down at himself, then up at Jodie. He grabbed his head. "No, no, Jodie, I am not OK, not at all. I'm just so confused right now I can't think straight. I think I've got the flu or something. I, uh, I don't know what happened. I don't know how *she* got here, or what. I don't remember, except that I was dreaming, and it all seemed so real."

"You're sopping wet," she said. "Why don't you go on upstairs and change. Stop at the desk and get some aspirin to bring down that fever." She touched his forehead with great care. After all, he was a priest. "No, Father, I think you should go right on upstairs. I'll stop by the desk. Then I'll bring some tea up to you, and some aspirin. That should do you good."

"All right, thank you. That's so good of you, Jodie," Chris said, pained all over, especially in his heart. "I swear I don't understand any of this. I must have been delirious. I thought I saw someone I knew, but I was wrong. Honest, I don't know how that girl got here. I know it doesn't look good, Jodie, but I swear I had no idea she was here. I didn't."

"I believe you, Father," she said, "I do." She needed to agree with him. She wanted so much to believe him. He was so sick, too sick to...If not, what could it mean? She didn't dare imagine.

"Thanks, Jodie," he said shakily. "I've got to get back to bed. I feel lousy. I'm sorry I caused you so much trouble."

"Don't give it a thought," she said. "I can handle everything myself. Just rest and feel better. I'll check on you later. Meanwhile try to sleep."

He heard those kind words. But how could he rest and could he ever feel better? He doubted it. If word got out, he feared, no one would believe him. He could even be arrested for child abuse or worse. All he could do was pray—but for what? That it was all a bad dream, that Jodie would keep this to herself, that he was totally innocent of any wrongdoing?

Glory thought all she had to do was tiptoe upstairs and sneak back into their suite. Her mother would be out cold. She had the key card in hand but her mother beat her to the door. She took one look at her daughter and gasped. She didn't know whether to hug or chastise her daughter.

At first Doug Sterling thought he was dreaming. Who would be calling him at this hour? It wasn't a workday, as if that meant anything. He'd often go into the office on weekends if there was pressing work to do—deadlines, contracts, or the like. Often Aggie would accommodate him as well. Finally he picked up his cell, and Belinda's image stared at him on the screen. Immediately he knew something was wrong. Of course, it was Glory, and she was missing, according to a shaken Belinda who had awoken with a start. Some noise, she guessed, had disturbed her. Her words were slurred from sleep. She was frantic. He couldn't understand how it could be possible for Glory not to be in their suite. They were miles away from civilization up in the mountains. Doug had Belinda check to see if Glory's jacket or boots or any outerwear was missing. And then she entered the room noiselessly like a specter, looking disheveled and sleepy eyed, not expecting to be face to face with her mother. Belinda dropped her cell.

She could hear her husband yelling for her to pick up the damn phone. She pulled Glory over to her bed and motioned for her to sit down, gesturing to the phone. "Your father," she mouthed to Glory. "I called him to tell him you were missing." Glory gasped. She wasn't missing at all. She knew exactly where she was. She was with him, with Father Chris.

"It's all right, dear, she's back...yeah, right here...OK, I will. Give me a minute." Belinda was quivering.

Glory had misery etched all over her face. She didn't have to speak. Her facial expression said more than words. But her father needed an answer otherwise why would his wife phone him in a frenzy, worrying him at an ungodly hour that Glory was missing, suggesting she might be kidnapped?

"I, uh, went for a walk around downstairs, in the lobby, I mean. I couldn't sleep. I heard people walking around in the halls. It was quiet downstairs and I, uh, sat down on the couch and, uh, fell asleep till now. Something must have woken me up and I came right back here. I'm sorry if you were worried. You were sleeping. I was fine. Nothing happened to me," she tried to explain. She had gotten very adept at excuses, making them sound credible. But this one didn't hold much weight, not this time. Glory's appearance told Belinda otherwise.

Her father could hear Glory's excuse at the other end of the line and was fuming. If he ever had any second thoughts about his decision to send her abroad to boarding school, this clinched it. "Belinda, now you just tell her I don't buy that excuse, not at all, or I can tell her myself." Both could hear him as though he was right there in the room with them. He sounded furious.

"Doug, look, the main thing is she's all right. She's safe now. Isn't that all that matters?" She didn't let on that Glory had on her nightie top, which was damp and wrinkled. Belinda pointed to dark splotches all over the back of it. Glory twisted her top to the front to get a better look at the bloodstains and seemed genuinely surprised. She just shrugged. How did she know where they came from? She was asleep. She wasn't hurt and she definitely had not been bleeding. The blood must have come from somewhere.

Doug Sterling mulled over his wife's words and seemed to ease off. Glory would be Glory, and Belinda would be weak and ineffectual. Powerless and overtired, he gave in. "Well, yes, I suppose it does. I'll see you both in a few hours, right?"

Relieved that her husband wasn't going to pursue matters any further, she said, with a sigh, "Sure Doug, after we have breakfast and pack, we'll check out. It's not the most luxurious place I've ever stayed in. Glory's choice, you know. Probably the best punishment for her is to end the ski trip right now. You know, Doug, I have no idea why she chose this one in the first place."

And with that, Belinda gladly ended both conversations, with her husband and with Glory, who was already curled in a lump on her bed, fast asleep. Belinda had had enough. She got into the shower and vowed they'd leave even before breakfast. They could stop somewhere on the turnpike if Glory was really hungry. As for Belinda, she'd lost her appetite. Their mother/daughter weekend had been a bust. But whatever unspoken truce they had between themselves must stay in tact. Both had so much to lose.

Hours later the trip had come to an end for the ski club. With the exception of the ruckus in one of the kids's rooms the night before and Father Tosi coming down with the flu, everything else went well enough, Jodie convinced herself. She thought maybe next year, however, someone younger could take her place as chaperone. She was leaving with a heavy heart.

Chapter THIRTY-TWO

THE NEXT WEEK A NOR'EASTER piled over two feet of heavy, wet snow in the western hills, putting a hold on quotidian activity. A sense of comfort, a lull, spread over Wexford Falls. Chris was unable to keep his garden paths cleared for the brave souls who'd like to have meditated there. They could go into the church instead. With restoration in progress on the stained glass panels it remained open longer hours, and Bernie was there to supervise as much as time allowed. Father Will assumed Chris's duties as he was still down with the flu with some lung complications. Dr. Dillon, their physician, actually paid a house call to check on both Chris and Bernie, at Chris's request. Bernie's remark was the usual, 'Not a damn thing wrong with me, doc.' Dillon had Chris on Tamiflu but it didn't stop Mrs. Hopkins from filling him daily with homemade chicken soup, which she claimed could cure any respiratory ailment. Marie would have sent over some of her concoction but the roads became drifted with lake effect snows that blew over most days of the week, making travel hazardous.

If Chris wasn't up and around soon, Bernie mentioned getting Father Rollo Donavan over to give a hand. Neither Father Will nor Chris was at all fond of that idea. They understood that Rollo could be available for a week or two, if needed. It was enough to get Chris back on his feet.

Chris was feeling well enough, however, to invite Marty over for a visit if he could spare the time away from Sylvie. Chris could always count on his old friend and he really needed a sounding board after his tumultuous night in the employees' lounge at the ski lodge. His mind was tortured ever since he found himself asleep with Glory ensconced in his embrace. Did he really have his arms around her? Could delirium really do that: betray your sensibilities, test your moral fiber, cause you to...?

Marty sat at the wobbly kitchen table in the upstairs kitchen and enjoyed a cup of chicken soup. The sooner they finished it up the better, Chris told him. He said he'd be clucking before long if it wasn't gone by that night. Bernie was out attending a diocesan dinner. He knew the bishop and others in power would be there and Bernie would be gone for at least another good hour. So the kitchen and front room in their living quarters would be available. They could talk freely, in private.

Marty had stopped by Chris's parents' house to return some casserole dishes Marie had left at his house. He gave Fred a hand clearing the drifted snow from the driveway, with Paddy's help. Chris thought Marty must still harbor some guilt about his own father's heart attack from shoveling, but then maybe not. He was just a good guy, helping his best friend's father, and the Tosis have been almost indispensible to Marty and Sylvie, surrogate parents, the very words Marty had used in referring to Chris's parents. They told him to tell Chris that Paddy could stay forever, but Chris knew otherwise. Paddy already had a good home.

"Hey, not bad soup, Chris. Your mother puts noodles in but I like it this way as well with the rice," Marty said, wiping his mouth on a paper napkin. With Chris in charge, no cloth napkins tonight. Why bother? "You know, Chris, this may be even the best I've ever had."

"Better not tell Mom or Sylvie, for that matter," Chris said, hoping to delay the inevitable topic. "Thanks for helping me use it up. It'll warm you up after all that shoveling out there in the cold." He was relieved that Marty could get away for a while. He was the only one besides Bernie he could pour his heart out to, and what he was about to disclose was not for Bernie's ears.

"Oh, it wasn't all that much," Marty said as he attacked one of Mrs. Hopkins's lemon bars. "Hey, this is delicious. How do you stay so thin eating these things?"

"You get the flu, I guess," Chris joked. "Kills most of your appetite, except for these." He gestured to the dessert. Mrs. Hopkins was a good baker, but he was partial to his mother's specialties. No one could match them. Then he put on his serious face.

"Oh, oh, here it comes," Marty said, half in jest. "So what's ailing you, Father Tosi, besides the flu?" Marty sensed something was up.

"I'd like to say 'nothing much' but I'm afraid I can't," Chris began. It would hurt to share this with anyone. Choosing his best friend would be the easiest and the least embarrassing. After a deep breath, Chris relived that night at the ski lodge he'd sooner forget. He knew that being febrile could erase or distort the details but he would relate as much as he could recall. Besides being a good friend, Marty was a sensitive listener, non-judgmental. Chris wouldn't expect him to react with shock or disgust. He figured the skill in part came from his being a caring teacher, and the rest perhaps from courses in active listening, a valuable skill for dealing with people. But in this particular instance, Chris couldn't be so sure how Marty would react, or what advice he could possibly give him.

It seemed as though Marty had paused forever, weighing Chris words, to take in the gravitas of Chris's revelation. All the light had faded from his usual cheerful demeanor. Finally, he began, "Chris, the main concern of the moment should be: can you trust Jodie Hopkins? I would ask myself that question. If word gets out this could blow up into huge proportions. It could be very, very serious for you. And although I don't know her, I don't see Glory bragging to anyone, from what I've learned about her through you," he said, hoping anything he said would help ease Chris's pain. He wanted to add, 'but who really knows'? "Now I know Jodie fairly well, from ski trips, that is. She's not a biggie for gossip, and she's really good with the kids, as you would have noticed. Remember, that night she only saw what she saw, or better still, what she thought she saw." He waited a moment, gauging Chris's reaction. He was just listening. Marty continued, "No matter how you look at it, it was a situation where two persons, namely you, a priest, and Glory, a minor, were discovered together in a locked room in what you described as a cozy arrangement, both of you sound asleep. It would be so easy to jump to, shall we say, logical conclusions. Jodie has no right to read anything more into what she saw. You were very sick, remember, or..."

"Or what, Marty?" Chris interrupted, a look of pain overtaking him.

" I guess the scary thing is the adage that comes to mind: a picture is worth a thousand words. If she thought about what could have ensued sometime before she came in..." Marty said, thinking about what those words could possibly be.

"Yeah, I know where you're going with that," Chris said. He picked at his finger where the scab had formed and reformed. It wound up being Chris's reminder of that night—the dream and Glory's presence next to him. "You don't think she'll say anything to anyone, do you?"

"You mean Jodie? You know as well as I do," Marty responded. He couldn't be sure, one way or the other. "I sure hope not...for your sake, Chris."

"She has no real reason to," Chris said, offering another lemon bar to Marty. Chris had hoped to feel relief after unloading on Marty, but what he felt was a growing sense of uncertainty and distress.

"Unless it slips out at the wrong time with the wrong person, though not very likely, knowing Jodie. You did say she believed what you told her," Marty said, intoning a question. He wanted to set his good friend's mind at ease but he understood Chris's concern.

"What she saw was what she saw then and there, at that very moment, and nothing more. I certainly wasn't doing anything. It's what she could read into it, but she seemed more concerned with my physical health than anything else. I had a raging fever. I was anything but clear-headed," Chris said. Chris knew in his heart of hearts that he would not have betrayed his vows. He felt at that time that Jodie had faith in him. Glory alone was the wild card. But for some inexplicable reason he believed he could trust her.

GLORY HAD DONE NOTHING to annoy anyone at home or at school for almost the entire school week. Just one more day to go. What with the weather, there wasn't much she could get into. She hoped if they took notice of this positive attitude her father would drop the idea of a Swiss boarding school, not that she wouldn't mind getting the hell out of Wexford Falls where the most exciting thing you could do there was catch a film at their two-theatre cinema, or maybe go to dinner at the Olive Garden in the next town, but then that wasn't even Wexford Falls, so it didn't count. She was hoping they'd hurry and finish repairing St.

Aeden's stained glass windows. Passing by there and seeing the broken panels all covered in plastic reminded her of her caper to spite Father Bernie, but not Father Chris. Never him. There was something so special about him. No, she'd never do anything to hurt him.

SMITTY HAD JUST ABOUT arrived at the conclusion that Spencer aka Spike Gilbert must have played a role in the vandalism at St. Aeden's. People had seen him in the neighborhood that night around the time the windows were broken. The assistant manager of the Dunkin Donuts said he saw Spike sitting with a pretty teen, some ritzy looking girl, who, he'd remembered, treated him to a latte. He said the boy was no stranger there. He came in now and then, walked with a swagger and acted like a big shot, especially if there were girls around. That night the two looked 'pretty cozy' to him, he told Smitty. Although they didn't arrive at the same time, they did leave together maybe an hour or so before the call came to headquarters reporting the sound of glass breaking at St. Aeden's. Could that be a coincidence? Smitty couldn't be sure. He needed proof. If he brought Spike in, he'd deny any part in the act. He knew Spike's kind.

SATURDAY AFTERNOON Carl Hopkins, Senior, phoned his son, whom everyone called just plain Junior, to ask him a favor, and Junior said sure, of course. He'd do anything for his mother. Sure, he'd give his father a hand to move the out-dated den set downstairs into the basement. Thelma Hopkins told Carl Senior it was high time for them to buy some modern looking furniture for the den since he spent most of his free time there glued to the tube. She'd already picked out the perfect thing—a green leather sectional with electrically operated dual recliners, armrests with cup holders and USB ports, whatever those thingies were. She thought he'd be impressed, and he was until he heard the price Wagner's Furniture Company was over charging for the ensemble pieces. He told her to look again in one of the big box stores to get a sweeter deal. Finally after getting Carl in just the right mood as she could with just the right dish—she knew the way to his heart—she got him to compromise. And so they chose a smaller, less pricy version of the original. Good enough, Carl relented.

Junior was salivating. He'd expected one of his mother's signature meals waiting for them in the warming oven. Instead she told him and Jodie that with all the moving and fussing around, she'd had to do some on the spot dusting and cleaning. There was no time to cook up a gourmet meal, she said as she thrust copies of Chin's menu at them. "Chinese OK?" she asked, and her answer was quizzical expressions, shrugs, and finally heads nodding in assent. Well, it had to be. It was OK for Jodie. She was nowhere near as fussy as Junior.

The problem was that the den would be empty until Monday so they'd have to watch TV in the bedroom. Thelma told Carl that would just have to do, and what was two days in a whole lifetime? He was inclined to agree with her. It was always in his best interest. She was a good, hard working woman, he'd tell anyone who'd listen to him.

As they shared a medley of Cantonese dishes from cartons and mounds of sticky rice she'd heaped into small bowls, the conversation shifted from the usual family topics to beyond. Junior and Senior were best friends; they shared the same pastimes—hunting and fishing, so there was never a lull in their conversations. Besides, there were always NCIS episodes to dissect if it was out of season for the outdoor activities. They both said they missed the character called Ziva. Together, as cohorts, they composed a cogent albeit simplistic letter to the producers of the long running CBS series urging them to bring back Ziva—if not possible, then why not a long lost twin sister, whom they said could be called Riva. They never sent out the letter though. Thelma and Jodie kept their comments to themselves, which was in *their* best interest.

Thelma had cemented a warm relationship with Jodie over the years. Mrs. Hopkins Senior had met Mrs. Hopkins Junior well before they became in-laws. Jodie's parents had drowned in a boating accident leaving their only daughter to stay with friends while she finished high school in Wexford Falls. Back then Jodie spent her Saturdays working in Tom's IGA where Thelma grocery shopped each Saturday morning. Over time the two got to know each other and became friends as they shared common interests, mostly crafts, with Mrs. Hopkins Senior as the mentor.

Thelma finished eating first. Then she turned to focus her attention on her daughter-in-law. "Say, Jodie, how did Junior here survive with you and Father Chris up there on your ski trip? Did you leave him enough food?" She smiled.

Jodie tried to crack a smile, "Of course, Mother Hopkins, why wouldn't I? And if he ran out, he's always got you." Junior gave his mother an exaggerated loving look. She returned the look to him, and held it a long moment for maximum effect.

"That's my boy, Junior," she cooed. The two could be very playful together, which Jodie envied. Carl and Thelma had become real family rather than just in-laws, the term of which so often conveyed pejorative connotations. She believed that getting to know your in-laws really well or anyone else for that matter was the key to understanding and accepting their differences. It certainly made for healthier relationships.

After a while, Thelma dug into the bottom of the take-out sack and pulled out the fortune cookies, which everyone had overlooked. The fortunes were not the unexpected kind and yielded typical little smirks, but somehow inexplicably Jodie heard herself reading her fortune aloud—'you are keeping a life-changing secret that you must reveal.' When the impact of the message hit her, she gasped; then she paled.

Thelma picked up on Jodie's shocked reaction. She could only think of one thing, something she'd been hoping for years. "Could that be true, Jodie? Are you really harboring *that* kind of secret? Oh, please share it with us. I'm so excited." The Hopkins men paid no attention. They were munching on the cookies, plus there was a platter of homemade cookies, hermits, on the table, which were up for grabs. They hadn't yet moved the furniture. There was plenty of time for that.

Jodie seemed to panic, and merely shook her head 'no'. She chewed her lower lip, and looked at her watch. She was edgy. Did she want to leave already? She would have liked to but, no, there was work to do, furniture to be moved. She was squirming just enough for Thelma to seize the opportunity. "Say, Jodie, how'd you like to come into my craft room and see what I've been up to lately? I'll teach you how to make them if you're interested. I've got lots of extra material. Come on now." Jodie gave her a pained look in response.

"You boys can have a beer now if you want, unless you want some more of that nice Chinese tea. There's a few more tea bags left. I guess they were overly generous. Hot water's on the stove top." Carl made a face; then he jumped at the chance to enjoy his favorite beverage and headed for the fridge. Thelma was such a hawk, surveying his intake of the brew. Junior didn't mind much either. Sure, he'd join his father. He saw Jodie raise one finger and he knew what that meant. One, only one.

Once the two women were out of earshot, Thelma whispered as though the men could still hear them over the din of the TV,

"OK, Jodie, what's bothering you that you didn't want to mention in front of the boys in there? What's the secret? I hoped for a second it was what we've been waiting and praying to hear, but...I guess it's not. You seem upset. I can tell." Jodie blanched. Thelma studied her daughter-in-law. It wasn't only the discomfort after reading the fortune. Jodie hadn't cracked a natural smile once during the visit, which was so uncharacteristic of her. She seemed preoccupied.

Thelma had known Jodie so long she could tell when she was distressed. She was a good, solid girl. The Hopkins Senior couple were delighted when Junior asked how they'd feel if he asked Jodie to marry him. The way things were, he couldn't ask *her* parents. Thelma told him he could do a lot worse, that Jodie was a decent girl with a good sense of integrity, and *that* was very important. Pity, still no children yet, but she asked no questions. There was plenty of time. The kids were still young enough to start a family.

"You've got a sixth sense, Mother Hopkins," she said with a sigh, not knowing exactly how to broach the subject, or even if she should. She hoped she wasn't making a mistake that she'd regret. She wanted to brush the whole thing aside as though it had never existed but she couldn't keep inside what she'd seen—not for another minute. It was making her come unhinged, and who better to share it with than her beloved mother-in-law?

"It's about Father Chris and the, uh, ski week-end, the one we just chaperoned," Jodie said, fiddling with her fingers, interlacing and unlacing them. She was anguishing over how she would relate what she had seen. She was beginning to feel like a barrel rolling downhill, out of control. "Mother Hopkins, this is got to stay between you and me, what I'm going to tell you. You've got to promise me."

"I guess so, sure, I promise. This sounds very serious. Father Chris, you say?" she said warily. Then all of a sudden she remembered what she wanted to forget. Father Chris...She was standing by the sink in the downstairs kitchen hoping to catch a glimpse of Father Bernie, whom she adored, as he left on a short visit to his sister Molly's. He had told her of his mission—to convince his sister that assisted living would be best for her at this stage of her life. Thelma had waved to him and he signaled back to her with a smile and a wink. She'd also noticed a stunning looking young woman enter the garden about the same time. She thought nothing of it; then she resumed her duties. About a half hour or so later she espied Father Chris in the garden entrance with a different female visitor, a pretty girl, obviously a teen-ager. In high heel boots she was nearly as tall as he was. She could tell because when they kissed on the lips, unimaginable, he had his arms firmly planted on her waist and she didn't have to go up on her tiptoes. Should she tell Jodie what she saw? No, why should she? Must be a reason for that, but she couldn't imagine what that could possibly be. Didn't look very good to her, no way, not very priestly behavior in her opinion. Priests didn't go around kissing a teen girl like that—no way.

"Well," Jodie began, not sure what it would lead to. "He came down with a terrible case of the flu on the ski trip, that's Father Chris, I mean. Seemed like it came on all of a sudden during the night—Saturday night. He was OK the night before at supper but he didn't look very hale and hearty. I figured he was just beat from skiing all day after so many years. But when I saw him the next morning, he was sick as a dog—maybe even worse."

"How well I know, dear," she said glibly. "I've filled him with my chicken soup, enough to float the QE2, I'd say." Then she laughed at her funny. Jodie didn't. She was dreading what she was about to reveal.

"Yeah, he looked pretty sick to me, feverish, you know, the usual stuff," she resumed. Then she told her mother-in-law the story, the whole story, she said, as she saw it. Thelma's eyebrows did a quick lift. She mulled over what Jodie had just told her. Jodie wasn't putting two and two together yet, but her mother-in-law was, and it added up to trouble with a capital 'T'.

"Remember, I was only there a second or two, and both of them were sound asleep until I let out what had to be a deafening yell. You can well imagine that. All I really saw was a very sick person and a sleepy girl. Father Chris looked astonished, and, uh, the girl, she just got up and, uh, well, left," Jodie said. "I ordered her to," she went on to sum up.

"Sure leaves you with a lot of unanswered questions, don't it?" Thelma Hopkins said looking her daughter-in-law directly in the eye. She wondered if she'd purposely omitted any incriminating details. But 'no,' Jodie wouldn't do that.

"I suppose so," she answered, wondering where or what this could lead to. She wished she'd kept quiet about this. She didn't feel any of the relief she'd hoped for. All right. It was out now. If only her mother-in-law hadn't found the fortune cookies, and that she herself hadn't read her 'fortune' aloud. If only...What if her mother-in-law couldn't keep the secret, as she herself hadn't been able to do? And whom would she dare tell, swear to secrecy? Hopefully, not the authorities. Oh, the damage it could do. She could feel panic settling in.

"Well, I hope it's nothing, but, it sure leaves you with far too many questions and no good answers at all," Thelma said, pausing, moving her closed lips to the side in contemplation, as she did when she was puzzled. "This could very well add up to no good, you know. You know, I wonder..."

"Please don't," Jodie interrupted. "I doubt it will lead to anything, Mother Hopkins. Father Chris is a good, decent person. You should know that."

Thelma wished this conversation had never taken place but it did and something had to be resolved, she thought, but kept it to herself. "You know how much I love Father Bernie," Thelma was whispering again. "He's such a dear man, and, oh, how he thinks the world of young Father Chris. I do, as well, but things may be adding up, I fear."

Jodie looked perplexed at her mother-in-law's last statement. Then Thelma poured out the story of Chris and Glory in what she had referred to as a long, passionate kiss. Jodie just about fell over.

Could this be something sordid, illegal or immoral? Jodie was hard to convince, though. Thelma thought otherwise. Her decision was to, gently, that's how she'd put it, say something to Father Bernie about what Jodie had seen. Jodie, at first, said she did not want to be quoted, but her mother-in-law insisted, saying it wasn't right for a young priest, for any priest for that matter to, uh, carry on with a girl, and a girl of that age. It was deplorable, she added. Then she remembered the little gold violin ornament on the poinsettia plant, which was just about ready to die until she came back to work and revived what little was left to salvage. The little violin thing, hmm, a telltale reminder, now took on a different meaning.

Thelma had decided to wait until after the weekend to talk to him. Yes, that's what she'd do. Father Bernie heard confessions in the afternoon today and said masses the next day. She didn't want to interfere with his regular schedule. Monday would be soon enough. She dreaded it with all her heart but she felt it was her duty. Something was going on and it had to be stopped.

Chapter THIRTY-THREE

LIFE AT ST. AEDEN'S gradually returned to normal. The supply of Mrs. Hopkins's chicken soup was finally depleted and, according to Chris, a return to real food and restored health was cause for celebration. Fred had dropped off Paddy who couldn't decide whose lap to leap on first—Bernie's or Chris's. He came with a canister of Marie's doggy biscuits. It was as though the rectory pet had never been away, or as though Chris had never been out of commission with the flu.

Saturday was Saturday, which meant their agenda included a well attended four o'clock vigil mass and confessions from five-fifteen to whenever. For reasons incomprehensible to priests in other parishes, that unconventional schedule seemed to work best with the priests at St. Aeden's and the majority of its parishioners.

It was Chris's first mass in a week and he actually felt weaker than he thought possible. He'd had no recollection of ever being so sick before. He'd hoped the after effects of the flu would magically disappear just as the fever had. Then he realized that if it took forever for bad memories to fade away then the body might be no different. He'd always valued strength and control of body and mind, *mens sana in corpore sano*, a sound mind in a healthy body, but things don't always play out the way we anticipate. His shaky limbs would not cooperate with his will. So he cut his homily short, leaving out many of the details to support the crux of his message. He was hoping his line for confession would be short as well. Actually both his and Bernie's lines were.

It seemed like the longest hour of his life. He usually waited in one of the pews, meditating as Bernie finished up, but this one afternoon he headed back to the rectory to rest until seven, their mutually designated Saturday dinner hour. All they had to do was turn on the oven. Everything was ready to go. Mrs. Hopkins saw that they were well taken care of on the weekends.

--- ✦ ---

THE LIGHTING IN ST. Aeden's was growing dim. The face of the tall girl in a bulky blue hooded parka was partially obscured. Then the setting sun shot a last blinding glint of daylight. It pierced through the leaded glass window panels, illuminating them, casting eerie shadows of long ago saints, aglow as though resurrected for only a brief moment, then it spilled their images into elongated shades of darkness, a blurry palette onto the pews and aisles below in its path.

The girl came forward from a pew in the rear of the church, slowly, deliberately, her head lowered, as she made her way down the side aisle to the confessional box, Father Bernard Monahan's, according to the engraved plaque. She'd checked in advance to ensure it was his, and not Father Chris's. Her eyes were blinded for a moment as she walked in the bolt of light. She bowed her head to avoid the sun's assault and kept on going. She did not genuflect. This act of reverence was not customary for her, and if she noticed others doing so, she disregarded it. She had been instructed how to do it, confession, that is. All was uncannily quiet. For a moment she didn't think she could utter a word. Normally audacious, she froze, listening to her breathing; then a moment later she yanked aside the draped entrance to the tiny room and entered.

She knelt and waited for Father Bernie to say something after he'd slid aside the little door, and he, in turn, waited for the girl to speak through the opaque screen separating the two of them. He listened for her to tell him what penitents should, what they'd learned as children, rote learning with the necessary adjustments. Then to spill out what they believed to be their sins, after examining their conscience, and to ask for forgiveness.

Finally he cleared his throat, and said in a whisper, "Well, come now. I'm ready for you." He blessed himself and expected the girl to do likewise. When she didn't, he said, "Don't be afraid. You may begin. Let me help you. Bless me Father..."

Still she said nothing. She was going over in her mind what her Grandmom had told her, recalling that she'd said the priest wouldn't hurt you. They just forgive you for whatever you've done, no matter how awful it is. You just have to tell them and you'll feel really good after. Then you have to say some prayers. Glory would have to make them up. There was no way she could remember the prayers Grandmom had given her to learn.

Father Bernie had experienced enough frightened people in the girl's position in his lifetime as a confessor to realize that this one needed some guidance and support.

"I'm going to start now, OK?" she said. Her quivering voice told him she was indeed terrified.

"Ah, yes, please do," he said. He wanted to assure her that everything would be all right. "Bless me Father..." He'd hoped starting her off a second time would tweak her memory and get her to continue.

"There's no one else in line. I waited to be last," she said, redoubling her courage. She couldn't figure out why this was making her so nervous. Grandmom made it seem so easy when they practiced together.

He answered, "Well, that's very good to know that no one else is waiting for me. All right. You may begin." He had the feeling that she just might run out before she lost her nerve. Probably hadn't been to confession in years, he thought, but her voice was youngish. It sounded a little familiar. She was definitely not an adult.

Finally the voice came out louder than either of them expected, as though a phantom hand had turned up the volume. "Bless me, Father...." She hesitated but before he could say anything, she asked, "Can I say this my way instead of the stuff I'm trying to memorize?"

Father Bernie thought a moment. "Is this is your first? Your first confession, my dear?"

Glory answered weakly. Lying came too easily to her. "Oh no, I think that was years ago. I'm not sure how many. You forget, you know. Like stuff you had to learn to recite in class? You, uh, learn it and then, poof, it's gone. You know what I mean?"

He wasn't sure what to believe. That voice was sounding more and more familiar, but no, he must be mistaken. "I suppose so, you may be right, but go on, please. You're here to confess your sins and obtain absolution, forgiveness. Am I not right?"

"I guess that's why I'm here. I'm a little nervous. Can't you tell?" she said with a giggle, a reflex.

"Well, you need not be," he said. "I can't see you. I'm behind this screen."

She went on. "But you can hear me good, right?"

Father Bernie almost laughed aloud. "Of course I can. I'm not deaf, even if people whisper I can hear them or I wouldn't be able to hear their confessions. Some even mumble so they can say to themselves, 'I confessed my sin. No matter if he'd heard me clearly or not.' Heh heh."

Glory could have cared less about any other people, let alone the whisperers. "OK. And you won't know who I am," she said warily. By now, he had a pretty good idea of who was at the other side of the screen. She'd not called him 'Father' as others always do, and she's so unsure of herself. How could she have had enough time to learn what she called Catholic? She must have made her Holy Communion years back and forgotten everything since. A lapsed catholic, he assumed.

"Your confession is confidential and anonymous, as it should be," he reassured her. He heard his stomach rumble in the quiet.

Glory sighed. "Good. That's a huge relief. Like with a shrink, or something?" She recalled that her therapist was sworn to secrecy. Confidentiality, he told her, which he hoped would free her up when she would be willing to spill out her guts to him, which was only if she cared to. She'd never told him about her mother, what she'd seen in her parents' bedroom that summer day she'd caught her and...She didn't know if she'd ever reveal what she'd seen to anyone. She owned that secret, it was hers and she kept it locked up, imprisoned in her mind. What good would it do to tell him, that stranger, her therapist, whom she'd never warmed up to? He never helped her much anyhow which was why she'd only keep an appointment when her father threatened. Her mother would let them slip. Glory never wondered why.

Father Bernie was growing impatient. "Yes, a shrink or someone like that," he answered. "And now tell me your sins, please?"

"What if I tell you just the big one? The little ones are nothings, like lying to my parents, and fighting with my brother. Stuff like that happens all the time," she rattled off with ease, sounding more and more like the Glory he'd encountered in the garden. He wondered if they should go on with this but decided to give her the benefit of the doubt.

Father Bernie said, "Well, in any event, you want to commit these little sins, venial ones they're called, less often, if not at all. That should be your goal. You need to pray to eliminate them."

Glory was adamant. "Even if I tried and tried hard, it would be almost impossible. Those guys, they're always in my face when they're around. That's the way it is in my house."

He sighed. "I see. Well, now why don't you tell me your big sin?" He was weary. His stomach growled a second time. He remembered he didn't bother to have much for lunch today and his head was beginning to ache.

Glory said nonchalantly, "Oh yeah, my big sin. Well, uh, I seduced someone. There, I said it. Whew. That was hard to say. I hope I said it right."

"Excuse me, my dear, did I hear that correctly?" he asked. Learning closer to the screen that divided them.

Glory snapped, "I thought you said you could hear good." She hesitated then spoke softly but clearly against the screen. "Ok, I'll say it again. I seduced someone...slept with him, spent the night with him, OK?"

"Hmm. Do you, uh, mean, you seduced him, uh, sexually?" he asked. He needed to hear that.

Glory asked, "Does it matter?" It came out petulant.

At this point Father Bernie's concern mounted. He felt a prickling on the back of his neck. "Well, yes it does. Are you, um, a minor?"

"Yup," she said. "I'm almost seventeen. So that makes me still a minor. I don't like to admit it, but numbers wise, I am. People say I look a lot older though."

Bernie went on, ignoring her prattling. "I see, a minor, you say. This someone, is a male, I presume..."

Glory admitted boldly, "Well, duh, yeah, he sure is."

"Is he also a minor?" Bernie asked, thinking it was hanky panky with another teen friend of hers.

"Oh God, no," she said amused. Her tone lightened even though to her it was getting to feel like 20 questions that her family played to pass the time when they took a long car trip. "He's a man, a really good looking man."

Bernie was fearful of where this was going. Could she be putting him on just for kicks, if she was indeed that girl, which by now he was fairly certain. He knew she was capable of almost anything, but he persisted. He had to know. "And you, uh, seduced him, you say?"

"That's right." Her boldness shocked him.

Bernie continued, "Is it someone who lives in your household?" He as well did not like the idea either that this was turning out to be a quiz game of sorts.

Glory laughed a little too loud, "Nooo. Are you kidding? That would mean my father or my brother. I'm not that crazy. He's a man, a very handsome man, not a family member."

He needed to quell any growing suspicions. He hoped to see through any lies or exaggerations. "And he, uh, cares for you?" Bernie asked weakly.

Glory was wary. "Seems to. Yeah, I think he does. You sure you don't go telling stuff that you hear in that little box you're hiding in?"

That remark hit a sore spot. "My dear, I'm not hiding. This is for confidentiality. Remember we talked about that. This is between you, me and God."

Glory said, "OK, then, if you say so. Yeah, like my shrink but God's not in on that, that's for sure. I get it. Bet my parents would like to know what I tell him. Actually, I tell him only what I feel I have to, and sometimes it's not very much."

Father Bernie later regretted that he'd asked this next question. "Is there, uh, anything else you want to tell me?"

She really didn't want to go on with this confession. It was becoming uncomfortable to her. It didn't feel as though she was talking to her shrink. When she kept her appointments, he'd just looked at her and gabbed, hoping to get her to open up. When she did open her mouth, he'd nod until she grew tired of it. She figured it was a huge waste of her father's money. But she knew how Father Bernie felt about her and figured by now he'd guessed her identity. "Um, not really."

But since she was there, the opportunity existed, and he persisted. He had to know. "Do you think this, uh, man, will continue to, uh, see you?"

"He should. He's a good friend of ours, yours and mine. He's a priest," she admitted blatantly.

Bernie was incredulous. He gasped. "Are you telling me that you seduced a priest?"

She told him he should get his hearing checked.

But he needed to know more. "Are you..."

Glory interrupted him. "If you're going to ask me if I'm sorry, I can't truly answer you. I just came here because it's the right thing to do in confession."

"You come here to tell me you seduced a priest and that's it? And you take the blame for it?" he asked. "You must or you wouldn't be telling me it was your big sin." His head went from a dull ache to a nagging throbbing.

Glory didn't know what to say by this time. She was flustered. "Yeah, sorta, I guess. I don't know. Maybe, maybe not. I don't know...I can't do this any more. I told you what I did and that's it. I'm outta here."

Before Bernie could probe any further, she got up abruptly, thrust open the curtain and headed to the side door of the church, leaving Father Bernie in a stupor. He heard the clickity click of her boots and the heavy wooden door clang shut behind her. It felt like a backhanded swat across his face. The sound reverberated in his head. He sat for a moment, deep into himself, tears welling in his eyes. He rose gingerly and exited the confessional slowly.

Thankfully, the church was deserted. He couldn't bear to face another human being after what he'd just heard. He started to shake. He somehow managed to steady himself. Then he looked upward and grabbed his head. He limped over to the front row, knelt and uttered a prayer before collapsing.

GLORY MULLED OVER WHAT had transpired as she descended the dozen concrete steps to the street. That afternoon she'd told her parents she was meeting a few friends for a latte, but she really had no plans after the confession. Lies to her came as naturally as flying does to a bird. It became her means of protection and survival to thwart reality with its harshness and its consequences. She began to feel a sense of triumph emerging from the chaotic experience of her confusion. But somehow in her convoluted reasoning, she told herself, 'I went to confession. I did it.' But that feeling was short lived. Little could she anticipate the impact of what she had instigated.

She checked her pocket of her jeans and fished out a rumpled twenty. That should do it. She headed to Dunkin Donuts, only a block away, before going home. She'd told her parents that she might be studying over at a friend's house later on. She wasn't sure. She'd let them know. That always worked. She didn't want to upset them if she got home too late.

The chill of early evening had set in, so a latte would warm her up and take her mind off the unpleasant experience of confession. Somehow, verbalizing the words she'd heard herself tell the priest unnerved her more than she'd anticipated. Those thoughts dissipated as she approached the restaurant. There she spotted Spike outside with a few of his 'customers'. When he saw her entering the Donut shop, he called out to her, and she grinned. His friends scattered. It wasn't a good idea in the first place for all of them to be seen together.

"Hey, Glor," he said in his 'I'm talking to Glory voice.' "I got you in my head, really, and what happens? You show up, just like that. See, we were meant for each other."

"She gave him a smirk and mumbled 'sure' to herself. She tossed her head and responded coolly, "Yeah, don't you wish." They both laughed. She did not want to get on his wrong side. It was not to her advantage so she played along.

"My treat, this time," he said glowing, taking out his wallet. He waved a folded fifty at her. Maybe he had a chance with her after all. "Get anything you want."

"Whoa, business must be booming," she said *sotto voce*. She didn't want the wrong person to hear and put two and two together.

When they settled into a corner table, the assistant manager, a recent graduate of WFHS, approached the pair. "Hey, you guys. You better watch out. Smitty's been snooping around here asking questions, you know, and the boss, old Buster boy, he don't like that at all. Bad for business, you know, so I'll pretend I don't know you guys."

"Well, it ain't gonna work," Spike said, craning his neck over toward Buster Greenleaf who was looking right at them. "Check it out, man."

The assistant manager whose badge read 'Oscar' pretended to be cleaning off their table. He was actually brushing crumbs onto the floor. Then he left without a word.

Spike ordered two lattes. Glory told him she wasn't very hungry. "If I don't eat dinner with family tonight, I'll stay on the shit list forever. Plus I don't want to get fat on junk food."

"Oh, OK," Spike said, suddenly at a loss for words. He wasn't going to contrary her. "Cool."

They sipped their lattes in silence for a few minutes. It was fine with Spike as long as he could be with her, look at her, watch her mouth when she spoke. It didn't matter what she said. Glory broke the silence. "Hey, Spike, tell me, are you Catholic?"

"Huh? Me? I'm not much of anything. My mom neither, so I guess we're not," he answered. "My old man? Who the hell knows what he was or is? I haven't seen him in forever." She noticed he had a latte moustache and gave him a private joke kind of look. He took that to mean she was warming up to him.

"Oh," she said. Her thoughts were all over the place. She was reliving her experience in the confessional.

"Why, what's up, Glor?" he asked, draining his cup noisily. Glory laughed. If she and her brother did that at the table they'd be reprimanded. That practice ended by the time they'd entered elementary school.

"I just asked. That's all, I could care less," she said, but she did care. She wanted to talk. She needed to unleash what was inside her. But how much? She wasn't sure.

"You're such a babe," he said, studying her face. To him, even her 'I don't care' look was captivating.

She ignored his comment. "I, uh, just went to confession at St. Aeden's." She said to him as though it was a regular practice of hers, though he knew better.

"Oh, you did?" he said with a shrug. "That's weird, coming from you especially."

"What do you mean by that?" she asked pretending to be wounded.

"Oh, yeah, sorry, I remember now, you were studying to be Catholic. So, what's in it for you?" he asked with a chuckle.

"Not enough, I guess," she said still sipping. Then she added, "Hey, Spike?

"Yeah," he said, gazing into her hazel eyes. "You know, you've got the most beautiful eyes I've ever seen."

"Well, then I guess you've never been around much," she said with a smile. She liked to tease him but knew the limits. She didn't want to lose her supplier. He returned her smile.

"I was trying to ask you something, OK? Can I tell you about sin?"

"Well, that's a shocker. I didn't expect that," he said, running his finger through his spiky hair. He had a habit of doing that when he was with Glory, had no idea why.

"I gotta tell you about sin," she insisted, placing her elbows firmly on the table, ready to impart her knowledge.

"OK, Glor, sin, hmm, let me see now. Sin can be cool," he interjected before she had a chance to explain. "Like stuff you're not supposed to do, not really breaking the law all the time, but you can feel OK when you're doing it. Sometimes it feels really good if you know what I mean. See, I know all about sin. So what about it? What more can you tell me?"

"Well, Spike, did you know there are two kinds of sin?" she informed him. She was looking him squarely in the eye.

Spike looked astonished or else he pretended to be for enhanced effect. "Only two? Come on, Glor. I can count up to eight or ten, maybe more, if I think real hard, like hey, the ten commancments. Wanna hear them, then I can give *you* a lesson?"

"No, why should I?" she snapped. This was her subject. She wanted to own it. She'd studied it.

He faced her squarely. "Because you brought up the subject, didn't you? Come on, tell me now."

She sighed. He was right. "Yeah, I did. Well, Grandmom's Maryland's Catholic book of stuff is like the Catholic Bible, she says. It says that if you think the sin, like think in your mind of doing it, then you're as guilty as if you did the sin—and if it's a big one, mortal, that's what they're called, and you hafta confess it to a priest who's supposed to listen to you, maybe ask you a lot of questions, like 20 questions, or more like a police interrogation, I think, and then he forgives you. You gotta say prayers after or it won't work. With the big ones, you're gonna burn in hell if you don't. Scares the shit outta you, doesn't it? Grandmom said it feels good after you tell your stuff to the priest, but I can tell you from experience, it does not."

"Wow, Glor! Am I glad I'm not Catholic," he said, sounding serious, or so she thought.

"Right," she agreed. "Yeah, like if I plan out in my mind to kill Glen Thomas, my stupid ass brother, and see myself choking him and killing him, then I'm as guilty as if I'd killed him dead. So I'd hafta go to the priest and say, 'I killed someone.' Plus you gotta be sorry. He'd ask you that. That's the hard part."

"No way," he said. "That's how it goes?" Glory's lesson was having an impact on him, she felt, or maybe he was agreeing with her because he always did.

"Way," she said nearly out of breath from her recitation. "It's in Grandmom's book. No wonder why my father's against that religion. Too bad because the young priest here is really hot. Remember the night we visited his garden?"

"Oh, yeah, I sure do," he said. "That dog sign we broke..."

"Yeah, and you smashed it nice with your big old boot," she whispered; then she shushed herself. She noticed the restaurant was getting crowded.

"And the snow ball fight. That was a blast," he said, lowering his voice. He was fingering his hair again, "And look what we did."

"Shush, be quiet, Spike," she said. Her brow wrinkled. "We don't know anything about it, right?" She watched him mime 'zip your lips' and gave him a relaxed smile.

Chapter THIRTY-FOUR

BY SEVEN-FIFTEEN CHRIS was becoming worried. He had set the oven timer and dinner was just about ready, but no Bernie. Chris wondered who or what was keeping him. He decided to walk over to the church, to Bernie's confessional, and that's when he spotted him, drooped like a rag doll across the front pew. Chris's first reaction was panic. He leaned over to feel Bernie's forehead. It was clammy; then he felt for a pulse. Instantly Chris breathed a sigh of relief. He spoke to him in a booming voice as though Bernie was in a coma. At first, nothing, then, Bernie being Bernie opened his eyes and spoke.

"What do you mean, can you hear me? Of course I can hear you. Even the saints can, and they're not among the living. I'm not deaf...or dead, for that matter." He told Chris that he only felt a little dizzy, probably had a little spell and nothing more. Chris knew the drill from a course in health. He asked Bernie what day it was, and Bernie just about blew his lid. He insisted there was nothing wrong with his memory. He said he'd heard confessions as usual today, Saturday. He stressed the day for Chris's benefit. When Chris told him the time of day, he expressed some degree of surprise; then he promptly squelched his reaction. He told him that he must have dozed off or something. Chris didn't buy that at all. He feared the 'something.'

Chris was going to be extra careful. "All right now, Bernie, please, I really would like you to come over and sit here next to me and take a few deep breaths."

Bernie balked. "Chris, take it easy. I just had a little dizzy spell. Plus I haven't eaten much today. That's all. Nothing more. Aren't you going to ask me who the president is?"

Chris smiled. He was feeling better already. Relieved. "No, I think you know."

Bernie said, "You know dang well that I know. I could say "Bush" just to rattle you, but I won't. Then you'd be carting me off to the hospital."

"My line was shorter than yours was today," Chris said, getting back to the issue. "When I left, you had three people waiting in line."

"So my line was longer. I guess they like me better than you. Heh heh," Bernie said.

Chris wouldn't let that one go. "Or else I'm quicker." He chuckled. "I should have waited for you but I decided to get a head start on the meat loaf and baked potatoes. They're probably cold now. I just took them out of the oven."

"Oh no, I'm glad you didn't wait," Bernie said. Then all of a sudden, he looked distressed.

"Oh? If I had waited," Chris told him frowning, "I wouldn't have to be worrying about you. Dinner's going to have to be reheated. It's probably all dried out now. Wait a minute, you're glad I didn't wait for you? What do you mean by that?"

"Oh, nothing really. I'm just babbling." As Chris looked more closely at Bernie, he thought he looked a little peaked.

Chris proposed giving Dr. Dillon a call, to be safe rather than sorry, he explained before Bernie could protest. He'd have him stop by and check out Bernie who was totally against that. He reminded Chris they'd both seen the doctor just days earlier, but

Chris retorted that yesterday didn't count since today was an entirely different story.

Chris had Doctor Dillon's cell number in his speed dial and contacted him immediately. The doctor was out for a jog and would stop by in half an hour unless it was a true emergency. Chris told him most likely it was not, but then you never know for sure. He also told the good doctor that jogging at dark in this cold weather with slippery walkways was not in his best interest. As he puffed along, Doc told Chris he would take that under advisement.

Once back at the rectory, Chris tried to help Bernie up the stairs to the kitchen but Bernie told him he could handle himself, hang onto the railing. That's what they were for. Didn't he know? They could smell the cooled meatloaf, which wasn't very enticing. Chris was starved. Bernie was not, but should have been. He asked Chris to remind the doctor that he'd already answered questions and he didn't need to have his intelligence put to the test again. Chris said it had little to do with intelligence as to short-term memory. Bernie ignored that. When Chris asked Bernie to refresh his memory as to what had happened, he merely said that he got upset—nothing more, though Chris doubted that. There had to be more, but Bernie wasn't talking.

Chris's 'oh?' got little response from Bernie. The more Bernie hashed it over in his mind, the more upset he became. He made it clear he couldn't and wouldn't discuss it. He mentioned the confidentiality factor, punctuated with a look that said, you should know better. Chris got it. Bernie hoped Chris hadn't spotted Glory in church. Most likely he didn't or he would've said so.

As Chris picked at the crumbly tepid meat loaf, Bernie remarked, "By the way, Chris, you heard my confession today, but I didn't hear yours." He hadn't touched his plate.

"Right. But never mind me. I didn't think it was necessary. You were so busy and we see each other all the time," Chris said. He plucked out the dried potato from its shriveled jacket, sprinkled pepper on it and took a few bites.

"It's been an unusual few weeks," Chris explained in a tone tinged with emotion. He avoided eye contact with Bernie. "First you were away, then I was, and then I got sick, and well you know the rest." He hoped Bernie knew only what he should know and nothing more. Bernie seemed to be fading right there at the kitchen table. He simply nodded. Chris went to the fridge and poured him a glass of juice. Bernie took a sip and made a face—too sweet or too sour? Hard to tell. Some fruity mixture that Mrs. Hopkins had left for them. What had possessed her to buy that nectar of some exotic fruit? She probably had a coupon, he guessed. Next time Bernie would tell her to stick to orange juice—plain and simple, and no pulp, please.

Chris informed him, "Anyhow yesterday was my first real day up and running, and I had to do a hospital run, yeah, I did. I didn't tell you? And I ran into Father Domenic. We had a nice little chat, catching up on all the news. Well, he heard my confession and I heard his. We're good buddies, you should know that. He's got a real challenge in his parish, being in the inner city and all. But he's trilingual. He can communicate well enough with lots of his parishioners who'd be lost if he weren't so linguistically gifted. At lease he tries. You have to give him credit. Says we've got it cushy here."

"Oh him, Father High and Mighty, he is," Bernie huffed, placing the glass down. He refused to eat cold meatloaf, and the shriveled baked potato remained untouched as well. He picked at a few buttered carrots and that was all. He pushed his plate away. Even the basket of rolls held little appeal to him.

Chris told him he didn't know Domenic well enough, that if he did he'd have a better opinion of him. Bernie then said Chris would change his mind if he sat in diocesan meetings with Father

Domenic. You just need to get to know him better in that kind of setting, that's all, Bernie added. They decided it was a draw, end of topic.

Bernie began, "Not to change the subject," but he did, saying, "I have to ask you, Chris, is there anything you need to tell me? Say, uh, did anything happen over the past two weeks, like when I was away, for example, that you need to tell me, to, uh, get something off your chest?"

Unnerved, Chris was quick to say, "I thought I was the one asking the questions." Did Bernie have an agenda of sorts? What was he driving at, Chris wondered.

Still pale and frail looking, Bernie insisted, "Look, Chris, I'm really fine. We don't even have to bother Doctor Dillon. He's got better things to do than bother with me. I'll let you know when and if I need him to tell me what I already know."

Chris decided to answer Bernie's question. He would have to weigh his words carefully. "So you want to know what happened that week. Hmm. I guess it wound up being only a few days." He watched Bernie's reaction, wondering if Molly had overreacted about her brother's symptoms the day she called him sounding so frantic. Maybe she'd had it with him, bringing up the idea of assisted living, but no, that couldn't be. "Well, Bernie, you lucked out. You left in the nick of time, missing out on Aleks, and then your favorite teenager, Glory."

Bernie couldn't take another dose of that girl. He dreaded what Chris could be revealing. He uttered weakly, "Glory? Her?" The mention of her name left a sick feeling in his mouth on top of the juice. He wondered if he'd heard her right, if she could be telling him the truth in the confessional. But then she had no reason to make that up. But, it couldn't be, not Chris, not the priest he knows so well, whose reputation he could vouch for.

"Oh yes, her, too, " Chris said. "Remember when Aleks came to see the garden? Well, you escaped her. How I wish you hadn't. It would have cut her stay short if you'd been there. Well, as luck would have it, doesn't Glory show up? It seems that she'd eavesdropped on Aleks's and my, uh, conversation—if you want to call it that. But I've already told you that. It was quite nerve-wracking with the two of them at me. I don't think I left anything out, anything of any import. As far as the parish is concerned, all went well enough with old Will and me, as I said."

Bernie tried to focus on what Chris was saying, on the words he saw coming out of Chris's mouth. He was beginning to experience some difficulty concentrating. Thoughts of what went on in the confessional still hounded him, and so he persisted, "So you have nothing to tell me? There must be something more you need to tell me." Bernie did not have the stamina to press any further for an answer and Chris wasn't talking. So Bernie rose to clear the dishes against Chris's protests. His job was his job. Chris had other duties, Bernie reminded him. Chris told him to sit down and to stay put.

Minutes later Doctor Dillon arrived, his face red and his forehead dripping with perspiration. After a cursory neurological check, which did include a few of the usual questions, Dillon told Chris to meet him at the emergency room as soon as they could get there. Bernie was spouting, insisted he was perfectly fine, but it was clear to Chris and the doctor that he was not. At best, Dillon told Chris, it was more than likely a TIA. He explained to Bernie that it means a little stroke, but only maybe. They would just run some tests to be sure. Bernie corrected the doctor telling him it was no stroke of any size, just a big shock.

Chapter THIRTY-FIVE

CHRIS TOOK ADVANTAGE of the thaw Sunday afternoon. He cleared the pathways in his garden and checked the plantings for signs of damage from the heavy snows. The hollies were beginning to pop back into place, even the one that had been bent the night the windows were broken. The Christmas rose bush was thankfully and miraculously intact. If that plant's blossoms could survive in the Alps, then why not in Wexford Falls? In his beloved garden, Chris could sense his energy returning. If only his thoughts could be healed as easily, and peace of mind could return to normal the way his hollies had. What persisted even as he prayed and inspected his plantings was that annoying tugging at the back of his throat. He knew what it was. It haunted him. He was beginning to think that that could be the seat of his conscience, then he laughed at the very thought.

Bernie was held over night at the hospital for observation and routine tests. It was confirmed that he did not have a stroke. He was furious, said he may never speak to Doctor Dillon again, but then in his more rational moments he realized that they don't put you in the hospital for no reason at all, not these days. But his absence and weeklong recuperation meant that another priest had to take his place. It wouldn't have been so bad if it was Father Will, whom Chris stopped referring to as Old Will. The man could do the job, albeit slowly, and he wasn't at all unpleasant, except maybe for his unnatural phobia of Paddy. But Paddy was back and the replacement, per the bishop, turned out to be Father Rollo Donovan. He claimed he was allergic to Paddy but Chris knew he really wasn't. The man was just contrary. The only consolation was that Rollo Donovan was there on a per diem basis, so Paddy could have a run of the rectory evenings and whenever His Majesty wasn't around. Bernie had warned Chris not to even dare to call Rollo that even behind his back; it could slip out, he feared. Chris told him not to worry. He knew better.

--- ✺ ---

MRS. HOPKINS CAME IN early Monday morning. It upset her that Father Bernie had had a spell, as she referred to his ailment. That meant that no way could she burden him with what her daughter-in-law had revealed about Father Chris. Imagine that! What a mess he'd gotten himself into at the ski lodge, and with a teenager to boot! The shock of that could kill poor Father Bernie in his weakened condition. So she decided to wait a week or two until she judged him ready to face the bare, cold facts, as she referred to the incident. The very thought of what Jodie had seen made her shudder at what the consequences could be. The parish would suffer as well. She dreaded the whole thing, but Father Bernie must be informed. And it was her duty to do so. And Jodie doesn't lie, she said to herself. This must be told and dealt with. Withholding that information was not right, not at all.

If she'd known in advance that Bishop Miles would be paying a visit so early on a Monday morning of all days, and with another priest in tow, she would have baked his favorite muffins, orange-cranberry. She figured judging from his paunch that he'd accept lemon-blueberry, as she had an affinity for anything lemon, and Bishop Miles would enjoy them. As for the softened butter, she didn't have much time so she microwaved a stick. She made sure it was not totally liquefied. Coffee was hot and cream was poured. It was OK for her to offer real cream to guests, especially the bishop. She believed in her absence that Father Bernie must have gotten into the real cream as there was only about a quarter of the container left.

She greeted the priests and the bishop with a wide smile, although that was hard for her to manage, as she was still reeling from Jodie's revelation. She didn't like the way Bernie looked, pinched, a grayish cast to his skin, a little older looking, too. So hers was a worried smile, a little forced. Her whole face wasn't into it. She held onto the smile as she placed the silver tray on the coffee table; she was trying to be as gracious as possible. Then she moved the ailing poinsettia plant from a table back onto the floor by the window. It bothered her that the little violin was still there. It took on a new meaning now that she was in the know. She noticed the bishop was still smiling, so true to form. It seemed so natural to him and it did put people at ease, she thought. Smiles were contagious. She wondered what he did with his smile when he had to break bad news to someone. She'd only seen that one cheery face he showed at the rectory.

Father Donovan sat on one of a pair of overstuffed chairs. If he knew how to smile, he was certainly out of practice. Bernie may not have looked very chipper but he did his best to act like himself, which was so endearing to his devoted housekeeper. This had to be something more than a social call.

Chris had said the morning mass and opted to have his breakfast alone in the upstairs kitchen. This meant Rollo could have his time with Bernie and the bishop. The less Chris interacted with Rollo the better, but then in the presence of Bishop Miles, Rollo had learned to be reticent. It must have pained him to just sit and listen.

Chris had no idea what they were saying, and he wasn't about to eavesdrop, not with Mrs. Hopkins dashing all about, even popping in upstairs to inventory pantry supplies or for some other reason. It would be typical for her to be in and out of the sitting room, and she would glean snippets of information from their visit. There had to have been an agenda. Bishop Miles didn't come there exclusively to visit Bernie. He could have gone to the hospital yesterday, but here he was in consort with Rollo Donovan.

But during the week when Chris and Rollo did spend some time together, talk centered on the parish, Bernie's overall prognosis, and religious matters, as one would expect. Rollo hinted that there would be some strategic moves down the pike, his exact words. He said that they wanted someone younger and more energetic over at St. Damian's. Chris knew that it involved a high school as well as one church, possibly even two. Not for me, he mused, but if the bishop says go, you go. That's the way it goes. Did he need another layer to heap onto his troubled thoughts? He prayed any time he could. He told himself that Rollo was just being a bore, a nosy body. What could he know?

Rollo told Chris over a club sandwich, his mouth half full of chicken, "You know, Chris, if I wind up here, they'd have to hire a gardener. I'd die of anaphylactic shock, that's fatal you know, if I had to fiddle around with all those flowers and plants like you do—I'm so allergic, as you well know." He punctuated his statement with a sniff and a feeble laugh, more annoying habits for Chris to add to the growing list. Prior to this week, Chris didn't know Rollo very well, just enough to realize that they couldn't share quarters. Bernie was of the same opinion. He didn't have to say so but it was apparent. However, this week Bernie bit his tongue, for the sake of his health and his sanity. After all, Rollo was doing the job that Bernie couldn't wait to return to. Parishioners had taken Chris aside, asking when Bernie would return. They weren't fond of Father Donovan. They preferred someone more personable. Chris did not press for details. He knew what they meant.

———— ✣ ————

WHEN OFF DUTY, SERGEANT Robert Smith made his presence known in Wexford Falls, here and there, in shops and businesses, even schools. At times he was seen in town taking his sons for a walk, sometimes pulling them up and down the streets in their little red wagon. That way he could keep his finger on the town's pulse, spend time with the boys, and get some exercise at the same time. And he accomplished this without arousing suspicion, most of the time. This day, however, he left the boys with his mother-in-law. And so he thought he'd pay a visit to Sterling-Baie Enterprises, by all appearances, a social call, since they were generous benefactors.

A radiant Agatha O'Toole led Smitty into Doug Sterling's inner office. She figured the sergeant was making an appeal for more support for the Boys Club or some other civic charity. On second thought, however, a simple phone call would have sufficed and Agatha could have handled it herself. In any event, Doug emerged from his inner sanctum and greeted Smitty with a firm handshake and a pat on the back. After idle chat, which in winter centered on weather, snow removal and rough travel, Smitty brought up the topic of snowball fights to see if Doug Sterling would react.

And react he did. He admitted that he had sent an anonymous donation to poor Father Monahan to help defray expenses for that awful accident, or act of vandalism, whatever you might call it. No one had said for sure, so he'd thought. But once revealed, his donation would no longer be anonymous. He told Smitty he preferred to keep it 'under wraps', but he acknowledged that word does get out. Smitty said nothing for a moment. He just kept studying the executive in his designer suit, that probably set him back four figures, in the midst of office furniture that probably cost as much as Smitty's whole house.

"That was very kind of you," he said obligingly, still taking in the splendor of the private office. His own was bare bones, by contrast, but it served the purpose. But Smitty was at Sterling-Baie Enterprises because he hoped to learn something. There were so many charities, some much more deserving than St. Aeden's. Why did Sterling choose to help out Father Bernie Monahan? Smitty calculated his comments. "I didn't know you were a member of St. Aeden's."

"I'm not," Doug said brusquely, fumbling with a gold pen he was holding. He didn't want to say any more than he had to, plus he was a busy man and he tried to give that impression at this moment. Doug had a good idea that Smitty knew why he'd been the one who'd made the donation.

"Must cost a bundle to repair all that breakage. Those windows are ancient, originals maybe, hard to match, I would think," Smitty continued. He was studying Doug's body language. It was talking to him, and Smitty was listening.

"Yes, very expensive and the match is proving to be a challenge, but you have to understand, my men are good. They're experts in the field." He paused. "And that Father Monahan's a good man, the other priest too, from what I hear," Doug said.

"That would be a huge unexpected expense for them," Smitty said. "Plus it would undoubtedly hike up their insurance premiums. And I'm sure they wouldn't welcome any negative publicity either." He wanted to hear more.

Doug feared what Smitty was driving at. Let him get to the point. Enough of this shadow dancing. "To whom do I write out the check, WFPD?" Doug asked the sergeant.

Smitty ignored the question. He had other things on his mind. Then the zinger came. "Say, Doug, tell me, does your son or daughter know a kid named Spencer Gilbert? Goes by the name of Spike. He's a junior at the high school in town."

Doug thought a moment, "Well, I don't recall Glen bringing anyone home by the name of Spike. He's at the Academy, you know." Doug had an inkling of the direction this was heading "Glen's here at the office much of his free time. Can't learn the ropes too early, can you? I've got great plans for the boy." With Doug approaching sixty, he hoped his son would take over the business after college.

Smitty just listened, and nodded. He was studying Doug.

"As for Glory, well, I couldn't say. You know teen-age girls. They're a breed unto their own. She can be quite a handful. She goes to the high school now, been there only a few months, but maybe she knows him. She's a junior too. She may know who he is, but after that I can't say. Why do you ask?"

Easy, Smitty, he told himself. Go easy. "I'm not so sure you'd want your daughter to know him. What I mean is to be a friend of his." Doug tried not to react. He could sense where this was heading.

After this little stall, Smitty let it out. "OK, I'll be frank. People saw your daughter and Spike cozying up together in town a few times."

Doug froze. He believed that the check would end any possible investigation, formal or otherwise. This seemed to fall under the category as 'otherwise,' so he hoped.

"The two were seen near St. Aeden's Church the night of the breakage not long after they left Dunkin Donuts," he said. "Now I know that doesn't mean they set out to smash three stained glass windows, but..."

"You're saying it looks suspicious," Doug finished the thought. It wasn't quite a question. He decided to let Smitty respond to that."

"'Fraid so. Rumor has it they're friends, very good friends, as a matter of fact, and you do not want your daughter hanging around with the likes of him. I've gotten to know him, had him in a few times for questioning but he's stayed under the radar, his mother, too. They are not pillars of the community, not by a longshot," he said.

"I suppose you could have said he was a degenerate?" Doug quipped to conceal his mounting attack of nerves. He had learned to control himself. It worked to his advantage in many a business deal.

"Nah, I wouldn't go that far. He's just a kid, and with a kid I like to think there's always hope. Gotta have faith in the next generation, don't we?" Smitty said, half seriously, knowing his sons will be teens sooner than he'd like to believe. Cut them a little slack when they're older until they prove otherwise.

Doug could have kissed Agatha when she nudged into his office after a gentle knock. She was balancing a tray of coffee and almond biscotti. Doug was pleased, even a little relieved that Smitty helped himself. It loosened the tension that was mounting. Agatha was amazing. She had a sixth sense, Doug believed. She left as quickly as she had entered.

When both were seated in comfortable chairs, Smitty asked, "Say, Doug, would you mind bringing your daughter Glory downtown to headquarters, say, tomorrow morning? I'll be on duty then, around, uh, sevenish. I need to ask her a few questions. That's all. Then she'll still make it to school on time and it won't eat too much into your busy day."

Doug swallowed hard. "Oh..." He paused to take in what Smitty had just said. It threw him for a moment. Then attempting to regain a sense of equanimity, he asked, "By the way, Sergeant, has, uh, that boy uh, Spike been in yet? I mean have you spoken to him yet about this, uh, situation?"

"I'd really like to talk to her first, if you don't mind. You or your wife would have to be with her," Smitty explained. He knew what he was doing. Next, Doug feared, he'd ask them to bring in a lawyer as well.

"Can I ask you a favor, Sergeant?" Doug said with a sigh. "It seems I'm always the one doing favors for someone. Now I'm asking you to do one for me." He was used to bargaining in his capacity as a businessman, a CEO. But he was unsure it would work in this case.

"Depends," Smitty answered coolly, then, "aw, shoot, I'm listening." And police business was business too, he reminded himself.

"If I can get her to admit she played some part in the snow ball escapade, which I'm sure was an accident, and if I pick up any additional expenses, can't we just bury the whole thing?" Doug was pleading now. He clearly wanted to keep this matter under wraps. He didn't need that kind of publicity, should this make the papers. He didn't know how much more he could take, but Glory did have to be taught a lesson, and nothing thus far was working. But she was his daughter, and yes, there was always hope. Didn't Smitty just say that about Spike? And maybe, just maybe, Glory was not involved, and if she was, that it was just an accident. Sure, he told himself, like all the others—just happenstance.

"So if I bring in Spike and he admits that he incited Glory to have some fun with him at anyone's expense, then what am I faced with?" Smitty asked, expressing his situation aloud.

"Well, somehow I don't think Father Monahan will press charges," Doug said, clinging to the hope that was true.

"All right for now, Doug, what I'm asking you to do is have a heart to heart with Glory and get back to me tomorrow. I'll put a hold on bringing in Spike for now," Smitty said, hoping he wouldn't regret this.

"And now the real reason you came here was for a check for the Boys Club, am I right?" Doug asked. He was sincere, and Smitty was just paying a social call, wasn't he? He was off duty.

"Let's wait a while on that. I know you're good. The fundraiser doesn't get under way for another few months, I believe. I'll have to check on that," Smitty said, relieved for the change of topic.

"You know, sergeant, this very morning I wrote the second check to a Swiss boarding school for Glory, for next year that is. I missed the deadline for this term," he said. He was ashamed that whatever he did for his daughter, it failed. Glory was just Glory. She was a force.

Rather than congratulating him, Smitty pitied him. The man cared, but his daughter was a tough case. Checks couldn't be the answer, not always. The visit was over. Smitty wiped the crumbs off his lips and set down his coffee cup, thanking Doug for his time. Yes, they would touch base first thing in the morning. They shook hands and Smitty left.

Belinda was shocked to see her husband return from the office in the light of day. He gave his wife a perfunctory hug. She knew him well enough to tell that something was on his mind, something grave, she feared. No, he wasn't sick. He was just fine. And so what if dinner wasn't ready. He wasn't very hungry, he said. He asked where Glory was and she told him it was too early for her to be home on a school day. No, she didn't know where her daughter was at the moment, probably at a friend's house, maybe at Dunkin Donuts. Doug made a sour face and told her he was going upstairs for a quick shower and to let him know the minute Glory came home. He paused to ask her where Glen was. Upstairs in his room with a friend at the computer working on a project for history, she told him. Was the friend expected to stay for dinner, he asked as he started up the stairs? When she said 'no' she saw relief on his face. Something was up.

Glory bounded into the living room in an unusually up mood. Minutes later she and her father had the dreaded *tete a tete*, dreaded more by Doug since Glory had no inkling what it would be about. She told her father the sergeant was out of his freakin' mind. Sure, she knew Spike Gilbert, everybody at school knew him, and he only played up to her in front of his friends to show them how cool it was to get a pretty, rich girl's attention. It was no more than a silly game for her. She told her father she played into his hands because it was cool, and coming from the Academy, she wanted the public high school kids to accept her, which was a boldfaced lie. She felt superior to them. The less she had to do with them, the better. She had trained herself to tell her father what he wanted to hear. She always felt bad when she hurt him, but she had to save her skin. As for her mother, she could care less.

Life is so boring, she said to her father, looking him directly in the eye. If anyone broke the windows it was probably a bunch of bratty kids out to raise hell. No, she would never do that. She liked Father Monahan and Father Tosi. Everybody did, she added. When her father told her he'd written an anonymous check for the restoration of the window panels, she just shrugged, saying that it was really nice of him. She wasn't going to change her story. Nice, she said...what was he going to tell the sergeant tomorrow? He'd surely summon Glory and himself to headquarters if they didn't show up. What if Spike and his mother were there as well? He didn't want his daughter charged with a crime. She was young. She will change, he hoped. Doug felt a wave of nausea envelop him.

Glory slept on it. She announced at breakfast the next morning that she would go to headquarters with her father if that was what he wanted. She said it in the same tone she might have used saying she was going on a field trip. He just about choked on a mouthful of bacon when he heard her say that. Belinda was dead set against it, but held her tongue right after Glory agreed to comply. Glen Thomas chimed in saying Glory was pathetic and should get what she deserves. She gave him a jab under the table and called him an asshole. She said she knows what she's doing.

--- ⚬ ---

SERGEANT SMITH STUDIED his Timex for the third time as though it held the wisdom of an oracle. It was seven-forty, and they were finally entering headquarters—Douglas Sterling looking like a Wall Street executive and Glory dressed like the little rich girl that she was. He couldn't help noticing how pretty she was—too bad her personality didn't match her looks. She was indeed a handful, as her father had told him just yesterday. Word of Glory's doings were not kept secret in the Wexford Falls community. Various versions of the truth meandered from one end of the town to the other.

Smitty was shocked when Glory freely admitted to breaking the church windows, with no compunction, adding that her father's check should take care of the costs of restoring the windows, as though it was the most logical, normal thing to do. Her tone changed as she pleaded with Smittty not to bring in Spike. She told him he was innocent, totally innocent, she stressed. She would swear to it. She admitted she was on the outs with Father Monahan, but she didn't want to discuss it. Her father knew the reason why. Spike, she insisted, took a walk with her, but didn't touch any of the rock-laced snowballs. She told him she and her brother used to make their missiles with rocks when they were younger, said they'd fire them at targets, bottles and stuff, on their backyard fence. She said Spike tossed a few snowballs at her, messing around, but not near the church windows. She said he didn't want to say anything to the authorities because he'd get her in trouble, and he wasn't a rat.

Glory's admission of guilt surprised Smitty, and he thought he knew teens. He figured he'd have to grill her. She gave it up much too easily. Something told him she was covering for Spike and may have been afraid to implicate him as an accomplice, but why? What was her reason? Glory's father was angry enough at her, but he bought the story—anything to end this matter, if indeed it was over and done with.

"What about Father Monahan? Do you think he'll press charges?" Doug asked the sergeant. He was visibly worried about repercussions. Glory just sat there bored, playing with one of several bangles she slid up and down her forearm.

"I suppose I'll have to talk to him but I hear he's just come out of the hospital," Smitty said. "I might wait a little."

"Oh, I hadn't heard. Will he be all right?" Doug asked the sergeant.

"From what I've heard, yes, with some rehab, they hope. They say he keeled over Saturday afternoon at the end of confessions. Can you imagine that?" he said. Glory paled when she heard that. She hoped neither the sergeant nor her father took notice of her reaction. But the sergeant could read something into that. He trained his eyes on her and she looked away.

But he's going to be OK?" Doug asked more so to reassure himself. He imagined Father Monahan was still coping with the after effects of the vandalism.

"Chris, I mean Father Tosi's been sick all week with a nasty bout of the flu and complications on top of that, so maybe Father Monahan was doing too much. He probably got himself overtired and such," Smitty explained. "I sure hope it's nothing more than that."

There was an uncomfortable minute of dead silence. Smitty took a deep breath, deep in thought. Then he spoke. "All right, folks, let's leave things as they are, at least for the time being. I'll pay a visit to Father Monahan in a few days."

"You'll tell him?" Glory said in a panic. "Does he have to know?"

BERNIE WAS GAZING OUT the window from his sitting room where he'd spent much time since Rollo Donovan and Chris were handling the parish duties. He couldn't understand why he had to lay low, as they said. He felt well enough, fine. As he watched passersby he spotted an airport limo pull up in front of Swenson's Hardware. The Swensons had just returned from Florida. Ingrid came dashing out, her oversized red smock blowing in the wind. She hugged her grand-parents and grabbed the handles of the two suitcases the driver had left at the main entrance, and wheeled them inside. The Swensons both looked tan, from what Bernie could see. Mrs. Swenson glanced over across the way and saw that Bernie was waving to her. It looked like a signal. She paused a second, then ran across the street to the rectory. Mrs. Hopkins was already at the door to let her in. By then Bernie was there to greet her.

"You should hang out a shingle, Father Bernie," she said, hugging him. "You shoulda been a shrink. Best advice I ever got, and from a Catholic priest, too. Can you imagine that?" She laughed. "Father, I sent you a big box of citrus fruits from Indian River, oranges and grapefruits. It'll do you good during the winter months, keep you nice and healthy, right?"

"That was generous of you, Eva. You didn't have to. Well, I guess the mister did OK," he said with a smile and a twinkle in his eyes recalling the reason the couple went on vacation in the dead of winter.

"Oh, yes. We both did. Look at me. When have I ever had such a tan? I'm orange like the fruits," she said, gushing with excitement.

"No more episodes?" he asked with a grin. He prayed Swen wasn't seeing dead people any more, or talking to them.

"Not a one," she said smiling and nodding. He thought she looked youthful when she was happy, or maybe it was just the warmth of her personality. "Like I just said, Father Bernie, you shoulda been a doctor or a, uh, shrink."

"Nah, not me," Bernie said. "I got enough to handle. I'm a doctor of the soul." He paused a second to contemplate what he'd just said. "Don't need people pouring out any more problems than I already deal with. And then, what if I give them the wrong advice?"

"Well, whatever," she said. "Now, Father, I gotta get back to business. Really, I do. I think the old boy missed it a little, the store, I mean. He worried that maybe it was too much for Ingrid to handle, not that we don't have good folks to help her out. I said to him, 'Take it easy, but you know how people don't listen."

Bernie nodded. Oh, yes, he knew only too well.

"So you been OK, yourself, Father Bernie?" she asked. "You're usually out and about this time of day, winter or not, yah?"

"I am, but...as for OK...depends who you're talking to. I'm fine, I tell them," he said, trying to convince himself. "The rest of them will tell you I'm not. Just had a little spell over the week-end and I'm on a little, uh, staycation—that's what they call it these days. Heh heh."

She raised her eyebrows, then figured she wouldn't pry. She excused herself said 'good-bye,' and scurried across the street, back to business.

Chapter THIRTY-SIX

BERNIE WAS BEGINNING to lose steam after Mrs. Swenson's visit. Mrs. Hopkins scrutinized him as she did too often for Bernie's liking, suggesting that he lie down for a rest. He admitted to himself that he was 'sagging' as he called it. No, he did not want to sleep. He'd just curl up the on sitting room sofa for a few minutes, and would Mrs. Hopkins kindly bring him a soft pillow? She frowned, her typical look of disapproval, and told him that that sofa was only for sitting. It's too stiff. 'Why do you suppose they call this a sitting room? That's the sole purpose, Father.' She punctuated her appraisal with another Hopkins frown. He knew she always had his best interest in mind, but he knew what he wanted. He did not want to fall asleep. He did not want to give in.

Stretched out on the sitting room sofa with his head at an awkward angle, he had just about nodded off when he heard the buzzing of the front door bell. It seemed to come from another world. Mrs. Hopkins called out to him in a loud whisper—she wasn't sure he was awake and if he was asleep she would tell the visitor to come back another time. Bernie bolted upright when he learned the identity of his afternoon caller.

"Sergeant Smith," he said, stifling a persistent urge to yawn. He smiled and extended his hand. By now, he was fully awake, stretching his neck and moving it in little circles to get the kinks out. "A social call, I take it. Nice to see you. And how're those little ones doing? Strapping young lads by now, I would guess. They'll be outgrowing their wagon before you know it."

"Well, not quite yet, thank goodness," Smitty said, exchanging pleasantries with Bernie. "Um, Father, I hear you've been under the weather lately."

"So they tell me," Bernie said with a huff. Smitty could tell this was not a topic for further investigation. Bernie would always downplay any reference to his health. He was fine, in his estimation. "Good of you to pay a social call before your shift."

"Oh, yes, thank you, Father, so I really can't stay more than a few minutes, plus I don't want to tire you out," Smitty said. He wasn't sure what action Bernie would be inclined to take after hearing what he had to say.

It didn't take very long. Bernie sensed this wasn't solely a social call. "All right, sergeant, you may tell me. Go ahead. You've got something on your mind."

The muscles on Smitty's face relaxed. "Yes, I do. Good news and, well, we'll see where if anywhere it goes from here." He still was still unclear as to who was and was not guilty, and who was protecting whom, and for what reason.

"I, uh, ran into Doug Sterling, you know the developer from Sterling-Baie Enterprises?" He continued, watching Bernie nod in recognition of the name. "And, uh, somehow it came out in our conversation that he was the anonymous donor to the, uh, window cause." He observed Bernie's eyebrows travel up as one would expect from such a revelation. But Bernie already knew or had surmised as much. That Smitty could tell.

"Well now, that does not surprise me a'tall. I don't know if you heard but his men are doing the restoration, says they're the very best in the business," Bernie said, as though it was obvious. Wexford Falls folks could attest to the quality of their workmanship throughout the town.

"Come to find out why he gave you the check," Smitty said. He glanced at his watch, which told him he should get to the final matter. Father Bernie looked weary and Smitty wanted this to be effortless on his own part, which it wasn't turning out to be, and speedy so the priest could get back to his nap.

"Father, I'll be blunt. Sterling's daughter did it. Her name's Glory," Smitty said trying not to sound so blunt. "She admitted she was the one who threw the snow balls that broke the windows."

"OK, hmm, now shall I say I'm surprised?" Bernie asked the officer a little too calmly. He took in a deep, contemplative breath before continuing. "I suppose I am surprised that anyone would inflict damage on a sacred place...but that it was *that* girl, I am not very surprised, not a'tall." This was payback for his tattling on her to her father about the poem she'd written for Chris, but he had to do it. The matter had to be addressed. Of course, he wasn't about to share this with Sergeant Smith.

"Well, Father, I wondered all along why you didn't seem to want me to pursue an active investigation, so I just went around asking questions to this one and that one. I'd be remiss if I didn't," he said. He was fiddling with the buttons on his shirt.

"Well, I'm not sure how you did it, but you sure did," Bernie said. He was ready to end this encounter.

"She actually admitted her guilt. I didn't have to press," Smitty informed him, searching his face for any reaction.

'Hmm,' was all Smitty heard him say.

"So Father, will you be pressing charges, or do you want some time to think it over?" Smitty asked with no preamble.

Bernie hesitated. "I need to know more, if you don't mind," he said. This visit was unanticipated. He'd been through so much. The windows had been broken—maliciously. They were being restored and paid for by a benefactor, Glory's father. The main problem was the inconvenience of having his church disrupted. Plus it didn't look good for the church and the community.

Smitty figured Bernie would want to know if it could have been accidental. He strongly doubted Bernie would think that. Or was it truly a vengeful act on the part of an angry person.

"I think you should know that Glory has been what Sterling says is a 'handful,' which, I know is putting it mildly, so to speak," Smitty began. "He hoped the check plus his assurance that the restoration would be done to your satisfaction would ease some of the pain you've suffered."

"Not just me, our whole church community. To think someone is so angry at you that she would set out to destroy church property, holy works of art, if I must remind you," he said, reddening.

Smitty could see the effect this was having on Bernie, and in no way did he want this discussion to exacerbate Bernie's condition. Maybe he should have waited a few days. "What would you like me to do? Will you, uh, be pressing charges, Father?"

"No, I do not believe so, no," he said with conviction, reiterating the negative. He had his reasons.

Smitty looked askance. "You know the girl, then?"

"We've run into each other at times," he admitted. Smitty waited. It was clear that Bernie did not choose to elaborate.

"Well, I think you should know that Sterling is pulling her out of our local high school. She was thrown out of the Academy in the fall, you know. Because of her, uh, infractions this year, he is placing her in a foreign boarding school for her own good. He's already made deposits, so the guy is not putting me on," Smitty explained, watching for a change in Bernie's expression. But all he noticed was Bernie's fatigue, increasingly apparent as the visit wore on.

"I suspect the poor man has done his best. He seems to me to be a good and generous soul. But does money buy everything? That girl, however, needs guidance, but I'm not sure who can provide it," Bernie said. "Only a higher power can help straighten her out."

Smitty didn't know if Bernie was serious. But he seemed to know her better than he thought, which was probably why he wouldn't press charges.

"Is there anything I can do, Father?" he asked. Something was off, in his estimation. Glory was getting off too easy, and another thing bothered him: why wouldn't she finger Spike? Too much of this didn't make sense, or did it?

Bernie thought a moment, then, "A warning to keep her off the property would be my first reaction, but no. Let her go at that. You can tell Doug Sterling I am very grateful for his generosity, and I'm sorry for what he has to deal with, but she is his child, and he is a decent man, so I will pray. That's about all," Bernie said. What more could he do?

Smitty had more admiration than ever for Father Bernie. He realized that Chris, his basketball buddy, was so lucky to be with the older priest, his mentor. Actually, he conceded, the two were good for each other. Smitty too would pray in his own way that Glory Sterling gets on the right track, but any alliance she might have with Spike Gilbert would send her off course and into a free fall. He doubted her father's money would always provide a safety net for her.

Chapter THIRTY-SEVEN

LIFE WENT ON IN WEXFORD Falls without a major hitch, in Chris's estimation. The memory of that fateful episode in the ski lodge seemed to evaporate from his mind. He couldn't even delineate its sequence of events, partly because he was delirious when it happened, and partly because Jodie kept what she'd seen to herself, as did Glory. At least no one had brought it up, thank you, Jodie Hopkins. The pulling at the back of his throat had eased up as a result. What did bother him, however, was sharing parish duties with Father Rollo Donovan. Because of his Rollo's niggling, Paddy had to take an extended sleep over at the Tosi home. Everyone else missed his presence, Mrs. Hopkins, included.

Chris often considered getting his parents a puppy, but tabled the idea for the present time—maybe he'd reconsider in the summertime. If they kept on dog sitting which would be the case for now and possibly in the future, house training a puppy might be too much for them to handle. Rollo may have been allergic to flowers, but Chris did not believe he had a pet allergy or he'd be sneezing his brains out from the pet dander that would be embedded in nearly every fiber in the rectory as no rooms were off limits to Paddy, not even Bernie's sitting room.

Chris wasn't happy to hear that Rollo had been added to Matt's visitors' list at the prison, which meant that he himself was removed from the list for now. He assumed that happened when he was nursing the flu. Plus he'd heard from Muriel Symond that Matt was 'losing ground,' as she called it. When Chris pressed for more information, she said to ask the priest who was in to see him. Chris would not deign to do that. He decided to place a call to Ruthie, who sounded even more uptight than usual. She told him she wouldn't visit her fiance again unless he got 'undepressed' as she referred to his emotional state. She told Chris it made her more depressed just being in his presence, as she'd told him on other occasions. Chris made a mental note to get back onto the visitors' list some time soon and see for himself. He wondered how the appeal was going, if there was even a chance Matt's case could be reopened. He planned to stop by Ruthie's for a little chat when he could find some time.

Without the team of Fathers Monahan and Tosi, things at St. Aeden weren't running quite as smoothly as Chris would've liked. Parishioners were still getting Chris aside and asking when the 'other priest' would be leaving. Rollo was either 'too this' or 'too that.' Chris would only smile, a knowing smile, and say, 'soon.' Then he would stress one of Rollo's positive traits. For reasons that Chris couldn't fathom, Bernie tolerated Rollo well enough. Chris wondered, did Rollo and Bernie know something that he didn't?

Rollo would be sticking around for another few weeks and Paddy would be romping up and down the cellar stairs at his parents' home as Chris's vacation time had been approved, and Bernie would be back running St. Aeden's. Chris looked forward to a carefree existence in a tropical setting. Anton Drobec, his high school basketball buddy, had underwritten all expenses for the ten-day Caribbean cruise. It would be Chris's first vacation in a long time. The good thing was that Bernie was looking better each day, and by taking a late winter vacation, Chris would be back in plenty of time to prepare the garden for the springtime explosion of blossoms and new growth. In the meantime, any work that needed to be done, including clearing the walkways, would be taken care of by Millicent Tewksbury and the Garden Club members. Heavy snow removal was assigned to one of their older sons.

———— ⟨∿⟩ ————

EACH DAY WHEN THELMA Hopkins drove to the rectory she rehearsed what she was going to say to Father Bernie and how she was going to say it. And each day when she arrived she became tongue-tied. No day or time seemed quite right. First, she thought that it would be better if Father Tosi were there so the two priests could process the situation together, if that could even be feasible. But then, given the gravity of the situation, she wasn't so sure. She really had no name for what might have happened between Father Tosi and that girl. Was it a fling, an affair, sexual abuse, or something else? And it wasn't she after all who had witnessed the scene; all she could do was relate what Jodie had told her, verbatim. But then her better judgment told her Chris should not be present. She wouldn't be able to speak freely with him there. She would be too embarrassed. Father Bernie could then handle Father Chris at another time, however he'd choose to do so. After all, it would be his responsibility to do something. She would have done her duty. So the rest was up to him. And so on day nine of Chris's ten-day cruise, she convinced herself to dive head first into uncharted waters and hope she didn't drown.

Father Donovan had a dinner engagement and wasn't expected back to the rectory much before eight p.m. He'd been staying at the rectory over night during Chris's vacation, but today he was all packed and ready to leave the next day. Thelma Hopkins checked Father Bernie's calendar, twice, to be sure. Yes, the time was right, she told herself. They would be alone. But she could not have anticipated his reaction or the consequences. She merely thought it was incumbent upon her to share what Jodie had confided in her weeks ago. It was behavior unbecoming to a priest, she said to herself, but Father Chris? How could it be possible? She'd tried her best to assume her regular duties as housekeeper since Jodie's revelation, so no one would suspect anything was amiss.

And so at zero hour she asked Father Bernie to come join her in the sitting room. She had something to tell him. She'd already laid out a tray of hot tea and cinnamon scones fresh out of the oven. If nothing else, that told him something was up. He feared she was buttering him up to give him her notice. What else could be on her mind? He didn't know what they'd do if she left. Would they ever find another Mrs. Hopkins? He doubted it.

They sipped their tea, just the way Bernie preferred it, with a little milk and one half teaspoon of sugar, none of those sickening sweet substitutes that she kept in the pantry should a guest request some. She divided the two scones in half, and they ate one half at a time in silence, savoring each mouthful. The silence was palpable. The softened butter dripped onto their plates, forming little yellow pools. Thelma had reached over for the teapot, ready to pour a second cup as Bernie set his cup and saucer aside. They could hear cars passing by, the sound of a siren approaching the intersection. She set the teapot back on the shamrock shaped ceramic trivet. It settled with a little rattling sound, breaking the stillness of the moment.

Bernie spoke first. "Something's on your mind, Thelma." Bernie hoped with all his heart it was anything other than her leaving St. Aeden's. Maybe she was about to request some time off now that Father Chris is returning. He figured it would do her good especially since her bout with the flu had taken so much out of her. He supposed they could find a temp for a few weeks or so. Then he noticed a tremor in her usually steady hands. "OK, now, Thelma. Out with it. I can tell. You're much too quiet. Heh heh." This time it was a nervous laugh.

"Well, Father," she said with a sigh, "I do have to tell you something, and I'm afraid it's very difficult for me." She was looking down at her plate, swirling the butter drippings with her knife, making little designs until the squeaking of her butter knife became unpleasant to the ear—strident. She couldn't face him. He would be heart-broken and she would be the bearer of ill tidings. She recalled the famous line, "Don't shoot the messenger," appropriate but unsettling.

Here it comes, he thought. I'll bet I'm right on the money. She's going to give her notice. "Would you prefer waiting until Father Chris comes back? Would that be easier for you?" he asked, hoping she'd make eye contact.

"Oh, dear God, no," she answered with too much haste. She was upset, breathing heavily. He could sense fear in her eyes when she looked up at him. "It's got to be now. It can't wait, Father."

"Very well, then. Tell me, Thelma, are you, uh, leaving us?" Bernie asked haltingly. He reached out to touch her hand. He'd come out with it if she herself couldn't verbalize it. "Are you retiring or taking a job somewhere else? Is that what's making you so uncomfortable?"

"Oh no, Father, I'm not, unless you'd rather have someone else here in my place. I like St. Aeden's very much. It's become my second home," she said, tears welling in her dark eyes. She removed her glasses and set them on her lap.

"Now, now, Thelma, if you'd rather, you can go to confession. Father Donovan or any of us can hear your confession," he said, hoping to ease her distress.

She daubed her eyes with a tissue she withdrew from her pocket as tears trickled down her face. Her lips were quivering. She held onto her glasses a moment, then set them back down. "Oh no, that's not it, not at all, Father. Going to confession is not going to help," she said, weeping.

"Then you have to tell me. Come out with it. You'll feel better, I assure you," he said with a hint of a smile. He took her hand, hoping to calm her. She pulled it away to grasp her other hand, not so much as an act of rejection but in supplication. She hoped it would calm her sufficiently to begin her story.

"I don't think so," she said. Then she looked over at him. She thought he looked so vulnerable. "Part of me says Father Chris should be here, and, uh, my daughter-in-law Jodie as well, then all parties could speak, or almost all of them, and, uh, say what they need to say," she said, causing Bernie to look perplexed, verging on fearful.

"So this involves more than just you and me?" he asked, rubbing his chin, still trying to anticipate what this could be about. Finally, he sat back and braced himself. It was the fear of the unknown, or in this case the unspoken. He was ready.

"It involves Father Chris, I'm afraid," she said after taking a deep breath. Then she cleared her throat.

"Well, then, shouldn't he be present?" he said, wondering how serious this really could be, and involving Jodie Hopkins somehow. Then he thought 'ski week-end,' ah yes, that had to be the connection, but Chris was so sick that weekend. Something must have gone wrong, very wrong.

"I wasn't sure it was a good idea, so I decided against it for a while," she said. She blew her nose gently into another tissue, balling it before stuffing it into her apron pocket.

"Well, then please tell me what's on your mind, Thelma. Get it off your chest," he said. "Then you can move on, feel better."

"I have no idea how I'll feel or how you'll feel but you need to hear this, Father," she said suddenly redoubling her courage.

He remained silent at this time. Let her talk, and talk she did.

"You know that girl Glory, the one who gave us the poinsettia plant with the little violin attached to it?" She did not wait for an answer. All she had to do was observe his reaction. Oh, yes, he knew her. His countenance told her so. It was that frown that she recognized when he was displeased.

"Well, first thing, the day you were leaving for your sister's house she, uh, Glory went into the garden. Father Chris was out there showing Aleks Powers around. You met her at Christmas dinner at Father Tosi's parents' house, right? I remember you told me about her. Not a very nice person and for you to say so, it must be true." She watched him nod affirmatively, patiently.

"Well, that girl Glory was out there in the garden, too, like I said," she said. Her eyes flashed. "And I saw..."

"I know she was there. Father Chris told me all about it," he interjected.

"Well, maybe his version, whitewashed obviously," she said, her voice gaining strength. "I was right there at the kitchen sink at the window, that is, scrubbing up some pans, shining them like I always do before I hang them up, and I happened to glance up and, uh, saw Father and Glory in a passionate kiss, lasting, uh..."

"Just a minute. Hold on, please, Thelma," Bernie interrupted. "A passionate kiss, you say?" A vein began to pulsate on his forehead.

"It sure looked like that to me. She had her arms around his neck and he was holding her tight at the waist, and they were really going at it, kissing I mean, not a good-bye peck on the cheek," she said. She was breathing rapidly now.

"That Powers woman had already left, you said?" he asked as though he hadn't heard everything she'd just told him. He was leaning forward at the edge of his seat. What Thelma Hopkins hadn't noticed was that Father Bernie's respirations had increased. Had she left it at that, and not continued, he'd have broached this to Father Chris the next day and there would have been an explanation, a credible one, he hoped.

"Oh, yes, I watched her leave. She got in her car and took off. Oh, hang on, now, there was another kiss as well," she said, adding more fuel to the fire. "Sure was, I could just about see her from where she was standing, but I caught a glimpse."

Bernie was at a loss for words. He seemed to be weighing and measuring his thoughts. "So what do we do?" he said, trying to be as calm and patient as possible. "Could all be quite innocent—possibly. Don't take this the wrong way, Thelma, but women can be very assertive, maybe even aggressive in some cases. Back in my day..."

"Father, are you kidding yourself?" she interrupted him, then immediately felt sorry for speaking to him in a harsh tone of voice, but her emotions were overtaking her reason. She had more to say, and say it, she did. "With Ms. Powers maybe so, innocent enough. You said he made it very clear to all that he had no interest whatsoever in that woman from his past, his high school days. But with Glory, I think you'll find that is quite another story," she said, almost triumphantly.

"And is there another story?" he asked, praying for the discussion to be over. Sure, he'd bring up the matter to Chris when he got back. Then the poem Glory had written came to mind. It got him thinking, worrying, fearing what else Thelma Hopkins was going to reveal.

"Oh, how I wish there wasn't, Father," she said, in words tinged with sadness. "It pains me to have to tell you this."

Bernie blanched. He swallowed hard. "Go ahead, Thelma. It better be good." He was not a gossip -monger and frowned upon those who were. This was not typical of Thelma, not at all.

"Well, Father, it was when Father Chris was chaperoning on the ski trip with my daughter-in-law, Jodie. She's the one who saw everything. She told me all about it," she began. She was betraying a confidence but it was time now; she plunged right in to those uncharted waters, but once she'd begun, there was no turning back. "Jodie really didn't want to say anything but then she couldn't hold it inside any longer. She, uh, felt she had to say something, as do I." Bernie was quiet. He knew she'd go on and she did after a pause to catch her breath.

"And you waited till now to tell me something so important that Chris should not be present to hear what he allegedly did or did not do? Shouldn't he be here to, uh, defend himself, if he needs to?" Bernie was doing a slow sizzle.

"Oh, Father, please, please hear me out," she said urgently. Her nerves had left her and she was determined now more than ever to tell the story. "You need to hear this, Father. Let me finish, please."

After he nodded with a look of resignation on his face, she began, "It all happened at the ski lodge, as I said, that weekend. Jodie woke up early Sunday morning, say, around five a.m. and since they don't serve breakfast till six-thirty or so, she needed her coffee to get going. It's an old habit of hers. At that lodge chaperones are given special key cards to the employees' lounge so they can get a snack or a drink any time of day or night. It's a little perk they get from the management. Well, she used her card to get into the private lounge, around five a.m., she estimated, and that's when she, uh, saw what she saw, what she could not believe before her eyes. She was shocked out of her mind."

"OK, Thelma, what was it she saw?" he asked urgently. He was fidgeting. "Hold on, you said that Glory was involved somehow, if I heard you correctly. She wasn't supposed to be on that ski trip. You had to be a member of either parish to go. What could she be doing there?"

"Oh, plenty, Father, besides skiing," she said triumphantly. "She was there all right, came on her own I would guess. And...she was with *him* in the lounge...asleep in his arms, uh, in his embrace, on the couch in there." Thelma could only envision what had transpired beforehand.

She observed Bernie who had moved to the edge of the sofa. He was incredulous—eyes wide open, brows nearly up to his hairline. "And what else did Jodie tell you she saw? If I remember correctly, Father Chris came down with the flu on that trip. He couldn't have been feeling very chipper at that time. That flu hits you like a ton of bricks. You should know. You just had it yourself, Thelma, knocked you out clear out of commission."

"Oh, yes, it sure did, but Father Chris," she began; then she paused again to rethink the situation she had put herself in. She was thinking, If only I'd kept my mouth shut maybe this thing would have blown away—gone and forgotten, but if...' No, she convinced herself that she had to finish the story. "No, not at all, from what she told me, he was quite sick. But she did tell me he had a cut on his finger and there was blood all over her, uh, pajama top, so, uh, he, uh, must have touched her," she added feeling a modicum of guilt or was it betrayal, for maybe revealing a little too much. This was gossiping, but no, she was telling her priest what he should know about his associate: Father Chris was cavorting with a minor. Thelma Hopkins hung her head low.

Father Bernie shook his head in disbelief. Jodie would not have spread a false rumor and certainly not to Thelma, whom she loved and trusted. She'd spilled out what she'd seen to her mother-in-law, a trusted member of St. Aeden's staff, and Thelma Hopkins felt it was her duty to inform her pastor. Now what could he do? What should he do? The reel of his mind's data stopped its forward progression, and clicked into the rewind position—back to the confessional, that Saturday afternoon when he'd heard Glory's confession. He had no doubt. It was indeed Glory. She was the one who'd confessed to sleeping with a priest, of seducing him. Those were her exact words. She'd all but mentioned Chris by name.

Bernie remembered the effect it had on him, on his health, on everything. He had a long time to contemplate that. But finally, he arrived at the conclusion that Glory had lied in the confessional, made everything up. After all she wasn't a very trust-worthy or upright person. But then he replayed Thelma's words—her sentences, her intonation—the sum total of the horrifying message over and over in his mind. Is there a chance it could really be true? Was there really something going on between the two of them, a priest, Father Chris of all people, and a minor girl, *her*? He didn't like what the evidence shouted at him. It left him emotionally over wrought. His head was spinning as though he was on a merry-go-round, spinning faster and faster, out of control, taking him from anxiety and disbelief, to fear and then to shock.

"No, no, it can't be," he said in a hoarse whisper, "Not our Father Chris, not *him*. There has got to be an explanation. There's got to be much more to this than meets the eye. There must be."

"Well, Father, there very well could be," she said, but quickly added, " but it could be even more damning, or..." she said in a whisper, hoping to cushion the effect, but her words pierced his heart. It pained her to look at Father Bernie. He had retreated somewhere deep inside himself.

"Father," she said weakly, painfully aware of the effect her words had on him, "Do you, uh, want me to go over what she told me again? I have notes here in my apron pocket. I was afraid I'd miss a point, uh, a detail, so I wrote down what I remembered so I wouldn't leave out anything, but I think I told you everything, as much as what Jodie told me. You can talk to her if you want but it would upset her very much. She only told me because she, uh, had to. I could tell something was eating her from the inside, and I, uh, encouraged her to tell me what was on her mind. She feels terrible. No one else knows anything except, uh, Glory."

Thelma Hopkins did not feel anything resembling relief after spilling it all out. She believed she had done her duty but she felt empty and sad. She couldn't imagine the grief Father Bernie must be feeling in his heart. Was he such a poor judge of character? Couldn't he tell the difference between a pious person and a charlatan? After all, he lived with Father Chris, trained him, made him the priest he has become, loved him like a son. How could he not know this side of him?

"I, uh, think I'll rinse these things out and be on my way, Father," she said weakly, gathering up the dishes onto a tray. "Dinner's in the fridge with instructions for heating it. And Father Donovan won't be here for dinner if you remember." She cleared the dishes and set them on a tray with trembling hands. For a moment she just stood there, searching for the right words to make everything all right. She asked herself, 'what have I done to this poor man'?

Father Bernie at this moment couldn't remember a thing if he were asked. He was still back in the confessional replaying Glory's damning words. Then an obsessive thought overtook him: if she told him she slept with Father Chris, whom else might she have told? Each time he spun it over in his mind he felt a jab, and another jab, but this time it was in his head. He suddenly grew weak.

"Good day, Thelma, thank you," he managed to say softly but garbled. Then to himself, he mumbled over and over again, 'and he never said a word to me, never.'

She wished him a good evening and dashed out of the room. Minutes later or could it have been an hour or so later, he heard the engine of her car or was it the sound of Rollo Donovan's in the driveway. He couldn't be sure which. He had dozed there in the sitting room on the stiff old sofa not fit for sleeping. Dinner was still in the fridge, untouched. He had lost track of time and place...

Chapter THIRTY-EIGHT

HE MAY OR MAY NOT HAVE heard the rectory phone ring. There was an extension phone in the sitting room, but he assured himself that Mrs. Hopkins would take it. She always did and if she deemed it important or pressing, she'd call him. So he just lay there and drifted in and out of a fitful stupor. At times he'd hear himself laugh. Other times he made whimpering sounds. Or maybe that was Paddy he was hearing looking to go out and do his business. Everybody had business with someone or another, he thought. The dark shadows on the wall told him it had to be night time so he should be sleeping but it didn't feel much like his bed, and his pillow was way too small; it had clumpy, bumpy threads here and there, embroidery, he guessed. He remembered his mother used to embroider pillows and such, she'd say, to pass the time. And when he tried to roll over to get more comfortable, he couldn't. His mind and his body did not seem to work together. He felt as though he was suspended in time and space. He thought he could hear his mother's voice in the distance calling out the litany of names, his siblings, in the evenings to come home for supper.

AFTER THELMA HOPKINS had returned home, she thought she'd better check on Father Bernie. She needed reassurance that he was OK—if that could be possible after what she had told him.

She phoned the rectory and received no answer, only the recorded message that she herself had made. Once, twice, then a third time. Overwrought with guilt, she made a snap decision. She tapped Carl Senior on his shoulder, telling him she had to take a ride over and see Jodie. Her husband was so engrossed in a CSI episode, more than likely a rerun, that he wouldn't be fazed if she'd told him she was going to the moon, so he didn't give it a second thought that his wife was going over to see the kids. She was always paying them a spur of the moment visit for one reason or another. She preferred face to face rather than phone conversations. This time it was under the guise of bringing them some home baked dessert, a Dutch apple pie she'd stored in the pantry. Jodie didn't bake much and when she did the product was fair to middling, as Thelma described it, which was a backhanded compliment at best. To boot, her daughter-in-law bought readymade pie crusts which to Thelma was anathema.

Jodie heard the jingle of the front door bell. She looked quizzically at her husband, who shrugged and shook his head. He wasn't expecting anyone. She put down the book she was reading, took off her glasses and strode across the room to unlock the heavy wooden front door. She peeked through the tiny peek hole and discerned a distorted version of her mother-in-law balancing a Tupperware container in one hand. Her other hand was already turning the knob. At that instant, Jodie was overtaken with an uncomfortable feeling. She'd never told Junior what she'd seen at the ski lodge, only Thelma, and now fearing the worst she thought, 'uh-oh, the rumor mill's beginning to turn, and I'm the one who set it in motion.' She tried to act casually so as not to arouse suspicion in front of her husband. "Mother Hopkins," she said feigning delight at the surprise visitor, "what brings you here so late? Was I supposed to be expecting you?" She noticed Thelma was out of breath.

Thelma pretended everything was fine as she barged in, her usual style of entry. "Oh, hello Jodie, Junior," she said, setting the pie down on the coffee table. She gave both a big hug, a little longer one for Junior. "Look, I've brought you two a nice pie. I'd made two of them so I thought I'd share." She gestured at the dessert.

"Well, isn't that nice, but we, uh, ate hours ago, dessert too," Jodie said with a worried look on her face. It was after eight o'clock already. Thelma looked pained. "Come, sit down. Let me take your coat."

Thelma told her she was freezing cold. She'd keep it on. She asked if she could talk to her. From her expression, it should be private. Junior like Carl Senior was wrapped up in probably the same show as his father was. He told the ladies to go into the kitchen if they were going to yak, which was just fine with him. He didn't want to hear women talk when he was watching TV.

Thelma finally let loose and poured out what had happened earlier at the rectory. Jodie was aghast, infuriated at what she might have set rolling. She was very fond of Father Chris and couldn't imagine that there'd been any illegal activity, as she called it, just some freaky thing that happened, but then again, you never know. It didn't look good. Thelma could only stare at her daughter-in-law. She was babbling. Jodie hoped to conceal the maelstrom of emotions she was experiencing. She told her mother-in-law Chris was much too sick for you know what, plus he was a priest and always conducted himself like one. He would never disgrace himself or knowingly allow himself to be put in a compromising position, she was sure of that. Furthermore, he would never take advantage of a teen-aged girl, a minor. That was a crime. Thelma told her daughter-in-law she always felt the same about him too, but... Jodie winced. She felt clawing pangs of guilt for telling Thelma what she'd seen that night, and now Thelma was just plain scared. She feared it might have shocked Bernie more than she could have imagined. But with the arrival of Father Donavan, she believed that would divert his attention from her startling revelation. They'd have parish matters to discuss. Was she kidding herself, she asked? The damage was already done.

Jodie punched the rectory number and hit redial. Each time the ringing seemed like an eternity. She was pacing. The same message played, her mother-in-law's voice. Thelma was so much a member of the St. Aeden's family. Jodie told her mother-in-law maybe they should make a trip over to the rectory but that might look strange if they just up and went out under some guise. They'd have to think one up fast so Carl wouldn't suspect anything amiss. Thelma said Father Donovan should be getting back to the rectory any minute, and she did have his cell number, but she figured he wouldn't pick up if he was still at the meeting. Her better judgment told her to make the call and he answered. He said he was pulling into the driveway this very minute. Thelma tried to sound calm as she asked him if he would please check in on Father Bernie and see if he's all right? Understandably this lead to questions: why wouldn't he be OK? Wasn't he well when you left him?

Thelma handled his interrogation with, "I just wanted to make sure. He had been ill if you remember, and no one else has been there since the afternoon." She didn't say what time she'd left. Knowing he'd see Bernie in just minutes gave her some degree of comfort. She could have just let things pass but she was pained, worried. She'd wounded Father Bernie, and she bore the entire brunt of it.

When Rollo Donovan entered the rectory he was surprised to find it in total darkness. He had no idea where Bernie might be in the dark. It was too early for his bedtime and certainly Bernie would stay up till he got back. Rollo was spending the night. He called out to Bernie as he went from room to room, turning on lights. Finally he heard a feeble cry from the front of the house.

When he lit the ceiling light in the sitting room, he found a very confused, disheveled Father Bernie, rubbing his eyes, and staring into space, mumbling to himself. Rollo could have been a burglar standing there pointing a gun in front of him. It wouldn't have made any difference to Bernie.

After fruitless attempts to reach Bernie's conscious mind, Rollo gave up. He had no idea how long Bernie may have been in that state of confusion, possibly hours, since he didn't know what time the housekeeper had left. Like Chris, he had Doctor Dillon in his contact list and speed dialed the number. He grabbed Bernie's topcoat from the vestibule closet and told him they were going out for a little ride. Bernie did not ask where, nor did he offer any resistance. The destination was the nearest ER. Doctor Dillon would meet them there, and he arrived as ER nurses were 'working up' the patient. Once more Father Bernie Monahan would be held overnight for observation. By then, he was conscious enough to begin fuming.

Rollo's next order of business was to get Father Will over to spend the night in case Chris's flight from Florida was delayed for some unforeseen reason. He guessed the cruise ship would be on time getting back though, first thing in the morning.

WILMA SANGER, THE SCHOOL nurse at the high school, took a coffee break with Sergeant Smith's wife Paulette who was asked to come in to work a little early. They were short handed in the cafeteria with two workers out sick. She told Paula she'd heard through the grapevine that Father Bernie over at St. Aeden's may have had a stroke the night before. He'd been taken to the hospital and they were running tests on him all day. Paulette immediately texted Smitty who had been in contact with the priest not so long ago, she recalled. She thought he might be interested in hearing the news. Smitty was still at home with the boys until his mother-in-law would come to fill in. He didn't have to go on duty till three p.m. so he had some time to spare.

He phoned his mother-in-law who arrived minutes later so Smitty could run errands, so he told her. He felt it was timely to stop by Sterling-Baie Enterprises to see Doug Sterling. Once again, Agatha O'Toole greeted him warmly. She checked with her boss who told her to send him in in a few minutes. Doug was just finishing up a call. Then he would make some time for the good sergeant. Smitty told her with a smile that this time he couldn't stick around for coffee and cookies. She returned the smile, but didn't tell him that the cookie supply needed to be replenished, which was her fault for letting it run out. She made a note to pick up some more after work. Doug would insist on having goodies on hand, claiming they had the power to 'sweeten' any deal he might be negotiating. Agatha would only laugh at that. She knew it took more than biscotti.

Doug feared the worst when Smitty came to his office—again and so soon. This was beginning to wear on him. Then he remembered that the sergeant was going to check with Father Bernie about Glory. Doug could never figure out what had caused such a radical change in his daughter's behavior over the past several months. She'd always been a good girl. Belinda had just shrugged when he asked her if she had any idea. How would she know? She said something about adolescent rebellion or some developmental phase, and that their daughter would grow out of it some day. But it was so much more than rebellious behavior in Doug's opinion. It was unconscionable.

Doug looked pained as he stood behind his desk. He wasn't so sure he wanted to hear what the sergeant had to say. He wasn't able to read Smitty's expression at the moment. What he needed to know was if Glory was off the hook or what. When Smitty told him that Father Bernie was not going to press charges, Doug could have just about kissed the sergeant, who backed up when he saw Doug approach him. He insisted he deserved no credit for it; Father Bernie is the one to thank. Smitty's expression changed, however, when he told Doug he had not such good news about the priest today. Possibly a stroke, he said. Doug felt sick when he heard that. The first thing that came to mind was Glory. Could she have played any role in it whatsoever? Somehow she seemed always to be in the middle of problems connected with St. Aeden's or the priests. To his knowledge, there was only one exception: both priests had bestowed lavish praise on her for saving the midnight mass music program with her violin playing. But could that ever be enough to offset the all the harm she'd caused there? Not by a long shot, he told himself.

Doug thanked Smitty for all that he did and for coming to his office to reassure him. He believed the good sergeant was the best go-between he could hope for, not that Smitty actually interceded in any way. He just asked questions and got answers, most of the time. Intuition played a major role, as well. He'd always say, 'just doing my job.'

———— ∞ ————

IT WAS ANOTHER EARLY arrival for Doug at the Sterling home within such a short period of time. Belinda knew something was up. This time Glory was home, upstairs in her room with a textbook open. So she told her father when he knocked at her door. Could he have a few minutes with her? She saw no reason why not. Her untroubled conscience told her not to worry, but she was mistaken. For some reason she couldn't fathom, he brought up the ski weekend. Glory blanched, and pretended to be studying, but he noticed the book was upside down and he figured she lacked the skill to absorb information that way. He took that as an indication that there was more to tell about the night he was out of his mind with worry that something had happened to her. He asked her to relate what she'd told her mother. He wanted to hear with his own ears what had happened early that Sunday morning when she was missing from the room she'd shared with her mother. When she asked her father why he wanted to hear her retell it to him, he told her he had his reasons. He'd tell her if he thought it was important. Glory balked. So many things were stacked against her. Her father didn't need one more behemoth of an issue.

She argued that it must be very important or he wouldn't be up here grilling her. She was growing defensive and his patience was being tested. She had to think a while. Then she related the version she thought she'd told her mother. Since what she'd said then was obviously an edited version of that night, it didn't come out quite the same when she told her father. There was a lapse of time in between so she'd forgotten what she'd told and what she'd changed or left out. She definitely would not mention Father Chris. Doug grew suspicious, remembering that Glory was Glory. She was skilled at prevaricating. It pained him to think she'd lie to him right to his face, but history too often told him otherwise. He remembered asking her when he returned from France that summer if anything was new, and she answered that her mother had fired her shopper. Nothing more. He thought that was a strange answer. He wanted to know about his daughter, not get trivial news about some dismissed part time employee, which had no bearing on the family, so he thought.

Doug pressed his daughter for more details about the night at the ski lodge. What about the blood stains on her nightie top? How could she explain that? At that, she squirmed and stalled. She told him she must've forgotten, oh yes, she must have cut herself on something and it must've gotten on her nightie. She didn't know, she told him. She'd fallen asleep on a couch in the lobby and the desk clerk was asleep. She told him not to make a big deal out of nothing—just a silly act of carelessness. And that was exactly what Doug was afraid of. He'd let things go at that. He wasn't getting anything more from her. Her story was her story and if she stuck by it, so be it. He'd gotten his answer. Glory was surprised when he walked out of her room and told her he'd see her in half an hour at dinner. Once she was alone, she panicked. What was happening? The only one who could have seen anything or have read something into it was young Mrs. Hopkins, the chaperone. Chris called her Jodie and when she came into the lounge she was more concerned with his health than anything else. Glory was driven out as though she was a poisonous snake.

Chapter THIRTY-NINE

CHRIS HAD THE BEST time imaginable on the seas. He and Anton renewed their friendship, picking up where they'd left off ten years ago. The long hiatus did not affect their comfort level as the former high school basketball stars got acquainted with their grown-up selves, and shared how their lives had diverged. What could be farther apart than a pro basketball player and a parish priest? But they soon discovered it didn't matter at all. They were fast friends and it was their old teen-age selves that had formed the bond in the first place.

Beth too was a common thread in their relationship. Chris had such fond memories of the tutoring sessions in the Tosi dining room after school well before basketball season had even begun. As a National Honor Society member Beth had volunteered to help Anton with his English. Although Anton had studied English in Croatia, he found spelling and pronunciation unreasonably inconsistent, and the laughter Chris often overheard caused him to reprimand Beth. No, she was not ridiculing Anton. She explained that she and Anton got hysterical at some of his goofs. They couldn't help it. Marie too would come into the room to tell Beth to ease off. She'd ask her daughter how would she fare if she were learning Croatian? And Anton would answer that she might find it very difficult, starting the language at age eighteen. He told Beth that it would be more difficult, more complex for her than, say, learning Spanish or French. He'd begun his English studies in elementary school and hoped to gain fluency in English, as it has become such an important language in the world.

In any case, Anton made progress in the language thanks to Beth's efforts and his perseverance. He did not request another tutor after Beth's passing. Although he returned to basketball and led the team to victory, he missed his good friend Chris whose position on the team he had once replaced. Chris never held it against him. Anton was just an all around better player.

His success in pro basketball in Europe is testament to that. He boasted that his team had won a silver medal at the 1992 Olympics in Barcelona, but that was years before he'd joined them. He told Chris he'd continue playing basketball as long as he could. After that, he aspired to go into a career in international business. He had hoped it would fit into future plans but now he had a wife and children to consider. Things could change, he admitted. That was life. How well he knew. He recalled the strife that had befallen his beloved country and their fight for independence and freedom. The blood and the losses. He tried to erase those early memories. They only served to upset him.

After the tragedy in Chris's life the two friends saw each other regularly at school, but not socially. Chris focused primarily on his studies, on graduating and moving on, but he didn't know on to what. He had retained few social ties. He was so deeply affected by the reversal of fate that he was never the same. How Chris made it through high school puzzled Anton. When June came around, Anton 'graduated' with his American class and left Birch Valley High School for Europe. He was relieved that there was no longer mandatory conscription in Croatia so he was able to move on to university. He vowed he would never forget Chris and the Tosi family and he didn't. The two young men exchanged letters a few times a year when they were in college. Before long, it was just the annual Christmas card and message. But this most recent card contained the invitation to accompany him on the cruise, and it could not have come along at a better time for Chris who still hadn't been able to shake off a nasty cough, a lingering effect of the flu. Doctor Dillon reassured him. It was nothing more.

Mostly Chris and Anton took in the full array of activities on board as the cruise ship took them from one tropical island to another. Each day there were new and different adventures. Chris thought scuba diving was something he'd like to do again. When he was younger and feeling sad at times, his mother would tell him 'you'll never find a rainbow if you're looking downward'. She might have followed her own advice, though, he thought. But looking down, down beneath the sea was where he discovered a whole new world, a kaleidoscopic burst of color—sea plants and magnificent creatures in motion, an exciting new world of wonder for him to explore. So who needs rainbows anyway? Next time, he told Anton, we'll be sure to do that again. Bring along your family, too, and Anton said they should toast to having many next times together.

"How about you come to my country one day. It is so beautiful. We have thousand islands and nice coastline on Adriatic Sea. It is warm country. We can go sail. Ana and I have boat. Beautiful Catholic churches, you can do mass, but language may be big problem." Anton paused to chuckle. He would have gone on and on. He could see Chris was with him, and then Chris drifted off to a far away place in his mind.

The last day aboard ship the two men stood apart from the others passengers in silence on the top deck, gazing out into the azure vista of sea and sky. Mists were beginning to descend upon the horizon.

Chris broke the silence. "You see those low wispy clouds over there?" He pointed in that direction. Anton turned slightly and nodded in assent.

"You know, Chris," Anton began with a wistful look in his eyes, "Beth taught me the word 'mist'. I think those are mist out there. Is correct? 'Mist' was easy for me to say and to spell too." A hint of a smile lit up Anton's tanned face. Thus far they had not mentioned either Beth or Kendra. It was safer that way. He watched a smile brighten Chris's face and noticed for the first time how much he and his sister resembled one other, but only when they broke into a smile.

Anton laughed aloud, "Oh Chris. I remember this. Listen, this is funny. 'Mist', remember the word now. My host family, they take me to New York for the weekend and a school day, too. When I get back, Beth tell me, 'Anton, I missed you.' I laugh because I think in my mind she put water on me, a mist. And I say, 'no, you not mist me. I do not want to get wet'. Finally she get it and we laugh for a long time. So you see the word 'mist' has special memory of your sister for me."

Chris smiled slightly and looked out at the sea. "When Beth and I were little." Chris said overtaken with sadness, "we'd be outside playing on our swing set and thin wispy clouds or mists would begin to descend, to come down on us, almost wrapping us inside them, shielding us. Our mother used to tell us they were angels with their wings spread out, enfolding us in their arms. We told her that was not possible because they didn't have any faces, but then she'd give us this look, which told us a lot—I think that they were there to protect us."

"Angels, you say, mist—clouds," Anton said taking in all that Chris had said, probably doing some translating in his head. His English was halting, simple, but what he lacked in eloquence, he more than compensated in insight and empathy.

"Yes, guardian angels. We believed her since we believed everything she said. You could see them in the mists." Chris said softly. "If you look and believe."

They both thought a long moment watching the clouds move and disperse, assuming different shapes and then vanishing from sight. Chris could not verbalize what came into his mind, his little boy mind. Because he and Beth were twins, fraternal, but it was still a single birth producing two children. Maybe, just maybe he and Beth shared a single guardian angel, and maybe on that tragic night...a tear formed in his eyes. That guardian angel stayed with him on the basketball court that night and not in the car with Beth where she was needed for protection from disaster. He had indeed lost a part of himself when...anything else was best left unspoken.

"Tell your parents I am sorry," Anton said all of a sudden, ending Chris's reverie. I will not be able to visit Connecticut this time. Maybe next time, Chris. I need to get back to my family. I miss them. I had wonderful time with you, my friend, but I belong with Ana and the children. I am so often on the road, so you say."

Chris stared out, lost in the flow of the eternal sea. He felt some relief. Beth and Kendra were held in the embrace of the angels. They were safe. Anton could imagine where Chris's thoughts were, but Anton himself had long ago put the sound of Beth's laughter in his heart. There was no room there for strife and regrets. He'd seen enough of that in his own country so he opted to hang onto the good memories. He hoped that his friend could do so as well. Chris tried to, but then Anton did not know the whole story.

Anton saw the need to transition to some other spot, lighten the mood. "Come, my friend, time is getting short. Let's go."

Chris faced him and nodded. He felt as though he'd just awakened from a dream. "Where to?"

"Shoot hoops, OK?" he asked. "Let's see if we can get into friendly game, I think they say."

"Only if I'm on your side," Chris agreed. "You know, Anton, I think I'd like that very much."

Chapter FORTY

AFTER THE EUPHORIC feeling of being at sea, Chris looked forward to returning to the rectory and back to reality with the Tosi and Monahan team running St. Aeden's. He hoped he'd seen the last of Rollo Donovan for a long time and was anxious to get Paddy back where he belonged. He'd imposed on his parents long enough. But what he didn't know was that Fred spent less time in the basement with his woodworking tools and Marie made fewer trips to the Tisdales. She figured the expectant couple needed their privacy, so she made large batches of food that would last them for days. That extra free time was spent in the pet store buying different kinds of treats for Paddy to sample and toys he could enjoy during playtime. They would miss Paddy when he left but they had to keep reminding themselves he was only a guest. It did not disappoint them at all when Chris phoned and asked if they'd keep Paddy one more day if it weren't asking too much. They were thrilled. Chris explained he was tired from all the travel and relaxation. He'd come by and get Paddy after a good night's sleep.

But how could Chris get a good night's sleep? When he got back to the rectory, no one was there, not even Mrs. Hopkins. Something was wrong, and then he spotted it. There was a note affixed to the back door that put Chris into a tailspin. He hauled his suitcase upstairs to his bedroom and without unpacking, set out for the hospital. A second thought occurred to Chris: Father Rollo

Donovan would not be checking out today, maybe not for a long while.

What in the world could have happened when he was away? The tests thus far were inconclusive, Father Rollo Donovan told him. As if he were the spokesperson. He was only a substitute, thank God, Chris thought. They had run into each other in the visitors' lounge. Rollo informed him that Bernie presented symptoms of a stroke, but they were waiting for definitive test results. Chris wanted to see Bernie, but was told to wait until they told him Bernie could have visitors. He wondered if anyone had contacted Molly. Rollo told him he would since he was the one who found Bernie in that state of confusion. Chris felt slighted. He *knew* Molly. He wondered if Rollo had even met her.

Chris was finally allowed to see Father Bernie. After all, he was not only a priest but also Father Bernie's associate and close friend. That's what he'd said to the head nurse who apologized for having him wait so long. She asked him not to tire Bernie, to only stay a few minutes in his room. She told him Bernie might drift in and out of sleep.

It was a one-way conversation at best. Chris wasn't even sure Bernie had recognized him. He looked so pale and frail. His wiry hair was splayed all over the pillow, which made him look distressed. At one time Bernie opened his eyes wide and seemed to register a thought in his mind, which seemed to trigger a powerful emotion. Chris couldn't imagine what it was. Then Bernie made a moaning sound as though in pain. Chris patted his hand and said he would come back tomorrow. He fought back tears. He hoped there would be a tomorrow and many more for Bernie. Chris couldn't have anticipated this would have happened to Bernie. He seemed to be on the mend or Chris would never have gone on the cruise. Chris was beginning to feel that tell tale tug at the back of his throat.

At morning mass Chris asked the congregation to pray for their beloved pastor. That was one day Agatha O'Toole came into Sterling-Baie Enterprises a little late, with Doug's consent, of course. She told him how sad everyone over at St. Aeden's was feeling and hoped Father Monahan would recover soon and be able to assume his duties. They couldn't imagine St. Aeden's without him. She added that Father Chris is beloved by all, but Father Bernie Monahan is the backbone of their parish community, had always been so for years. She told her boss she wished that he knew the man. There were tears in her eyes. He patted her shoulder and gave her an empathetic look. 'Oh yes', he said to himself, 'I do know the man. I certainly do.'

AGATHA SHARED HER FEELINGS about Father Bernie with her old friend Jodie Hopkins at the monthly book club meeting in the town library conference room. About twenty readers took up half of the chairs set up for the meeting. Coffee 'and' was set up on a side counter. Many residents, mostly women of a certain age and two men, showed up mainly for the refreshments and the socialization, so it seemed. Agatha and Jodie held a side conversation as best they could over the discussion of the latest novel they'd read, *A man called Ove.*. Neither was paying much attention to the readers' comments—some inane, some insightful—none really noteworthy.

Agatha knew that Jodie's mother-in-law was the housekeeper at St. Aeden's. She asked her friend if Thelma had noticed any tell tale symptoms, if Father Bernie had been feeling ill, if he'd given any indications of an impending stroke. Agnes was surprised. She'd heard he was doing much better since his spell that time, but then after what she'd just heard...Jodie's shrug told her she didn't know. Agatha told her that she'd keep on going to mass there as long as Father Chris would be there, but the new priest, Father Donovan, wasn't to her liking, not at all. She told Jodie he seemed to be going through the motions at mass but seemed to lack the true piety of the other priests. She said she could be mistaken but she couldn't deny how she felt. She said others she'd spoken to felt the same. She went on to say that his homilies were forgettable, much too preachy, and not very inspiring. She saw that Jodie wasn't very interested in what her friend had to say. After all, Jodie wasn't even a parishioner. She didn't go to church regularly anyhow. What astonished Agatha was that Jodie suddenly looked very uncomfortable, edgy. She grabbed her tote bag, got up abruptly and excused herself, saying she really had to be going. Agatha had no idea why Jodie left the room like that. The discussion wasn't over yet, and the two women usually stayed on after the meeting to socialize.

Agatha rose and followed her to the front door. "Hey, Jodie," she called after her in a library quiet voice. "What happened? Is anything wrong? Are you all right?"

"I'm so sorry, Aggie. I just couldn't sit there another minute," she explained, pausing by the door. They stayed inside to avoid continuing their conversation out in the cold.

"I suppose I was boring you with my ragging on and on about Father Donovan. Why should you be interested? Sorry I was boring you so," Aggie said, oblivious to Jodie's true feelings, to what she was hiding.

"No, of course not, Aggie," she said calming herself. This was her trusted friend. "I knew, uh, I had learned that Father Bernie had had a stroke. It was terrible. I know how he is regarded in the community. It's just too bad that it had to happen to such a good man."

"Well, sure you'd know. Your mother-in-law would have told you. I should've known better. By the way, how is she taking it?"

Agatha asked innocently. How would she take it? She'd be sad for her priest, blaming herself, as well. She could have kept things to herself, but then...

"Oh, awful. You can't imagine," Jodie said, wishing she could share what she knew but determined never to speak of it again. She wished with all her heart she had not seen what she'd seen at the ski lodge, that she hadn't spilled it out to her mother-in-law. "She's a mess over it. She was the last person to see him before..."

"Has she gone to visit him in the hospital?" Agatha asked, again innocently enough.

"Visit him? Are you kidding me?" Jodie snapped, but then of course, how could Aggie know that it was her mother-in-law that set the downhill slide in motion.

"Right, I should have known better," Agatha said. "They're probably only letting in family, maybe the priests. That's all."

"Uh, right," Jodie agreed. "Yes, I imagine." It was easier that way. This wasn't the time or place or even the right thing to do—to tell Aggie. Who knows? Maybe some time, she said to herself. After all, her boss will know what's going on once this thing blows up.

Chapter FORTY-ONE

---❦---

(Weeks later)

DOUG STERLING WASN'T able to find a suitable temp when Agatha took a rare personal day so he resorted to calling in Belinda. For her, it could be an exciting change of routine. But today was different. She complained about having to cancel an hour-long appointment with her personal trainer and a luncheon with a few socialite friends to show off an outfit her designer had created just for her, and, oh yes, she told her husband, a shopping date with a new friend to help her pick out new window treatments. That last one was a lie. She just needed to get some spring clothes and her personal shopper was not available.

There was little for her to do at the office other than answer the phone. Agatha ensured that everything would be taken care of when she'd left the night before. She would go directly to a book club meeting. It was one of her few social activities. She'd brought a health food bar to snack on with the coffee that the library provided for its members. So she wasn't overly concerned with Belinda having to make any work related decisions. She only hoped that the boss's wife would leave things in order. Doug was such a neatnik.

Belinda would practice her secretarial voice whenever she answered the phone. She tried to sound cheery like Agatha, but it came out stilted. Doug didn't mind for one day as long as he had a front person. When she dialed his extension rather than enter his office, he opened his door and she put down the phone.

"Doug," she said in a tone laced with annoyance. After all, it was a little after ten, she'd checked her watch, and she was missing that session with her trainer. She was sifting though his mail. "What's this bill here? It's from Hillside Manor. You know that tony rehab place up in the hills?" She watched him study the invoice and nod slightly. He didn't want to have to explain it to her. What she didn't know wouldn't hurt her. Actually no one needed to know. It was only for short term care, the sooner the better he hoped for the sake of all those concerned. No, he didn't have to explain.

"Just write the check, dear, will you please? I'll sign it," he said, leafing through a stack of papers. He tried so hard to look busy. He didn't need to engage in conversation with her at work. All he needed today was for her to answer the phone. He said, toning down his mood, "Why don't you head out early today, dear? I can handle what's here."

"Well now Doug, I'd like to stay since I went and cancelled everything for the entire day. I suppose you want me to go and uncancel them now, right?" she asked, getting up from her chair. She made her perturbed face at him. Right then, she reminded him of Glory.

"Well, go to your lunch appointment, go on ahead," he said, glancing at his watch. "You've got time. I'll see you for dinner, say, around six. I'll get by. It shouldn't be too busy today. Agatha would never take a day and leave me in a lurch if she thought I'd be swamped."

Belinda was annoyed. She wondered if her friends would have already made other plans? But she did take a few minutes to straighten out the desk and prepare to leave. For a brief moment, it struck her that something might be going on with Doug. He was looking so strained lately, and what's with Hillside Manor? It seemed as though he was keeping someone there unbeknownst to her? Could it be...? She convinced herself that he would hardly have time for an affair. She smiled at the very thought then dismissed it as quickly as it sailed into her mind. She yelled a cheery good-bye to her husband and noticed he was deep in conversation on his private line. He blew her a kiss.

Certainly no one needed to know Doug was underwriting expenses to keep Father Bernie Monahan at Hillside Manor. He had put the pieces together and came out with something that involved his daughter—again. What he'd heard through the grapevine got him to realize that though there was some buzz, nothing was confirmed and much remained unspoken in the community at large. At least to his knowledge, there was hope for Father Bernie and Hillside Manor had the best reputation for stroke rehabilitation. If personnel didn't know Doug Sterling personally, they knew his generosity. He made sure two bouquets of flowers arrived weekly, one for the front desk and one for the patient in Suite 115, the most posh suite available, and Father Bernie's *temporary* residence, so he hoped. He was relieved that Belinda wasn't there when the bill for the flowers arrived. Then he would really have some explaining to do. He laughed to himself, thinking Belinda would most definitely jump to the wrong conclusion.

Once Belinda left for lunch at the country club, Doug typed up a letter on plain stationery. He had a such a supply for anonymous donations, and Belinda didn't have to know everything, even if Agatha probably did. She kept what went on in the office to herself. He could always trust her. Twenty years to her credit. He was a lucky man to have such a faithful assistant.

This donation was for the diocese in Bishop Gregory Miles's name. The letter mentioned that it was on behalf of Fathers Monahan and Tosi and St. Aeden Church, for all that they do for the parish community. It was signed 'A devoted member of St. Aeden's parish'. The cashier's check was for one thousand dollars. Although Doug was not a religious man, he had taken a quiet moment and had a little talk with God, a prayer of sorts for the healing of both Father Bernie and Glory.

Chapter FORTY-TWO

WHEN CHRIS GOT A YELL from Mrs. Hopkins that there was a call from the hospital his stomach did a flip. But this time, it wasn't about Bernie. He said a prayer of thanks to God and to his favorite saints; it was Marty who could use prayers too. His friend sounded more excited than worried which could only mean one thing. Sylvie was in labor, and a full four weeks early, her obstetrician estimated.

Mrs. Hopkins got into the habit of speaking to Chris only when absolutely necessary these days and this time he was sure he couldn't attribute her frostiness to after effects from the flu. One of these days he would get her aside and they'd have a good talk, but not now.

Marty's excitement was contagious and Chris found himself chatting easily with him as they did during their college days. It was a welcome distraction for Marty who alternated between pacing and nibbling on snacks that Sylvie would not approve. He rationalized that this was different. How many times was he becoming a father, he said.

"Would you like me to come by and pace with you?" Chris offered. "Unless she's about to deliver I can stop by the hospital after dinner. Rollo will dine by himself tonight. Can you believe it: he even complains about Mrs. Hopkins's cooking. Crazy! We've got a deacon helping out but we've got to share him with St. John's.

Nice guy, married with grown kids. You know, Marty, you and I have got some catching up to do and it will help you pass the time."

"Sounds like a great idea, Chris, because she's able to doze a little between contractions—at least for now. Once they get closer together, I'll be staying with her. She'll need me," Marty said. There was a combination of nervous energy and trepidation in his voice.

Chris could understand. He prayed that Sylvie would deliver a health baby after all she'd gone through with her history of miscarriages and disappointments. The prayer brightened his thoughts. He was going to be a godfather, a role he would take very seriously, in the old-fashioned way. The Tosi family was like that. Your god-parent played a special role in your life if you were like the Tosi clan.

The labor wore on into the night and both Sylvie and Marty were exhausted. Marty told Chris to go back to the rectory and get some sleep. They'd be fine. There was no need to worry, the doctor assured them. But there *was.* Sylvie's blood pressure had spiked and her cervix wasn't cooperating the way it should. She wound up with a caesarian section in the wee hours.

Marty held off phoning Chris who would need his sleep to fulfill his parish duties. But when midnight rolled around Chris was still awake. He prayed that all would be fine and finally fell asleep until the call awakened him at six a.m., informing him that he is soon to be the god-father of the most beautiful baby girl in the world. She was as yet unnamed. Marty was going to go home for a nap and let Sylvie rest after she talked to her mother in France. Clothilde was jubilant and cancelled her classes for the day. For one afternoon the Sorbonne could function without her. She and her new husband Amir were going to celebrate the birth of their first grand-child, and the champagne would flow like a fountain. Chris was sure Sylvie's mother was a wonderful person, but he hoped that the baby would not bear her grand-mother's name.

———— ⌘ ————

WEEKS LATER THE CHRISTENING took place at Marty's church, St. Joseph, after the noon mass. Marie Tosi served as proxy for the god-mother, Sylvie's Aunt Anne, Clothilde's younger sister. Little Marie Christine slept soundly through the entire sacrament of oil and water. She made up for her quietude the rest of the afternoon. But it didn't bother anyone. They just felt blessed for the Tisdales. Chris gave the baby a tiny gold cross necklace that he had blessed. A reception followed at the Tisdale home.

Everyone knew that Sylvie needed her rest so it was over by mid-afternoon. The Tosis had to leave early to tend to Paddy, so this time Marie got to take food home for a change. Chris started to leave when his parents did. He had other duties to fulfill, he told them. But his heart was full. He was overjoyed at being a god-father to his best friend's baby girl. He could only imagine the joy Marty and Sylvie felt at welcoming their precious gift of life. He also believed that Marie and Fred would be frequent visitors, as the birth of little Christine was proving to be joyful for them in a different way. They would embrace their role as surrogate grand-parents.

Marty stopped Chris at the door. The new father looked ecstatic. "Hold on a sec, Chris," he said hugging his friend. "I want to share something with you before you go. Do you remember Dr. Forbes-Marshall, our old ecology prof?"

Chris gave him a strange, inquisitive look. "I can't say I've ever thought about him since college. But, yeah, I do. Weird little guy with bushy dark hair and thick glasses, but nice enough. Why do you ask? Was he supposed to be invited to the christening today but had to buy out because he was going to be on some expedition in some God forsaken place?"

Marty laughed through a yawn. He looked exhausted. "Yeah, sure. Seriously, Chris, don't you remember that class where he expounded on the fairy circles phenom in the Namib Desert? Really mystical, if you remember, but telling just the same. Well, I'm getting it better than ever now." Chris shot him a look that said, 'uh-oh, there he goes again.' Unfazed, Marty resumed, "Yeah, I'm waxing philosophic, again. I can draw a parallel between what happens to the circles of sand. You know, the ones that come and go from pure sand to full vegetation, and then back again to total sand again? Well, I can relate that to life, to my life and yours, everybody's for that matter, the way life goes with its rhythms. I see it now, going from all the heartache...losing the babies and my parents...from all that sadness to pure joy, with the birth of our healthy little Marie Christine. Let's hope it stops there, at the joy level, I mean. We don't need it to revert to sadness and desperation." He straddled the doorway studying Chris, waiting for a reaction from him.

Chris only stared at him, pondering. What is he thinking? Sure, that's how things seem to go. "OK, if you say so, but I can't say I remember those, uh, fairy circles in some desert or another. You're the guy who ties all these strange things together. No wonder you're such a good English teacher. You make things relevant and interesting, to use a word you despise."

"Right, I tell my students there are better words than 'interesting,'" he said. "Anyhow I was thinking about you and me and the direction of our lives have taken, what you're going through now. It seems so different but the same as well, like those desert circles that mysteriously appear, disappear, then reappear."

"Now, I'm getting lost in that desert of yours. Where did you say it is?" Chris asked.

"Namibia, southwest coast of Africa, but no matter, my point is that because of so many things out of our control, order emerges somehow out of chaos," Marty said. He was serious. Chris was becoming impatient.

"Or that's the ways things go, cyclically, I mean, like you said." Chris needed to get going. "I'll let you share that with your AP students."

But Marty wasn't leaving the topic, not yet. "Alan Turning, you know, the theoretical computer cryptologist. Remember the guy who cracked the Nazis' coded messages in Britain? How do you think the Allies won the war?" Marty went on. "Well, this theory can explain just about everything in the universe."

"All well and good, my friend, but I wish it could explain Bernie's situation," Chris said buttoning his coat. "Now that little Marie Christine is here, I've got to focus on getting Bernie back where he belongs. Pray for his healing, Marty."

He left Marty with a sleepy grin on his glowing face, basking in the joy of fatherhood. And for the moment Chris was over the moon to be a god-father. But his euphoria was soon dampened by his concern for Bernie's condition. Something was wrong. Where was Bernie the prize fighter? Things have got to change, he told himself.

Chapter FORTY-THREE

(Later that winter)

THERE WAS NOTHING ABOUT therapy that Glory liked, or even tolerated, but she owed it to her father to return to regular sessions. She recalled once seeing a split sign over a door bearing the word *the-rapist* fractured just so in an old Benny Hill skit on TV, and she couldn't hold back a chuckle. But that was where the mirth began and ended. Dr. Polman's sign simply read Morton J. Polman, Ph.D., family relations. Had it read *Family therapist* she might have been tempted to take a black sharpie and sketch in that ignominious crack. But in Glory's estimation, Dr. Polman was clearly not a rapist or much of a therapist, for that matter. The thought of the former was ludicrous; it grossed her out, and, as for a therapist, he was pretty much of a bust, according to Glory. He'd never manage to get into her head; she wouldn't let him in, at least, not willingly. She figured he'd try to trick her into revealing her innermost thoughts. So, in part, she feared him, but only a little. She liked to be the one in control.

She found the décor of his office totally distasteful. When she vocalized her disapproval of his furnishings, he told her bluntly that the style was termed 'eclectic' and that eclectic was in. He told her that people need to respect 'differences,' which yielded an eyeroll and a sigh from Glory. She told him it was distracting to be around such hideous, uncoordinated furniture. He replied that she needed to focus only on him, as he would focus on her. She was there for a purpose. He would impart wisdom and guide her into making wise choices and she would listen and focus, focus, focus. Only then would the odd shaped green chair disappear, as would the lumpy aqua and orange print sofa. Fat chance—Glory got tired of focusing on Dr. Polman, or Mort, as he allowed her to call him.

Although Dr. Polman told Glory to think of him of as 'Mort the Sport,' the well-meaning therapist and good guy, she saw him through her myopic view as 'Mort the Wort.' And so she finally came around to focus on him, or rather on the mole, which she playfully referred to as a wort, on his left cheek. This distraction worked to her advantage. He now had her attention.

At one time she would have preferred changing therapists but she chose to comply with her father's wishes. Doug Sterling was at his wits end with all the damage his daughter had caused, and was willing to pay a yearly tuition of $80,000 for the Swiss boarding school, the last straw to save his daughter from herself. Although her exile, as Glory referred to it, could result in even more problems, he was willing to take that chance. Blood ties run deep.

Over the past few months the whole family had been concerned with Doug Sterling's demeanor and his haggard appearance. New, deep lines were etched on his forehead and he wasn't as chatty as usual at the dinner table when he did manage to show up for the evening meal *en famille*. Even Agatha O'Toole, who saw him daily, noticed a change in her boss. Unless he made a conscious effort to stand erect, he looked as though he was bearing a Herculean weight on his shoulders; his stature and bearing had always been a mark of his confidence and youthful appearance. Too often, lately, he was curt. At one time, Agatha, like Belinda, had suspected he was having an affair, but when would he have the time, the opportunity? He buried himself in his work. Then she too dismissed that thought. He was a good man with solid values. She knew it in her heart. But he had been through so much.

The family dynamic had changed. Glen spent less time shadowing his father at the office or on site and Belinda found more creative excuses to spend time in the 'city,' fashionista that she claimed to be. Grandmom, however, remained Glory's most trusted ally, but then Glory white-washed whatever she shared with her. Grandmom was just grateful for any communication from any of the family members. So out of love for those who deserved it, and out of guilt for all the harm she had inflicted on unsuspecting, innocent people, Glory began seeing Mort Polman again. Prior to that, her visits had been sporadic, yielding virtually no success. This time Dr. Polman laid the onus on Glory's shoulders, insisting on consistency, continuity and more willingness on her part to open up and come to grips with her insecurities, as he referred to them. He told her that he, however, was the 'catalyst' in their sessions, but she didn't bother to ask him what that meant. She'd heard it before but figured it was some 'shrink term' with an incomprehensible explanation.

Glory had attended sessions for the past few weeks and, if nothing more, gave the impression of listening, but still sharing next to nothing. If only she could concentrate on his eyes or the sound of his voice instead of on the mole/wort, as she persisted to call it, unspoken of course. Her eyes were riveted on the mole that must have been nicked mercilessly each time he shaved. She felt sorry for it, anthropomorphized it, giving it life apart from Dr. Polman, not unlike the ventroloquist's dummy. Maybe that was where the wisdom lay, she deluded herself, in that part of him. It became a game for her and it fascinated her. Before, she had been responding to him in monosyllables, and realized that it had to change if any real progress was to be made.

"You did the right thing, coming back to therapy, let's see now, three weeks in a row. I'm proud of you, Glory," he cooed at her in his soothing therapist voice. She made a feeble whoopee-doo face in response. Then he leaned toward her, supporting himself on one elbow, mimicking Glory's posture. She changed it and Pavlov-like he responded in like kind. He was determined to stay one step ahead of her. He would tolerate her perverse behavior and get results.

"Good. I'm glad someone is. But you're not my father. What right do you have to be *proud* of me?" Glory shot back.

The mole slid slightly to the right as his facial expression slid into a slight smile. He was making every attempt to understand this strange girl. Rapport was what was needed and she was a tough one, although she *was* looking at him now and not at the floor or the ceiling or picking at a cuticle as in past sessions.

"You may not see it, but I am seeing progress, Glory. Good job," he replied nodding, careful not to gush. This wasn't the appropriate time.

"Well, Mort, I'm here because of my father, and I don't know what 'job' that I did was 'good', if you must know," she said defiantly. Her features twisted into a look that told him he'd used the wrong choice of words. "He's the one who needs to be proud of me, no one else, and I know he's anything but proud of me, of what I've done." Her thoughts drifted to Sergeant Smith and what he'd intimated to her father. Out of fear or more likely dread, she cooled her relationship with Spike Gilbert. If her father found out she spent any more time with such a bad influence, he'd leave her to face the consequences alone, so he told her.

"You're right. So, tell me, what do you need to do to make him proud of you? Now remember, only you have the answer," he stated calmly. The last thing he wanted to do was get her agitated. She'd walked out on him before.

"So for a starter, I'm here, and I'll probably be stuck coming here till I go off to Switzerland," she admitted. At times the European setting seemed more appealing as to what it could offer her, a change from Wexford Falls, from the charade of a life she was living, and a clean slate—a chance to be a new Glory.

"Do you think he'll change his mind, and send you back to the, uh, public high school?" he threw at her. He could anticipate the answer.

"No way. That stupid school? They're glad to get rid of me. I won't go back there anyhow. I'd run off somewhere first," she spouted, taken aback at the question. "But that's not gonna happen; he's already made payments to the boarding school, and I don't want to cause him any more grief than I already have. So, Mort, can we leave it at that? I'm going off to Switzerland. I'm getting used to the idea now, and it shouldn't be half bad," she said defiantly, hoping the change of scenery would be idyllic.

"So you're resigned to being sent to Europe to boarding school," he echoed, observing her intently.

"Got bad ears, Mort?" she said with a snicker, then, "I'm sorry. No, I know you're a good listener. You have to be to help people like me."

"So Glory, what *are* you like? Can you tell me in your own words?" he probed.

"Um, not really, I'd rather hear *your* own words, what I'm like, I mean," she teased. This wasn't half bad, she told herself.

"I don't think I can, but you can, if you'd only let yourself," he continued, leaning in so close that the wort seemed to dance for her when he vocalized. She liked it better when it stayed where it belonged.

"What am I like?" she thought a long moment, eying the wort for inspiration. Then, "Well, I'm lucky to be who I am, I guess. But I can't say I really know who I am. I do know that I'm scared," she answered almost robotically. There, that's exactly what he'd want me to say, she thought.

"Good, go on, that's the idea," he said in his cheer-leader voice which used to annoy her, but not so much this time.

"I'm scared to tell you what I should, and I won't," she said with a touch of petulance.

"You won't, like never?" he asked in his fake teen age voice, a real impressionist, she thought...must work in his favor, but she could see right through it.

"Some things just belong inside. They have to. You're human, Mort, and you're smart. You should know that," she stated. She watched him smile at her remark and again she followed the movement of the wort.

"Well, suppose now you share what you're scared of so I can help you. The stuff you want to keep inside, just leave it there...for now anyhow, OK, deal?" he asked, seeking her approval, feeling some progress could be made.

"Well, since I'm here, I'll try. OK, wow, God, this is starting to feel like confession, the, um, Catholic kind," she paused to laugh at herself, "except you can't forgive me. You're not a priest. I am sorry for some of the things I have caused, the expenses my father paid out to save my skin," she spilled out. She wasn't sure how much more to say.

"Good, good, Glory," Dr. Polman said energetically. "No, I can't forgive you but you can learn to forgive yourself, and move on from there." Encouragement helps. He just had to caution himself not to go overboard. "Go on, please."

"So in a way you are like the priest. You can't tell anyone what I tell you, not even my father, right?" she asked, knowing the answer in advance. She just needed more reassurance.

"Righto," he assured her. "Everything you tell me is in strictest confidence. I swear. I will not tell your father or anyone else. I'm bound by my profession—doctor/patient confidentiality."

"You better not or I'll go right out the door this very second," she stated boldly. Then, softly she added, "You do know him, don't you, my father, I mean?"

"Well, yes, but that's all I'm going to say about him," he answered. There was something cryptic in his tone.

Glory stopped a minute to analyze the homely shaped pattern of the sofa—three aqua triangles to one orange circle. She needed to chill a moment. She was going to ask him what kind of triangles he preferred and he was letting her explore her thoughts, whatever they might be, or maybe she was trying to rein them in.

"So you know him," Glory stated rather than asked.

"We've met. The town's not that big," Dr. Polman admitted. He'd leave it at that. "Hey, let's keep everything between you and me only. How about one thing you're scared of, let's start there."

"Oh, all right, if I must," she stalled to finger the gaudy, rough fabric. Then, "I'm afraid I've destroyed some people."

"Destroyed?" he repeated, wondering to what extent she'd exaggerated her answer. "You didn't kill anyone, I'm sure of that."

"Don't be so sure of that," she countered, "Not yet, at least. But destroyed in a way, yes, if you want to count causing someone to have a stroke."

"So you caused someone to have a stroke, am I right?" he asked, his cheek bent, suffocating the poor wort with his expression, a smile that wasn't really a smile.

"It seems like I did," she said, "although it wasn't my intention. I, uh, didn't really understand. But that's not all." She stopped to fiddle with an errant piece of piping on the couch that had come undone. Then, "Hey Mort, can't you afford anything better than this piece of crap? I think it affects my reasoning or something."

"Huh, yeah, sure I can, but I like it. It has a history," he answered lightly. Fine, let her digress.

"Yeah, an ancient one. Which dynasty does it belong to?" Glory lightened. "Can we talk about something else?"

Anything for progress, just communicate, he said to himself. "Anything you want, Glory. It's your dollar, I mean your father's," he agreed. He felt that they were on the right track. Finally, some semblance of rapport.

"One more thing I'm afraid of," she began. "I know I've hurt a very special person. Sure I've hurt my father, but I'm not talking about him this time. It's a younger person, and I can't ever imagine him forgiving me, even if he tells me he does, like in words, but not in his heart. He won't really mean what he'd tell me. Um, can we save that for the next time? OK, Mort?"

Mort nodded. He wanted to hear more about the stroke she says she'd caused. Progress, yes, progress. He was determined to crack the shell of this troubled teen who had so much going for her that she was blind to it.

───────── ◈ ─────────

DR. MORT POLMAN, SAT drained at his desk, rubbing his eyes after his last appointment of the day. By then it was a little after six p.m. He noted that the name plaque on his desk had fallen over, and he righted it. He was surprised Glory hadn't noticed. She would have commented, he was sure of that. She was so taken in with his uncomely décor that she failed to focus on the real reason she was there. One time she cracked up at his marble paperweight that read 'A messy desk is a sign of genius'. Her comment to that was, 'So that makes you a pretty mediocre shrink.' He laughed, as his desk was usually somewhat in disarray, but that day he'd just taken a few minutes to unclutter it when it was time for her appointment.

She puzzled him, defied classification. Her very name 'Glory' lent credence to what she could be if she could dispense with her fixation on men, that is if you could believe what's in a name. He chuckled to himself at the very thought. Today was promising. He pondered about the real breakthrough that would happen right there on his gaudy orange and aqua couch. 'Next time,' she'd said to him. He hoped she really meant it.

He figured he had a few minutes to unwind before catching up with Marion Sable, his 'significant other', a term he resented, but to refer to her as his long time girlfriend was silly, likewise was the term 'squeeze,' as his cronies referred to her. Marion accompanied him one day a week in her role as receptionist. They took a leisurely lunch from twelve to two the day he was up from the City, New York, his regular practice, where the luxury of time was next to impossible. He could thank Doug Sterling for that, for finding him an office he could use in a Sterling-Baie building, which housed doctors, a lawyers, and public accountants.

Mort and Marion lunched at the Country Club, thanks to Doug's generosity, and when possible, Doug availed himself of Mort's services when life was becoming unbearable for him. He thought he was putting up a good front, but those close to him could see the changes, at first imperceptible, then more obvious. And these were not restricted to his outward appearance. Doug had become impatient and testy, less personable. Mort thought the entire family would benefit from family counseling, both individually and together. When he mentioned that to Glory she just about hit the ceiling. Once he began to understand Doug on a therapist to client basis he could understand Glory's hyper reaction to the very idea.

Marion was late. She'd left him a note explaining she needed a few things at the Walgreen's before they headed back to the City. So Mort figured there'd be no harm in having a little nip of Jack

Daniels. It would put him in a good mood. Marion could drive as she often preferred. She liked the feel of his Lincoln Continental, made her feel that Matthew McConnaghy was seated next to her rather than short, pudgy Mort, a marked contrast to her tall, willowy blondness. But Mort was the one who was always there for her, loyal and dependable like the cocker spaniel she'd had for so many years.

Mort poured the bourbon into the crystal shot glass he'd kept in the back of his bottom desk drawer along with peppermint flavored breath spray, not that he could hide anything form Marion. But the drink helped him to relax, and he needed to do some processing of the notes he'd taken.

Finally the beginnings of a breakthrough, he said to himself, chilling in the green chair that Glory found so distasteful. She's finally facing up to the pain and grief she's caused others. 'Destroyed' he remembered her saying. The details will come out soon. But she's scared. If only she can learn to accept what she's done and forgive herself and others, but she sees the world so differently.

Mort was ruminating. Glory has no idea I'm also seeing her father. So I know a lot more about her thanks to him, but not enough. That's up to her and her alone. But her father thinks he can pinpoint the time that coincides with Glory's undoing, referring to the onset of her aberrant behavior. Even though Glory's mother deems it teen-age rebellion, Doug disagrees. He's long suspected his wife's infidelity but had no proof, just an inkling, a feeling that something's not quite right. He couldn't bring himself to hire a PI to tail Belinda. He'd often say that his suspicion was provoked by his feelings of guilt for being absent so often. But it was his hard work and the success of the business that buys his family what the average household cannot imagine. He told Mort that he was considering taking on a partner so as to spend more time at home, but was unsure that that was the answer.

However, Mort credited Doug with hiring a PI to investigate Spike Gilbert and what he discovered led him to warn Glory to break off any ties she had with him. He was bad news and would surely take her down with him. Doug had told Glory next time she got in trouble she was on her own, and she seemed to believe him. He really felt that if Glory came around he too would feel 100 percent better, and things would work out better with the whole family, Belinda included. Mort was with him for the most part, but as for Belinda, he felt that was another matter all together.

When he heard Marion enter the outer office, he gulped down the last swig of bourbon, squirted his mouth and shoved the glass unwashed into the drawer just as she breezed in. She told him she couldn't believe how outgoing his last patient, that Sterling girl, was to her. He had to pinch himself—Glory Sterling? Normally the teen ignored her as though she was just another piece of unsightly furniture connected with shrinkdom.

Chapter FORTY-FOUR

(Spring—weeks later)

AS CHRIS WAS LEAVING Hillside Manor, he couldn't help feeling discouraged from Bernie's apparent lack of progress from his stroke, or was that simply a side he'd chosen to show to Chris and to others? And if so, for what reason? What was really going on? He wasn't the old Bernie he had come to love and respect that showed him what being a priest was all about. He wondered how many times Glory had been there to visit Bernie. He couldn't figure out why she would want to see the 'old Father' as she referred to him. Oh, there was so much he didn't know. And when he encountered Glory at the Manor she was apologizing to Bernie, but for what? Chris asked himself so many questions, but who would answer them?

He was in a hurry to get back to the rectory. The sky was darkening, a storm on the horizon, perhaps, he wondered, as he headed over to his dusty old pickup. The rain would do it good. The weather this time of year could be so unforgiving. He heaved a sigh, and then there she was. Glory—leaning against the driver's side of his truck. He thought she'd be gone by now. But no, she was right there waiting for him.

"You'd better back away. It's all covered in road gunk," he said to her flatly. She stepped aside and he climbed up into the vehicle. Hoping to avoid any further interaction with her, he slammed the door shut. She was poison to him, to anyone she came in contact with.

"I have to talk to you, Father Chris," she said yelling through the closed window. She seemed frantic. "Can we get together, please? It's very important."

"Look, we really have nothing more to say to each other," he said, looking straight ahead, as he revved up the engine. She stayed right there, a supplicating look on her face. Finally he gave in and rolled down the window. "Glory, I don't know what in the world you're doing here. I'm sure Father Bernie does not need you visiting him. Upsetting him. How can you do this to him?"

"I've been here before," she admitted sheepishly. Sadness wrapped her features into a frown.

"You have? And why would you want to do that?" he asked. "Look, he needs to rest and we need him back at St. Aeden's. You don't want to agitate him. Anyhow, I've got to get back to the rectory. I can't talk now. "

"Chris, I mean Father Chris," she said. She swallowed hard. "I, uh, want to make a confession. Can I please come to the rectory tomorrow?"

"Are you kidding around again?" he asked her. He was impatient. He'd had all he could take of her. He rolled up the window.

"No, no, I'm serious," she insisted through the glass. "Can I meet with you and Mrs. Hopkins, the young one, you know, the one that was on the ski trip? She threw me out of the lounge that night, remember? It's OK if her mother is there too. I want to tell the truth—everything I know. I swear it will help." She was crying now. "I don't think anyone really knows what happened that night...except maybe me."

At the mention of that fateful night, Chris became uneasy. The memory of their encounter, of what did or did not happen, flashed in his mind. He turned off the ignition and stared straight ahead, his jaw set. "The other Mrs. Hopkins, it's her mother-in-law, our housekeeper," Chris said bluntly, correcting her error as if it made a difference. "Why do you want to talk to her too?" He asked, opening the window part way. Then he remembered how distant Mrs. Hopkins had been to him since the ski trip. Maybe Glory had a good idea after all, but how could he ever trust her? History had proved otherwise.

"Because I need to. I really do. You'll see. I promise," she said with conviction, wiping her eyes with a sleeve.

Chris thought for a long moment. Glory shifted her weight from one high-heeled boot to the other. An oversized SUV was pulling into the space next to Chris. Glory jumped aside and ran behind the truck around to the other side. She wasn't about to leave until she got her way.

"All right, OK," he called out to her. "Have it your way. Meet me at the entrance of the garden at three tomorrow afternoon. I'll tell Mrs. Hopkins to set us up in the sitting room. The other priest will be out; I will make sure of that. You'll be out of school by then, won't you?" He said, softening.

"Don't worry about that. I'm out of that school—period. I'll tell you about it tomorrow," she said.

"Well, three should be a good time for me. I can get ahold of Jodie Hopkins and we can go inside and you can do what you say you need to do," he said. Things couldn't get any worse. If she could straighten everything out, then maybe some good could come of it...as if this wayward teen-age girl could make things all right.

"You'll be glad to get rid of me after that. I just want to do the right thing before I go," she said in her sweet little girl voice, smoothing her hair. She could turn it on when it behooved her. "I'm really sorry. I had no idea of the damage I caused, but now I know."

All along, she'd had little faith in Dr. Mort Polman, but he did listen, and he didn't judge. She did open up—told him only what she felt she had to, what she could. But it was enough for her to muster the courage to do what she hoped she could do? Maybe then, and only then would Father Chris truly forgive her...and maybe...

Chapter FORTY-FIVE

THE FOLLOWING AFTERNOON, the threat of a chilling, icy rain loomed over Wexford Falls. The temperature had not risen above forty degrees. The onset of spring was off to a false start. Early morning temps could fall to the low thirties and below. Chris feared a frost could damage his plantings if the forecasters were right. But then this was New England. The weather could change in a heartbeat.

Heedless of the cold, damp weather, Glory appeared at the garden entrance about ten minutes to three. She seemed impervious to the damp chill. She was wearing jeans and a long tailored shirt, likely her brother's. Her hair was pulled back into a low ponytail. A pink pashmina was wrapped loosely around her hips. She didn't look like the Glory of the previous day. She stood there shifting her weight from one foot to another, staring up at the kitchen window. She hoped he wasn't called out somewhere on an emergency. She was ready to confront him and the others. If he had to cancel the meeting she wasn't so sure she'd have the courage to set it up for another time. It was now or never.

Chris was waiting too. He had been pacing upstairs, wondering if she'd actually show up, wondering what would be gained from this meeting. He peered out the kitchen window. When he spotted her he dashed down the back stairs, and loped over to the garden entrance. He unlatched the gate and motioned for her to enter. They had a few minutes to spare. Jodie hadn't arrived yet. Neither uttered a word. Then finally she said quietly, "Here, please come over here." She led him over to where she and Spike had shared a joint the night she had wantonly destroyed the stained glass panels.

"That was me and a friend over here," she said blandly, gesturing to a holly bush that had sprung back into place in all but one spot. "I'm guilty," she said with a sigh, looking down at her white and silver Skechers. No boots today. It made her seem smaller all around. She pointed to a few bent and broken branches, barely discernible.

Chris said, "I guessed as much." He knew all too well what harm Glory had caused him and Bernie. "You know you don't have to run through everything."

They strolled down the paths as though she was touring the garden for the first time, and she actually *was* but in the springtime and in the light of day. He showed her the new growth, the greening of the garden, patch by patch. The earliest spring flowers, daffodils and crocuses, were peeking through the newly mulched beds. He paused by the lilies of the valley, calling to mind their religious significance. He decided not to share the legend that tells of these tiny white inverted bell-shape flowers that symbolize the tears of the Virgin Mary at the Crucifixion. Not at this time, anyhow. Probably never. This was his prayer garden. It was an integral part of St. Aeden's, and it meant so much more to him than just a burst of flora.

Pride shone in him like a new father seeing his baby's face for the first time. But this was spring and the garden was faithful to him. It renewed itself without fail year after year, reviving and revitalizing what was dormant.

Glory gestured over to the explosion of blossoms on the arching branches of the only tree, which cowered over a corner of the garden at the far end. She asked pointedly, "What's that? It's really beautiful, like a canopy of flowers."

"I'm surprised you don't know. It's a fruit tree, crab apple to be exact," he responded. "It is pretty when it's in bloom but the fruit is not to my liking."

"Crab apples? That's a funny name. I've never heard of them. What are they like?" she seemed interested. "Do they taste anything like normal apples?"

"No way," he answered with a shy grin. "You couldn't bribe me to eat one." He made a sour face. It felt strange to be conversing with Glory today under these circumstances with the meeting just minutes away. He added, "They're not sweet, and their texture is very unpleasant, pithy, they say."

Glory made a face. "Well, then why do you grow them?"

"We're stuck with them, I guess. The tree was here before me and it *is* pretty when it's in bloom, as you can see. Only heaven knows why it happens to be here in my garden, or why my garden happens to house this tree. It's just there. The birds seem to like it well enough." He paused a moment. "And, oh, I almost forgot. Mrs. Hopkins, not Jodie, but our housekeeper, well, she makes crab apple jam out of the fruit. It tastes OK enough. I guess it's the sugar that makes it edible, or else Mrs. Hopkins's skill. Father Bernie slathers it on his English muffins." Glory seemed to be taking all that in, hoping that it wouldn't be too long before the old Father would be back upstairs in his kitchen by the window.

"Oh, Father Chris, you recognized the lilacs I borrowed from those bushes over there. I thought they'd make the old Father feel homesick so he'd get better and come back," she said. "I didn't think you'd mind since they also belong to him really. And I didn't know you would be there. I really didn't, but I'm glad you were."

"I think you mean nostalgic, not actually homesick," he said. Was this really the old Glory? He wondered. "I didn't know you'd be there either. Someone's been sending flowers to Father Bernie, every week—beautiful bouquets—anonymously. We didn't know whom to write thank you notes to. I didn't have any flowers to bring him until now. The lilacs from the garden were the first bloom of those bushes over there." Glory could guess who it was, the anonymous donor. He was the one who always picked up the pieces, trying to fix things, make them right, or make them better. It wasn't always possible to make things as they were before. No one knew better than she did.

It was time now. Jodie had just pulled up and entered the rectory. Chris escorted Glory out of the garden and over the gravel driveway to the front entrance. Glory hesitated at the threshold. Chris took a deep breath and let it out slowly. He felt uneasy all of a sudden. He stood there and waited until she was ready before escorting her inside, hoping that whatever revelation she'd make would achieve the desired results. He couldn't be sure. What if it backfired?

"Come on inside, Glory," he said to her finally. "Please. We'll talk inside. The Hopkins women are waiting for us, both of them. Father Donovan won't be back for at least an hour. And if he shows up early, I'll tell him I'm running a meeting and it's a private affair." He cringed—wrong word.

She didn't say a word. He led and she followed him through the vestibule into the sitting room. He had told Mrs. Hopkins they did not need any refreshments that it wasn't a tea party, but Mrs. Hopkins being herself had laid out a tray of brownies and cookies and hot chocolate. They sat around the coffee table, each of the four looking like death row inmates marking time before execution. He'd never seen Jodie's face so pinched, and an inscrutable look plastered on Thelma Hopkins face made her seem unconcerned, but her body language said otherwise. She was robotic in her movements. Each person in the room had a story to tell. Everyone hoped that the truth would out, but would it set all free...from their anguish?

After recognizing the two women, Chris tried to begin as calmly as he could. His insides were churning. He hoped no one could see how agitated he really was. What if Glory was about to launch a bomb and destroy him? What if this act of hers was only a pretense? For a long moment, he feared the meeting could end in disaster. Then reason convinced him to cancel those injurious thoughts. Glory did seem sincere, insistent, when she asked if they could all meet.

"Good afternoon, ladies," he began. "I am not the one who called this meeting. Glory Sterling asked me if all of us could meet. I don't have to tell you the reason why, so we won't beat around the bush." He was met with silence followed by nervous laughter. He was grateful Mrs. Hopkins Senior did provide refreshments after all. It gave everyone something to hold and to munch on, a welcome distraction. It would serve a purpose. Food always does.

Just then, as if on cue, there was a knock at the front door. Chris motioned to Thelma Hopkins to remain seated. He would get it and tell whoever the visitor was that there was a meeting in progress, to call for an appointment. But that wasn't necessary. It was Doug Sterling. He greeted Father Chris and said that his daughter needed him to be here at three o'clock, that it was 'extremely important,' her own words, he stressed. Chris invited him in and made the necessary introductions. Glory managed a weak smile. He didn't let her down. He never did. The Hopkins women didn't know whether to focus on Glory or her father. They seemed unnerved, restless. Chris nodded to Glory.

"I can start, OK, Father Chris, if, um, that's OK with you?" He detected a trace of hesitancy in her voice. He hoped she'd regained her courage. She had a story to tell and it certainly wasn't his place to start something that only she could explain. At this time he felt his life, his future, hanging in a balance that only she could set straight. No, nothing happened that night at the ski lodge, or yes, something incriminating did. He envisioned a black or white outcome. He feared that any shade of gray would indicate doubt and doubt would warrant further investigation, but into what? Could it all be like the spin of the pointer on a Ouija board? He hoped not. Certainly God was on his side, and truth, yes, the truth was about to come, if he could trust Glory, if those present would believe her. He only prayed that it was the *truth* and not a Glory contrived version to serve whatever purpose she had in mind.

She was seated across from him. If he felt anything positive at the moment, it was a modicum of relief on two accounts. She had volunteered to get things going and she didn't call him just plain Chris. He nodded gratefully.

"I've, um, got a lot to say but I'll just stick to what you need to hear so everyone can get things straight in their minds. That's what I, um, want to do." She looked over at her father. "I know, Dad, and you ladies think you know what happened at the ski lodge...but I'm the only one who knows the whole true story, at least as I saw it. And not Father Chris. Not even him. He was sick out of his mind with fever," she said. "And I didn't know what to do."

She didn't look at anyone in particular. She was swirling marshmallow goo round and round in her hot cocoa. She had acquired a filmy chocolate moustache, which made her look younger than her years, and vulnerable, as well. The silence around her was palpable.

"You have to believe me," she insisted, coming on stronger than expected. She would be defending herself as well as Father Chris. "He, that is Father Chris, well, um, he had no idea I was there in that room, that was a private lounge, where I should not have been. It was only for chaperones. I, uh, told my mother I needed to get away with her for the week-end, so I chose that ski lodge on purpose because I knew Father Chris would be there with the ski club, um, as a chaperone. I just wanted to see him, that's all, and, um, just be near him. I didn't want to cause any trouble, especially not for him. I'm very, very sorry. I can see now it was wrong, and it caused a lot of trouble." She took another sip of her hot chocolate and paused. At first Doug's look was inscrutable, but he did pause now and then to look his daughter in the eye. You could see the love.

"Go on, please, won't you? You got us here to tell the, uh, real story, if you can," Thelma said to Glory as she paused. Thelma was visibly uncomfortable with Doug Sterling in the room, listening to his daughter's words, possibly lies. How could anyone believe that girl? Thelma face sagged into that same dour expression that she'd worn for too long, according to Chris, after she believed him to be guilty of God knows what. If he could kiss that girl blatantly out in the open, in the garden, what could he have done in that chaperones' lounge?

Glory glanced over at her father and he nodded when their eyes met. She redoubled her courage and resumed. "Sure, OK, that night at the ski lodge, I, um, couldn't sleep. It was late. I don't know what time it was. It's hard for me to sleep when someone else is sleeping in the same room near you. And it was my mother," she added with a nervous giggle. "So I, um, opened the door to the corridor and looked all around for a long time. Seems like time crawls when it's dark." Another nervous giggle. "It was real quiet. Then I couldn't believe my eyes. I saw Father Chris come out of his room. He didn't have on his priest clothes, but I could tell it was him. I knew where his room was. I watched him tip toe down the big staircase into the main area. I figured he couldn't sleep either. So I thought he was going to sit down on the sofa in front of the fireplace. They kept a fire lit all the time, which was really nice and cozy. But no, Father Chris went somewhere else. I was barefooted so I decided to sneak out of our room and see if I could find him. I really like talking with him. Like if we both couldn't sleep we could, um, just talk. He knows so much about so many interesting things. I know now that wasn't the right thing to do. Anyhow the guy at the front desk was sleeping, which they're really not supposed to do if they're on duty. Like what if you needed something? So I went past that guy and I saw a door that said 'Employees Lounge'. They keep it locked. You need a key card to get in, but I saw a light under the door and the door wasn't shut tight, so I, um, just went in. Father Chris did not let me in. I let myself in. I figured we'd just visit, that's all." Glory paused to collect her thoughts.

As if on cue, the room darkened as the sun slid behind a storm cloud. All grew still. They could hear a clap of thunder in the distance. The rain held off. Chris hoped no one could hear his pulse quickening, his respirations increasing. Thelma's breath came out in little sniffs as she dabbed at her nose with a Kleenex. She glanced over at Jodie whose involuntary gulping drew unwanted attention to her, so she imagined. All she harbored now were regrets. And Doug was poised as though surveying his prey, ready to pounce. Chris was listening intently, fiddling with his napkin.

He felt the need to add something at this point, what he could recall, and so he spoke up. "Yes, you can only get into the lounge with a key card. Chaperones can enter and help themselves to a drink or a snack any time of day or night. Well, anyhow, I wasn't feeling great when I went to bed. When I woke up, I had no idea of the time except it was still night. My throat was on fire and my head felt awful, so I got up and tried to get a drink of water from my bathroom sink but I was shaking so bad I broke the glass and sliced my finger, and it bled forever." He raised his index finger. The scar was obvious. " Sorry, Glory, but I think everyone had to hear this." He glanced around, noting each one's reactions, listening to the street sounds, the hum of traffic, the chatter of children passing by, and then finally the onset of a pounding rain.

After a moment Glory directed her attention to him, seeming to ask, 'OK?' He nodded. "Well, I made sure it was him, Father Chris, that is. You know, you can make a mistake at night." She ignored the looks between both Hopkins women, and went on. " On the sofa, I, um, sat down next to him. I didn't say anything to him because he, um, he was already asleep. His eyes were closed and then, um, a few minutes later, he, um, looked like he was dreaming. I could tell. His arms were waving all over the place and he was yelling out. I thought he must have seen me, or at least figured out that somebody was next to him. I don't know. But he didn't recognize me 'cause he was sleeping. He thought I was someone else. That I knew for sure. I heard him call out, 'Karenda' or 'Karina' or some name like that. He said it over again. He was sounding kinda hoarse and gruff like and he said something like, 'Karenda, you've come back. You've come back to me. Oh, God. It's you—I can't believe it.' That was freaking me out but I was more scared than anything. I didn't understand what he was saying and, um, because he looked so sick, like he was there but not really there, if you know what I mean, and there was blood on his hand, I didn't know from where and I didn't know what to do."

She paused to wipe her eyes with her napkin. Then, "I shouldn't have been there so I thought, um, better not call anyone for help. My mother would kill me. But then all of a sudden, the yelling stopped. His head slumped over and I thought I better stay still and not move or he'd start getting into that weird yelling out and stuff, a nightmare I guess, all over again, the dreaming, I mean, calling out some girl's name, and like thinking she was there. I was really afraid to disturb him. So I just sat there and I guess I fell asleep on the sofa next to him, and then the next thing I knew Mrs. Hopkins, the young one, the chaperone, she came in. She must've used her key card because I think I closed the door tight when I came in and then, um, she saw us asleep together, and she freaked out. Father

Chris woke up, and I woke up too. It was like all of us were freaking out. But Father Chris was still real sick, and nothing happened between us that night, I swear to God. Nothing. That's why I came here to tell everyone here the truth, what really happened in that room at the ski lodge. Nothing happened. Not a single thing. You have to believe me."

If Glory had whitewashed her story you couldn't tell. She did a convincing job of retelling what had happened. Glory could not have made that up. Chris believed her account of the incident. He figured that her very presence must have triggered the dream. His nightmares would take on such proportions since the accident. He had not abused her, not at all, and had never led her on, and she came over to the rectory to tell her story. It was her confession, true and contrite. She backed him up and that was what mattered.

But Mrs. Hopkins Senior was not so easily convinced. When she accused Chris of kissing Glory passionately in the garden, Glory gave her a piercing look and shouted, "Hey, wait a minute, I was only doing what his old friend Aleks did when she was leaving the garden. She attacked him, grabbed him almost knocking him over, and kissed him hard. Whoa, she took him by surprise. I could tell he didn't like her very much. But when I kissed him, it was totally my fault. I only copied what she did. And I'm so, so sorry. I shouldn't have done that. But she shouldn't have either. Anyhow I had a huge crush on Father Chris from the time I saw his picture in the paper. For some reason my mother held onto the garden articles and I just saw them a week or so before Christmas. She had them in a corner on her desk with the Christmas mailings. I have no idea why. She does things like that. But you have to believe me. The only reason Chris, um, I mean Father Chris, um, had his arms on my waist was to push me off his face, and I was fighting with all my might. I didn't want to let go. I wanted that kiss to last forever, for him to know how I felt."

Thelma Hopkins was fuming. She decided she wasn't going to accept the entire blame for spilling to Father Bernie what Jodie had told in her in confidence. She couldn't have imagined it would provoke a cerebral hemorrhage. She looked intently at Glory, "Look me right in the eye, missy, and tell me you weren't going after Father Tosi. What are you sick out of your mind? My God, after all, he's a priest, and you're just a...a...no, missy, I'll bet you can't," she fired back at Glory. She was sputtering. Doug Sterling stood up. He was about to intervene but his daughter waved him back down.

"No, I can't," she said, meeting Thelma's harsh gaze. Doug could see how painful this admission was for his daughter. Tears formed in his eyes. She addressed Thelma, "I thought he was hot from the minute I saw his picture, like I said. I fell for him and he couldn't care less. It's the truth. I tried everything to get his attention, to get him to like me, I mean really like me. He was always nice and smart and so holy too. He was very special to me. But he wouldn't even look at me. Look, everything is my fault, all mine. And what's even worse, I even decided to learn Catholic to get closer to him, and my Grandmom taught me all the religious stuff she knew from when she was young. She, um, said if you thought the sin in your mind, you were as guilty as if you did it. So I, um, went to confession to the old Father and I told him my sin. I used to think of doing it with Father Chris so I told him I slept with a priest, which I sorta did, like at the ski lodge, but not *that* way, not like sex and stuff. Then I told him that I seduced him. The old Father knew who I was, but not at first. I thought I was changing my voice good enough, but I guess not. I got scared and ran out of there." She stopped short and took a few deep breaths. She recalled Mort's reassuring words after she'd finally opened up to him, the techniques he'd taught her, the deep breathing exercises that he made her practice in front of him and the visual imagery of healing thoughts. By this point in her confession, nothing was working for her, and she caved in, bursting into tears.

Chris did a double take. So she was the one but she didn't mean it, the confession. So that's what caused it. She didn't really understand confessing the sin at all. Thinking something and doing something are *not* the same thing. Jodie and her mother-in-law looked at each other aghast. They didn't have to say a word. Chris understood everything now. Bernie must have been harboring the thought that Chris had broken his vow, sinned, and worse. That explained the condition Bernie was in when Chris discovered him slumped over the front pew long after confessions had ended. All Chris could say under his breath was, "Poor Bernie. He must've taken her at her word. And, oh my God, what he must have thought of me, what he still thinks of me."

No one said a word. Doug was able to hold back his tears. He hid his shock well, but inwardly he was proud of his daughter for coming forth, for clearing the air. He had sensed a change in her recently. After all, he knew she had been going to see her therapist regularly. But she had no idea that her father was seeing Dr. Polman as well. It was better that way.

And now for the first time, Chris was able to look Glory in the eye without seeing Kendra. He went over to the poinsettia plant, its leaves shriveled and sparse, and detached the tiny golden violin from the ribbon. He handed the ornament back to Glory telling her he knew how much it meant to her, that she had earned it through her masterful violin performances. It belonged to her. She put it in her pocket and turned away. He heard her whisper, 'thank you'.

Chris wasn't so sure Mrs. Hopkins Senior was totally convinced. She was making her skeptical face, one that Chris had promptly recognized. He could sense her mulling over Glory's story in her mind, weighing what could be true, and what was not.

Glory's excuse seemed plausible enough to her but she thought it could also be a pack of lies, or at least an embellishment to exonerate the alleged guilty parties. She wanted it to be the truth for Father Bernie's sake.

But the distrusting side of her said what if Glory and Chris were really secret lovers, waiting it out until she turned eighteen, in what was very likely a little over a year. Not so long a time to wait, to keep things under cover until then. Then she looked over at Chris. Couldn't she see that Father Chris wasn't a monster? That he was a pious, dutiful priest, as she had always regarded him? Couldn't she see past her prejudices that so much was built on misconceptions? What more did it take for her to erase her doubts?

Chris bolstered his courage to address Mrs. Hopkins Senior. "Thelma, please try to understand my situation. That night in the ski lounge I had a nightmare that Kendra, my high school girl friend, came back to life and I believed I was reaching out to her, not to Glory. I did not know Glory was there or I would have asked her to leave immediately." Thelma was studying him the way she used to look at Junior when she doubted his version of the truth, but this was Chris, an ordained priest, who'd always done what's right in his capacity as a cleric. He had nothing to hide. He tried to avoid Thelma's painful glare. He paused to quiet himself. He was shaking. "She, Kendra, and my twin sister Beth were mangled and incinerated in a horrific car accident ten years ago. I wasn't with them. I was supposed to be. I could have saved them if I had been there, if I was the driver. It still tortures me, but mostly in my dreams. Kendra was the one I was going to marry. That was the name I must have called out thinking she was there with me. That had to be what Glory heard. I believe her account of that night. I have no doubt in my mind." He nodded towards Glory.

Thelma Hopkins was no longer looking at Chris; she stared into space as though trying to catch and hang onto his words, to test their meaning, their intent. She wanted so much to believe him. Jodie looked grief-stricken. No one moved.

At last, Doug Sterling rose and gestured to Glory. They were about to leave when he turned to face everyone. Brimming with emotion, he spoke. "I'd like to say a few words before we go if I may." Chris nodded for him to continue, noting the weariness in his voice. Glory walked over to stand by his side. He put his arm around her. She couldn't look at anyone. "I would like to thank all of you for hearing Glory's account of her wrongdoings. This could not have been easy for her. I want to tell you that I'm proud of her for owning up to her misdeeds and clarifying what I assume have been lots of misconceptions, that, uh, seemed to mushroom. But she has come to realize all the pain she has caused, and she is sorry.

"I sincerely hope that this puts everyone's mind at ease and I'm sure we will all do our best to facilitate Father Monahan's rehabilitation. I, uh, would like to offer my company's services to make any accommodations to this rectory should Father need them. And, on a final note, I would like to let you know that Glory's mother and I, uh, feel she will benefit from a change in environment, for obvious reasons, so she will not be finishing high school here in Wexford Falls. And so we are enrolling her in a boarding school in Switzerland this fall. It's got an excellent music program as well as strong academics. Oh, one last thing, Glory and I, uh, will be paying a visit to Father Monahan in a few days. I think it's something we both need to do—together."

Chris stood to shake Doug's hand. He felt unburdened at the moment but realized he had so much to process. He knew there was a long road ahead. So much healing needed to take place. He thanked Glory and Doug and wished them both 'good luck'. The Hopkins

women looked at one another, then they nodded, but said nothing. Their expressions said much more.

Mrs. Hopkins Senior who'd been avoiding a visit to Hillside Manor for reasons that are now apparent said she'd pay Father Bernie a visit tomorrow or the next day if she could be spared for an hour or so. She didn't want to make the trip at night and she certainly didn't want her husband to accompany her. The fewer persons who knew the real story the better. Chris said that would be no problem. He himself would get over to Hillside Manor later today. He had to. He would talk and Bernie would hear him. Once Bernie learned the truth, Chris had faith that he would embrace rehabilitation with all his forces. St. Aeden's needed him, and he certainly needed to be back at St. Aeden's. Paddy has missed him in the way that dogs do. Chris decided he'd take him along for a visit.

Jodie apologized profusely to Chris. He could feel her spasms of sadness and grief as she hugged him good-bye. She composed herself and told them she had to leave. She was heart-broken at what she had set in motion and assured him that her mother-in-law meant no harm telling Father Bernie Jodie's account of that night. She'd only felt compelled to do what she thought was the right thing.

AND SO LIKE THE FAIRY circles of the Namib Desert, whatever order seems to exist at one time or another will eventually revert to chaos and then reemerge as order. Thus goes the cycle of life here in Wexford Falls and beyond. This was truly evidenced in a voice message Chris played on his cell after all had dispersed. Ruthie Symond had just broken her engagement with Matt Barton who'd gotten into some big trouble in prison. Chris speed dialed Muriel Symond and held his breath.

Author's Note

A SEQUEL TO *"In the Garden of Aeden"* consisting of short stories set in Wexford Falls will be available in January, 2019.

COVER DESIGN BY CHEEKYCOVERS.com

PHOTOGRAPH BY W. PILOTTE

Did you love *In the Garden of Aeden*? Then you should read *Tales From Wexford Falls*[1] by M. Pilotte!

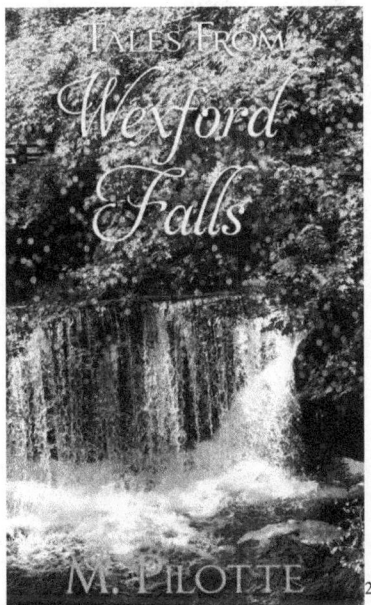

Tales from Wexford Falls

"Tales from Wexford Falls" is a collection of nine short stories featuring characters and familiar locales from Pilotte's novel "In the Garden of Aeden". Some stories can stand on their own, whereas others function as a sequel. Father Chris Tosi from "Garden" appears in some of the stories to offer wise counsel to those in distress, and his buddy Sergeant Smith (Smitty) is called upon when an officer of the law is needed.

The status quo is shaken as characters encounter life-altering experiences in this charming, typical New England town. Themes revolve around hopes and dreams, betrayals and disappointments.

---

1. https://books2read.com/u/mdLgwO

2. https://books2read.com/u/mdLgwO

Share Aggie O'Toole's journey as she copes with lost love and holds onto a secret that threatens to devastate her boss, Doug Sterling. In the final story, she joins him in making a monumental decision. Root for Ruthie Symond as she engages in a plan to rid herself of a unsavory former boyfriend and restore her imprisoned fiancé's reputation. Get acquainted with inn-keeper Clover Hollis as she finds herself with a grieving guest placed in an uncomfortable situation.

In this collection of short stories, the restorative power and catalytic role of art, poetry and nature provide distraction and comfort as hidden truths become known and characters remove blinders to the truth so as to embark on a new path in life.

Read more at https://www.mpilottebooks.com.

About the Author

M. Pilotte has always enjoyed writing, whether it be for academic purposes, newspaper reporting, or simply as a creative outlet. A lifelong learner, she earned a Ph.D. from UCONN. Following her retirement as an educator, she wrote several plays. She and her husband divide their time between Connecticut and South Carolina.

email: mpilottebooks@yahoo.com

Read more at https://www.mpilottebooks.com.

About the Publisher

Wexford Falls Independent Press is an independently owned company headquartered in Colchester, Connecticut.

Cover photo for Tales - W. Pilotte

Cover design - cheekycovers.com